THE WHITE WITCH OF
THE SOUTH SEAS

Gregory was far from rash by nature. To the contrary, on a score of occasions only the exercise of great caution had saved him from his enemies. But the decisive factor in this present matter was that he had become bored with life. Manon provided him with a new and delightful interest, but a love *affaire* was not enough. Another side of his mentality craved exciting situations in which he would have to use his good brain, and this quest for the treasure had unexpectedly developed into just that sort of thing. Moreover, if the gamble did cost him his life – what of it? He had hopes that death would reunite him with Erika.

D1421864

Dennis Wheatley

THE WHITE WITCH OF THE SOUTH SEAS

THE SHERIDAN
BOOK COMPANY

This edition published in 1994 by
The Sheridan Book Company

First published by Hutchinson & Co. (Publishers) Ltd 1968
Random House, 20 Vauxhall Bridge Road, London SW1V 2SA
Arrow edition 1970

© Dennis Wheatley Limited 1968

This book is sold subject to the condition that it shall
not, by way of trade or otherwise, be lent, resold,
hired out, or otherwise circulated without the
publisher's prior consent in any form of binding or
cover other than that in which it is published and
without a similar condition including this condition
being imposed on the subsequent purchaser

Printed and bound in Great Britain by
Cox & Wyman Ltd, Reading, Berkshire

ISBN 1–85501–640–0

For
PHYL

A small souvenir of our successful endeavours
to secure a show in Bond Street for the
paintings of the ex-leper, Semisi Maya.
And for her husband,
His Excellency Sir Derek Jakeway, K.C.M.G.,
Her Majesty's Governor of the Fijis.

Contents

1

Doomed to Die in a Ditch

Gregory Sallust was dining alone at the Copacabana Palace, the most luxurious of the many hotels situated along the great bay to the south of Rio de Janeiro, which is Brazil's most famous playground.

Since losing his beloved Erika he had spent much of his time alone; not from necessity, as he had many friends in Europe and, although no longer young, was still very attractive to women, but owing to a restlessness that impelled him to spend the greater part of each year travelling.

To most places where he intended to spend a fortnight or more he took introductions; but new acquaintances could not be expected to give him all their time and, as no woman could replace Erika, for him the casual *affaires* he had indulged in had been short-lived. In consequence, he had become quite used frequently to going to his room immediately after dinner and reading in bed.

But tonight he had an engagement, and one which promised to be very interesting. On arriving in Rio he had looked up an old war-time friend, Colonel Hugo Wellesley, who was now Military Attaché at the British Embassy. During the past few days Hugo and his wife Patricia had entertained him most kindly, and the Colonel had arranged for them to attend a *Macumba* ceremony.

Macumba is the form of Voodoo widely practised in Brazil, and ceremonies of a kind were put on regularly to attract tourist money; but this was to be the real thing, from which all non-practitioners were normally excluded. The all-powerful Chief of Police had secured agreement for Hugo

9

and his party to be present and, in case of trouble, they were being provided with a police escort.

Gregory's knowledge of the Black Arts was confined to his reluctant co-operation with a Jewish Satanist during the last years of the Second World War, when they had made use of Hitler's belief in the occult to drive him to commit suicide instead of leaving Berlin for the Bavarian Alps where, with a still undefeated army, he could have prolonged Germany's resistance.[1] Voodoo and its allied cults were entirely new territory to Gregory; so, although he had no intention whatever of allowing himself to become involved, he was looking forward to the ceremony as a fascinating entertainment.

At half past nine he asked the hall porter to get him a taxi. As he stood waiting for a few minutes outside the hotel, he could see the whole curving sweep of the splendid Copacabana Bay. It was early January, so in Rio high summer and during the daytime the long beach was black with people. Even at this hour innumerable couples lay scattered upon it. Thousands more, enjoying the comparative cool of the evening after the long, hot day, were strolling along the promenade, lit by the myriad lights from hotels, shops and cafés.

The city of Rio consists of several valleys which run like gaps between outspread fingers into the great mountain range that cuts it off from the interior, and Copacabana is separated from Rio itself by a lofty spur that runs right down into the sea; so Gregory's taxi took him through a long tunnel under the spur, then through the streets in the nearest valley to a small park with many lovely tropical trees. High up on one side of the park stood the President's Palace and, beyond it, still higher up and backing on to a mountain, the fine residential block in which the Wellesleys had an apartment.

On Gregory's arrival he found the small party already assembled. His host was a lithe, dark, handsome man in his late forties, his hostess a pretty blonde with merry blue eyes. When he had selected a daiquiri from a tray presented by a white-coated houseman, she introduced him to her other guests—a Brazilian couple named da Fonseca, a Madame

[1] *They Used Dark Forces.*

10

Manon de Bois-Tracy and Captain Candido Sousa from Rio Police Headquarters.

The da Fonsecas were middle-aged and, judging from the Senhora's jewels, very wealthy. For a while the conversation became general, then the da Fonsecas resumed an animated discussion they had been having earlier with Hugo in Portuguese. The Police Captain—a big, round-faced, jovial man— spoke only broken English, but in an unembarrassed spate of words was obviously endeavouring to impress Patricia; so, having accepted a second drink, Gregory turned his attention to Madame de Bois-Tracy, whom he had rightly assumed to be French.

She was of medium height and what the French term a 'belle-laide' when they wish to describe a woman who is not beautiful but definitely alluring. Her attractions lay in a pair of magnificent brown eyes beneath delicately tapering eyebrows and a pretty figure that her dress sense enabled her to display to the best advantage. Her nose was snub, with wide nostrils, her lips thick, which suggested a dash of coloured blood somewhere in her ancestry, and her complexion was sallow. Gregory put her age down as a little short of forty and was quick to realise that she was a sophisticated woman of the world who could prove intriguing and amusing.

The outer wall of the main room in the Wellesleys' apartment was one huge window which could be wound down during the great heats—as it was now, for the evening was oppressively hot and sultry. Having been there in the daytime, Gregory knew that from the window there was one of the finest views imaginable. It looked out over the President's Palace and hundreds of other roofs to the world-famous entrance to Rio harbour and to Sugar Loaf Mountain, the outline of which could still be seen against a background of blue-black sky, twinkling with a myriad of stars. Further off, across a wide sheet of water, lay another mountainous shore. The Portuguese explorer Gonçalvo Coelho had come upon this great area of bays, capes and estuaries on January 1st, 1502. On sailing up into it, he had assumed that he was entering the mouth of a broad river and so erroneously named it River of January. Darkness now hid a great part of this

11

magnificent panorama; but, from eighty feet above the park, which lay immediately below, thousands of lights gleamed in the dusk, giving this valley of the city a fairy-like quality.

By unspoken agreement Gregory and Manon de Bois-Tracy carried their drinks over to the wrought-iron balustrade installed to prevent children or incautious people from falling from the big window. Finding her English halting, he changed his conversation to French, as he was fluent in several languages. She told him that she was in Rio only on a holiday and that her home was in Fiji. Friends there had given her an introduction to the wife of the First Secretary of the British Embassy, and it was at dinner with them that she had met the Wellesleys. Afterwards she and Patricia had chanced to talk about the occult, and it was this that had led to her being invited to witness the *Macumba* ceremony that night.

As she talked, in an attractive, slightly lisping voice, she was studying Gregory acutely. Owing to the habitual stoop with which he walked, his lean head thrust a little forward like a bird of prey, he appeared shorter than his five foot eleven inches. His hair had turned nearly white, owing to the strain he had endured while a secret agent for long periods in Germany during the Second World War; yet his face belied his age. The only two furrows on it were deep laughter lines curving from nose to chin on either side of his mouth. An old scar ran up from the corner of his left eyebrow to his forehead, on which the thick hair came down smoothly in a widow's peak. From long habit, when speaking in a foreign language, he used his hands to stress the views he uttered. On international affairs his opinions were well informed, highly practical and always tinged with a cynical humour.

Gregory had not been talking to Manon de Bois-Tracy for very long before she decided that he was quite an exceptional man—considerably older than herself, but nonetheless attractive for that, and one with whom it might prove highly rewarding to become on intimate terms; while Gregory had come to the conclusion that she was the most unusual and intriguing woman he had met for a long time.

Both of them had been in Rio for some days and to begin

12

with they had compared their impressions of the city. She thought the main streets and shops unworthy of such a great metropolis, but the scenery superb. They had both been up the Corcovado, a rocky peak two thousand three hundred feet high dominating the whole area, from the top of which rises a one-hundred-foot-high statue of Christ, and agreed that the view from it must be one of the finest in the world. He found the obvious poverty of the masses depressing and spoke of the appalling shanty towns on the slopes of the mountains adjacent to the city, where tens of thousands of people lived without sanitation. But she shrugged that off, remarking that such a state of things was not unusual in countries as poor as Brazil, and that at least the people had ample food and appeared happy.

'I'll grant you that,' he said. 'And, anyway, Brazil can take credit for being one of the few countries in the world that have solved the colour problem. There really is equality here between whites, Negroes, native Indians and the people with an infinite variety of mixed blood.'

She then asked him what form he thought the ceremony they were to see that night would take.

'I have only a vague idea,' he replied, 'but I expect they will all smoke marijuana and dance until they have worked themselves up into a frenzy. Then some of them will have what appear to be epileptic fits, froth at the mouth, throw themselves on the ground, squirm about and prophesy.'

Manon nodded. 'When they behave like that they believe themselves to be possessed by one of their gods, don't they? But we won't be able to understand what they say, so if there is no more to it than that it doesn't promise to be very exciting.'

'You never know.' Gregory gave her a slow smile. 'I've heard that at times these shows end up in a general orgy.'

She raised one eyebrow, then said quite calmly, 'That would be fun and I'm all for it—providing I am not expected to participate.'

His smile widened to a grin. 'I'll see to it that you don't have to—provided, of course, there is some hope of your rewarding me afterwards.'

13

As she laughed, she showed two rows of even white teeth. 'I'll make no promises, but, to echo your own words just now, "You never know".'

Their attention was momentarily distracted by raised voices behind them. Turning, they saw that Captain Sousa was insisting that the Senhora da Fonseca should leave her jewels in the Wellesleys' apartment. Still protesting, she took them off. Manon followed suit with her more modest jewellery and Hugo collected the valuable pile of trinkets to lock up in his safe.

Captain Sousa then talked to them for a while about *Macumba*. He said that throughout the whole of Central and South America very similar cults had grown up from a blending of the religion of the native Indians, the superstitions brought over by the Negro slaves from Africa and the imposing on both of the Roman Catholic faith. The vast majority of the people in these countries would tell you that they were Christians, and they regularly attended the ceremonies of the Church; but they also continued to believe in the potency of the old gods and worshipped them during midnight meetings held deep in the jungle. How widespread the belief in *Macumba* was could be judged from Copacabana Beach on New Year's Eve, when the sea was white for a quarter of a mile out with the tens of thousands of lilies thrown into it by *Macumba* votaries to propitiate Yemanja, the goddess of the ocean.

These meetings were conducted by both men and women, who were known either as 'Godfathers' or 'Godmothers'. They said the prayers, invoked the spirits and, with a trident, stirred a cauldron from which rose lurid flames. Meanwhile, initiates of both sexes, already under the influence of drugs, performed a dance which continued for several hours. From time to time a spirit would enter into one of the dancers. He or she would then break from the ring, gyrate wildly and become the voice of the spirit, calling out messages from the gods. Then, exhausted, the possessed would fall writhing and jerking to the ground.

With one exception everyone wore white, as the symbol of good. The exception—a concession to the doctrines of the

14

Christian Church—was a representative of the Devil, who was painted red and wore red clothes.

Finally, Sousa told his listeners that they must make no comments, because the ceremony they were about to witness was normally attended only by believers and, should they be suspected of ridiculing it, there would be serious trouble. But provided they remained quiet all should be well. Recently quite a number of socialites in Rio had become converts to *Macumba,* so the good clothes worn by the members of the party would not alone give them away as non-believers.

After a last drink they all went down in the lift to two large, waiting cars. In addition to police drivers, a detective was in one and a police-woman in the other. Introductions were made, everyone shook hands, then the party of eleven squeezed into the cars and they set off.

They left the city by one of the tunnels and continued for several miles up into the mountains. It was now almost pitch dark, but on either side of the road they could make out dense jungle. After some twenty minutes they came upon a long line of parked cars. A few hundred yards further on, their cars pulled up and the party got out, to be led by Captain Sousa up a long flight of some sixty steps cut out of the bare earth, which was kept in place only by rough pieces of wood. On the steps they passed several chickens which had been decapitated, and, as they mounted, the rhythmic beat of many drums grew ever louder.

At the top of this flight they emerged on to a small plateau that had been made into a primitive auditorium. In the centre there was an oblong, open space about the size of a tennis court, surrounded by a waist-high wall. A line of tumbledown huts faced one side of the open space; on the side opposite there were benches for the congregation and, at the far end, where the ground sloped up, more benches. These latter faced the other narrow end of the 'court', the whole length of which was occupied by an altar. It consisted of long, white, draped tables, above which there were shelves to the height of about ten feet. Every inch of space was occupied with an extraordinary collection of objects, crammed higgledy-piggledy together—offerings of all kinds including

15

melons, bottles of rum and beer, sugar cakes, crude paintings, jam jars holding wilting flowers, a number of quite large figures, including those of the Virgin Mary, St. George and the Devil—the whole being lit by chains of fairy lamps.

Except for the open space the whole area was swarming with people, and Gregory had already noticed that the women of the congregation were separated from the men: the former occupying the benches to one side of the 'court' and the men those on the slope at its far end. When they reached the slope the police-woman led the other women of the party off, while Captain Sousa found places halfway up the slope for the men. As they squeezed through to them they were given some rather ugly looks and there were angry mutterings about 'Americanos'. But both Sousa and da Fonseca spoke to the *Macumba* votaries in Portuguese, the surly muttering was replaced by smiles and the party settled down without incident on a bench.

It was now getting on for midnight and the whole auditorium was packed. The majority of the people were apparently of pure Negro blood, but there were complexions of every shade, through coffee up to white tinged only faintly with yellow; quite a number had hooked noses and a few even had blue eyes and straight, golden hair.

Here and there among them were people wearing quite expensive clothes, but most of the congregation were poorly clad; many were barefooted and in rags. It was very hot. The atmosphere was most oppressive and unpleasantly acrid with the smell of stale sweat. Few jackets were to be seen; the rows of black faces stood out sharply against open-necked white shirts, and the native women appeared to have on only a single garment.

For a time the drumming contended with the noise and laughter coming from the crowded benches. Then, suddenly, there fell a hush and the tempo of the drums became faster. An elderly Negro walked a little unsteadily out into the middle of the open space. He wore dirty white cotton trousers, bagging at the knees, a sagging jacket and, at a rakish angle on his head, an old cloth cap. His grey hair was wavy and he had a beard. He was smoking a pipe and carried a

16

walking stick with a crook handle. After grinning round at the congregation he began gradually revolving in a very slow shuffle.

His supporting cast then appeared. It consisted of about twenty women, mostly black, but including a few near-whites. All of them were dressed in white, with high-necked bodices and long, full skirts that swept the ground as they moved. Forming a line, with their backs to the female congregation, they swayed, rather than danced, slowly backwards and forwards, gradually forming a circle.

The old 'Godfather' continued to puff at his pipe of marijuana while shuffling round and round, occasionally waving his stick and, in a quiet voice, calling out a few words. As he grinned after each utterance, Gregory thought it probable that he was making jokes, and he certainly had more the appearance of a clown than a witch-doctor.

Without any alteration, except for a slight acceleration in the pace of the shuffling and swaying, this went on for a good twenty minutes. Becoming bored, Gregory moved restlessly in his seat. Hugo, who was sitting next to him, leaned over and whispered:

'Pity we couldn't have come in later; but they wouldn't have that. I gathered that they don't really get going until about two o'clock in the morning, so we'll have to be patient.'

Gregory nodded, and lit one of his fat, four-inch long Sullivan cigarettes.

With little variation, the sombre dance continued for a further quarter of an hour. Then there came a spattering on the leaves of the trees that surrounded the enclosure. It had begun to rain.

Hugo swore under his breath. 'Let's hope this is only a shower. If it's one of our big tropical storms, we've had it.'

'With so much thunder about, I'll bet you it's a downpour,' Gregory replied. And after a few minutes it was clear that he was right. From large, scattered splashes, the rain rapidly increased until it was sheeting down. In tropical countries Negroes go about lightly clad, but they nearly always carry umbrellas. A solid mass of them shot up, obliterating the congregation, but the torrents of rain descending were such that the umbrellas offered little protection.

Thunder boomed like a broadside of heavy guns, temporarily drowning the sound of the drums. The strings of fairy lights above the altar suddenly went out, but great jagged streaks of forked lightning continued from minute to minute to light the scene. By their light, through the curtain of rain, it could be vaguely seen that the ceremony was still proceeding. The old Negro continued to stumble round, but was now waving his stick above his head and yelling at the sky. Captain Sousa leaned forward and shouted, "E is telling rain to go away, but I think 'e don't 'ave much luck.'

Within a matter of minutes everyone was soaked to the skin. As the rain was lukewarm, the discomfort it inflicted was minimised; but the storm showed no sign of abating and the congregation rapidly began to break up.

'No good staying on,' said Hugo abruptly. 'We must find the girls and get them to the cars.'

Leaving their seats, they began to struggle through the seething mass of people. Captain Sousa blew his whistle. There came a shrill reply from some distance off and, knowing that it came from the police-woman, they headed in that direction. Five minutes later, to their great relief, they found Patricia and the others. Taking the arms of the women, they strove to get them through the crowd to the head of the long flight of steps. At length they succeeded, but only to find that rain from the plateau was cascading down the primitive staircase like a waterfall.

Gregory was leading, with Manon de Bois-Tracy. In one swift movement he picked her up and plunged knee deep into the torrent. Some of the boards supporting the steps had already given way. The earth had turned to mud and was extremely slippery. Lurching from side to side and only just succeeding in keeping his balance, he got her down to the solid road and, gasping for breath, set her on her feet.

For several minutes they waited for the others. Stumbling, sliding, some on their backs, scores of the congregation were swept down the steep slope, but none of Hugo's party was among them.

18

With a frown, Gregory said, 'They must have decided that the steps have become too dangerous, and mean to wait up there until the storm is over. We had better try to find one of the cars.'

Like two drowned rats, their clothes clinging to them, while the rain still sheeted down, they set off along the line of motors parked at the roadside. A few, the owners of which had got away early, were pulling out and setting off for Rio, but the majority were lightless and unoccupied. Angrily, Gregory realised that the drivers of the police cars must have left them to go up and see the ceremony and were now trapped among the milling mob above the torrent. It was too dark for there to be any chance of identifying the cars, so for a few moments he stood silently cursing while wondering what best to do.

There came a deafening clap of thunder. Lightning streaked down from almost immediately overhead, a great tree nearby was struck and one of the larger branches was peeled off, to crash across the roof of a car. Manon screamed and threw her arms round Gregory.

'All right, all right,' he muttered. 'Don't be afraid. As long as we stay clear of the trees we'll come to no harm. But we must find shelter somewhere.'

Swinging her round, he drew her back up the road. After covering a hundred yards he glimpsed through the trees the white walls of a bungalow. Taking the path that led to it, they went up the steps to the porch and he banged on the door. There was no reply, but the door swung open.

Staggering inside, they found the place deserted, but an oil lamp that had been turned low was burning in the main room. Turning up the wick, they looked about them. The room was better furnished than might have been expected. It even had shelves on one wall, carrying a hundred or more books, and a writing desk in front of one of the windows. Exhausted after their struggle against the elements, they sank down on the sofa.

The rain drummed with unceasing ferocity on the roof, thunder continued to roll and every few moments lightning made the window a blinding glare that lit up every detail of the room.

Gregory soon pulled himself together, stood up and went to explore the other rooms of the dwelling. After a short absence he returned carrying a bottle three-quarters full of rum and two mugs. He had already taken a good swig himself and now he made Manon do likewise. As the fiery liquid went down her throat she gasped, but her sallow cheeks took on colour and she gave him a faint smile. Then she asked:

'What now? How will we ever get back?'

He grinned at her. 'All the odds are that the owner of this place went to the party and is still stuck among the crowd. When he does return we'll ask him to get a car for us or, if he can't do that, fix us up here for the night.'

'Perhaps he won't be able to get back,' she hazarded.

Gregory's grin deepened. 'I'm afraid that's too much to hope for. All the same, you ought to get those wet things off. There are some women's clothes in the second room on the right down the passage. In the circumstances, their owner is hardly likely to object to your making temporary use of them.'

As he spoke, his glance swept over her from top to toe. Her thin frock was so saturated that it clung to her skin, revealing every detail of her good figure. After a moment he added:

'It looks as if you are going to have difficulty getting that dress off. If you do, give me a shout and I'll come and help.'

'I'm sure you would like to,' she replied a shade tartly, 'but at the moment I'm in no mood to accept such attentions from a gentleman.'

'Now, don't pretend to be a prude,' he mocked her. 'No woman with such a lovely figure as yours isn't glad of an excuse to show herself off in a bikini or her undies. As for the "attentions" you appear to fear, you wrong me. I indulge in that sort of pastime only in warm and comfortable surroundings, with a magnum of champagne at hand and after having given my companion an excellent dinner.'

Before she could reply, sounds came from the front door and a little group of people came hurrying into the room. At their head was the old 'Godfather'; he was followed by a

20

gangling-limbed but quite well-dressed young Negro of about nineteen and three of the Negresses who had taken part in the ceremony, their long white skirts now slushing round their ankles.

The old man looked at Gregory, gave a sudden start and dropped his stick. Picking it up, he stared at Gregory for a moment as though seeing a ghost, then spoke to him in what Gregory took to be a bastard form of Portuguese. Hoping that one of them understood some English and choosing the simplest words he could, he explained that he and Manon had taken refuge there from the storm. Whereupon the youth said in a squeaky voice:

'Americanos, eh? I speek yo' language. Am educating at university. My father an' the womans not. My name Enrico.'

Gregory then asked if it was possible for him to get them a car, to which Enrico replied, 'I 'ave auto in garage. Later I takes yo' to city. But not yet. Much, much rain. Yo' wait here fo' while.'

Having thanked him, Gregory asked if Manon could be provided with a change of clothes. The youth translated to the women, who had been standing staring wide-eyed at them from the doorway. Their black faces broke into wide grins, then they beckoned to Manon and she went off down the passage with them.

Meanwhile, the old *Macumba* priest had seated himself in a rocking chair. He had a white film over one eye, but the other was as keen as that of an eagle. He was regarding Gregory in a by no means friendly fashion.

Glancing at Enrico, Gregory said, 'Please tell your father how distressed we are for him that the storm should have spoilt his ceremony.'

Enrico translated, then said in English, 'He much opset. He believe yo' an' yo' friends who come with Police enemies of him an' make bad magic that bring rain.'

Gregory raised his eyebrows in surprise. 'Please assure him that is not so. We came only out of scientific interest and were just as disappointed as he is that the ceremony had to be stopped.'

When he learned this the old man looked slightly mollified

21

and Gregory said, 'I would very much like to hear what would have taken place if the ceremony had continued.'

'Spirits enter bodies of some of the womans,' Enrico answered. 'Then spirits talk; denounce bad peoples, make prophecy, help father to tell future.'

Manon had just re-entered the room with the other women. She had not accepted a loan of clothes but stripped and wrung her own out, knowing that in the intense heat they would soon dry on her. Hearing Enrico's last words, she said with swift interest, 'So your father, 'e tells fortunes. 'E make me very 'appy if 'e tell mine.'

Enrico grinned at her. 'I make persuade him. That is, if yo' pay 'im good money.'

Turning to Gregory, she said in French, 'When you were carrying me down that stairway I dropped my bag. Could you lend me enough money for this?'

'I expect so,' he smiled, and took a two-inch-thick wad of half-sodden notes out of his jacket pocket. They looked to be worth a small fortune, as most of them were five-thousand-*cruzeiro* bills, the highest value normally then in circulation in Brazil. But, largely owing to the immense sums expended in recent years on the new capital of Brasilia, Brazil's finances have fallen into such a parlous state that the *cruzeiro* had slumped to over six thousand to the pound sterling. So, to the considerable inconvenience of people who live fairly expensively, such unwieldy packages of currency had to be carried about.

Peeling off five of the five-thousand-*cruzeiro* notes, Gregory offered them to the old man while Enrico was making Manon's request. His solitary eye glinting brightly, he stretched out a claw-like hand and took the money.

Enrico then walked over to the desk. From a drawer he took a canvas bag and a piece of similar material, both of which he handed to his father.

The 'Godfather' eased himself out of his rocking chair on to his knees and spread the piece of canvas on the floor. It was about two feet square and marked on it in black there were a number of crude symbols. Picking up the floppy bag, he began to mutter what was evidently an incantation, meanwhile shaking the bag gently up and down and to and fro.

With each movement something inside the bag made a soft clicking sound and, from what Gregory had read of Negro magic, he had little doubt that this descendant of long-dead African witch-doctors was about to 'throw the bones'.

He proved right. After chanting in a low voice for about five minutes, the old man loosened the string round the neck of the bag and tipped a score or more of small bones out on to the square of canvas.

For quite a while he silently studied the way they had fallen in relation to the symbols, while the three Negresses peered timidly over his shoulder. Then he looked up and spoke to Enrico, who translated:

'My father, he say yo' soon have new lover. But yo' very fond of another mans. Also, with him yo' have big money interest. So your heart divided; understand? Much happiness for yo' with new lover, but to keep much courage needed. My father then ask: "Have yo' ever kill?" Kill a man, that is. He think yo' have.'

Manon suddenly went pale and her brown eyes distended until they looked enormous. Giving a slight nod, she whispered, 'Yes, but—but only because I had to.'

The old man spoke again and Enrico interpreted. 'My father, he say, "Then yo' should kill again. There is a White Witch. She comes into yo' life. Yo' will lose yo's happiness —lose all, unless yo' kills her when yo' has the chance".'

There fell a sudden silence. Having understood what the 'Godfather' had said, the Negresses were regarding Manon with awed curiosity. Enrico had thrust his thumb between the first and second fingers of his hand, and was pointing it at her as a defence against her possibly malign influence. Gregory, hearing her confess to having killed a man, caught himself looking at her with increased interest. To break the tension, he again pulled out his wad of notes, peeled off another five and offered them with the request that the bones should be thrown for him.

The old man swiftly gathered up the bones and thrust them back into the bag, but he did not take the money.

Waving it away, he got from his knees and spoke swiftly to his son.

Enrico's mouth fell open and he gave a slight gulp. Then, recovering himself, he said in a tremulous voice, 'My father, he say yo' have no future to tell. Sometimes he have visions. Jus' now, when he come in this room, he have one. He see yo' this time tomorrow night as dead—dead in a ditch.'

2

His Last Twenty-four Hours

Again a shocked silence fell. They could hear the rain still pattering on the roof, but none of them noticed that its beat had lessened or had registered the fact that thunder now rumbled only in the distance. At length Gregory said to Enrico:

'Please thank your father for his warning. And now, with my apologies for having abused your hospitality while you were absent, do you think I could have a little more rum?'

'But yes!' The young man eagerly stretched out a hand to the bottle and poured a lavish portion into Gregory's mug, then he went on, 'I's sorry; mos' sorry 'bout this. But my father, he is very honest mans. He could not take money an' lead yo' up garden path.'

'It can't be true!' Manon burst out. 'It can't! This filthy old rogue is just being malicious. He is trying to frighten you because he believes we brought the rain that spoilt his ceremony.'

As she had spoken in French, Enrico remained unaware of her insult to his father. But Gregory abruptly waved her to silence and asked the young man, 'Does your father often have these visions, and do they afterwards always come about?'

Enrico shrugged. 'I regrets. I's mos' unhappy for yo'! His visions do not come frequent, but when he has them it is as seeing true.'

Gregory turned to Manon. 'Then things don't look too good. You remember what a shock he appeared to get when he looked at me on first coming into this room? Unless he

25

did see something unusual about me there's no accounting for that.'

'But it must not happen,' she protested vigorously. 'And it can't if you take care. From midday onwards you must not leave your hotel.'

He smiled at her. 'The Arabs have a saying, "The fate of every man is bound about his brow", and there is no escaping Fate. I've been mighty lucky. They say a cat has nine lives, but I've had at least a score of narrow escapes from death. And I'm not afraid to die. In fact . . . Anyhow, please don't upset your charming self about me.'

Silence fell again; then, after a moment, Enrico said, 'The rain, he has stopped. There will be much water still, but yo' wish it and I make try to get yo' home.'

Gregory thanked him and he went out to fetch his car. When he had brought it round to the door the visitors made formal adieux to the old man and the three Negresses, then went down the steps.

Water was still rushing ankle-deep down the sloping road, but the little car slushed steadily through it. Then, as they entered the tunnel on the outskirts of the city, Enrico asked, 'Where I drop yo'?'

'I stay at ze 'Otel Copacabana Palace,' said Manon.

Gregory turned to smile at her. 'Why, so do I. How very convenient.'

A quarter of an hour later Enrico set them down outside the hotel. Gregory had palmed twenty thousand *cruzeiros*. As he shook hands with the young man, he said in a whisper, 'Just for the petrol,' then added louder, 'Good night; we cannot thank you enough.'

With a happy grin, Enrico shook hands with Manon and drove off. It was by then after two o'clock in the morning, but Latin American cities are said never to sleep. There were still a number of people about and the bar was open. Their clothes were still damp but causing them no inconvenience so they went in. It was a long dimly-lit room, with white moulds of seahorses and starfish decorating the dark green walls. When they had settled in a corner, Gregory ordered

26

foie-gras sandwiches and brandies-and-soda for them both. Then he said:

'It's been quite a night, hasn't it?'

She nodded. 'Yes, but it is tomorrow night I am worried about.'

'Please don't be,' he urged her. 'Never meet trouble halfway. Tonight is far from over yet. Much better think about that. By the by, what is the number of your room?'

She hesitated, then fobbed him off by asking, 'Why do you wish to know?'

'So that I can tell the waiter to send a magnum of champagne up there.'

'No! No!' She gave a nervous little laugh. 'I hadn't even met you five hours ago. I'll admit that I have had a few lovers, but I'm not the sort of girl who is willing to jump into bed with every attractive man she meets. I require to be courted and get to know a man really well before I am prepared to play that sort of game.'

Gregory gave a heavy sigh. 'I'd be delighted to spend months escorting you about as your *chevalier sans peur et sans reproche*, given the prospect of eventually becoming your lover, but, unfortunately, it seems that in my case time does not permit such a prolonged wooing.'

'I cannot believe it. I simply cannot.'

He shrugged. 'I, too, find it difficult to resign myself to the thought that I'll be a lifeless body by this time tomorrow night. But the old man seemed pretty positive that I would be, so it is only sensible to regard this as my last night on earth.'

Turning his head, he gazed straight into her big eyes and went on, 'Try to look at it from my point of view. If you thought the odds were that in twenty-four hours you would be dead, would you be content to spend them alone, sleepless, sweating with fear at the thought of the unknown into which, within a few hours, you were to be precipitated; or, if you had the remotest chance, spend them in bed with a delightful companion who could make you temporarily forget?'

'Of course I'd hate to be left on my own. And I'm des-

27

perately sorry for you. But, really, you are taking an unfair advantage of your situation.'

'No,' he insisted, 'this is not blackmail. You are not a young, unmarried girl. You have admitted to me that you have had several lovers, so evidently your conscience is not troubled by that sort of thing. I am, too, somewhat of a judge of physical characteristics, and I would bet my last farthing that you love being made love to. So why not enjoy yourself and at the same time do me a great kindness? You like me, don't you?'

'Yes, yes; you must know that.'

'Then all I am asking is that you should skip the usual preliminaries and be generous. Take me as your lover tonight. Then, if I die tomorrow, you'll be able to chalk it up as one of the good deeds you have done.'

As she looked at his lean face, her full lips parted in a sudden smile and she murmured, 'I have never met such a persuasive man, and the circumstances being so unusual, my pride is salvaged for such a swift surrender. Very well. The number of my room is 406.'

Gregory took her hand and kissed it. 'That adds up to ten, which reduces to one—my lucky number. And I think you are adorable.'

When the waiter arrived with the drinks and sandwiches, Gregory gave him the number of Manon's room and ordered a magnum of Krug '59 to be sent up there. Suddenly they found that they were both hungry, and within ten minutes the plate of sandwiches was empty. They finished their brandies-and-soda, then he escorted her to the lift and whispered, 'How long?'

Her eyes narrowed but held a hint of laughter as she whispered back, 'Twenty minutes, and if you are a moment later you will find my door locked.'

Up in his own room, Gregory undressed, gave himself a swift shave, put on a dressing gown, then with long-practised silence made his way like a shadow up two flights of stairs and along the now deserted corridors until he reached the door of her room. Soundlessly he opened it and slipped inside. Only seventeen minutes had elapsed since they had

28

parted, but she was sitting up in bed naked, her hands clasped round her knees.

As they smiled at one another, he said, 'Come, jump out of bed so that I can enjoy the sight of all your beauties.' Without a second's hesitation she slid from between the sheets and clasped her hands behind her neck, so that her round, firm breasts stood out in full perfection.

His glance ran over her, noting the full hips, the triangle of thick dark curls that covered her lower abdomen, the flared nostrils, through which she was already breathing deeply, and her big eyes that had taken on an almost slumbrous expression. He knew then what he was in for; but as this boded to be the last woman he could ever have, he could have wished for nothing better.

Throwing off his dressing gown, he slid his hands down the satin-soft skin of her sides, hips and buttocks. She quivered as he did so and lifted her face to his. Her thick lips seemed to engulf his and she sucked avidly at his tongue. When he pushed her gently back on to the bed she was already gasping with uncontrollable passion.

It was close on seven o'clock in the morning when he left her. They had agreed to meet downstairs for drinks at midday, then lunch together. Back in his own room he hardly gave a thought to the prophecy that his life was drawing swiftly to a close. He had been faced with probable sudden death too often, and physically he felt not exhausted but wonderfully relaxed. Having cleaned his teeth and telephoned down to be called at eleven o'clock, he got into bed. Within five minutes he was sound asleep.

Manon had also ordered her *café complet* to be brought to her at eleven o'clock. Having munched a croissant, she poured her coffee, lit a cigarette and lay back to think.

Like a happy cat that has licked up all the cream, she smiled at her memories of the hours Gregory had spent in her bed. Within ten minutes of meeting him the previous evening she had made up her mind to get him if she could. She had been telling the truth when she said it was not her custom to hop into bed with men after only a brief acquaintance; but she was glad, in this case, that circumstances had enabled her to do so without loss of face.

Idly, she compared Gregory with Pierre, her current lover, and could not decide which was the more physically satisfying. Mentally, she found Gregory the more stimulating companion, but that might be because he was still like a book of which she had turned only the first page. In any case, Pierre was far away in Tahiti, so she would not be plagued by jealous scenes owing to their coming into collision.

Pierre certainly had his points as a lover, but the social graces were not among them. He would have had little chance of penetrating circles that she could hope to without difficulty; that was why she had reluctantly agreed to go to Rio for him. All had gone well. She had succeeded in making the personal contact he had considered so important and had good hopes now that the venture in which they were engaged would prove successful. If it did not, she thought bleakly, she would be in a fine mess.

Manon's besetting sin was extravagance. It had plagued her all her life, yet she never seemed to be able to control her impulse to squander money. Building a house on one of the outer islands of the Fiji group had been sheer madness. But for that, she would still be receiving a handsome income. As it was, ferrying the material over from Suva alone had cost a fortune. If the gamble that Pierre had persuaded her to finance failed she would have to sell the house, and how many people would want to buy a handsome property in such a remote place? She would be lucky if she saw a quarter of her money back. And what then? Unless they were successful she would be reduced to living on a pittance. She shuddered.

The thought of money brought her back to the present. She would never have gone to the expense of this trip to Rio had it not been essential to scare off the Brazilian. Anyway, she should have had more sense than to stay at this *grande-luxe* hotel; yet, after all, how could she have brought herself to live, even for a week, at some shoddy *pension*?

She had booked a passage back to Tahiti for two days

hence, but now this exciting Englishman had come on the scene. And she had gathered from something Patricia Wellesley had said that he was extremely rich. Somehow she must find the money to stay on for a while. If need be, she could sell a ring.

Suddenly it came back to her that Gregory was doomed to die within twenty-four hours. Could that possibly be true? Fortune-tellers often made false predictions. Yet the old man had been terrifyingly accurate about herself. He had told her she would have a new lover, had spoken of another with whom she had financial ties, which fitted Pierre and, *quel horreur*, had dragged up from the past the fact that she had killed Georges. At the memory of how she killed him, another shudder ran through her. Thrusting the thought from her mind, she jumped out of bed and ran herself a bath.

The Copacabana Palace formed a huge quadrilateral built round a large swimming pool. Three of its sides were many storeys high and looked down on the pool or across the fourth, much lower side, to the sea. This fourth side faced the promenade and contained the reception hall, bars, restaurant and grill room. But a wide terrace ran all round the pool and along it were set tables, under gaily-coloured umbrellas, at which guests could take their meals in the open while watching the bathers.

A little before twelve o'clock, Gregory, dressed in a bright blue open-necked shirt and a freshly pressed suit of pale fawn linen, secured one of the tables just outside the bar and ordered himself a Planter's Punch. His four hours' sleep had considerably refreshed him, although he admitted to himself that at his age he could not stand up to a succession of nights like that just passed. Having gratefully downed the first half of his drink, he smiled cynically to himself at the thought that it looked as though he would not be called on to do so.

Manon did not put in an appearance until nearly half past twelve. She looked as fresh as a daisy and came towards him with the faintly swaggering air of a woman who is extremely *chic* and knows it. The scarlet dress she was wearing suited her dark hair and bronzed skin to perfection. The skirt was short and flaring, displaying her admirable legs, and the

31

bodice had a deep 'V', showing the valley between her full breasts. Gregory would have bet good money that she had very little on beneath the dress; but the heat from the sun blazing almost directly overhead was excuse enough for that, and most of the people sitting nearby were wearing only bikinis or bathing shorts.

Seeing the circumstances in which they had parted only a few hours before, it was quite natural that anyone who observed them exchanging greetings would have taken them for old friends, but in fact they knew next to nothing about each other; and within a few minutes of Manon's having been provided with a drink, she said:

'I gave up blushing long ago, but if I hadn't I would now at the thought of what happened last night, and that we're practically strangers. I don't even know if you're married.'

He looked a little surprised at the question, then shook his head. 'No; I lost my wife some years ago.'

'Well,' she smiled, 'men have been known to travel without their wives and, er . . . How did you lose her?'

'We were guests with several other people on a private yacht owned by an old friend of mine, Sir Pellinore Gwaine-Cust, enjoying a round-the-world cruise. One night, on the run up from Tahiti to Hawaii, the yacht struck an uncharted reef that ripped her bottom out. It was all over in a few minutes and a high sea was running. Everyone aboard except myself was drowned, and I was washed up on a remote island.'[1]

'How awful for you. Were you very devoted to her?'

'Very. I still miss her terribly.'

'Had you been married to her long?'

'Since the end of the war, and we had been lovers from within a few weeks of its beginning.'

'Why didn't you marry her before, then?'

'For one thing she was already married. For another, there were various complications, which made it next to impossible for her to get a divorce.'

'Do tell me about her.'

[1] *The Island Where Time Stands Still.*

32

Gregory shook his head. 'No, my dear. The history of an old love would only bore you.'

'It certainly would not. You are a fascinating person and I want to know every single thing about you.'

He grinned at her. 'Then we are two fascinating persons. All right, if you insist. But let's order lunch first.'

When they had studied the long menu the waiter brought them, Gregory decided on cold *bisque homard* and *poulet Duc de Bourgoyne;* Manon on melon, followed by a *tournedos* done rare and a *caju* ice.

'I think I could manage an ice, too,' he said. 'But what is *caju*?'

'Cashew,' she replied. 'But this isn't made from the nuts. It is flavoured with the fresh fruit of the plant, and it's delicious.'

'Really! Then I'll try one.' Handing the menu back to the waiter, he went on: 'As a young man I was a foreign correspondent. Later I carried out several special investigations for Sir Pellinore, the grand old man I mentioned a few minutes ago. He was a banker and immensely wealthy. When the war came he asked me to go into Germany and attempt to get in touch with a group of Generals who were conspiring to overthrow Hitler.'[1]

Manon's eyes widened. 'So you became a secret agent. How thrilling!'

'That's it and it was on my first mission that I met Erika. She came from a famous Bavarian family and was the daughter of General von Epp. When I met her she was married to a Count von Osterberg. In the early days she had been pro-Nazi and was a great friend of Hermann Goering's, but she had quarrelled with Hitler about his persecution of the Jews and she proved to be my lead to the conspirators.'

'What was she like?'

'Golden-haired, blue-eyed and rather like Marlene Dietrich. She was said to be one of the loveliest women in Germany. We fell for one another right away, but she refused to leave Germany for England with me after the failure of the Munich Bomb Plot.

[1] *The Scarlet Impostor.*

'Instead, she took refuge in Finland. There we met again.[1] Later we were in Norway together, then in Belgium, where she was shot and badly wounded; but I got her off from the beaches of Dunkirk.[2] In due course I carried out many other missions for Sir Pellinore. On one occasion I went into Germany to get Erika out after she had been lured back there and had fallen into a trap.[3] Finally, we met again in Berlin in the last week of the war. The Russians were storming the city and we escaped only by the skin of our teeth.[4] You see now how it was that we couldn't get married until the war was over.'

'It all sounds incredibly exciting. Are you still a secret agent?'

Gregory laughed. 'Good gracious, no. I gave up that sort of thing long ago.'

'What do you do for a living, then?'

'Nothing. Sir Pellinore was a most generous patron. That enabled me to buy a charming estate in Dorset, and Erika and I settled down there. The old boy had no children and when he died he left me a large part of his fortune; so I can well afford to spend the greater part of the year travelling. Since I lost Erika I've done little else.'

Manon sighed. As Gregory's death was predicted for that night, his confirmation that he was very rich added insult to injury. That Fate should have sent her such a charming lover and one who could afford to indulge her every whim, yet rob her of him before she had a chance to make a bid to share his wealth, was doubly cruel.

After a moment he said, 'Now it's your turn to tell me about yourself.'

She shrugged. 'My story is nowhere near so exciting as yours. I was born in Algiers and come from an old French colonial family. I was only ten when the war started. It didn't make very much difference to our lives, although there was great excitement at the time of the Anglo-American landings.

[1] *Faked Passports.*
[2] *The Black Baroness.*
[3] *V for Vengeance, Come Into My Parlour* and *Traitor's Gate.*
[4] *They Used Dark Forces.*

After the war my parents sent me to Paris to complete my education, and I lived with an aunt. I liked Paris much better than Algiers; so when my schooling was finished I stayed on there, and as the family was not very well off I earned my living for six years working in an art gallery.

'Naturally my parents expected me to spend my holidays with them, and it was in Algiers that I met Georges de Bois-Tracy. He was a good bit older than me, but quite attractive, and he owned hundreds of hectares of vineyards in one of the best wine-producing districts. By then I was twenty-five and had had several *affaires,* but none of them with men who could afford to keep a wife with my extravagant tastes; whereas Georges could give me everything I wanted. At least I believed so at the time.

'That he didn't wasn't altogether his fault. It was mainly due to the increasingly troubled state of Algeria. From the time of the victory celebrations in 1945 there had been unorganised risings and an agitation for independence. These had been suppressed with a firm hand; but the agitation continued and in 1947 the Muslims, led by Missali Hajj, got the vote. Everyone in Algeria knew that they were living on a volcano, but it seemed that the Government had control of the situation and there was no reason to suppose that there was any serious menace to the white population.

'Matters still stood like that when I married Georges in June 1954. I had expected to spend most of my time living a pleasant social life in his house in Algiers and to be able to make trips to Paris two or three times a year. But on November 1st, less than five months after my marriage, there were simultaneous risings in seventy localities. Our estate was a long way from the capital and we were out there at the time. There was no trouble in our area, but the risings continued sporadically all over the country; and Georges decreed that we must remain on our property to protect it.

'We armed our employees and they were loyal to us, but they might not have remained so if Georges and I had left them on their own for any length of time. Now that bands of Arabs were carrying out organised raids on the isolated homes of the white Colons, to leave the place for even a few days was to risk returning to find it burned to the ground and every cask of wine in the bodegas stove in.'

'Surely,' Gregory remarked, 'your husband could have remained there and let you live in the city? In any case, he ought to have done that if the place was likely to be attacked, rather than expose you to danger.'

'Oh, he could have, but he wouldn't,' Manon replied bitterly. 'He was obsessed by jealousy and feared that if we lived apart even for a few weeks I would start an *affaire* with another man. So I was condemned to lead a dreary life out there in the country, miles from anywhere. And, of course, we were attacked several times. In the spring of 1956 the Front of National Liberation was formed, and things got steadily worse. Again and again I begged Georges to sell out for what we could get, as on the income from his investments we could have left Algeria and gone to live in reasonable comfort in Paris. But he had inherited his property from four generations of forbears and flatly refused to give it up.

'In 1958 the F.L.N. formed a Provisional Government of the Algerian Republic. Although it could not establish itself on Algerian soil, it was recognised by all the Arab States and by then was conducting widespread terrorist activities all over the country. But that same year Charles de Gaulle came back to power. We all took heart because we thought that, being a strong man, within a few months he would restore order.

'Instead, matters became even worse. The months dragged by and in 1961 he permitted the referendum on self-determination. The O.A.S.—of which, of course, we were members—succeeded in preventing the Arabs from getting a clear majority, but in '62 that *cochon* de Gaulle betrayed us and declared Algeria independent.

'To be left at the mercy of a coloured Government seemed the last straw, but Georges still refused to sell out and emigrate. Although I had no money of my own, I had practically made up my mind to leave him; but that summer he developed heart trouble, so I felt that I must remain with him, anyhow until he showed signs of getting better. But he didn't. In the autumn he had a fatal attack.'

36

Manon paused to light a cigarette. While she did so she recalled vividly the afternoon on which the attack had occurred. Georges had called to her to get from his desk the drops he took to counter such attacks. She had, and had actually given them to him. Then, on a sudden impulse to end matters and regain her freedom, she had snatched the bottle back from him, thrown it out of the window and, with distended eyes, watched him die in agony. For the thousandth time she cursed herself for her folly in not having simply kept the bottle. But that was another matter.

After a moment she went on: 'Georges' death meant liberation from my prison—an end to eight of the best years of my life utterly wasted. But he had left me the greater part of his money, so I was free to leave Algeria and make a home for myself wherever I chose.

'Naturally, my inclination was to return to Paris, but the idea of living in France as long as it was ruled by that traitor de Gaulle was repugnant to me, and the climate of Paris is horrid in winter. I have always loved the sun; so I decided to settle in Tahiti.

'At first I lived in an hotel, then I rented a small villa, as I meant to take my time looking for a really pleasant property. But after I had been in the island for six months the situation there rapidly began to deteriorate. Thousands of white Colons from Algeria, who had been dispossessed, were sent out there by de Gaulle. Very few of the poor wretches had any money, so many of them turned to crime and the streets of Papeete became dangerous at night. My own position, as a still wealthy French ex-patriate from Algeria, became, too, a specially awkward one, because I had quite a number of old friends and acquaintances among the new arrivals. I helped them as much as I could, but they were constantly borrowing money from me that I knew I should never see back, and I simply could not afford to go on like that.

'While I was wondering how to get out of this awkward situation, I took a trip to Fiji and fell in love with it. Some of the outer islands are absolutely heavenly, particularly those to the west. I bought one in the Mamanuca Group, and built a house on it. There, now you know all there is to know about me.'

Over lunch they talked on over their respective pasts with so much enjoyment in each other that they both temporarily forgot the shadow that hung over Gregory.

When they had finished their meal Gregory said, 'There is nothing I would like more than to ask you to dine with me tonight; but, unfortunately, I'm committed to dine at the British Embassy.'

Quickly she laid a hand on his. 'Don't go. Please don't go. I want you to stay here and lock yourself in your room.'

He shook his head. 'No, I wouldn't like to cry off at the last moment. Our Ambassador learned through Hugo Wellesley that I was in Rio, and he said how much he would like to talk over old times with me. You see, it was not until after the war that he went into the Foreign Service, and during the war he held a post that brought him into contact with many of my own activities. And this is to be a *tête-à-tête* dinner; just H.E. and myself.'

For some while Manon strove to persuade Gregory to change his mind; but, although he had long been out of the game, he knew, from what Hugo had said, that the Ambassador wanted a private talk with him about the world situation; so he remained firm.

At length she said with a sigh, 'Very well then. But at least let me see you again before you go. We'll go up for our siesta now, but come along to my room about six o'clock. I'll have a bottle of champagne on ice up there and we'll hang the "Don't Disturb" notice outside the door.'

Gregory needed no telling what she had in mind and, now fortified by an excellent lunch, he smilingly accepted the challenge.

That evening his session with Manon matured as he had expected, to their mutual delight. While he was dressing, she again pleaded desperately with him not to go out. But he told her not to worry, as the only risk he could think of was that of being attacked by thugs. As he would be going by taxi, such an occurrence was most unlikely; and if it did happen, few people were better qualified by long practice than he was to take care of themselves. At a quarter to eight, after a last lingering kiss, he left her to go to his own room to change.

Nevertheless, having survived so many perils only owing to his lifelong habit of never taking an unnecessary risk, he had been in half a mind to plead sudden illness as an excuse for not keeping his dinner engagement. His resolve not to do so had actually been determined by the fact that death had no terrors for him. On the contrary, as he had always been a convinced believer in survival after death, it held a promise for him of reunion with his beloved Erika. Even so, before he left he took the precaution of slipping a small automatic, with which he always travelled, into his hip pocket.

At four o'clock that afternoon it had again begun to rain, heavily and persistently. In fact, the downpour was such that, while in the taxi that took him to the Embassy, he could not see through the windows for more than a hundred yards ahead.

The British Embassy in the Rua Sao Clemente was a fine copy of Georgian achitecture. Built in the late forties, it stood well back from the street in a pleasant garden. The lofty, handsomely furnished rooms recalled the more spacious days of the past, but Gregory and the Ambassador dined in a small, well-stocked library.

His Excellency was a genial host and most knowledgeable; so Gregory thoroughly enjoyed an admirable meal and their long talk afterwards about the foreign policies of various nations which had resulted in trouble spots developing in so many parts of the world.

During the evening H.E. asked Gregory if he was going up to Brasilia.

'I don't think so,' he replied. 'The fantastic buildings in the new capital must be some of the finest examples of modern architecture in the world, but one can appreciate them well enough from photographs and, I gather, there is nothing else to see there.'

'That's true,' the Ambassador agreed. 'One must admire the Brazilians for their stupendous effort to show that they are no longer a backward nation, but the huge cost of it has ruined their economy and the city has become a white elephant. The Congressmen and Senators who have to hold their sessions there loathe it and positively fight for places on the planes to get back to Rio every weekend. It has, too, developed into a depressed area. The many thousands of labourers who were sent up there to build it are now mostly unemployed, so the suburbs have become huge shanty towns where poverty is rampant. However, should you change your mind, let me know and I'll furnish you with introductions to the unfortunate members of my staff who are compelled to live there.'

Soon after midnight a taxi was summoned to take Gregory back to his hotel. The rain was still coming down in torrents. After eight hours of steady downpour the drains were choked and the street, awash well above the pavements, looked like a turbulent river.

On being told to go to the Copocabana Palace, the driver, in a travesty of English flavoured with an American accent, said he would do his best but could make no promise, as the water was pouring in thousands of gallons down the mountainsides through the city to the sea. But it could not get away there because the tide was rising and blocking the escape of the flood-waters. In consequence they would be still deeper near the shore, and Grgeory might have to walk the last mile or more.

As they progressed at only a few miles an hour, Gregory saw that the man had good reason for his pessimism. Every street they entered had abandoned cars in it and when they reached the broad waterfront, two-thirds of the way along Botafogo Bay, there were long lines of stationary vehicles left awash by their owners. The water there was knee-deep and its height was increasing every moment. The taxi man succeeded in keeping going only by driving his cab up on to and along the pavement.

A few hundred yards further on they reached a big open space at the southern end of the bay, called the Mourisco. There the taxi should have turned inland in the direction of the tunnel, but it pulled up with a jerk. Turning, the driver made Gregory understand that he dared go no further. At such a slow pace it would take him at least another half-hour to reach the Copacabana Palace, and by the time he got back to recross the Mourisco, the water would have risen to a level that would submerge his engine.

The sight of the floods had at last made Gregory really uneasy. Now, cursing his folly at not having asked H.E. to put him up for the night at the Embassy, he reluctantly got out and paid off the driver. The water was well above his knees and he found it a considerable effort to splash through it.

Miles of the seafront along Rio's many bays consist of reclaimed land which has been laid out in long, broad lawns planted with ornamental trees. Some stretches are wider than others and the Mourisco is one of these. It forms a small triangular park with three main streets running into it. The whole of the area was inundated, so no pavements, street islands or flower-beds were visible. From between the blocks of buildings, several hundred yards away from where Gregory had left the taxi, the streets, seen only vaguely through pouring rain, had the appearance of rushing rivers. Behind him the flood merged with the sea, so the little park was one great sheet of water, from which rose only the trees and the upper parts of stranded vehicles.

Being unable to make out any of the paths, Gregory had no option but to head straight across the park in the direction in which he knew the tunnel lay. He had not gone twenty yards before he struck rising ground, so knew that he must be crossing a flower-bed. Next moment, as he plunged down its far side, he tripped and fell. As he was already drenched to the skin, that made him no wetter, but he had gulped down a mouthful of evil-tasting water.

Cursing, he picked himself up and stumbled on for a further thirty yards with the water sloshing about his lower thighs. Suddenly the ground seemed to give beneath his feet and he plunged in up to his armpits. He had walked into a hidden gully. Now using his hands and arms as well as his legs, he thrust himself forward until he had crossed the gully and mounted the far side. Resting for a moment, he drew in a few deep breaths while taking stock of his situation.

He was only a third of the way across the Mourisco and when he reached the far side he would still have to wade up the street leading to the tunnel. The water should be shallower there. But what when he came out at the far end of the tunnel? The deluge must have flooded the Copacabana waterfront as deeply as it had that of Botafogo Bay, and the promenade was much narrower there. The tide was coming in, but, even so, he might get caught in a current and swept out to sea. After a moment he decided that it would be much safer to take the right hand of the three streets and make his way back to the Embassy.

Altering his direction slightly, he set off again. Forcing his legs and knees through the swirling water, and breathing heavily, he ploughed on for another few minutes; then his left foot struck something and with a great splash he measured his length in the water. This time he had caught his foot in one of the low iron hoops that edged the plots of grass.

As he fell, he felt a fierce pain shoot through his left ankle, and knew that he had either sprained or broken it. When he stumbled to his feet and tried his weight upon it the pain was agonising. Setting his teeth, he struggled a few steps, slipped on the muddy slope of another flower-bed and sprawled face-down in another gully.

Fortunately, it was shallower than the first into which he had stumbled. Squirming round, he was able to sit up with his head still above the water level. Desperately anxious now, he began to shout for help. But no moving vehicle was in sight, nor any pedestrian. Through the half-blinding rain he could see the lighted windows in the not-far-distant buildings. There lay safety. In normal conditions the people in those rooms would have heard him. But the roar of the torrential rain drowned his shouts and the water was still rising. Grimly, he realised that his life now depended upon his ability to bear the atrocious pain in his ankle for another hundred yards until he was close enough to be heard.

Gritting his teeth, he prepared to make the effort. Then, just as he put his weight on his good foot to stand up, something hit him hard on the back of the head, knocking him forward and sideways. As he rolled over and under, whatever it was came to rest across his body. Thrusting his head above

42

the surface, he shook the water from his eyes. In the semi-darkness he peered at the thing that now pinned him down. It was a long wooden bench that had come adrift from its footings and was being swept out to sea. The bench was made of that heavy timber strangely enough known in Europe as 'Brazil wood' long before the Portuguese had discovered Brazil, but from which the country had taken its name. Strive as he would, Gregory could not lift it from his chest or squirm from beneath it. The water was lapping against his mouth and only by straining his neck could he keep his nostrils an inch or so above the wavelets.

Up to that moment Gregory had been no more than considerably worried and still confident that, as had been the case so many times in the past, by keeping his head he would find a way out of his dangerous situation. Now he knew that he was trapped with little hope of escape. Faced with imminent death, he endeavoured to resign himself to it by fixing his thoughts on Erika. For a while he lay there gasping and spitting as, every few moments, the water lapped against his mouth and nose. Suddenly, he felt that he could bear it no longer. Animated again by the will to live, he gathered all his strength and made a final effort. It resulted in the heavy bench shifting a little without warning, so that its weight forced back his head. Next moment, his eyes bulging, he was gulping down water. Before he lost consciousness his last grim thought was:

'So that damned *Macumba* priest was right. I've been doomed to die in a ditch.'

3

A New Interest

When Gregory opened his eyes he could not for a moment imagine where he was or what had happened to him. He was lying on his back on a surface of hard stone and a man was crouching over him, alternately, with widespread hands, crushing in his lungs and letting up.

Gulping, he moved his head unhappily from side to side and tried to lift his own hands to defend himself, but could not. Staring up into the face above his own, he was seized for a second with the wild notion that he was in Hell and being attacked by a demon; for, in the uncertain light, his torturer's head seemed twice the size of that of a normal man. Then he became conscious that it was pouring with rain and that he was soaked to the skin.

With an effort he gasped out, 'Stop! For God's sake, stop!'

The demon sat back on his haunches and exclaimed, 'So you speak English. How fortunate.'

'Where ... where am I?' Gregory wheezed.

'In the Mourisco, on the Praia de Botafogo. I was making my way back to my hotel when I noticed one of the park benches and decided to rest on it for a few minutes. I found you pinned beneath it and, although you were unconscious, I realised that you could not have been so for long, so I carried you here. We are now a few feet above the water on the base of the statue to Pasteur. I applied artificial respiration and after some minutes you came round. That makes me very happy. Where do you live?'

'Copacabana Palace.' Gregory's lungs were working again, but he was very far from recovered and could speak only

44

with difficulty. Struggling into a sitting position he knuckled the water from his eyes. Again he thought he must be dead or dreaming. The man towering above him was huge, and his head, now outlined against the light coming from the nearest buildings, was enormous.

At that moment his rescuer put a hand beneath his arm and lifted him to his feet. From his left ankle a ghastly pain shot up his leg. In his weakened state it was more than he could bear, and he slid into unconsciousness.

When he came to, it seemed that he had passed into another phase of his nightmare. He was lying face down, with his head hanging over what felt like an iron bar. His body was balanced on some narrow structure, on either side of which his arms and legs dangled, the latter trailing in water. At a steady pace, he and the contraption on which he lay were being pushed forward. As he stared downwards, the light from a nearby window glinted on curved black metal only a few inches beneath his nose. It was a mudguard and he realised then that he was spreadeagled face down on a motor-cycle. Even had he been in a fit state to talk, the fact that his throat was resting on the handlebars would have made it difficult to do so; but memory was seeping back. Rightly, he deduced that, after carrying him some way, the giant who had rescued him had come upon a machine that its owner had not had the strength to push home, and was using it as a means of transport.

Easing the position of his head from time to time, but still half comatose, Gregory let matters take their course. For what seemed to him an endless time, the machine continued to plough through knee-deep water, then it was thrust for some way up a slope on to a pavement, into a glare of light and brought to a halt. As the giant lifted Gregory from it, he saw that they were at the entrance to the Copacabana Palace.

Now, for the first time, he could see his rescuer clearly. He was a splendid specimen of manhood. Young, good-looking, with copper-coloured skin, but features more European than native; and from his head, which had appeared so huge in the semi-darkness, rose a four-inch-deep halo of black hair.

'Then I wasn't dreaming,' Gregory muttered. 'You really are a giant.'

The other grinned, showing two perfect rows of strong white teeth. 'I am six foot five. But that is nothing exceptional in my country. I have a cousin who is six foot seven. It was quite a struggle to get you home, but here we are.'

'I owe you my life,' Gregory said gravely. 'I can never thank you enough. Let's get inside. We could both do with a drink.'

As he spoke, his companion let go his arm to prop the motor-cycle alongside the hotel entrance. No longer supported, Gregory lurched, came down on his injured foot, lost his balance and fell forward, striking his head heavily against the door. Stars and circles flashed before his eyes and he again passed out.

When he regained consciousness he was up in his room, being undressed by one of the night porters and an under-manager. As they got him into bed, he enquired for his rescuer. The under-manger shook his head:

' 'E left without giving 'is name. 'E said only that 'e was sorry about your fall, but 'e did not realise you were so weak. What a fine young man. A South Sea Islander. We do not often see such in Rio. Lie still now, sir, please, for a few minutes. I 'ave telephone the 'otel doctor but the flood makes it impossible for him to come; so I appeal to doctor who is a guest here. An American. 'E is dressing and will be 'ere soon.'

Five minutes later, a tall, lean American arrived and took charge. Having examined Gregory's ankle, he said that it was not broken but very badly sprained and it would be some days before he was able to get about again. By the time he had finished dressing it, the under-manager brought Gregory a double rum on the rocks that he had ordered and with many expressions of sympathy, they left him.

As soon as they had gone, he put a call through to Manon. On hearing his voice, she gave vent, in her relief at knowing him to be safely back, to a spate of French, interlarded with many endearments. Then he told her of his hairsbreadth escape and how it had come about that the *Macumba* priest had seen him in his vision as 'dead in a ditch'. She wanted to

46

come to him at once; but he said that he badly needed sleep, and it was agreed that she should pay him a visit at ten o'clock the following morning.

When he awoke, apart from some soreness in the lungs, he had fully recovered from his night's ordeal; but his ankle proved a severe handicap in getting to the bathroom and he managed it only with the aid of a chair, which he alternately leant on and pushed in front of him. Back in bed, he telephoned the Wellesleys. Hugo had already set off on an attempt to get to his office in the Avenida Presidente Vargas, so it was to Patricia that Gregory related his adventure. She wanted to bring him books to read while he was laid up, but a glance out of the window had shown him that the rain was still descending in a solid curtain, so the floods must be as bad as ever; and he persuaded her to put off her visit, anyhow until the following day.

Manon had had the same thought about reading matter; for she arrived with an armful of magazines and three French novels, perched herself on the edge of his bed, embraced him with Gallic warmth, then made him tell her every detail of his near-drowning and rescue.

After a while she told him that she was due to fly up to Mexico, and thence home, on the following day; but many landslides had been reported and she was wondering if she would be able to get out to the airport.

Gregory said that, even if the road out to the international airport was blocked, she should be able to get a plane to it from the local airport on the waterfront near the city centre. Then he went on to say how distressed he was to think that their romance must end so soon, and he asked whether she could not possibly postpone her departure.

Screwing her full lips into a grimace, she replied, 'Chéri, I have fallen for you completely, so I would like nothing better. But, alas, it is a question of money. I brought with me only as much as I thought I would need, and to get a further grant of currency from Fiji would take a week at least.'

Patting her hand, Gregory smiled and said, 'Then, my sweet, don't give it another thought. You must stay on as my guest.'

47

Manon made a pretence of demurring; but she needed no great pressing, then accepted with becoming grace. Meanwhile, she had been thinking: 'How right I was to try it on. Now I won't have to sell one of my rings. And the danger to him is past, thank God. His ankle is a nuisance: but no, perhaps it is all for the best. While he is cooped up here I'll be able to find out all his likes and dislikes, and he'll have no chance to become interested in another woman. Oh, if only I can hook him.'

Her belief that she would have Gregory to herself for several days proved correct. When the American doctor paid him a visit he said that his patient would do far better to remain in bed, or at least in his room, with his foot up, rather than try to hobble about on crutches—even if a pair could have been procured—and that would have been far from easy, as few shops other than those supplying food had opened for business that morning.

For his part, Gregory was happy to accept Manon's administrations. It was much more fun to have a pretty woman support him while he shaved and help him have a bath, than to call on the services of a valet. Apart from the siesta hours and at night, when Manon returned to her own room, she never left him. They had their meals sent up, swopped stories, laughed and made love, hardly noticing the rain which continued mercilessly as though it meant never to stop.

He had noticed that she wore several rings and that one, on the index finger of her left hand, was an enormous aquamarine, in an old-fashioned setting of gold filigree work. On the second morning of the deluge she was sitting on the edge of his bed, enjoying a pre-lunch glass of champagne with him, when he asked her where she had found the ring.

'Ah!' she laughed. 'That is my Borgia ring and if you cease to love me I shall make use of it; then you will die in a fit.'

For a moment he thought she was joking about the ring's containing poison; but, taking it between the first finger and thumb of her right hand, she pressed a secret spring in the filigree work. The stone slid back, revealing a hollow cavity. In it there lay a small, round pill.

Closing the ring again, she smiled at him. 'Georges, my

48

late husband, gave it to me at the time when the troubles in Algeria became really serious. As I told you the other day, we lived for many months on his estate far up-country. Several times the house was attacked and if those devils of Arabs had overcome our people things would have gone ill with me. It is all very well for cynical people to say that if a woman cannot escape being raped she should "lie back and enjoy it", but after the first two or three times in quick succession there can be no more pleasure in it. Soon afterwards, I am told, it becomes agonising and after about twenty men have had a woman one after the other, she dies from it. As I was the only white woman there, you can be certain that every one of those brutes would have demanded his turn with me, and some more than once. That is why Georges bought the ring for me and made me promise to swallow the pill in it if I was captured. The pill is cyanide of potassium and would have killed me instantly.'

'And you would have taken it?'

She shrugged. 'Of course. I am not afraid of death, only of pain.'

That same evening their pleasant privacy was temporarily interrupted by a visit from Hugo Wellesley. With the initiative so frequently displayed by British officers when abroad —however reluctant to make themselves conspicuous when at home—the handsome Colonel had gone to the local circus and hired an elephant and its mahout to transport him about through the floods.

He had a depressing tale to tell of devastation and distress. Only the higher ground sloping up to the mountains now remained above water. Millions of pounds' worth of goods had been rendered useless by the flooding of countless basements. Still worse, many of the *favelas*—the sprawling shacktowns on the hillsides—had been swept away by the torrents. Thousands of people now had no roof over their heads, hundreds had been seriously injured and several score were believed to be dead.

Gregory was anxious to trace his rescuer and asked Hugo's help. Except that he was an exceptionally tall young man and a South Sea Islander, there was nothing to go on, and in a

49

city of nearly four million inhabitants this would be no easy task, but the Colonel promised to do his best. Then, after finishing his second drink, and being satisfied that Gregory lacked for nothing and was in good hands, Hugo took his departure.

For a further forty-eight hours the rain continued without ceasing. It was not until the fifth day that it eased to a drizzle, the low, black clouds remaining overhead. The four days' downpour had resulted in the worst disaster Rio had suffered for over eighty years. The only access to the city is along the coast roads. These had been cut, so it was isolated and food had become short. Over twelve thousand people had been rendered homeless and there were three hundred and sixty dead. The sewers had been disrupted, so there was acute danger of a serious epidemic. But the ever-generous Americans had rushed in teams of medicos with a newly-invented injection gun, which punctured arms and sterilised itself, so that a queue of a hundred people could be immunised in a matter of minutes.

As Gregory was rousing from his siesta on the fifth day, a page brought to his room a bouquet of flowers that had wilted a little from the intense humid heat. Attached to them was a card, inscribed *Ratu James Omboluku,* and beneath that was written: *I do hope you are fully recovered,* and an address: *Hotel Gloria.*

Gregory had a vague idea that 'Ratu' was the equivalent in the South Sea Islands to Rajah or Prince. Later that evening, after two unsuccessful attempts, he got on to James Omboloku and asked him to lunch next day; for he had already had the hotel carpenter make him a crutch, and with it was now able to get about without Manon's assistance.

Taking note of this, Manon had decided that her next move should be to make Gregory miss her. Actually she knew very few people in Rio; but she invented several whose invitations she said she could hardly refuse, now that the flood was subsiding. Gregory accepted the situation with a readiness that by no means pleased her; but he had become so used to making his arrangements without reference to anyone else that he was glad that she had already said she was

50

going out. Feeling no obligation to ask her to join them when he gave lunch to the Ratu, he had not even mentioned his own appointment.

It was on Wednesday, the 12th January, that the Ratu James lunched with Gregory. Jackets had to be worn when eating in the restaurant; but it was air-conditioned, so, in spite of the intense heat outside, they felt no discomfort while partaking of an excellent meal.

On seeing the South Sea Island Prince again, Gregory was more than ever impressed by him. His bronzed features had a noble cast and he displayed the quiet self-assurance that is the hallmark of the aristocrat whatever the colour of his skin. Gregory soon learned that his guest was the hereditary Chief of the Nakapoa Group, which lay between Fiji and New Caledonia, but was nearer the former although it had, since 1853, been subject to France.

When Gregory expressed surprise that he spoke English so well, he smiled and said, 'I have many relatives by marriage among the hereditary royalty of the South Pacific. Queen Salote of Tonga was my aunt and the Ratus of Fiji are my cousins. So, although I happen to be a French citizen, my family has always preferred to think of itself as British. I was sent to school in New Zealand and afterwards took my degree there at the University of Dunedin.'

Over their meal they talked of many things and formed an increasing liking for each other. Two hours had sped past very pleasantly and they were sitting over their brandy when Gregory remarked casually:

'I've no wish to pry into your affairs, but you say business brought you to Rio. You don't seem at all like a business man and I'd be most interested to know what your business is.'

The young Ratu hesitated for a moment, then shrugged his broad shoulders. 'Mr. Sallust, I feel that you are a man I can trust, but this should go no further. Off Tujoa, the main island of my group, there is the sunken wreck of an old Spanish ship. I have good reason to believe that when she went down she had aboard her a great fortune in gold. Should others learn of this, they might forestall me in retrieving it. I have come to Rio because there is a prospect of

51

forming a company here that would finance the salvaging of this gold.'

Gregory nodded. 'I see. You speak of a prospect. Does that mean you are fairly certain of getting all the money you require to finance this venture?'

'I would not say that. My prospective backer is very rich, but he is hesitating to assume the sole responsibility for this enterprise.'

For a moment Gregory remained thoughtful. For a long time now he had been at a loose end, with no interest to engage his mind fully. The vivacious and attractive Manon had dropped into his lap, but, as far as he was concerned, after Erika no woman was capable of doing more, for any length of time, than assuming the role of a pleasant playmate. The retrieving of sunken treasure offered both activity and excitement. At length he said:

'I happen to be fairly rich. And I owe you a debt that no money could repay. Unless you can get all the finance you require without difficulty, let me know, and I'll consider rowing in with a few thousand.'

4

Spanish Gold

The Ratu gave Gregory a look of pleased surprise. 'You really mean that?'

'Yes, providing there is a reasonable prospect of getting my money back. What evidence is there that the ship does hold a cargo of gold?'

'She is in fairly deep water, but not too deep for our best native divers to have gone down to her many times during the years, and several of them have brought up gold coins. Last year I bought an aqualung and went down to her myself. In one of the stern cabins I could see several chests. One of them had broken open and had spilled on the floor a crucifix, a chalice and other items, which undoubtedly are treasure. But I could not get at them because part of the roof of the cabin had fallen in, blocking my way. To move those heavy beams without endangering the lives of the divers will require special machinery: powerful cranes and so on.'

'That certainly sounds promising. What share are you prepared to give your backers for providing the machinery and expert divers?'

'Forty per cent.'

Gregory gave a sudden smile. 'In the event of success, the other sixty per cent might make you a very rich man.'

The Ratu shook his head. 'It is not for myself that I wish to do this, but for my people. For many centuries they lived happily, the produce of our islands supplying their simple wants. But that is so no longer. As is the case in many Pacific islands, we are being swamped by immigrants from India. The Hindus are clever and industrious. Already they have bought up much of my people's agricultural land. This has led to the dispossessed then being exploited by the Indians, and having to work for a pittance which buys them barely enough food to live. Still worse, the Hindus breed like rabbits. Soon they will outnumber the islanders and by their majority vote have laws passed that will turn us into an underprivileged minority.'

'Indeed! That really is a bad business. It is quite shocking that an immigrant race should become the masters. Surely the French Government will give your people some form of protection?'

'No. I have pleaded with them to give us a new Constitution, similar to that which the British are about to institute in Fiji, but they have remained deaf to my appeals.'

'What sort of Constitution are the British giving the Fijians?'

'They have been faced with the same problem as my people. The Indians there already outnumber the natives. But in future, however the population may vary, the Indians and the Fijians will have the same number of representatives in the Assembly. In addition, half a dozen or so representatives are to be elected by the British and members of other races living in the islands, and that small block will hold the balance of power; so, however much the numbers of the Fijian natives decline, their rights will always be protected.'

Gregory nodded. 'That seems very sound. But, tell me: should you succeed in raising a fortune from the galleon, how would that enable you to prevent the Indians from exploiting your people?'

'I would use the money to modernise our native industries,' Ratu James replied eagerly. 'There are good markets in Australia, New Zealand and America for many of our products. But at present most of them are still made by hand. Given money, I could buy machinery which would greatly increase the quantity that could be turned out. That would lead to a greater demand for raw materials and so provide employment at a fair wage for natives who would otherwise be exploited by the Indians. I would also like to build a fruit-

54

canning factory and a refrigeration plant for the export of prawns and other shellfish with which our coasts abound.'

Regarding the handsome young man with admiration, Gregory said, 'I think your ideas laudable and your plans for carrying them out excellent—if only that treasure can be raised. Perhaps you would care to tell me now about the man you have come to Rio to see, in the hope that he will finance you.'

'Why not? He is Valentim Mauá de Carvalho. His second name comes from his mother—a descendant of the great industrialist and associate of the Rothschilds, who flourished in Dom Pedro II's reign. The Emperor made him a Viscount and the whole family is still extremely rich. Senhor Valentim owns many properties and he likes the South Seas, so he keeps a fine yacht at Fiji in Suva harbour. From time to time he cruises among the islands. A few months ago he visited the Nakapoa Group and I entertained him and his wife in Revika, the capital of Tujoa, our largest island.' Ratu James paused to raise his eyes and give a sigh. 'The Senhora de Carvalho is a most lovely girl—or perhaps I should say woman —although she is not much older than myself.'

Much amused, Gregory asked, 'And how old are you?'

'I am twenty-three. But to continue. Some weeks ago, this idea came to me of helping my people by salvaging the gold. I searched my mind for a means to raise capital, but could not think of one. Then the wealth of de Carvalho recurred to me and I wrote to him. He replied that I should come to Rio, and we would discuss the matter. I came. He was greatly interested, and we have had several talks. The last was three days before the beginning of the flood. He said then that those of his financial associates whom he had approached had not proved enthusiastic, but he would think the matter over. He was shortly leaving Rio on a business trip to Guatemala, but he will be back at his country estate, up at Vassouras, by now. He and his charming wife live there for most of the hot season and he invited me to spend Saturday night up there with them. By then, he said, he would be able to give me a definite answer.'

'I see,' said Gregory thoughtfully. 'Then, if his pals are reluctant to come in with him, he might welcome the idea of taking me as a partner.'

The young Ratu leaned forward eagerly. 'Exactly. The thought came to me immediately you said that you might be prepared to put up some of the money. Your offer might even make the difference between his turning me down or agreeing to back me. You see, he was very keen to start with, and has only become doubtful because others have poured cold water on the idea.'

'How far from Rio is Vassouras?'

'About sixty miles, I think.'

'One could drive that distance in two or three hours, so it might be an idea if I hired a car and went up with you. I'm not suggesting foisting myself on the de Carvalhos for the night. I would drive back the same day. But I'd like to meet de Carvalho and my personal word that I was prepared to help finance you would carry more weight than your just telling him that you had found someone willing to do that. What do you think?'

'It is an excellent idea. At the height of the flood, most of the telephone lines were out of action, but by now many of them will have been repaired. I will try to get through to him this evening and ask if I may bring you with me.'

When they parted, Gregory felt that he had received a real tonic from the youthful enthusiasm of his young guest, and James was filled with admiration for the knowledge and *savoir faire* of his much-travelled host. This mutual attraction led to their taking leave of each other as though they were old friends.

That evening James rang up to say that he had succeeded in getting through to de Carvalho and that the financier would be pleased for Gregory also to spend the Saturday night at his *fazenda*. Gregory then insisted that he should hire the car to take them, and it was agreed that they should set off from the Copacabana Palace at nine o'clock on the Saturday morning.

The call had come through while Gregory was dining with Manon in the restaurant. When he returned to their table he told her only that on Saturday he was going up-country on

56

a business matter, so would be away that night and most of Sunday.

At that she pouted. But, with a laugh, he reminded her that she had lunched with friends and for the next few days had accepted several other invitations. Swiftly she decided that she would be wise to reverse her policy and remain with him as much as possible, so minimising the risk of his becoming interested in anyone else.

The Wellesleys had rung Gregory up several times to enquire about his injured ankle and, now that the floods had subsided, they were to lunch with him the following day. Manon made a fourth, and once more they enjoyed the brilliant sunshine on the terrace round the swimming pool, making a jolly party.

During the meal Hugo said that he had failed to trace Gregory's rescuer, to which Gregory replied, 'Please don't bother further.' But when the girls left them to powder their noses he told Hugo briefly about the Ratu James and the project of salvaging the gold from the Spanish galleon. Then he went on:

'Do you happen to know this chap Mauá de Carvalho, or anything about him?'

'I've met him at functions a few times,' the Colonel answered, 'but that is all. It is quite true that he is very rich and dabbles in all sorts of ventures. But I suggest that if you do go into partnership with him you should employ the Embassy lawyer to draw up the contract. The Brazilians are most likeable people, and the great majority of the businessmen I know are entirely honest. But, as in every other country, some of the big financiers here pull a fast one at times, and in a speculation to retrieve sunken treasure you can't be too careful.'

'Thanks; I'll certainly do that.' As Gregory spoke, the two girls emerged from the hotel and Hugo remarked with a smile, 'You seem to be making the running very well with our little French friend.'

Gregory laughed. 'You've said it, chum. It's a pity her complexion is so sallow and that her chin is inclined to recede. But she is devilish *chic*, highly intelligent and great fun.'

57

In the afternoon the Wellesleys took Gregory and Manon for a drive through the lovely jungle forests outside Rio. The leaves of the colossal tropical trees displayed a great variety of shape and colour, and giant butterflies—bright blue, red, orange and yellow—flitted about the roads along which they drove.

The following day, although Gregory was still using a crutch, his ankle was mending so well that, as a change from the luxury of the Copacabana, he took Manon to lunch at a typical Brazilian middle-class restaurant called the Churrasaria Gaucha. From a passage, having a narrow cactus garden on one side, they entered an area two-thirds of which was shaded from the sky only by awnings. In the centre there was a round thatched grill, and all the way down one side a food counter at which people perched on high stools were helping themselves from a great variety of dishes. But there were also scores of tables, some seating as many as twenty people. These tables being occupied entirely by men, one or other of whom was constantly on his feet addressing the others, were evidently used for club lunches. At another big table beyond the grill a wedding breakfast was in progress; frequent toasts' were being drunk there, followed by much cheering. The babel of sound was such that one could hardly hear oneself speak and the place was so packed with people of all shades of colour that Gregory and Manon had to share a table with two enormously fat, colourfully-garbed Negresses.

As they could neither read the menu nor find a waiter who could interpret it for them, they had to take pot luck. When the dishes they had chosen arrived they proved so highly spiced that they only toyed with them, and made up on fruit and ices. The quality of the wine, as is nearly always the case with those produced in Brazil, was negligible; but so also was the bill.

Manon did not attempt to hide the fact that she found the atmosphere of the place far from congenial, but Gregory only laughed at her. The motley throng of poor, but laughing, noisy, cheerful people, the men nearly all in shirt-sleeves, represented, he felt, the real Brazil, and it pleased him to see them enjoying themselves.

Later in the afternoon they drove right through the city to visit the National Museum, formerly the Royal Palace, which stood in the centre of a very fine park. Gregory had hoped to see a fine collection of the gorgeous featherwork cloaks once made by the Brazilian Indians, but there were few exhibits and those were disappointing. He had also expected to see cases filled with shrunken human heads, but could find none. When he asked one of the curators about this, the official told him that the heads had been withdrawn from public exhibition, but he kindly offered to take them to the gallery in which they were stored.

There he produced from a drawer a dozen or more of these gruesome relics. Certain tribes of Indians, believing that to retain the heads of enemies they had killed gave them special powers, had developed the practice of boning these and shrinking them by filling the resulting cavity of flesh with hot sand. This reduced the size of the heads, some of which still had remnants of hair and beards, to the size of very small coconuts. The extraordinary thing was that the shape of the noses, lips and other features had been retained, so that people who had known them in life could have recognised them.

On Saturday, Gregory and James duly set off for Vassouras. At first the way wound up through jungle-clad slopes. Before they had gone far they feared they might never reach their destination, for every few miles there had been a landslide and the road was partially blocked; but the Brazilian Government was dealing with the situation most efficiently. Wherever a landslide had occurred there were bulldozers and gangs of men shovelling hundreds of tons of yellow earth off the road and down the slope opposite that from which it had fallen. At these places there was one-way traffic and the car had to crawl or skid through half a mile or more of greasy mud, but their driver was a good man. He also spoke enough English to point out to them places of interest along the way.

About twenty miles out of Rio they had climbed high enough to leave the jungle behind and entered an area of lofty, wooded slopes running down to broad lakes, so that in places the road formed a causeway between hundreds of acres of still water. On leaving this delightfully picturesque district they came to a town, to get through which they had to make a considerable detour, in order to reach a bridge that spanned a wide river. The river was still a torrent, the yellow waters lapping the fairway of the bridge, and all the houses along the low river-front were still half submerged by the flood.

They had done about two-thirds of their journey when their driver pointed out a house just visible through the trees on a hill-top to the right of the road, and said, 'The *fazenda* of Dom Pedro Enrique.'

'He is the Pretender to the throne, is he not?' Gregory asked.

'Yes; he and his cousin, who live in Petropolis, are Pretenders equally,' the man replied. 'Both very popular.'

'It speaks well for the broadmindedness of a Republican Government to allow Pretenders to reside in their own country,' Gregory remarked.

Ratu James took up the subject. 'The Brazilians are most tolerant people. Their Government even goes so far as to pay respect to the two Pretenders. At every State function they are invited to be present.' After a moment he asked, 'Do you know much of the history of Brazil?'

'Not much,' Gregory admitted. 'Only that in the early days both the French and Dutch endeavoured to oust the Portuguese, but failed. Then for some two hundred years it became a neglected colony ruled from Lisbon. If I remember, it was the Napoleonic wars which led to the Braganza monarchs taking refuge here.'

'That's right.' James nodded his head, crowned with the enormous halo of soft, black hair. 'It was the British who pushed Dom Joao, the Prince Regent who was then ruling Portugal in the name of the mad Queen Maria I, into coming here instead of remaining on and becoming a puppet of the French when they invaded his country in 1807.

'As a result of the French Revolution, there had, some years before, been a movement here to break away from Portugal and achieve independence. The revolutionaries were known as the Minas group. They were intellectuals and several of them were poets of some distinction. Their leader was a Lieutenant named Joaquim José da Silva Xavier; but occasionally he practised dentistry, so he was given the nickname of "The Toothpuller". The conspiracy was discovered and he was hanged and quartered, but the Brazilians still honour him as a great patriot and "Toothpuller Day" is celebrated as a national holiday.

'The arrival of Dom Joao and his court set Brazilian independence back for thirty-three years, and even after that the country remained a monarchy for a further thirty-four. But perhaps I am boring you with all this?'

'No, no,' replied Gregory. ''Please go on.'

'Well then, squeezed into some forty vessels, fifteen thousand Portuguese nobles and their servants set out as refugees. After fifty-two ghastly days they landed in Brazil and made their way to Rio. Naturally, they hated the primitive conditions they found here, but gradually they settled down and with excellent results for Brazil. Formerly no trade had been allowed with any nation except Portugal. Dom Joao opened the ports to all nations. He established a printing press, started the iron and textile industries and encouraged the arts and sciences.

'In due course, the mad Queen died. Dom Joao became King. Napoleon had been defeated and by 1820 it became clear that if Portugal was to be prevented from becoming a Republic, Dom Joao must return and occupy his throne. But he left his heir apparent, Dom Pedro, in Brazil. Unfortunately, the Prince had been badly brought up. He was a kindhearted young man and wanted to be a good ruler, but he was unstable, dissipated and a neurotic.

'Not long after Dom Joao had returned to Lisbon his Government began to restore the old restrictions on Brazilian commerce and advancement. Then a despatch arrived, ordering Dom Pedro to come to Europe to complete his education. He received the despatch on the bank of the Ipiranza river. Having read it, he rebelled, drew his sabre and cried, "Independence or Death!" This became known as the *Grito,* or "Cry of Ipiranza", and led, in this strange way, to Brazil becoming independent of her mother country.

'Dom Pedro was proclaimed Emperor, but he reigned for only nine years. On his father's death, he became the titular King of Portugal. Being averse to leaving Brazil, he ceded the crown to his daughter, Maria da Gloria; but his younger brother, Miguel, contested his right to do so and civil war broke out. Pedro sailed for Europe to champion his daughter's cause, leaving behind, as Regent of Brazil, a son of only five years, who became Pedro II.'

'He became a most unusual monarch, didn't he?' Gregory put in.

'He did indeed. Physically, he was imposing.' Ratu James paused to smile. 'He was six foot four, nearly as tall as myself. But mentally, for Royalty, he was outstanding—far in advance of his times and capable of speaking many languages. He held liberal views and gave his people a generous Constitution. After thirty years of rule he felt free to travel. Leaving his heir apparent, the Princess Isobel, as Regent, he went incognito as Dom Pedro da Alcantara to Europe, the United States, Egypt and the Holy Land, mixing with their people as a modern Haroun el Raschid. But, of course, wherever he went his real identity was known. He sought out and talked with every great literary celebrity of his time, visited synagogues and held learned discussions in Hebrew with their Rabbis. Everywhere he was admired and respected for his good humour, boundless energy and as the most learned monarch of his day.

'Back in Brazil, with the aid of Mauá, he established banks, started railways and encouraged the investment of foreign capital; but his one failing was that, although he had given Brazil a Constitution, he continued to rule as virtually an autocratic monarch.

'The prosperity that he had hoped to bring to Brazil was thwarted by two wars: the first in 1851-2 against the Argentine in an attempt to destroy the brutal regime there; the second against Paraguay. It dragged on from 1865 to 1870. But the real cause of Dom Pedro's downfall was his attitude to slavery. He had freed his own inherited slaves as early as 1840. Then, in 1871, he decreed that all children born of slaves after that date should be free. Finally, in 1888, he forced through a law for complete abolition of slavery.

'That spelled ruin for the owners of the great estates and a hundred million pounds' worth of property was rendered valueless. At the time, the Emperor was again in Europe. On his return, he received a great ovation. But in his absence the ruined landowners, the industrialists and the Army had combined against him. Without warning, there occurred a bloodless *coup d'état*. With great dignity he accepted it, refused a large sum of money that was offered to him, and returned to Europe to spend the remainder of his life continuing his studies of Asiatic languages and Comparative Religions. That is how the monarchy ended and on May 13th, 1888, Brazil became a Republic.'

As the Ratu fell silent, Gregory said, 'As a visitor, you are remarkably well up in the history of this country.'

James shrugged a shade self-consciously. 'I hope I haven't bored you, but it was the Senhora de Carvalho who aroused my interest in Brazil and told me all this. She is a most knowledgeable girl and has a special interest in the history of her country because she has the Royal Braganza blood in her own veins.'

Some miles further on they left the highway for a side road that was ill-kept and extremely bumpy. Eventually it brought them to the de Carvalho *fazenda*. On either side of the approach to the house there were many barns and outhouses. Crossing a bridge over a shallow ravine, they drove round to the entrance of the house, which was on its far side. From there, across a lovely sloping garden, there was a magnificent view of rolling pastures with grazing cattle and patches of woodland.

As they drove up, their host came out and gave them a smiling welcome. He was a short but sturdy man in his middle forties; black-haired, dark-complexioned, with a square face, forceful chin and heavily-lidded eyes.

The house was a one-storey building containing many large, lofty rooms, At that altitude air-conditioning would have been redundant, but there were gently-moving fans in all the ceilings, to circulate the pleasantly warm air. The bed-

63

rooms to which de Carvalho showed them were sparsely furnished, but the living rooms displayed wealth and good taste. They contained many examples of antique Brazilian pottery, well filled book-shelves and paintings that must have been worth several thousand pounds.

When Gregory and James had refreshed themselves by a wash, their host provided them with Planter's Punches and, soon afterwards, his wife joined them. Her name was Olinda da Conceiçao—the beautiful one of the conception—and at the first glance Gregory saw that she did justice to her name.

She was an exceptionally tall girl—slightly taller, he judged, than himself—with broad shoulders and big hips. Her skin was golden brown, her hair copper-coloured, her mouth full but not thick-lipped like Manon's, and beautifully curved. In her eyes there lay a slumbrous fire and her firm, almost aggressive chin showed that she had plenty of determination. Recalling that James had said that Dom Pedro had been six foot four and that Olinda had Braganza blood, it occurred to Gregory that she had probably inherited her height from the Emperor.

Lunch proved to be one of the best meals Gregory had enjoyed since arriving in Brazil, and a pleasant change from restaurant food. It was not too heavy but suggested that the de Carvalhos had a French chef or, anyway, a French-trained cook; and with the meal they drank a good Moselle.

Over lunch, no mention was made of the treasure. They talked only of the country and what the visitors had so far seen of it. Afterwards they walked round the garden, heavy with the scent of magnolia blossoms, then retired for their siestas.

When they met again they drank *maté* which, among the lower classes of Brazil, takes the place of tea. In this case Olinda had ordered the brew only because her visitors had not yet tried it. Gregory thought it like very strong Indian tea and rather unpleasant, but he admired the vessels in which it was served. They were cow-horns, beautifully embellished with gold filigree work, and the liquid was sucked up from them through a silver 'straw', called a *combello,* with a filter tip to prevent the leaves from getting into the drinker's mouth.

Afterwards Olinda, Gregory and James bathed in the swimming pool. Gregory had never cared for big women but, on seeing Olinda in only a bikini, he freely conceded that she was a truly magnificent creature, and he did not wonder that James was obviously attracted to her. In bathing trunks, the rippling muscles of his pale-brown body now exposed to view, the young Ratu made an equally striking figure, and it crossed Gregory's mind how much better suited they would have been as a couple than Olinda and her squat, middle-aged husband, who was lying in a hammock—a means of taking one's ease invented by the Brazilian Indians—near the pool, smoking a cigar.

A delicious iced cup made from soursops was brought out to them, then they went in to dress for dinner. The meal was a long one and again admirably chosen, but it was not until they were served with old brandy in the drawing room that de Carvalho spoke of the business his visitors had come upon.

After swirling the liquor in the balloon glass, and sniffing its bouquet, he said to James:

'My dear Ratu, I fear I have bad news for you; but I did not want to spoil your day here by speaking of it earlier. I have decided against financing the project you put up to me.'

James's face fell a little as he asked, 'May I ask why, Senhor?'

'Because enquiries lead me to believe that there is very little likelihood of any substantial amount of gold being in your sunken galleon. Great quantities of gold were taken by the Spaniards from Peru, but they sent it home to Spain across the Atlantic. It is true that their ships were constantly crossing the Pacific, to the Philippines and other countries in Asia. But there was no gold in such places for them to bring back, and no point in their sending any large sums out. The only purpose of these voyages across the Pacific was to send supplies to their colonists and return with cargoes of spices, silks and ivories. Therefore, I am now convinced that, should you succeed in bringing up anything there is to bring up, it will be only a few bags of doubloons that were being sent out

65

to pay the Spanish garrisons. That is why I am not prepared to back you.'

Suddenly Olinda, her dark eyes flashing, leaned forward in her chair and cried, 'That is not true! You are refusing because you are a coward! You are backing out because you have been threatened.' Her voice rose in a sneer. 'Yes, you are letting the Ratu down because you have allowed yourself to become scared—and by a woman!'

5

A Midnight Visitor

Valentim de Carvalho's swarthy face flushed and his heavily-lidded eyes narrowed. For a moment he looked as though he was about to burst with rage, but he controlled himself, managed a slightly twisted smile and said acidly:

'My dear, I understand your disappointment. You are a born romantic and had set your heart upon this quest for treasure. But I am a financier, so naturally am opposed to throwing my money down the drain. That is my reason for refusing to finance the Ratu, not because I was warned that if I backed him certain people would make serious trouble for me.'

There was a moment's silence, then Gregory said, 'I have been considering offering to participate in this speculation; so may I ask who was this woman who threatened you?'

De Carvalho shrugged his broad shoulders. 'I don't know her name, but I met her at a reception at the British Embassy just before I went up to Guatemala. Our conversation was very brief. She came up to me and simply said, "I happen to know that you are thinking of financing the Ratu James Om-boloku in his project of securing sunken treasure. Others are interested in this affair, and I have been instructed to give you warning that, should you do so, it will be the worse for you. The people I represent will stick at nothing to gain their ends, and unless you keep out of their way it may well cost you your life."

'I was about to question her when the Ambassador's wife beckoned to me. As I acknowledged her signal, the woman slipped away and became lost in the crowd. Later I tried to

67

find her, but failed. Evidently she had left soon after conveying her warning to me. I enquired of the Ambassador and several other people who she was, but no-one could put a name to my description of her. That was not surprising, as at this reception there were several hundred people. More than that I cannot tell you.'

After a moment, Gregory asked, 'Was the woman British or Brazilian?'

'Neither. Most of the people at the reception were, of course, talking in English, and it was in that language she addressed me. But she did not speak it very well. She was of medium height and I judged her to be in her middle thirties. She had dark hair, very fine eyes and a good figure. In fact I thought her quite striking; so I was all the more surprised later that no-one should be able to tell me from my description who she was. I have no idea of her nationality, but she was a Mediterranean type—Italian, French, Greek, or perhaps a Spaniard with a dash of Moorish blood.'

Gregory looked across at James. 'Have you any idea who this woman could have been?'

'Not the faintest; and this occurrence astounds me. Until now I was entirely unaware that anyone else was interested in the old wreck and her gold.'

Standing up, de Carvalho said:

'Well, there we are. If Mr. Sallust still feels inclined to put up money for this treasure hunt, that is his affair. But you must count me out. And now, let us not spoil our evening by discussing this affair further. As my withdrawal must be depressing for the Ratu, instead, over a magnum of French champagne, we will talk of other things.'

The magnum was brought and for two hours that quickly slipped away de Carvalho laid himself out to be pleasant. He was extremely knowledgeable about Brazil's chequered history and the succeeding waves of fortune and misfortune that had sent its economy seesawing. First, during the seventeenth and eighteenth centuries had come the sugar boom which made the owners of many great estates fabulously rich, but it was killed by the competition of the Caribbean Islands. Next, wealth came to Brazil as the world's greatest source of rubber; but by 1910 the planters of Malaya and the Dutch East Indies were underselling her, so that the flourishing towns on the Amazon soon became dying communities. Then Brazil held almost a monopoly in the export of coffee, but the competition of the African growers led in 1950 to vast, unsold surpluses having to be burned and many plantations being abandoned to return to jungle. Lumber, too, had had its boom and the country still had vast resources of timber, but transport made it difficult to exploit fully this source of wealth. Diamonds, tobacco, cotton and bananas all helped the economy, but Brazil's greatest wealth lay in iron and other minerals. Two hundred miles north of Rio there was a mountain, composed almost entirely of iron ore, and so far only the top four hundred feet had been shaved off. The un-exploited riches of the country were fabulous; hardly yet touched, and the vast interior, where primitive Indians were the only inhabitants, had, even yet, not been fully explored. Every endeavour to develop the country was thwarted by lack of capital and the scarcity of modern roads.

Olinda took little part in the conversation and at eleven o'clock went off to bed; but Valentim was obviously enjoying himself and when they had finished the magnum, insisted on making a King Cup, of more champagne laced with brandy. Gregory had a head like a rock, so survived the party; but, by the time it broke up, James, who was not accustomed to heavy drinking, was obviously very tight.

When the three men met next morning at breakfast, poor James was still very much under the weather, but de Carvalho said he would soon put him right and produced for him a drink made from the ground berries of the *Guaranà* plant. This he declared to be a sovereign remedy for a hangover and, as he added cold water to the powder, he remarked with a laugh, 'Many Brazilians drink this every morning, as it is said both to aid longevity and to be a mild aphrodisiac.'

Breakfast over, Valentim went to his study to write some letters. As soon as he had gone, Gregory asked James, 'Have you still no idea who this woman is who threatened de Carvalho?'

James gave a rueful grin. 'As far as my head permitted, I

have been puzzling about that ever since I woke up. Who the woman was I haven't a notion, and I can think of only one person who would like to thwart my plans. That is old Roboumo, a witch-doctor who lives on a small island near Revika, the capital of Tujoa, and has great influence over my people.'

'Why should he be opposed to your bettering their lot?'

'Because he would stand to lose by it. He controls a gang of badmen, and runs what, in modern terms, could be called a protection racket. They blackmail the superstitious into handing over a percentage of their slender earnings. If I could bring a modern way of life to Tujoa the people would no longer be superstitious, and would defy him. He would lose his power and he is determined to cling on to it.'

'Have you not sufficient influence to break the hold he has over your people?'

The Ratu sighed. 'Unfortunately, no. As is the case in most of the South Sea Islands, the people still have great respect for their hereditary rulers and accept their guidance in the majority of matters. But *draunikau*, as witchcraft is called, still plays a great part in their lives. They are frightened of the curses this evil man might put upon them, so still remain subservient to him.'

'That is quite understandable. But it is difficult to believe that a witch-doctor on a remote island in the Pacific could have the sort of connections that would enable him to threaten a financier in Rio de Janeiro. And the woman did not threaten de Carvalho with a curse. She said she represented people who would stick at nothing, which is a very different matter.'

'I agree. But as far as I know I have no enemies except Roboumo, and I doubt if more than a handful of Europeans have even heard that there is gold in this sunken ship.'

'Well, it seems certain that somebody is taking an interest in her, and that someone must have known that you had come to Rio in the hope of getting de Carvalho to finance you.'

'True, but that gets us nowhere. The whole island knows that on and off for several weeks I have spent my time skin-diving to explore the galleon, and I discussed my plans with my Council of Elders before leaving for Rio; so anyone might have become aware of my intentions.'

'If these people's Intelligence is good, they'll soon send a threat to me,' Gregory remarked.

'Then you still mean to find the money for me,' James said with evident relief. 'I was afraid that after last night you might decide not to.'

Gregory laid a hand on the young man's arm and smiled to soften the blow he was about to deliver. 'I've never definitely said I would, only that I was very interested and greatly inclined to. I still am, and no threats would frighten me off. But I couldn't help being impressed by what de Carvalho said about the gold from Peru always being sent across the Atlantic and never the Pacific. Like him, I am averse to very risky speculations in which my money is likely to go down the drain, and . . .'

'But wait!' James interrupted. 'He wasn't altogether right about that. Lately, I've been reading quite a lot about the Spanish Conquest. From Mexico they did ship the gold they got there direct across the Atlantic, but they couldn't do that with the gold from Peru. In those days there was no Panama Canal, and it was impossible for them to transport it across the Andes, then through hundreds of miles of unexplored Brazilian jungle. They had to ship it from Lima, up the west coast of Central America to Acapulco in Mexico; so at least half of those treasure galleons' voyages did take place in the Pacific.'

'No dice, dear boy.' Gregory shook his head. 'Admittedly they had to sail right up the Pacific coast of Central America but that is five thousand miles from your home town, and you can't tell me that any ship was ever blown that far off course.'

The young Ratu's face fell, but Gregory gave him a friendly pat on the shoulder and continued, 'Don't be downhearted. I've not said no yet; but before I say yes I do want to secure further information.'

'I don't see how you can.'

'Well, I do. In the days when the greater part of America

71

was ruled by Spain it was run by the Council of the Indies, which sat in Seville. Even the Viceroys took their orders from the Council and it recorded in detail every transaction that took place here. I know that for a fact because when I was in Seville I was shown some of the vast collection of documents. You told me that this ship was not a high-pooped galleon of the old style, but you judged her to be a warship of the type used towards the end of the eighteenth century. That narrows the search, and in the records there should be an entry of such a ship being lost off the Nakapoa Group with particulars of the cargo she was carrying. It will mean my going to Spain; but time is my enemy these days, so I have no objection to making the trip. Now, how about a dip in the pool?'

Much cheered, James agreed, and ten minutes later they were disporting themselves in the water. Shortly afterwards, Olinda joined them and, when Gregory went in to dress, James remained out there with her. As the window of Gregory's room looked out on to the pool, from time to time he took a look at them. After a while he observed with interest that James was no longer displaying his ability to make complicated dives and swimming for three lengths under water. He and Olinda were sitting close together on the side of the pool, with their feet dangling into it, engaged in earnest conversation.

Gregory had shrewdly assessed that Olinda's attack on her husband had been caused not so much by annoyance at being deprived of participation in an exciting undertaking as by anger at his refusal to finance James. Gregory thought it probable that she had little interest in retrieving the gold but had been greatly looking forward to a long stay on Tujoa in James's company. Anyhow, he felt certain now that she was just as much attracted to the handsome Ratu as he was to her; and he wondered how far, had their association been likely to continue, de Carvalho would have allowed this budding romance to go.

During their conversation the previous evening it had emerged that neither Gregory nor James had yet visited Petropolis, the Versailles of Brazil, where the Emperors used to hold their courts during the great winter heats, and de Carvalho had said, 'I intend to return to Rio tomorrow, but had not meant to leave until the afternoon. Instead, we will set off earlier, take a picnic lunch and, as Petropolis lies about twenty miles north of Rio, make a big detour so that I can show you this charming little town.'

In consequence, at midday the two cars left the *fazenda*. Gregory, with his young friend in mind, asked to go with Valentim, thus enabling James to have Olinda with him in the hired car.

It was another lovely drive through mountains, beside lakes and over swollen rivers. But again they had to slow down every few miles owing to landslides, so it was not until four o'clock that they reached Petropolis.

The town lay in a depression surrounded by wooded hills. Its centre of interest was the Palace, now a museum—a long, one-storey mansion in the style of late eighteenth-century Portuguese architecture. They spent half an hour looking round it, then drove on a mile further and pulled up at a huge, timbered building that looked like a gigantic Swiss chalet. It had, de Carvalho told them, been a Casino but, since the Government had prohibited gambling, was now a Country Club.

In front of it there was an artificial lake, on which there were boats, rafts and every device for water sports. Inside, on the ground floor, there seemed to be an endless succssion of lofty halls, restaurants, ballrooms, swimming baths and bars. As gaming was no longer permitted, Gregory wondered that such an immense establishment could continue to support itself. But de Carvalho told him that everyone who was anyone in Rio belonged to the club, and there were certainly plenty of people in it.

After drinks there, they took the road to Rio. For several miles it wound down the wooded mountainside, revealing a succession of deep gorges beyond which lay lovely vistas, then they reached the narrow coastal plain with its seemingly endless suburbs sweltering in the heat. At the Hotel Gloria on the baia de Guanabara, where James was staying, the two cars pulled up and he took a reluctant farewell of Olinda.

73

She joined her husband, good-byes were said, then Gregory took her place in the hired car and was driven on to the Copacabana Palace.

When he had washed and changed he went down to dinner. Manon was seated at the table they had been sharing for the past few days and, not knowing what time he would be back, had just started. Elegant and piquant as ever, she received him with delight, said how greatly she had missed him and asked if his trip had been successful.

'Interesting, anyhow,' he replied with a smile. On the way back he had been considering whether he should tell her about the Ratu James' sunken galleon. Obviously the fewer people who knew about the possibility of its containing gold the better; but if he did finance the venture he would be going to the South Seas, and Manon lived there. He was thoroughly enjoying their *affaire,* and to have a charming mistress within easy flying distance of the operation would provide him with delightful relaxation during the time that must elapse while preparations were being made and, later, during periods when rough weather made diving impossible. So he had decided to take her into his confidence.

To begin with, as she listened, her face remained grave and intent. Then, when he told her of his intention of going to Tujoa, she exclaimed with delight, 'To have you come to the South Seas would fulfil my dearest wish. The islands are unbelievably lovely and you must stay with me in my home. No matter what the gossips may say, I will willingly sacrifice my reputation for you.'

'Darling, how sweet of you,' he replied. 'I'm greatly tempted to accept if we could find a way to get over that. No doubt I could hire a motor yacht, lie off your island and let it be thought that I was sleeping aboard. But once we've got the apparatus for the job, I fear my visits would be for only a day or two now and then, as I'll have to spend most of my time on Tujoa.'

At that she frowned, then said rather diffidently, 'It's not my business, of course, but do you think it really wise to sink a lot of money in such a speculative venture? The Pacific is littered with sunken galleons and for generations past any number of people have attempted to recover treasure from them. But I've never heard of anyone bringing up more than a few odd coins and things like weapons and bits of armour. That can be fun if it entails no more than skin-diving; but you say you'll need pontoons with big cranes, and that sort of thing means a considerable capital investment.'

Admiring her French shrewdness, he nodded. 'You're right about that, my sweet; and, as a matter of fact, I'm not going into this thing until I have found out a bit more about the prospects of getting a fair return for my money. In a few days' time I mean to fly to Seville and consult the records of the Council of the Indies. With luck, I'll learn from them what cargo this ship was carrying.'

She made a little *moué*. 'So you mean to desert me so soon. How horrid of you.'

'Only temporarily. I'll be back inside a week.'

Leaning forward, Manon said earnestly, '*Chéri*, why waste your time and money in this way? The odds are enormous against your succeeding where so many other people have failed. This poor young Ratu is building castles in the clouds. It would be much kinder to refrain from encouraging his hopes now rather than allow him to be grievously disappointed later. Put this foolish business out of your mind and, instead, come to stay with me in Fiji.'

Gregory took her hand and kissed it. 'My love, you are most persuasive, and you are probably right that I should be an ass to go further with the matter. But I feel I owe it to young James not to back out until I have a valid excuse for doing so. I mean to book a passage to Spain tomorrow morning. You will stay on here until my return, and if I learn when I get back that you have been hitting it up with some other chap I'll smack your lovely bottom until it's purple.'

She laughed uproariously. 'What fun! You certainly tempt me to. That sort of beating puts fire into a girl. The following morning your legs would give under you. But seriously, *chéri*, have no thoughts but nice ones about me. As I have told you, I am not a woman who takes lovers after only a short acquaintance.'

75

'Except myself,' Gregory grinned, kissing her hand again.

Nevertheless, he was not destined to go to Spain. On the following day they had both been invited to lunch with the Wellesleys. Knowing that anything he confided to them would go no further, Gregory told them about Ratu James and the quest for treasure which he was thinking of financing.

Hugo reinforced Manon's opinion that there was small hope of recovering a large quantity of gold from any galleon sunk in the Pacific. Then he went on:

'Anyhow, I don't think you need go to Seville to find out what your chances are. In the old days the whole of Spanish South America was ruled from Antigua, in what is now Guatemala, by a Captain General. The city was destroyed by a terrible earthquake in 1773, but it was rebuilt some twenty years later. If your ship was not sunk until the 1790s, or thereabouts, the records of the cargo it carried are certain to be in Antigua.'

Manon clapped her hands. 'How splendid! From here to Fiji the quickest route is up to Mexico City, then on by QANTAS, and Guatemala is on the way. We would go so far together, Gregory. That would be most pleasant.' She did not add that she hoped he would accompany her for the rest of her journey, but he realised the implication and smiled at her.

Next day Gregory telephoned James to tell him what he intended to do, and it was agreed that the Ratu should accompany them to Guatemala. On Wednesday the three of them left in a VARIG aircraft for Lima. It was the first time that Gregory had crossed the Andes and, peering down through the cloudless atmosphere, he was fascinated by the extraordinary barrenness of the lofty mountains and desolate valleys. He would have liked to stop off at Lima and spend a few days going up to Cuzco, the thirteen-thousand-foot-high capital of the Incas, to see the ruins there, composed of twenty-ton blocks of stone, reminiscent of the Mycean civilisation in pre-Hellenic Greece; but now was not the time to do so.

They spent the night a few miles outside the modern Peruvian capital, at a delightful Country Club, with acres of tropical gardens, three swimming pools and every other civilised amenity.

On Thursday they did the short trip to Panama, again by the Brazilian line VARIG, which Gregory found put many other lines to shame. Instead of the horrid little vinegary kickshaws offered before a meal by most of them VARIG gave its passengers slices of genuine pâté de foie gras, cold crawfish and a big tin of caviare in which to dip. The wines were from first-class European vineyards, the meals excellent, the service impeccable; and the line prided itself on arriving on time.

They could have gone on to Guatemala the same day, but Gregory wanted to see the Panama Canal; so they had engaged rooms at the 'Siesta' Airport Hotel. The heat was terrific and humming birds zoomed over them as they bathed that afternoon in the palm-shaded hotel pool. But the rooms were air-conditioned and their twenty-mile drive the following morning to Panama City and the Canal Zone was a most interesting expedition.

Late in the afternoon they flew on to Guatemala and it was already dark when they landed. Antigua, the old capital, lay twenty-five miles inland and five thousand feet above sea level. A hired car took them up gradient after gradient and, looking back from an ever-greater height, for a long while they could see the lights of Guatemala City spread below them like a fairyland.

For the rest of the way the car roared along an almost deserted road between banks of now-black forest or high bushes. Overhead, the night sky looked like a blue-black ribbon on which were floating thousands of bright stars.

The main building of the hotel appeared to have once been a spacious, one-storey, Colonial mansion; but there were no bedrooms in it. These, again one-storey buildings, were set in blocks of four round a two-acre garden. As they were led to their rooms, they approached an oval swimming pool. Beyond it, over the garden wall, there reared up the ruins of a once lofty church which, as they were floodlit, formed a lovely backdrop to the scene.

They found the bedrooms clean, roomy and well fur-

77

nished, with bright, chintz curtains and, in one corner—an incongruous note for that part of the world but a pleasant amenity against cold weather at five thousand feet—a stone fireplace with a fire already laid.

As is the custom throughout Latin America, dinner did not start until nine o'clock, so when they went into the restaurant numerous other guests were still lingering over the meal. While they were ordering, two men got up from a nearby table and left. One was a very tall and bulky man with fair hair and a flowing fair moustache, below which was a row of slightly protruding teeth. He looked about forty-five. The other was younger, much shorter; broad-shouldered, dark-haired and with a swarthy complexion. As they passed, James remarked, 'I'm sure I've seen that tall, fair-haired man somewhere before, but I can't think where.'

Tired after their long day, as soon as they had finished dinner they went to their respective rooms. As the hotel was nearly full, to Gregory's annoyance, they had had to accept rooms in separate blocks; but he did not anticipate much difficulty in finding Manon's in the dark should he wish to do so.

Having undressed, he went to bed, read for a quarter of an hour, then put out the light. Some time later, he awoke. Long years of living in acute danger had enabled him to train himself to become instantly alert when suddenly awakened. No sound came from near the door, but he felt certain that someone had entered the room stealthily and was standing there.

6

The Ambush

Many people habitually lock the doors of their rooms at
night, particularly when in hotels. But Gregory had been told
when young that it was better not to do so as, in case of fire,
one might half suffocate while still asleep and wake already
befuddled by fumes. A locked door would then make any attempt at rescue much more difficult. It would, therefore, have
been easy for anyone to get into his room almost noiselessly.

During his secret missions he had always slept with a small
automatic beneath his pillow and, as a precaution against
sneak-thieves in hotels, he had resumed the habit during his
travels.

Now he slid his hand beneath his pillow, withdrew the gun,
pointed it towards the door, then suddenly sat up and
switched on his bedside light.

At once he recognised the uninvited visitor as the tall, fair
man whom James, at dinner, thought he had seen somewhere
before.

The intruder had one hand on the light switch beside the
door. With the other he swept up his long, fair moustache,
smiled disarmingly and said in French, 'You forestalled me,
Monsieur. Pray pardon this visit. I intend you no harm—at
least for the moment.'

'Do you presume to threaten me?' Gregory snapped. 'Try
it, and I'll put a bullet through your leg; then say I woke and
found you here and took you to be a hotel thief.'

The man gave a low laugh. 'If you did that, my friend Jules
Corbin would call in the police, and you would find yourself
under arrest. But your hostile attitude is uncalled for. I have

come here only because it is necessary for us to hold a short private conversation.'

For a moment Gregory considered telling him to go to hell but, on second thoughts, decided to hear what he had to say. 'Very well,' he snapped. 'But be brief. I have a rooted objection to being disturbed in the middle of the night.'

Ignoring his remark, the other replied, 'Allow me to introduce myself. My name is Pierre Lacost. I and several friends of mine are interested in the sunken ship off the coast of Tujoa. It came to our knowledge that Ratu James Omboloku was about to approach the Brazilian financier Valentim Mauá de Carvalho with a view to his financing a company that would attempt to salvage the gold believed to be down in the wreck. We sent an associate of ours to Rio to warn de Carvalho that if he agreed it would be the worse for him. Very wisely, he accepted the warning and declined to play. We then learned that you have now become interested in this project. I am here to give you the same warning. If you value your safety you will forget this matter, Monsieur. Go where you will when you leave here, provided it is not to the South Seas. Your presence there would bring you into grave danger.'

Lowering the barrel of his automatic a little so that it pointed at Lacost's left knee, Gregory said quietly, 'And I warned you what would happen to you if you threatened me. Now get out.'

The big man shrugged. 'I am told, Monsieur Sallust, that you are very far from being a fool, but you would be one if you carried out your threat. In the first place, prisons in countries such as this are not pleasant places. I am unarmed and have robbed you of nothing. If you shot me you would undoubtedly be held, perhaps for months, while a full inquiry was made into your having used a firearm on another hotel guest who only walked into your room in mistake for his own. In the second place, I should so strongly resent a serious injury to my leg that soon after you left prison I should arrange for you to become the victim of a fatal accident.'

Gregory had never had any intention of using his weapon unless he was attacked, and he felt that, in the circumstances, it would be wise to find out all he could about Monsieur Pierre Lacost; so, to encourage him to talk, he replied in a much milder tone:

'There is certainly something in what you say about the unpleasantness of being held in a Guatemalan prison while an investigation is being carried out; and to be set upon and perhaps seriously injured by one of the thugs you appear to control strikes me as a high price to pay for a trip to the South Seas. But you will permit me to point out that if there is treasure in this ship the only person who has a legal right to it is Ratu James, as the hereditary ruler of the Nakapoa Group; so should you attempt to deprive him of it you will be committing a felony.'

Again Lacost gave a low laugh. 'Might is right, Monsieur. I and my friends have suffered much. We need money and we mean to get it.'

'Do you mean that you have suffered at the Ratu's hands and are taking this way of avenging yourselves upon him?'

'No, no! From all I have heard, he is a pleasant young man and we have no quarrel with him. I have no objection to telling you my own story, and those of my friends are very similar. In fact, by doing so I may persuade you to retire gracefully from this business. That would save me some trouble and you considerable pain. You must know of the unrest that beset Algeria from the fifties on. I was the owner of a big estate there, but that *sale type*, de Gaulle, let us Colons down. After Algeria was given independence the Arab Government dispossessed me of my property. Like countless others, from a comparatively wealthy man I was reduced to near poverty, and had to leave my country for France. To escape the trouble that our bitterness would have caused us to make, de Gaulle shipped several thousands of us off to Tahiti, with promises of a bright new future there. But again that unscrupulous traitor let us down. Next to nothing has been done for us. We were left to rot in poverty and idleness. Now do you understand why we feel entitled to mend our fortunes in any way we can, even if it entails taking strong measures against people like yourself who would thwart us?'

'I do,' Gregory agreed. 'And I sympathise with you. But

81

there is another side to the matter. Are you aware how the Ratu intends to use this gold, should he secure it?'

'I neither know nor care.'

'All the same, I will tell you. The natives of the Nakapoa Group are rapidly becoming dominated by Indian immigrants. Unless something can be done for them they will soon be reduced to poverty and semi-slavery. The Ratu plans to establish industries in the island that will save his people from being exploited and provide them with a means to make a decent living.'

Lacost shrugged. 'The natives of the South Seas are a lazy, shiftless lot. It is their own fault if they allow the Indians to buy their land, then turn them off it. Anyhow, they will be little worse off in the long run. In fact, they are far luckier than most races. They have an abundance of fruit and fish to live on. Even if they were offered work in industries they wouldn't take it. To use the money as the Ratu plans would be only to waste it.'

'There I do not agree,' Gregory said quietly. 'Even a chance to better the lot of a whole people, or at least a proportion of them, is infinitely preferable to allowing the money to fall into the hands of a small group of unscrupulous adventurers.'

Lacost's light blue eyes took on a stony look and, with a sudden change of manner, he cried harshly, 'Then you refuse to back out of your understanding with the Ratu?'

'I do.' Gregory's eyes were equally hard, as he went on: 'And now I'll give *you* a warning. In my time many people have found me a very dangerous enemy. In fact I've killed more men than I care to remember, and I'd not scruple to kill again. So it is you and your friends who would be wise to throw in your hand. Given cause and opportunity, I'd not hesitate to stick a knife in you and throw you to the sharks. Good night, Monsieur Lacost.'

For a moment Lacost glared at him, then, without another word, turned on his heel and left the room, slamming the door behind him.

Switching off the light, Gregory replaced his little pistol under his pillow, and for a while lay contemplating this new development. From his early twenties he had lived dangerously, so he found the situation far from upsetting. It titillated his lifelong craving for excitement and offered an opportunity to pit his wits against an unscrupulous enemy. He decided now that, even should the Antigua records provide no evidence that the sunken ship had a cargo of treasure, he would back James just for the fun of the thing.

Meanwhile, Pierre Lacost had silently slipped into Manon's room. She had been expecting him and at once switched on her light. 'Well,' she asked, 'I take it you have had a talk with him? How did things go?'

He shook his head, with its crop of straight fair hair. 'Not well. He is a tough one, and I fear we will have trouble with him unless you can persuade him to change his mind.'

'I doubt if he will. As I told you in my cable, I tried several times while we were in Rio, but failed. The trouble is that, since his wife died, he has become foot-loose. He is his own master, has any amount of money and has been an adventurer all his life. The Ratu James's proposal intrigued him because it offered him a temporary escape from doing nothing and simply travelling here and there while brooding about his loss.'

'We must rid ourselves of him somehow, and the sooner the better.'

Manon remained silent for a moment, then she said, 'I am not prepared to stand for that. By all means stall him off if you can. But I won't have him harmed. He is as rich as Croesus and he has fallen for me. Given a little luck, I'll hook him. Then I'll be able to live in the luxury that I've always longed for.'

Lacost's pale blue eyes narrowed. 'So that is your game. Good luck to you then, but only provided that you can keep him out of this present business. Until we get the gold you will continue to take your orders from me. Understand?'

Sitting up in bed, she gave him an angry look. 'Why should I? You couldn't even start the job until I had half ruined myself to provide you with the money to hire your salvaging equipment. I am still with you as far as getting the gold for ourselves goes. But I'm not such a fool as to allow you to do him some injury that might sabotage my chances of his marrying me.'

With a toothy smile, Lacost replied, '*Mon petit chou*, be pleased to remember that I still have that bottle. So long as I hold it, you remain in my power, and should I require your help to eliminate him, you will give it.'

His words caused Manon's mind to flash back to that fatal, sweltering afternoon when, maddened by the heat, boredom and years of frustration, she had snatched from her husband the bottle containing the drops that would have nullified his heart attack, flung it from the window, then watched him die.

It had been bad luck for her that Pierre Lacost had happened to be outside on the veranda and had picked up the bottle when it landed at his feet. He was Georges' estate manager, and for some months past Manon had been having an *affaire* with him. Their secret meetings had been infrequent and fraught with danger, owing to her husband's arguseyed jealousy. But, since his first heart attack, Georges had frightened himself into impotence. Manon's sexual craving had led her into letting Pierre have her from time to time in odd corners of the estate, outhouses, where the risk of their being surprised was small. As he had been aware how boredom with her husband had grown into hatred and a longing to be rid of him, no sooner had Pierre read the label on the bottle than he felt sure of the way in which it had come into his hands, and one glance through the window confirmed his belief.

After Georges' funeral Pierre had confronted Manon with his knowledge of her deed. She could produce no other explanation for the sudden arrival of the bottle of drops on the veranda and after a while sullenly admitted her guilt. Had he disclosed his knowledge to the authorities it could have led to her being charged with murder. As the price of his silence, Pierre had demanded that she should marry him. At that she had rebelled. She liked him well enough, and was even strongly attracted by his animal sexual vigour, but Algeria had become anathema to her. The idea of remaining on that isolated estate tied to another husband when she had rid herself of Georges was, to her, unthinkable. Neither cajolery nor threats could persuade her. In the end Pierre had given way and they had struck a bargain. She made over the estate to him and he left her free to leave Algeria.

As the state of the country had by then rendered the property almost valueless, except to a man long used to running it, Manon had considered parting with it a cheap price to pay for securing her freedom. In consequence, she had felt no rancour against Pierre for getting what he could out of her. On the contrary, her instinct as a Frenchwoman was rather to admire him for playing well the cards that had fallen into his hands; so before she left they again slept together several times and when they did take leave of each other they had parted as good friends.

She had never expected to see him again, but eighteen months later he had turned up in Tahiti. As at that time she had another lover, they had not resumed their *affaire,* but had met on friendly terms and he was one of the many people to whom, for old times' sake, she had lent money.

By then she was already planning her move to Fiji, and when she left Tahiti Pierre again passed out of her life for a while. It was not until a few months before that he had re-entered it. Knowing that she still had considerable capital, he had sought her out in her remote island home and put to her the project of salvaging the gold from the sunken ship off Tujoa. Already worried by the inroads that the cost of building her house had made in her small fortune, she had fallen for the possibility of recovering her outlay, and had agreed to gamble a sum to finance Pierre's venture that was greatly in excess of what caution demanded.

One disadvantage to her island retreat that Manon had soon discovered was that while living there the chances of coming into contact with an acceptable lover were almost negligible; and, from her late teens onward, after a few months of chastity she had always been beset by a craving to have a man in her bed again. It was not, therefore, to be wondered at that when the virile Pierre had re-appeared on her scene he had found no difficulty in persuading her once more to become his mistress; and during the visits he paid her while making preparations to retrieve the treasure they had enjoyed some very pleasant times together.

Now she cursed her folly in having renewed her association with him. Not only had be glibly persuaded her to jeopardise her financial security but, if she had turned down his proposition the odds were that she would have seen no more of him; so he would not be there in her room threatening to wreck her chances of securing Gregory as a husband. But then, had Pierre not induced her, for the protection of her gamble, to go to Rio, she would not have met Gregory; so he could not altogether be blamed for the situation in which she found herself, or the attitude he had taken up. Swiftly she decided that, while continuing to humour him, she must not allow him to believe that he could browbeat her into doing anything he wished.

Staring up at him, she said in a voice that conveyed more sorrow than anger, 'Seeing what we have been to one another, Pierre, I feel terribly upset that you should even think of threatening me. After all, it is very far from certain that I can succeed in manœuvring Sallust into marrying me; and should I fail in that I'll be ruined unless we can secure the treasure. So I'll still do everything I can to aid you, short of luring him into a trap. And don't think I'm influenced by your bringing up that old business of Georges' death. Had you accused me at the time, I would have been hard put to it to defend myself. But not after all these years. Then, the Arab servants could have been brought as witnesses to give evidence that I had grown to hate my husband. But they can't now. Having the bottle proves nothing. You might have got it anywhere. If you charged me it would only be thought that you had hatched up this story owing to jealousy, and you'd be laughed out of court.'

'Perhaps, but, as the saying goes, there is no smoke without fire, and to be accused would be most unpleasant for you. Besides, I wouldn't need to do that. Instead I could give Sallust chapter and verse about the whole affair. Even if he did not entirely believe me it is pretty certain that he would decide against marrying a woman accused of murdering her former husband.'

Instantly Manon realised how fatal this new threat could prove to her plans. Her mind flashed back to the *Macumba* priest. To him she had admitted in front of Gregory that she had killed a man. She had given no explanation of her act, except to say that she had killed in self-defence, and left it to be supposed that she had probably been saving herself from rape. But if Pierre told Gregory how Georges had died it was certain that he would put two and two together, and all hope of her marrying him would be gone.

While these shattering thoughts were rushing through her mind, Pierre was going on, 'But please believe that I have no intention of doing anything of the kind. After our long friendship the last thing I would do is to queer your chances of securing a wealthy husband. I mentioned it only to show you that I could be nasty were I that sort of man. You have already said you will continue to give me your help and do your best to persuade Sallust to throw in his hand. That is all I ask. Now, my sweet chicken, it is over a month since I caressed that lovely body of yours; so take off your pretty nightie.'

As he spoke he was getting out of his jacket, but she checked him with a swift, low cry. 'No, Pierre, no! You have already been here much too long. Since you woke Sallust up, if he can't get off to sleep again he may decide to pay me a visit.'

His eyes narrowed again. 'So you have already *trompé* me with him?'

She nodded. 'Yes, what did you expect?'

'I've always supposed that when a woman wants a man to marry her, her best policy is to keep him wanting her until he does.'

'Not a woman like myself. You should know how good I can be in bed. That is my strongest card. When a man has spent a few nights with me he realises that he's got something that he would be very reluctant to give up. But Sallust must not find you here and he might come in at any moment; so, for God's sake, get out.'

Suddenly he grinned at her. 'Well, I don't mind his having you as long as I continue to do so. And from the moment I set eyes on you again this evening I've been feeling as randy as an old goat. I tell you what. Slip out of bed, put on a coat and come along with me to your room. If in the morning he tells you that he came to your room and you weren't here, you can say that you couldn't get to sleep, so went for a walk round the garden.'

For a moment Manon hesitated. Gregory made a delightful lover, but he was no longer young and he had been far from sustaining the prowess he had displayed during their first night together; whereas Pierre was nearly as insatiable as herself, and it would be good to feel his weight on her again. With a low laugh she threw back the bedclothes and jumped out of bed.

In the morning Gregory told Manon and James about his midnight visitor. Both showed grave concern and Manon took the opportunity to plead long and earnestly with him to abandon the quest for treasure and, instead, go straight to Fiji with her. But finally he said:

'No, my dear. Naturally I am hoping that in the records here we will find confirmation that there was a cargo of gold in the ship. But even should we not, I've a mind to go through with this thing now. You see, this man Lacost's threat was more or less a challenge to me, and it is not in my nature to refuse a challenge. In fact, pitting my wits against his will be rather fun.'

Being eager to learn as soon as possible what the records held, they had agreed the night before to breakfast together in the dining room at nine o'clock. As soon as they had finished their meal they walked the short distance to the main square of the town.

They already knew that in 1773 Antigua, then a city of fifty thousand people, had been totally destroyed by a terrible volcanic eruption. The two volcanoes that had wiped it out stood grimly beautiful in the near distance against an azure sky. One was called the Mountain of Fire and the other the Mountain of Water—the latter because it had an underground lake inside it. When they had erupted simultaneously, the city had not only been swept by fire, but also deluged by torrents of boiling water and mud.

For twenty years the site had been deserted, but was then rebuilt in the Spanish style of the late eighteenth century. As no additions or alterations had since been made, it contained not a single glass and concrete building, so remained a remarkable and charming example of the architecture of that period.

One side of the main square was occupied by the arcaded Captain General's Palace; opposite was another long, arcaded building that held the Library. On a third side stood the imposing Cathedral. Few of the buildings were more than one storey high, their sides facing on to the streets, with small windows protected by grilles of fine, scrolled ironwork. Through the arched entrances of the larger buildings could be seen sunny patios, gay with flowering trees and shrubs, on to which the principal rooms of these one-storey mansions looked out.

The old capital was made even more romantic and a thing apart from the modern world by the fact that here and there among the houses rose the roofless ruins of big churches, the lower parts alone of which had escaped destruction. The Cathedral was so vast that only one-third of it had been restored, yet that could accommodate a congregation of several hundred.

When they reached the Library they met with disappointment. As it was a Saturday, it was closed. Crossing the square to the Palace, a part of which was now occupied by the local tourist agency, they enquired there how best to spend the week-end. A most helpful little man who spoke good English told them that they must not fail to visit Lake Atitlan and Chichicastenango. And to see the latter at its most interesting they must go there that day, because the market was held on Saturdays. It was a fifty-mile drive, but he said that if they were prepared to leave at once they could get there by lunch-time. Deciding to go, a car, with a driver who spoke a little English, was summoned from a rank in the square and they at once set off.

Within a few minutes they were out of the town and soon enjoying some of the finest mountain scenery they had ever seen. In the distance there were whole chains of volcanoes,

89

many of them still active, with plumes of smoke drifting up into the sky. A considerable part of the land on either side of the road was well cultivated, with crops of sugar cane, maize and barley. Now and then they passed groups of paw-paw, apricot, cherry and apple trees. The villages were well kept and the little people who lived in them, all of whom were of pure Indian stock with no trace of Negro blood, were better dressed and more prosperous-looking than those they had seen in Brazil, Peru or Panama. At times they ran through patches of woodland in which they were amused to see every few hundred yards, nailed to a tree trunk, an advertisement for Andrews Liver Salts. This considerable advertising expenditure in sparsely-populated districts, innocent of all other advertisements, implied such large sales as could be explained only by the Indians having given up their local distilled liquor because they had found Mr. Andrews' health-giving tonic more to their taste, and a drink for all occasions.

They saw evidence on the last ten miles of the road to Chichicastenango that the stamina of the Indians was quite extraordinary. In single file little groups of small brown-skinned men and women were making their way to market. On the heads and shoulders of all of them were balanced enormous loads of fruit, vegetables, woven cloth or pottery, some of the men carrying as many as forty or fifty weighty, hand-made pots; but they were trudging along quite happily and, as the car passed, invariably turned to grin at the occupants and call friendly greetings.

As they neared their destination, the way became frighteningly twisty and precipitous. The car plunged down into valleys, skidded round hairpin bends and roared up slopes with steeper gradients than any Gregory could recall having previously encountered in a motor vehicle.

Chichicastenango stood on a plateau seven thousand feet above sea level and from its outskirts there were splendid views of the surrounding country. It consisted solely of one-storey buildings, mostly constructed of wattle and daub, but the inhabitants numbered many thousands.

After Planter's Punches and a very satisfactory lunch at the pleasant little hotel, they went out to see the famous market in the large central square. The stalls were so numerous that it would have taken hours to inspect them all, and the variety of goods offered showed the strangest contrasts. Jackets, skirts and aprons, beautifully embroidered in the gayest colours, such as the peasants had made for many hundred years, were displayed alongside radio sets; palm-leaf hats beside electrical appliances; native musical instruments of a long-past age beside up-to-date arrays of patent medicines, and hand-made crockery pots beside aluminium cooking utensils. There were buckets and bags, bead necklaces and raw tobacco, sandals and patent leather shoes, wonderful arrays of tropical fruit and revolting-looking lumps of meat, nuts by the million and gaudy sweets, chewing gum, underclothes, formidable knives, fountain pens and scores of other items; while here and there among the stalls tables had been set up at which little parties of Indians were joyfully guzzling hot messes and swigging down draughts of raw red wine.

At one side of the square there stood a fine church, and on the flight of steps that led to it several Indians were swinging bunches of burning leaves. Their driver had accompanied them as guide. Leading them towards the church he said:

'We make visit. Very interesting. Mornings seven o'clock priest he say Mass. Then go home. Rest of day church place for worship of old gods. Men on steps go up very slow. Reach top and families allowed in with them. Inside all burn candles. Pray to ancestors for good crops or bad luck to enemies. With each group you see magic man. He take money to see prayers answered. Inside church you look only at saints, carvings, altar. Not to look at people. They not like, might make trouble for us.'

Greatly intrigued, they followed him into the church by a side entrance. There were no pews and nearly the whole of the stone floor was occupied by many small groups of Indians, most of whom were kneeling. While pretending to admire the architecture of the church, the visitors covertly observed the pagan rites that were in progress. The kneeling Indians had lit hundreds of short candles, among which were scattered rose petals and many small, unidentifiable objects.

91

From each group a constant mutter went up and, evidencing the strong double faith resulting from the Spaniards having imposed a veneer of Christianity on the natives, many of them were frequently crossing themselves.

As they left the church, Manon said, 'Well! I should never have believed it. The higher clergy in Guatemala must know about this, and Mass is celebrated here every morning. How can they possibly permit its being turned over to witch-doctors for the remainder of the day?'

'That is their policy,' Gregory replied with a cynical little laugh. 'They know jolly well that unless they closed their eyes to the fact that a majority of the people are still fundamentally pagan they wouldn't get them to come to Mass at all. And I suppose they vaguely hope to get a genuine convert now and then.'

'As many people go to Mass as worship old gods,' their guide remarked. 'Good thing to "hedge", as you have expression. Then when dead you win either way. But in real trouble people think old gods best. From here they go up mountain to old sacred stone. Sacrifice chickens, goat, pig. If man's vigour lost he smear blood on private part. They say certain remedy. Better much than burning candles to Virgin. That not logical, I think. But me very modern man. Better I think to spend money at drugstore.'

Gregory grinned at him. 'I'm sure you are right. I must bear your tip in mind.'

Manon drew him back a pace and whispered in his ear. 'No, darling. You might do yourself harm if you stimulate yourself beyond your normal powers. Please don't. I'm perfectly content with the loving you can give me. As things are you are wonderful and you satisfy me completely.'

Nevertheless, she spent a good part of the night in big Pierre's bed. Before she left him the previous night he had made her promise to report to him what success she had had in dissuading Gregory from financing James, and she had felt that she must do that.

Soon after dinner they had all retired and about ten o'clock Gregory had come to her room, but he had spent only an hour making love to her. As they lay embraced, she had again

92

done her utmost on Pierre's behalf. This time she took the line of endeavouring to convince Gregory that he would be running into really grave danger. Had she known her man better that was the last thing she would have done.

He listened patiently while she talked of the Colons of Algeria: how for years they had had to defend their properties, then engaged in a vicious hit-and-run war with the Arabs; how they had come to hold life cheap and killed without mercy. She pointed out that he would not be up against only Lacost and his companion, the swarthy Corbin. There could be little doubt that Lacost was the leader of a gang of unscrupulous toughs. They knew the South Seas and Gregory did not, so he would stand no chance against them.

Gregory was far from rash by nature. To the contrary, on a score of occasions only the exercise of great caution had saved him from his enemies. But the decisive factor in this present matter was that he had become bored with life. Manon provided him with a new and delightful interest, but a love *affaire* was not enough. Another side of his mentality craved exciting situations in which he would have to use his good brain, and this quest for treasure had unexpectedly developed into just that sort of thing. Moreover, if the gamble did cost him his life—what of it? He had hopes that death would reunite him with Erika.

Gently but firmly he told Manon that his mind was made up. He had become very fond of young James, so would not disappoint him. In fact, should the treasure after all prove a myth, he had decided to use part of his wealth to enable James to establish industries on Tujoa that would save his people from exploitation. Then he fondly kissed Manon good night, and left her.

Soon afterwards she joined Pierre in his room. To have attempted to deceive him would have been pointless, as he must soon have discovered that she was doing so. In consequence, when he asked her whether she had been successful, she replied:

'No, and for that you have only yourself to blame. To have threatened Sallust is the worst thing you could have done. He is a very brave man and a born adventurer. Your threats put his back up and he has taken them as a challenge. He is now determined to go through with this business, and nothing I can say will deter him.'

Lacost shrugged. 'Then the more fool him. But we'll talk further about it later. I could hardly wait for you. Get your things off and jump into bed.'

Three hours slipped by, then as she was about to leave him she asked, 'What do you intend to do about Sallust?'

Pierre gave an ugly laugh. 'I must put him out of the ring and the sooner the better.'

'No!' she pleaded. 'No! Please do nothing here. Wait till we get to Fiji or one of the other islands. Out there I may be able to turn him into a lotus-eater who will become content to laze in the sun and let everything else go hang.'

'That would not ensure our coming out on top,' Pierre argued. 'By then he will have provided the Ratu with the money to get on with the job. While you are playing Circe to Sallust, young James will be working like the nigger he is, and may forestall me.'

Suddenly inspiration came to Manon and she said, 'James is the king-pin in this whole business. Why concern yourself with Sallust? Get rid of James and you will have a free field. Why not do that?'

'You've got something there,' he agreed. 'I'll consider it. Perhaps there will occur a chance to throw a spanner in his works tomorrow. Have you made any plans to go sight-seeing?'

'Yes, we are going up to Lake Atitlan and making a trip in a motor boat across the lake to the village of San Antonio Palopo to see some wonderful carvings in the church there.'

Pierre fingered one end of his long moustache thoughtfully for a moment, then he said, 'There are plenty of lonely places on the way there. Perhaps Jules Corbin and I might stage a hold-up and put the Ratu out of the running.'

'You won't harm Sallust, will you?' she exclaimed in sudden alarm.

'No, my little one; no,' he assured her with a smile. 'If we can render young James *hors de combat* for a few months his backer will be stymied too. Besides,' Pierre's smile became a grin, 'I would hate to deprive you of the embraces of your Casanova.'

Manon shrugged off the jibe at Gregory's now limited sexual activities and soon afterwards she returned to her room.

When she woke in the morning she felt extremely worried. She knew from long experience that Pierre never hesitated to lie to her when it suited his book. She knew, too, that he was completely unscrupulous and had a malicious streak in him. If he did hold up the party on their way to Lake Atitlan she felt certain that Gregory would not stand by and see his friend injured without endeavouring to prevent it. That would be excuse enough for Pierre to shoot him, too. And, although he had said that he had no objection to sharing her with Gregory, that might not be true. Quite possibly he would be delighted at the chance to put her other lover out of the way. Again, he might not hold up the car but, concealed in the bushes along the roadside, shoot into it. She knew him to be an excellent shot, but would he be able to obtain a rifle? If not, his aim with a pistol at a moving target twenty or more feet away must prove uncertain. He might miss James and hit Gregory—or her.

Instead of breakfasting with the others at nine o'clock, as they had arranged, she remained in bed. When Gregory arrived to enquire why she had failed to join them she had almost made up her mind to tell him about Pierre and warn him of his danger. But at the last moment she was deterred by the awful thought that if Pierre found out what she had done he might tell Gregory about her having killed her husband.

As an excuse for still being in bed, she said that she was suffering from an appalling migraine. Then she asked Gregory to postpone the expedition to Lake Atitlan and remain with her.

To her distress he said that he did not think that would be a good idea. 'If I could help to get rid of your migraine quicker,' he declared, 'I'd willingly stay with you. But I know from experience that doesn't help. Talking to anyone only makes things worse, and the best cure is to lie silent here in a semi-darkened room. That being so, it would be absurd for

James and me to kick our heels about the hotel all day; so we'll adhere to our plan of going up to the lake, and I'm only sorry that you can't come with us.'

She then pretended a fit of temper, and abused him as an unfeeling lover. But that got her nowhere. She was already aware that once he had made up his mind about a thing he was as stubborn as a mule. With gentle mockery he told her that she was behaving like a spoilt child; then he saw to it that she had everything she might want, kissed her and departed.

The first half of the way to Lake Atitlan was the same as that to Chichicastenango, then the road branched off to the north. Again they drove through magnificent scenery with ranges of volcanoes outlined against the blue sky, forming a backdrop in the distance. Soon after midday, at a place high up in the mountains, their driver pulled up and they got out to enjoy, from the edge of the cliff on which they stood, one of the finest panoramas in Central America. Far below them the great inland lake shimmered in the sunshine. It was ringed with six volcanoes—one of which was eleven thousand six hundred feet in height—descending steeply to its shores. Here and there along the lake edge there were clusters of seemingly tiny white houses and, leaving furrows on the still surface of the lake, a few boats that looked no larger than beetles.

Having gazed their fill they returned to the car, and for another half-hour it wound its way down into a lovely valley where lay the pretty little town of Panajachel. Two miles further on they came to the lake shore on which stood the Hotel Tzanjuya. There they lunched off freshly-caught lake fish that tasted like bream.

James was in great heart. Until that morning he had been far from happy, because he feared that, should the records in Antigua fail to provide definite evidence that the sunken ship had carried a cargo of gold, Gregory would decline to finance him. But on the way to the lake Gregory had told him that he meant to do so in any case. Over the meal they talked of the gear that would be needed to raise the heavy beams that blocked the way to the cabin in which were the chests that, it was hoped, contained the treasure.

Pontoons and a crane could, James thought, be hired in

Suva. If not, they might have to be brought from San Francisco. But nothing could be gained by writing to the harbour authorities to ask if they had such equipment, as if they left for Fiji within the next week they would arrive there sooner than a letter.

When Gregory enquired about divers and labour, James assured him that there would be no difficulty about that; his people would willingly co-operate. But it was certain that a professional diver would have to be employed, as moving the beams would be a tricky operation.

After the meal they went aboard a small motor launch to make the trip across the lake. The crew consisted solely of the owner. Smilingly he welcomed them aboard but, looking at his wrist watch, conveyed to them in broken English that he wished they had made an earlier start, instead of lingering over lunch. Apparently, while the lake was always as placid as a mill pond in the mornings, a change of temperature in the afternoons caused winds to come rushing down the valley between the volcanoes, and disturb it to such an extent that at times the waves could become twelve feet high.

Chugging away from the hotel, for a while they hugged the shore, on which there were a few pleasant villas scattered along a bathing beach, then they turned out and crossed an arc of the lake, to arrive an hour later at the rickety landing stage that served the village of San Antonio Palopo. Going ashore, they made their way up a narrow, winding, potholed track to the church. It was an empty, barn-like structure and proved disappointing. The carvings which had been so cracked up turned out to be eight or ten wooden figures obviously intended to represent saints. In a group they leaned disconsolately against one wall, with no altars or candles burning before them. They were unquestionably old, but no-one could honestly have considered them fine works of art.

After a glance at these dusty, neglected relics, as the village was no more than a cluster of hovels, they returned to the boat.

The surface of the lake had already become choppy and the boatman, anxious to get back before it became really rough, set a direct course for the hotel, which could be picked

97

out as a white blob several miles distant. Between it and San Antonio lay three wide bays, separated by two rocky capes that projected a good way out into the lake.

For a while the nearest cape gave them some protection, but when they had passed it the launch caught the full force of the wind. The waves did not rise to dangerous heights, but were large enough to lift the little boat so that every other minute her bottom boards smacked down on to the water and clouds of spray hissed up on either side of her.

They were about a third of the way across the middle bay when they noticed another launch coming towards them. Two minutes later it looked as if it would pass within ten feet of them. Instead its engine was abruptly cut. Apparently the only person in it was the man at the wheel, but as it drifted past another man, who must have been crouching behind the gunwale, suddenly bobbed up. With a swift movement he lobbed what looked like a small tin of soup across the few feet that separated the two boats.

At that moment, through a gap in the flying spray, Gregory got a clear view of the men in the other launch. Corbin was at the wheel and it was Lacost who had thrown the missile. Only seconds later it landed in James's lap.

He and Gregory were sitting one either side of the boatman in the fore part of the boat. Instantly guessing that the missile was a home-made bomb, Gregory threw himself across the boatman and snatched it up. As his fingers closed on the tin his heart seemed to come up into his throat. At any instant it might explode. Unless there was just time for him to throw it overboard all three of them would be torn to ribbons.

Gregory was sprawled right across the astonished boatman, so to pitch the bomb clear meant an awkward movement. With all his force he jerked up his hand. But in plunging sideways he had knocked the man's hands from the wheel and the boat was already beginning to veer off course. The boatman made a grab at the wheel to bring her back on to it. Just as Gregory was about to release his grip on the tin, their arms came into sharp contact. Instead of going over the side, the tin shot up into the air. It landed with a thud on the roof

98

of the cabin behind them, then rolled away to the stern of the boat.

Springing to his feet, Gregory yelled, 'It's a bomb! Over you go!' Still shouting to the others to save themselves, he threw himself into the water. Next moment there was a shattering explosion.

The water heaved and he was thrown half out of it. Falling back, his weight carried him deep down. As he became conscious of the coldness of the lake water, it added to his fears for himself. They were in the middle of the bay and must be a good mile from the shore. If the boat had been wrecked there was small likelihood that Lacost would take them aboard his and there had been no other in sight. He was a good swimmer, but in cold, rough water he greatly doubted if he could cover such a distance.

As he came gasping to the surface, he saw that the bomb had blown the stern of the launch away and that the boat was sinking. Grimly, he turned on his side to strike out for the shore. Suddenly a shot rang out, another, another and another. Bitterly he realised that he was to be given little chance to reach the shore. Without even glancing over his shoulder, he knew that both Lacost and Corbin were shooting at him—and shooting to kill.

7

Death on the Lake

Gregory needed no telling then that his situation was desperate. Lacost's threats had not been idle ones. He clearly meant to rid himself of any rival seekers of the treasure, even if it meant committing murder. And he had been not only swift to act, but clever. Here, out on the broad lake, there were no witnesses to what had taken place. Even if the explosion had been seen from the distant shore it would be thought that some carelessness, perhaps the throwing away of a cigarette butt, had caused the petrol tank to blow up. In due course the bodies of the victims would be washed ashore, but in that sparsely populated area it could be days or weeks before they were found. It would naturally be assumed that they had drowned, and any wound inflicted by a bullet would be thought to be a gash caused by the body having been hurled against a jagged rock. In any case all the odds were that, by the time Gregory and his companions were washed up, Lacost and Corbin would long since have left Guatemala.

From Gregory's swift glance at his would-be murderers he derived only one ray of comfort. Shooting with pistols from a heaving boat, their aim must be uncertain. Even so, there was a very nasty chance that they might get him, so he promptly dived. A dozen swift strokes took him under the sinking launch. With aching lungs he surfaced on its far side. But he knew that it could give him only temporary protection.

Anxiously he looked round for his companions. The boatman, emitting a stream of curses, was clinging to the other side of the launch, but James was nowhere to be seen. Gregory was now faced with a choice of remaining where he was, or striking out for the shore. If he did the latter, it seemed certain that he would be spotted and the Colons would come in pursuit of him; so it seemed safer to remain under cover, anyhow for as long as the wreck stayed afloat. Just then she swung a little, revealing beyond her stern a box-like wooden structure that was floating a few feet away from the main wreck. It was the roof which had been blown off the cabin.

Striking out, Gregory swam towards it. He had barely reached the half-submerged roof when he caught a glimpse of the Colons' launch. They had switched on the engine and had come round the wreck to hunt him down. Knowing that his life now hung by a thread, he ducked and thrust himself sideways so as to come up beneath the cabin roof. While under water, he barged into an obstruction. Coming up, he shook the water from his eyes. To his delight, the obstruction proved to be James, who had already taken cover under the floating roof.

Finding that it was Gregory who had joined him, James began to speak; but, fearful that they would be heard and discovered, Gregory quickly put a hand over his friend's mouth. Under their hideout there was barely enough room for both of them to lie floating on their backs, and between the top of the roof and the water there were only a few inches of air space. Their faces were half submerged and wavelets constantly slapped over them.

They had been reunited for no more than two minutes when three shots rang out, followed by a piercing scream. That told them without a doubt that the Colons had spotted the boatman clinging to the wreck. To make certain that he did not survive to bear witness against them, they had killed the poor fellow in cold blood.

This brutal act was the final confirmation of Gregory's fears that they would not be satisfied and head back to land until they had killed James and himself; and every moment their position was becoming more precarious. To prevent themselves from floating out through the open end of their box-like cover, each of them had to hold on to the underside of the roof, and their weight was dragging it down. Another few minutes and there would be no air space at all left. Then they must either drown there or come out to face a hail of bullets.

Minutes that seemed an eternity dragged by; then, blinded and half suffocated, Gregory could bear it no longer. Ducking down, he came up outside but still clinging to their cover. Staring apprehensively across the choppy waves he drew in a succession of deep breaths. To his infinite relief, the launch was not in sight. Cautiously he peered round the side of the roof and there she was, obviously still hunting them as she circled slowly not more than a hundred yards away. He had been lucky to surface with the roof between him and her, otherwise he would certainly have been seen. But how much longer could his luck last? Even as he wondered, the launch turned in his direction.

At that moment James came up beside him and gasped, 'The roof served us well but . . . but it's no good any longer. Too low in the water.'

'Only chance left is to make a dash for it,' Gregory muttered. 'But with luck they won't get us both. You strike out in one direction, I'll take the other.'

As he spoke there sounded a drumming on the roof, but both of them were so concerned about what might happen in the next few minutes that neither of them took any notice of it.

James put a hand on Gregory's shoulder. 'No, I'm a much stronger swimmer than you. Stay here behind the cover the roof still provides, while I give them a run for their money. Then, when you see them going after me, you'll have a much better chance of getting away.'

Before Gregory could protest, his young friend had submerged and was swiftly swimming off under water. In an agony of apprehension he awaited the outcome. His eyes only just above water level, between each wave-crest he snatched anxious glimpses of the oncoming launch. As the seconds passed, he began to breathe a trifle more freely. Suddenly a cry went up and the launch swerved in the direction that James had taken. But no shots were fired. Having come up for air, James must have dived again, and they had temporarily lost sight of him.

Only then did Gregory realise that the drumming on the roof had been rain. A minute passed, two, three. Still no shots, and the rain had increased to one of those unexpected downpours that are frequent in tropical countries. Another minute and he could no longer see the launch. With a great sigh of thankfulness, he realised that, now she was no longer visible, it was quite certain that the men in her would not be able to spot James' dark head in the tossing waters.

A great surge of joy flooded through Gregory. He was seized with an impulse to shout aloud at this triumph of the brave young Ratu over their enemies, and cheer him on. But his elation was short-lived. Like a douche of icy water, awareness of the desperateness of his own situation returned to him. For the past quarter of an hour his thoughts had been so engrossed with keeping out of sight of the two murderous Colons, and anxiously awaiting the result of James' gallant attempt to leave him a free field, that he had forgotten that he was a mile from the shore and, pulled down by his waterlogged clothes, would almost certainly drown before he could reach it.

The idea that he and James should strike out in different directions for the coast had seemed sound when they had exchanged their few hurried words. But to risk putting it into practice was a very different matter. As long as he hung on to the cabin roof he could keep afloat, but once he abandoned it his chances of survival seemed terrifyingly slender.

Yet even to remain there was fraught with peril. Tropical storms were usually of short duration and ceased as abruptly as they started. In another few minutes the protective curtain of rain might dissolve and the sun break through. It seemed certain that the Colons would then return for a last look round the wreck to make sure that he was not clinging to it. So far, it was only by sheer luck that they had overlooked the possibility that one of their intended victims might have taken cover beneath the cabin roof. On their return, the luck might turn against him. Then he could expect a bullet fired at close quarters.

The rain was already easing. Inaction being abhorrent to him, he forced himself to make up his mind. But his decision was a compromise. Instead of abandoning the roof, he would endeavour to get it as far as possible away from the danger area of the wreck. Still clinging to it, he kicked out with his legs, pushing it before him.

As it was quite light and the downpour had rendered the lake calmer, he made good progress. By the time the rain ceased altogether, he had covered some two hundred yards. Peering round the side he could again see the launch. She was slowly patrolling about halfway between the wreck and the shore, evidently still searching for James.

Slightly altering his direction to keep well away from her, Gregory kept going for a further five minutes. Then he saw the launch turn towards the wreck and suddenly increase her speed. His heart lifted, for this new move indicated that the hunt had been given up and James had got away. But in a few moments now he would be in deadly danger. The launch must pass within a hundred yards of him. Unless he could keep his head under water for several minutes he would be spotted. Or they might alter direction slightly to find out if he was clinging to the roof. In either case the game would be up.

With bated breath he watched her approach while preparing to duck under the roof. Just as he was about to do so, to his amazement and relief she suddenly altered course again, heading across the lake in the direction of the hotel.

For a moment he was completely puzzled by this swift change of intent. Then, as he pushed the roof round a little, so as to head for the nearest beach, a sideways glance gave him the explanation. The wreck had disappeared. It must have sunk only a few moments before and, seeing it go down, Lacost had decided that there was no point in returning to it.

The best part of half an hour had elapsed since Lacost had thrown his bomb. During this time Gregory's mind had been constantly occupied with the urgent question of what next to do that would give him the best chance of escaping with his life; so he had given little heed to his physical condition. But, now that immediate peril of being murdered was past, he was again beset by acute anxiety about his staying powers.

In spite of the distance he had pushed the roof it was little nearer the shore, as a current had swept it in a sideways direction. His water-filled shoes felt like lumps of lead, the muscles of his legs were aching badly and, most menacing of all, the lake water was very cold.

Even if he ceased thrusting with his legs, sooner or later the roof must drift ashore, provided he could continue to keep his hold on it. But his hands were becoming numb and the explosion had thrown a film of oil on to the roof, making it slightly slippery. So could he cling on for an hour, two hours, three perhaps? That was the awful question.

For what seemed an endless time he struggled on, alternately pushing the roof before him for some fifty yards, then resting. From time to time he let go of it, trod water and clapped his hands vigorously to restore their circulation. But now each breath he drew pained his chest, and by the time he was halfway to the shore he decided that he had little chance of setting foot on it.

When he had lost Erika he had himself narrowly escaped drowning in the Pacific. Just over a fortnight ago in Rio he had been saved from drowning only by a miracle. Now he was again faced with drowning. It seemed that he was fated to die that way. In his case it would not be 'third time lucky'.

Then an idea came to him. If he stopped swimming, and instead used the roof as a raft, there was just a chance that it might have sufficient buoyancy to bear his weight until it was washed up.

After two unsuccessful attempts he managed to turn the roof over so that it formed a shallow, oblong-shaped boat, one end of which was missing. He then had to get into it. As soon as he put his full weight on one side that side went under. Four times it overturned completely, so that he gulped in water and came up beneath it. But persistence was second nature to Gregory. At the fifth attempt he managed to spreadeagle himself upon it, half submerged in the water with which it was filled. Only the broken edges of the three sides now showed above the surface, but at least it kept him afloat. Near the end of his tether, he lay there face down, fighting to keep conscious, as he knew that if he passed out, even for a moment, the least shifting of his weight would cause the roof to overbalance.

As time passed, now that he no longer had to make any considerable effort, he gradually got his breath back and his condition improved a little; but whether his endurance would have proved sufficient for him to maintain his precarious position until wind or a current carried him to land remained open to question.

He was roused from semi-lethargy by a shout and, lifting his head, saw James swimming vigorously towards him. From the shore the Ratu had sighted the roof and wondered if Gregory was still clinging to it. He had already made up his mind to swim off and find out when he saw Gregory struggling to turn the roof into a raft, and set off to his rescue.

As the raft was still a quarter of a mile from land, it was hard work to push and tow it to the beach; but James was a magnificent swimmer and at length the two friends staggered ashore, worn out but thankful to be still alive.

It seemed to them that many hours had elapsed since they had left San Antonio Palopo; but Gregory's waterproof watch showed it to be only a little after five o'clock, so they could not have been in the water for much more than an hour and a quarter. Fortunately, they had landed on the promontory furthest from San Antonio; but, even so, as they would still have to go round the furthest bay, they were several miles from the Hotel Tzanjuyu.

As the sun was no longer sufficiently strong to dry their clothes on them, they took off all but their under-garments. Then, when they were well rested, carrying their other things, they set off on their long tramp. It proved far from easy going, as there was no path along the shore. At times they had to scramble over patches of rock and at others, where precipitous cliffs came straight down to the water, make their way up steep slopes, then through long patches of scrub to the next beach.

Every twenty minutes or so they sat down for a breather and discussed what they should say about their recent experience when they reached the hotel. As there had been no boatman in the Colons' launch, it seemed probable that they had stolen it from one of the villas on the foreshore. If so, the odds were that they would beach it somewhere not far distant from the road, regain a car that they had left in some secluded spot, and by now be well on their way back to Antigua without anyone in Panajachel having seen them. As they had set out intending to commit murder, it could also be assumed that they had arranged some form of alibi. In consequence, if a charge was brought against them, it might be impossible to prove that they had even been in the district.

In any case, bringing a charge would mean Gregory and James being detained in Guatemala as essential witnesses, perhaps for several weeks, which would seriously interfere with their own plans, and be a foolish thing to do if there was little hope of bringing the criminals to justice. They therefore decided to make no mention of having even seen the Colons or their launch, and simply say that their own boat had blown up without warning, leading to the unfortunate loss of the boatman.

When they had accomplished about two-thirds of their trek they came upon a cluster of poor dwellings. From them a rough track led on round the lake, which was fortunate, as by then darkness was falling, and it was past eight when they came in sight of the first villa on the long beach outside Panajachel.

James' splendid physique had enabled him to come through their ordeal without ill-effect, but, fit as Gregory was for his age, his powers of endurance were no longer what they had been and he was drooping with fatigue. So, instead of continuing on the last mile to the hotel, they knocked up the occupants of the villa.

They proved to be an elderly couple and the husband was a German, so Gregory was able to tell him without difficulty about their boat having blown up. The man said that he had been resident in Guatemala for many years and had recently retired from the export business. No doubt that was true, although Gregory had a shrewd suspicion that he was one of the many Nazis who, after the defeat of Hitler, had emi-

grated to Latin America. But the couple could not have been
kinder and more helpful. Having refreshed their visitors with
drinks, as they had no telephone they sent a servant with a
message to the hotel; and twenty minutes later the driver
from Antigua, who had been very worried by his passengers'
failure to return, arrived with the car.

It was by then nearly nine o'clock and Gregory was feeling
terribly done up, so instead of setting out on the long drive
back, they decided to spend the night at the Tzanjuyu. There
they gave the manager their account of what had happened
and commiserated with him on the death of his boatman and
the loss of his boat. With Latin resignation he said that 'one
must accept the trials sent by the Good God' and that he
would break the sad news to the man's widow. Feeling himself responsible in part for the tragedy, Gregory produced
his book of traveller's cheques and cashed one for a considerable sum to be given to her. He then put through a call
to Manon.

It did not come through until they were finishing a belated
supper. On hearing his voice, she was infinitely more relieved
than he could know, but he put her breathless exclamations
of delight at his safety down to her perhaps loving him more
than he had thought. He told her only that the boat that
James and he had been in had blown up, but that they were
both unharmed and expected to be back by lunchtime the
next day.

Manon had no doubt at all that Lacost had in some way
caused the explosion to occur; and she hurried to his room,
intending to upbraid him for his callous disregard of her interests by endangering Gregory's life as well that of James.
But she found his room empty and, on enquiring at the desk,
learned that he and Corbin had departed that morning, leav-.
ing no address.

On his return to Antigua the next day, Gregory gave her
the full story of what had taken place. It did not surprise
her in the least but, wide-eyed, she listened with simulated
horror to his tale of Lacost's villainy. Then, when Gregory
had done, she burst out:

'But, *chéri*, you have only yourself to blame. That this terrible man would attempt to kill you I did not think. But injure you, and seriously, yes. Did I not warn you that these Colons are without scruple? Embittered by their misfortunes they have become hard, brutal men. Now that Lacost and his *confréres* have this chance to retrieve their broken fortunes they will stick at nothing to gain their ends. Already you have escaped death at their hands only by a miracle. Now that they have shown their determination to rid themselves of you, it is certain that they will try, again and again.

'I implore you to be sensible. Forget this wretched gold. What is it to you, who are already so rich? Give the good James a sum of money—a big sum—so that he can improve the prospects of his people. However large, it would be cheap as the price of your life. Instead, come with me to Fiji. We will laze in the sunshine, drink champagne together in the moonlight, make love under the stars. If you prefer, I will come to Europe with you. I'll do anything you ask. I am yours to do with as you will. You know that.'

He kissed her hand, finished his second daiquiri and said, 'No, darling, no. You are sweetness personified and I adore you. Perhaps I would have been wise to listen to you in Rio, or even after Lacost threatened me here. But now the game is set and must be played out. Those two rogues did their best to kill James and me. And they did kill that poor devil the boatman. Now I mean to kill them, even if I swing for it.'

After the siesta they paid their delayed visit to the Library. The chief librarian proved to be a charming and cultured man who spoke several languages. Willingly he shuffled through the piles of yellowed parchment records until he turned up an entry made in 1796.

In the autumn of that year a thirty-six-gun ship, the *Reina Maria Amalia,* had sailed from Lima for Manila. On board had been a newly-appointed Bishop of the Philippines and the long overdue funds—then eighteen months in arrears—for the payment of the administration of the colony and its garrison. The ship had taken on water and provisions at Tahiti and again at Bau in the Fijis. After that no more had been heard of her; so it had been presumed that she had struck a reef and gone down with all hands.

Gregory smiled at James. 'Congratulations, my boy. You are proved right that she had a cargo of gold aboard; and a big one. By 1796 the Spaniards had been established in the Philippines for over two hundred years; so it was then no little outpost of Empire but a large and thriving colony. In addition to the back-pay of a year and a half, it is reasonable to assume that enough money was sent to keep the place going for another year or more. With the price of gold today, it must amount to a tremendous sum. No doubt the delay in sending supplies had something to do with the wars of the French Revolution.'

James beamed back. 'I felt convinced of it. And the Bishop's presence on board would explain the chalice and other religious objects that had fallen from the burst chest.'

The elderly librarian gave Gregory a speculative look and said, 'I find it interesting that, while no enquiries have been made about the *Reina Maria Amalia* for many years, I should have received three in the past two months.'

Turning to him, Gregory asked, 'Could you give us the names of the people who have made enquiries, or describe them?'

'The first came here in December. He was a tall, powerfully built Frenchman, with a fair, flowing moustache. The other's visit was more recent—early in January. He was a shortish, middle-aged Brazilian. But I do not recall the name of either.'

Gregory nodded. 'Thank you. I'm not altogether surprised. Now that modern diving apparatus enables previously inaccessible valuables to be brought up, quite a number of people are interesting themselves in wrecks sunk in the Caribbean and other places.'

During the hour that followed, the librarian showed them his great treasure—the third oldest printing press in the New World—and his fine library which contained many rare editions; then he took them round the adjacent museum, which housed a fascinating collection of ancient artillery pieces, Spanish armour and Indian weapons.

As they left the building, they paused for a few moments in the shade of its long, low, graceful arcade before crossing the sunlit square; and Gregory remarked, 'It is very understandable that Lacost should have come here to make certain that the *Maria Amalia* really was carrying a cargo of gold, before scraping together the money needed for an attempt to salvage it. But I find the second enquiry puzzling.'

'That must have been made by Mauá de Carvalho,' said James. 'We know that he came up to Guatemala from Brazil early in January, and the description fits.'

'Oh, it was de Carvalho without a doubt. But why, having verified that there was gold in the ship, should he have gone to such pains to persuade us that ships carrying any quantity of treasure never crossed the Pacific? And that was after he had been here, you will remember.'

James shrugged. 'To take that line was the only way he could save face after Olinda had accused him of having been scared off by that woman.'

'Perhaps,' Gregory said thoughtfully. 'But he came up here after, not before, he had been threatened. That's what strikes me as queer. Why should he have done that if he had already decided to throw in his hand?'

'He may have had to come to Guatemala in the course of his normal business,' Manon suggested, 'and, happening to be in Antigua for a night, made his enquiry only out of curiosity.'

As that seemed the most likely explanation, they pursued the subject no further and returned to the hotel.

Over drinks they discussed their next move. James pointed out that it had now developed into a race between themselves and the Colons: so they ought to get to Tujoa as soon as possible, in order to be first in the field.

But Gregory objected that they could do nothing until they had secured salvaging machinery. Therefore they ought to go to Fiji; as being the most likely place in that area of the Pacific to procure it.

Manon was aware that Lacost had already hired the necessary pontoons and crane in Tahiti and would by now have been on his way to Tujoa with them, had not her cable from

111

Rio brought him to Antigua for the purpose of scaring Gregory out of the game. Moreover, the Colons had at least a clear day's start. They would, of course, have further to bring their salvaging equipment; but, even so, by the time Gregory had secured his in Fiji and reached Tujoa with it, she thought it highly probable that he would find Lacost's party already at work. But, naturally, she said nothing.

James left them to go to the office to find out about air flights. When he came back he said, 'As I thought, the only direct service from Central America to Fiji is the QANTAS flight, which leaves Mexico City every Saturday. There is a PANAM flight from Guatemala City at six-forty-five tomorrow evening, which gets us to Mexico City at nine-five but we'll have to spend two days there.'

Gregory nodded. 'We'll get off a telegram to QANTAS right away, and telephone the PANAM people in Guatemala first thing tomorrow morning.'

At ten o'clock on the Tuesday they left for Guatemala City. As they had previously arrived there after dark, they had not so far seen it, so they spent an hour driving round. It had a fine central square and the National Museum was so admirably arranged that it would have been a credit to any country; but otherwise they were not impressed. There were few old buildings and the area outside the immediate city centre seemed to consist of endless, sprawling suburbs, with one exception—a splendid, broad, tree-lined boulevard that ran through the best residential district. Out there they lunched at the Biltmore Hotel. Behind it lay a fine big swimming pool and they had their lunch beside it, under a striped umbrella; then, as it was intensely hot, they lazed away the rest of the afternoon there.

Their short flight to Mexico City was uneventful, but when they came down at the air terminal they found it a scene of utter chaos. No fewer than four large jet aircraft had landed there within the hour; so the Customs and Immigration departments were a seething mass of between two and three hundred people.

Having at last secured their luggage, they drove to the El Presidente Hotel, where Gregory had stayed on a previous

112

occasion. Fortunately he had made a good friend of the manager, as the desk clerk told them that the hotel was full. But, on being sent for, the manager came to their rescue and fixed them up, although Gregory had to share a room with James.

The following day, having learned to their relief from the QANTAS office that they had seats on the flight to Fiji, they spent the time renewing their acquaintance with the splendid modern city. Then, after an early dinner on the Saturday, they drove out to the airport.

When their baggage and passports had been checked they went into the departure lounge. As Gregory thought quite a possibility, Lacost and Corbin were standing there, obviously about to fly out on the same plane.

The faces of both showed almost comical surprise as they caught sight of Gregory and James. Corbin made a movement as though about to take to his heels in panic; but Lacost recovered swiftly, grabbed his companion by the arm, said something to him in a low voice then, without the least embarrassment, walked up to Gregory and greeted him with a toothy smile.

'I had thought, Monsieur Sallust, that our meeting on Lake Atitlan was to be our last. Had it not been so brief, I could have saved your heirs the cost of this journey you are obviously about to make to the South Seas. That you are making it shows that you are slow to learn; but, since you insist on tempting fortune, I can promise you one thing.'

Turning on his heel, he threw a twisted smile over his shoulder and added, 'You won't need the return half of your ticket.'

8

Of Cannibals and Paradise

As Lacost moved away, James' dark eyes flashed with anger
and he shot out a great hand to grab the Colon by the shoulder. But Gregory was quicker. With a swift movement he
knocked up James' arm and said sharply:

'Don't act like a fool! If you start a brawl here it would
lead to our all being pulled in by the police and we'd miss the
aircraft. With luck we'll get him in a quiet corner sometime.
Provided there's no risk of your being found out, I won't lift
a finger then to prevent you from strangling the swine. He's
asked for it by killing that poor boatman.'

On seeing Lacost approach, Manon had kept her eyes
averted, fearful lest anger at finding her two companions still
alive should lead him, in a fit of spite, to disclose that she was
his mistress and that they had been working together. Having heard him utter his new threat, she was greatly tempted
again to urge Gregory to abandon his plans while there was
still time. But, knowing that almost certainly it would be useless, she resisted it and decided to hold her fire until they were
in Fiji.

Twenty minutes later they boarded the aircraft. The economy section was full, but the first-class compartment, in
which Gregory had asked for seats, half empty. As the
Colons were travelling economy, the two parties did not even
see each other again until they arrived in Tahiti soon after
half past five the following morning. Dawn was coming up
and the mountains behind the airport provided a wonderful
backdrop. Lacost and Corbin disappeared into the Customs,
while Gregory and his friends went into the cafeteria to re-

vive themselves, after their night flight, with coffee laced with cognac.

There, Manon ran into a woman she had known well during the months she had lived on Tahiti; she was about to take a plane for Hawaii, where she intended to settle permanently. The friend said that, since Manon had left, conditions in Tahiti had worsened considerably.

Not only were they still saddled with thousands of down-at-heel, often dangerous, Colons, but de Gaulle was now using the island as the headquarters of his nuclear-bomb experiments in the Pacific. Why he should require such great numbers of troops for security purposes no-one could imagine, but he had recently increased the garrison of the island by thirty thousand men. Added to that, France's great new aircraft carrier, with an escort of destroyers, was due to arrive shortly, and to remain stationed there indefinitely. This big influx of Servicemen was leading to an all-time-high boom in the bars and nightclubs, but had already become a terrible infliction on the residents. With so much easy money about, the shopkeepers had become insolent, menservants could earn more doing jobs for the Army, and it was now almost impossible to get maidservants because so many of them had become prostitutes.

After the usual hour for refuelling, the QANTAS aircraft left for Fiji, arriving at 7.40 a.m. Fiji time. And there it was still Wednesday, for some four hundred miles to the east they had crossed the Date Line; thus theoretically, having gained a day in their lives.

Suva, the capital of Fiji, lies at the eastern end of Viti Levu, the largest and most populous of the three hundred islands in the group, but its airport is not big enough to receive jet liners, so these come down at Nandi, a hundred miles away at the western extremity of the island.

From Guatemala, at Manon's suggestion, Gregory had cabled Hunt's Travel Service to make all arrangements for them, so they were duly met, seen through the Customs and promptly whisked away to the Mocambo Hotel. To Gregory's surprise, it was not simply a hostel for the overnight convenience of air passengers, but a luxury resort where

115

scores of wealthy people were enjoying the attractions. After a good breakfast they went to bed, having agreed to meet again for drinks before dinner.

As soon as they had settled down in the dim, cool lounge over their Planter's Punches, Manon endeavoured to persuade Gregory to go with her next day to Lautoka, the principal port at the western end of the island, where they could hire a boat to take them to her home in the Mamanuca Group, which lay only twenty miles to the west. But he firmly declined her invitation, on the grounds that they must secure salvaging equipment as soon as possible; and that he had already asked Hunt's representative to secure seats for them on the local flight to Suva the next morning.

They had just ordered their second round of drinks when they were joined by a Mr. and Mrs. Ronald Knox-Mawer, whom Manon had met soon after coming to live in Fiji. It emerged that he was the Puisne Judge, who administered justice throughout that part of Viti Levu, and that his wife, June, was the author of a recently published book called *A Gift of Islands*, describing life in Fiji. They had previously been stationed for several years in Aden, about which she had written an earlier book, *The Sultans Came to Tea*. Gregory happened to have read it, and greatly enjoyed its interest and humour, so he was delighted at this opportunity to talk to her and her husband for he felt that few couples could tell him more about this colony in which he expected to make his headquarters for several months.

They all dined together, and afterwards, over their brandies, the young Judge told Gregory about the islands. The Dutch explorer Tasman had been the first, in 1643, to discover the Fiji Group; but the whole South Pacific remained on the imaginative maps of those days for another one hundred and forty years, under the description 'Here be Dragons'. It was not until 1774 that Captain James Cook learned of them in Tonga, but only touched upon them. Then, fifteen years later, Lieutenant Bligh, of *Bounty* fame, when put overboard off Tonga by mutineers, with eighteen loyal officers and men in a six-oared boat only twenty-three feet long, had become the real discoverer of the Fijis. Tahiti had been

116

nearer, but the winds contrary, so with great courage he had decided to attempt the three-thousand-miles voyage to the Dutch East Indies. During it he had passed right through the Fiji Group and in 1792 he had returned to chart many of its islands.

This led to European and, a little later, American ships calling fairly frequently at the Fijis. Then, early in the nineteenth century, they began to arrive in scores. The reason was the discovery of sandalwood at the south-west end of Vanua Levu, the second largest island. The wood was greatly prized by the Chinese for making articles used in religious ceremonies, and its dust was turned into joss-sticks. The profits in this trade were enormous, six hundred per cent being the average. One ship, the *Jenny*, traded fifty pounds' worth of trash for a cargo of two hundred and fifty tons which realised twenty thousand pounds.

Eventually the supply of sandalwood gave out and new sources were found near Noumea. But in the 1830s and 40s the Fijis enjoyed another boom, owing to the discovery that the rocks in their innumerable shallow lagoons were great breeding grounds for *bêche-de-mer*. These are the sea-slug Holathusia, about eight inches long and three thick, having rough skins thickly coated with slime. Before shipping, the slugs were cleaned, par-boiled and smoked. Again the Chinese were eager buyers, because when the cured slugs had been made into soup it was believed to be a marvellous aphrodisiac. At small expense native divers could be paid to collect the *bêche-de-mer* and in less than a year a Captain could sail away with a cargo of them worth sixty thousand pounds.

Before the coming of the white man, and for nearly a century afterwards, the Fijis were peopled by innumerable small and large tribes, ruled over by independent hereditary chiefs. They were nearly always at war with one another, although there was little loss of human life. Often, for months at a stretch, a war would consist of small parties creeping into their neighbours' territories, surprising a few of them cultivating their vegetable gardens, clubbing the men and carrying off the women. Occasionally, there would be a great gathering of ferociously-painted warriors who, after much

117

shouting and boasting, would set off in their canoes. This could lead to 'battles' with a thousand or more men on either side. When the clash came there was more shouting and still more boasting, but when half a dozen men had been killed—or, to the superstitious terror of all concerned, a Chief had by accident been struck down—both sides called it a day. Eventually, one side gave in and brought baskets full of earth to the enemy in token of submission. The victors burned the huts and destroyed the vegetable gardens of the defeated, then went home happily declaiming on their bravery, taking with them the bodies of the slain to be cooked and eaten at a joyful celebration.

With the arrival of the traders, matters changed for the worse, because the most prized objects they had to offer were firearms. The possession of even a few muskets meant that the warriors could kill without risking their lives in personal combat. So the wars became more frequent and casualties much more numerous. By the fifties there were occasions when over a hundred victims were eaten after a victory.

Smiling, Gregory put in, 'No wonder the Fijis became known as the Cannibal Isles.'

June Knox-Mawer laughed. 'There is a nice story told about Ratu Edward Thakobau, the great-grandson of the King of Fiji who ceded the country to Queen Victoria. Once, when he was on his way to Europe, a stupid woman at the Captain's table expressed her horror at cannibalism and would not leave the subject alone. Ratu Edward sent for the menu, read it right through, then said to the steward, "Is this all you have?" As the menu listed about a hundred items, the man looked very surprised, as he replied, "Why, yes, sir." The Ratu shrugged and handed the menu back. "It all looks a little dull, and I am rather hungry. Please bring me the passenger list".'

'Another about him,' the Judge followed up, 'is of his meeting a lady who asked his nationality. He replied, "Half Fijian and half Scottish". Naturally she was surprised to hear that he had Scottish blood, so he explained, "You see, in my great-grandfather's time quite a number of Scottish missionaries came to Fiji and our people found that they made

118

a very pleasant change from pork." Then he added with that charming smile of his, "But perhaps I should have said, 'Scottish by absorption'." '

'He sounds a most delightful man,' Gregory remarked.

'He is, and a brave one. He won both the O.B.E. and the M.C. in the last war. The Fijian Chiefs are splendid people. Ratu Penaia has the D.S.O. and the O.B.E., and both the Ratu George and the Ratu Mara are O.B.Es. Ratu George is the direct descendant of the hereditary King of Fiji. He is greatly respected by everybody. The Ratu Mara rules the widespread Lau group to the east of Fiji, and is the Chief Minister under the new Constitution.'

James grinned at Gregory. 'He is the cousin I mentioned when you remarked on my height that night we met in Rio. Mara stands six foot seven and his wife, the sweet Adi Lala, is taller than you are. The Fijian Chiefly Families are all highly educated, modern in thought and wise in their decisions. They are greatly honoured by their people, who still have the good sense to be guided by them in everything.'

'I find it a little surprising,' Gregory said, 'that a family who were cannibals only one hundred years ago should have developed into such cultured people.'

'That, I think,' said Knox-Mawer, 'is due to their being largely of Polynesian descent. As you doubtless know, the line dividing the Polynesian peoples from the Melanesians runs only a little to the east of Fiji, and they are utterly different races. The Polynesians of the Eastern Pacific are light-skinned, comparatively gentle and evolved a high culture of their own. Based on root similarities in language, there is even a theory now that Scandinavian Vikings came via South America to the Pacific and were among their ancestors. The Melanesians, on the other hand, infiltrated into the Western Pacific from New Guinea and came of Negroid stock. Until comparatively recent times they remained cruel and primitive savages.

'The Fijians were originally pure Melanesians. But Tonga lies not very far to the south-east of Fiji, and the Tongans, a very brave and adventurous people, are Polynesians. For many years they not only frequently raided the Fijis but established permanent settlements in some parts of the Group. At times some of the leading Fiji Chiefs secured them as allies against their enemies. That led to intermarriage between the ruling castes of the two countries and, of course, the Tongan warriors often had children by the Fijian women they captured.

'The present people of Fiji include many of mixed blood, and it was not only the Tongans who account for that. The white man made his contribution. Then those who settled here found the Fijians unwilling to work on their cotton and sugar plantations, so in the 1860s they began to import labour from the islands to the north and west of Fiji, where there were great numbers of hardy natives for the taking, I say "taking" because it virtually developed into a slave trade. Thousands of them were kidnapped and many thousands more induced to agree to work here for six years for what seemed to those innocents a good wage, and a promise to be shipped home when their time was up. But the planters played the wicked old game of selling them goods that got them into debt, and very few of the poor wretches ever saw their homes again.'

After pausing to light a cigarette, the Judge continued to tell Gregory how Fiji had achieved civilisation the hard way.

'The traffic had raised such indignation in the United States that there had been talk of America putting a stop to it by annexing the Fijis; but nothing came of that. Yet with every year it became clearer that the country needed some form of stable government. It had developed into a positive hell, where every man was a law unto himself. Half the white inhabitants were the dregs of humanity: castaways, deserters, escaped convicts and beachcombers who had brought with them liquor, firearms and disease. With whip and gun they terrorised the natives and battened upon them. The more prosperous defied the local Chiefs and ignored their ordinances. The warring feuds continued and tribes who were victorious carried out orgies of cruelty.

'There had already emerged two major, if small, powers in Viti Levu: the people of Bau Island, which lies some twelve miles off the east coast, and those of Rewa, who occupied the delta region in the south-east of the island, where afterwards Suva was to become the capital of the whole group. In 1843 a war between them broke out. As usual, it did not concern the interests of the common people on either side, but was brought about by a quarrel between two High Chiefs.

'The Principal wife of Tui Tanoa, King of Bau, happened to be a sister of Tui Dreketi, King of Rewa, and she was unfaithful to her husband. On being found out, she fled to her brother. Instead of returning or punishing her, Tui Dreketi gave her in marriage to a Rewa Chief. In the light of Fiji customs there could have been no greater insult. Tui Tanoa called on his son, Prince Thakobau, to avenge him.

'Thakobau was an outstanding personality. He was brave, cunning, wise within the limits of his upbringing and by nature as well as birth an aristocrat. The war with Rewa went on for years, and in the end Thakobau won it, but only through the backing of King George of Tonga, who allowed Prince Ma'afu to bring a Tongan army to Thakobau's assistance.

'On his father's death, Thakobau conceived the ambition of becoming King of all Fiji, and this turned Ma'afu into his enemy. The Tongan Prince was a man of great ability. As his King's representative, he controlled the greater part of the islands in the north of the group and had a powerful army. There followed more years of wars, intrigue and treachery. There were still forty petty Kings in the Fijis, but real power lay in the hands of fewer than a dozen. At length these were brought together, Thakobau and Ma'afu agreed to sink their differences and in 1860 the Fijis were made a Confederacy.

'Unfortunately, it did not last, because Thakobau and Ma'afu quarrelled again. Meanwhile, a reign of anarchy continued. A British Consul had long been resident in Fiji, but he had not been given the powers even of a magistrate over his own nationals. The white settlers rode roughshod over Thakobau's laws and American traders blackmailed him into making over to them large tracts of land in exchange for weapons to fight his wars against the tribes up in the mountains. Up till 1854, deaf to the pleas of missionaries, he continued to feast off his captured enemies. But in that year he suffered a sudden change of heart. The missionary Waterhouse succeeded in converting him, and on Sunday, April 30th, he was baptised into the Christian faith as Ebenezer.

'His conversion made no difference to the universal strife. In 1867 a Confederacy of Western Fiji was formed, Thakobau gave his people a constitutional government and was formally crowned King in Bau. But the British Government refused to accept his jurisdiction over their subjects and he came no nearer to controlling his own.

'For some years past the more responsible settlers had agitated for Fiji to be annexed by Britain. Thakobau, although not liking the idea, had been persuaded to make offers of cession in both 1858 and '59, but the British Government had declined. Early in the seventies, as the only means of establishing law and order, another appeal was made, and backed by the probability that if Britain did not take over Fiji, either America or Germany would, Ma'afu at last consented to accept Thakobau as his overlord. In 1874 Benjamin Disraeli, the champion of British interests throughout the world, placed Fiji at the feet of his Queen as another jewel in the Imperial Crown.

'Sir Hercules Robinson, the Governor of New South Wales, arrived in H.M.S. *Pearl* to represent the Queen and the cession took place on October 10th. Thakobau, by then an old, white-haired, bearded, but still stalwart man, was at last to find peace and honour after a lifetime of troubles. With great dignity he declared, "We give Fiji unreservedly to the Queen of Britain that she may rule us justly and affectionately and that we may live in peace and prosperity." Then, with true nobility, he handed his old and favourite war club to Sir Hercules, saying that it was the only thing he possessed that might interest Her Majesty, and that he sent it to her with his love, confident that she, and her children who succeeded her, would watch over the welfare of his people.'

It was a touching scene that Knox-Mawer had evoked, and after a moment his wife went on to speak of the passionate loyalty that the Fijians felt towards the present Queen. In the fifties, when the British forces had been hard-pressed by the

Communist revolutionaries in Malaya, volunteers had been called for. The word had gone round, 'Our Queen needs us', and boys of sixteen had made their way from the outer islands to volunteer. Many of the Chiefs had led their troops in person. Skilled in jungle warfare, the Fijian battalions had become the terror of the enemy and had covered themselves with glory.

Next morning, as Manon was loath to leave Gregory, all three of them took the aircraft for Suva. The Dakota flew only at a few thousand feet; so, during the short journey, Gregory was able to get a good view of the country over which they passed—the blue sea creaming white on reefs and beaches, then dense forests both down in the valleys and clothing the slopes of high mountains, until on lower ground patches of cultivation could be seen, and soon they were coming down over the great arc of Suva Bay to the little airport.

Hunt's had secured them rooms at the Grand Pacific Hotel. On arriving they found it to be a happy mixture of the old and the new. The centre of the main block was a series of spacious, lofty chambers leading into one another—hall, lounge, bar and dining room overlooking the bay. There were white-clad Indian servants, and fans in the ceilings, which gave it the atmosphere of old Colonial days; while adjacent to it there was a three-storey modern block, in which they were given air-conditioned rooms looking out on the pleasant, palm-fringed garden and an oval swimming pool.

After lunch it was much too hot to go out; but at four o'clock Gregory and James had a swim in the pool, then drove the half-mile into the town to Hunt's Travel Agency. At their request, Mr. Hunt himself saw them. He proved to be a big, cheerful man and they learned that he had formerly been a Police Inspector. No doubt it was his police training which had made him such an efficient business man, for in fewer than ten years he had built up an organisation that could offer every amenity in the island at a few hours' notice.

But Gregory's request was unusual. He said that later he might want to hire a motor cruiser and make use of Hunt's fleet of cars, but for the moment he wanted the name of the

123

firm most likely to be able to provide equipment for salvaging a wreck.

Mr. Hunt at once got on the telephone and made an appointment for them to see a Mr. Trollope down at the docks in half an hour's time, then drew a sketch map showing how they could reach his office.

As it was not far, they decided to walk, so that Gregory could see something of the town. For a capital it was small, with only one main street. There were a few modern blocks, most of the buildings were in the Edwardian Colonial style, or earlier. The first thing that struck Gregory about it was its cleanliness and orderliness, in contrast to the cities in Central and South America from which he had come, and the sight of the six-foot-plus Fijian policemen in their smart uniforms gave him real pleasure.

The shops were adequate but not impressive. Nearly all of them were run by Indians or Chinese. Souvenirs and native work were to be seen in abundance, also beautifully-embroidered silk wraps, jackets and blouses at incredibly cheap prices. But it was the polyglot population in the streets that interested Gregory most. Hindu ladies with caste marks and wearing colourful *saris*, bronzed Britons in bush shirts and khaki shorts, Chinese in shoddy European suits, and tall Fijians, made still taller by their enormous puffs of thick, silky, black hair and wearing kilt-like *sulus*, jostled one another on the pavements.

Crossing a bridge over an inlet from the sea, they passed the big covered market, and soon afterwards came to the docks and Mr. Trollope's office. He was a small, sallow-faced man who looked as though he had a dash of native blood. After stating the business he had come upon, Gregory left most of the talking to James, as he was better able to describe the equipment which would be required.

On learning that James was a Ratu, Mr. Trollope treated him with considerable respect, and for a while they discussed the technicalities of salvaging. In due course it emerged that Mr. Trollope could find the gear that was required, with a professional diver named Hamie Baker, and would be willing to hire out these facilities for three months. Gregory then agreed the price asked, and his willingness to put down a substantial deposit.

But when it came to transporting the gear to Tujoa, Mr. Trollope said that ships big enough to carry a large crane and pontoons sailed only occasionally to make a round of the outer islands to the west, and a special arrangement would have to be made for such a ship to go on to the French-owned Nakopoa Group. It would be a fortnight or more before the material could be sent on its way, so it could not be expected to arrive in Revika until about the middle of February. Gregory was not aware that Lacost had already secured salvaging gear, but assumed that he would do so in Tahiti and, as Tahiti was two thousand five hundred miles from Tujoa, there seemed a good chance that they would get there before him. In any case, that was the best Trollope could do, so a brief letter of agreement was typed out and Gregory wrote him a cheque.

That evening at the Grand Pacific they enjoyed a pleasant dinner, at which Manon, now on her home ground, displayed even more than her usual sparkle and vivacity. Then, after the meal, Gregory succeeded in telephoning to the home of a solicitor whom Knox-Mawer had recommended, and arranging an appointment for ten o'clock the following morning.

The solicitor, a Mr. Firebrace, turned out to be young and keen. He said there would be no difficulties about drawing up the simple articles of a company such as Gregory and James required, and that he would at once set about it. Having given him particulars, they had another stroll round the town and, to Gregory's delight, he found that it had one really good bookshop. It was owned by a Mr. Desai, a short, portly, cheerful and most knowledgeable Indian. In addition to thousands of paperbacks, he stocked all the latest novels and a fine selection of large, illustrated books.

Gregory and James made several purchases, to be sent to the hotel, then, on Mr. Desai's suggestion, went on to spend half an hour in the city aquarium. It was quite small, but contained a wonderful variety of brilliantly-coloured tropical fish.

Over lunch, they discussed future plans. As there was no

likelihood of the salvaging equipment reaching Tujoa in much under three weeks, Gregory happily accepted Manon's renewed invitation to stay for a while at her home. But James felt that he ought to return to Tujoa, both out of duty to his people and in order to be present to stall off Lacost and his gang, should they arrive there before the machinery being sent by Trollope.

Inland, opposite the hotel, there was an open space of several acres. On the left stood the Government buildings, overlooking the cricket ground, and on the right the Botanical Gardens, which sloped up to the Governor's Residence. Late in the afternoon they took a stroll in the gardens to admire the magnificent specimen trees, then up the hill to the Museum. In it there were weapons galore, native basket-work, *tapa* cloth and a collection of the most beautiful shells, but the really impressive thing was several wood carvings, four to five feet in height, of men and women. They had been brought from Samoa; and Gregory felt that they could have held their own with anything produced in Europe during the past fifty years.

Next morning they said good-bye to James, and Manon was by no means sorry to see him leave. The sight of his big, muscular body and bronzed, strongly-cut features, surmounted by the great puff of black hair which, refusing to become conventional, he had never had cut had stirred her sexually from time to time, and he was an amusing and charming companion. But, quite unconsciously, he had time and again played the unwelcome role of 'gooseberry' when she was with Gregory. And it was in his interest that Gregory was determined to expose himself to grave danger. Now, at last, she would have Gregory on his own.

She would have liked to carry him off that Friday. But he was enjoying Suva, and had a perfect excuse for staying over the week-end, as the articles of the company, which he wished to take with him, would not be ready until the Monday morning.

Gracefully Manon resigned herself. Together they visited the cemetery, a mile or so on the far side of the town. It was of interest because it had several sections: Protestant,

Roman Catholic, Chinese, Hindu. Occupying a sloping hill-side, it was unusually attractive, as there were a number of large trees in it clipped like yews or boxes into immense, flat-topped drums.

The Knox-Mawers had said that they must go to the St. Elizabeth's Home for Cured Lepers to see some remarkable paintings, so they drove out there on the Sunday. In recent years leprosy has happily come under control, but there are still victims of earlier years who have to be cared for, and the Home was run for that purpose by the Sisters of Mary.

The paintings that the Knox-Mawers had felt would interest them were by a man named Ṣemisi Maya. In 1938 he had contracted leprosy and had been sent to the Leprosarium Island of Makogai, where in two periods he had spent fourteen years of his life. After his discharge he returned to his village, but his fingers were so contracted in towards the palms that he could not hold a brush. In spite of that, he started to paint using his knuckles and the stumps of his fingers, and with the hairs on his forearms he produces fine lines. The result is the most delightful pictures, both of Fijian scenery and abstracts with rhythmic lines in brilliant colours.

Thirty or forty of his paintings, about fifteen by nine inches, were for sale. Manon, having worked for an art dealer in Paris, was immensely impressed; so Gregory bought several of them for her.

On Monday morning Gregory received the articles of the company from Firebrace and, on telephoning Trollope, learned that the salvage gear would be shipped in another week, on February 7th, so should arrive at Revika about the 11th. He at once got on to Hunt's, arranged for them to book seats for Manon and himself on the afternoon plane to Nandi, and to have a cabin cruiser at his disposal next day at Lautoka.

Instead of staying again at the Mocambo, from Nandi they drove up the coast the twenty miles to Lautoka, where Hunt's had booked them rooms at the Cathay Hotel. To their amusement they found that, down to the minutest particular, the bedrooms were replicas of those at the Grand Pacific; so that on waking in the morning, for a moment they might well imagine themselves back in Suva.

That evening they took a stroll round the town. It was quite small, but again impressive by its cleanliness. Next morning they drove down to the harbour and went aboard the cabin cruiser *Firefly*. Her Captain was a middle-aged, lanky man named Clarke. He welcomed them with a grin and a bone-crushing hand-shake, and told them that he had emigrated eighteen years before from Australia. His crew consisted of four Fijians, all fine-looking fellows with enormous gollywog heads of soft, frizzy hair. There were four cabins and a small saloon. The after deck was covered with an awning, beneath which there were a table and comfortable basket chairs. Across the stern was slung a small speedboat for going ashore.

Soon after they sailed it began to rain, and within a few minutes it was sheeting down so hard that visibility was reduced to a matter of yards. But half an hour later the rain ceased with equal suddenness, overhead the sky became a harsh blue and the sun blazed down so fiercely that deck rails outside the shade of the awning became too hot to touch.

Early in the afternoon they approached the Mamanucas. The group consisted of one large island and several small ones, some of which were no more than atolls. Gregory had often read about the beauty of the South Sea Islands, but he decided that no author, however gifted, was capable of conveying their superb loveliness.

Against a background of bright blue sky they stood out extraordinarily clearly. In places either the jungle, or great rocky cliffs, came right down to the water; in others there were stretches of glaringly white beaches, formed from millions of small, crushed shells. All of them were palm-fringed, the trunks often leaning right over from the force of many hurricanes, their fronds a vivid green. The sea was a deep, rich blue with, here and there, streaks of turquoise in the shallows. A shoal of flying fish flitted by and, as they neared the beach and the launch reduced speed, over the side they could see thirty feet down to the fans of coral and fantastic forms of seaweed waving from the rocks.

Manon's island was quite a small one, only about twenty acres in extent. When they came opposite her home, the cruiser dropped anchor a quarter of a mile off-shore, and the speedboat was lowered. In a matter of minutes the steersman beached her gently. Lifting Manon as though she weighed no more than a sack of feathers, another of the Fijian sailors carried her ashore through the foaming surf. Then he returned and, with equal ease, sloshed through the water to set Gregory down beside her.

They were welcomed by a grinning group of native house-servants, headed by her top boy, Joe-Joe. He was a skinny figure, his black face covered with a network of wrinkles, his great puff of hair measuring a good two feet from side to side, and gold rings in his ears.

The house was like those in which lived the native Chiefs. The main building was a big, oval *bure*. Palm thatch sloped down from a great ridge pole thirty feet up, to within ten feet of the ground, so that inside it should remain cool in the great heats. Near it there were other, smaller, *bures*, for use as bedrooms and servants' quarters. The kitchen was a long lean-to at the back of the main building.

Entering the main building Gregory looked about him with delight. The walls were covered with thousands of bamboo canes of varying thicknesses, lashed together and arranged in geometrical patterns. Mighty beams, rough-hewn from tree trunks, supported the roof, the acute interior angle of which could be seen only dimly far above. These beams were covered with *tapa* cloth—a speciality of Fiji, which is made from the white bark of a tree, hammered out until it is thin and supple, then dyed black and brown in patterns. Super-imposed on the cloth there were rows of lovely Pacific shells. The great room was dim, cool, spacious and only sparsely furnished with low tables of rare woods and comfortable chairs.

Wiping the perspiration from their faces, Gregory and his smiling hostess subsided into two of the chairs. Silent, bare-footed, Joe-Joe appeared beside them with long tumblers of pineapple and fresh lime juice laced with rum. Manon had given her servants no notice of her coming, yet she had been expected and everything was prepared. From previous experience she had known that warning was unnecessary How such foreknowledge of events is obtained is one of the great mysteries, but it is almost universal among the older people of the islands.

After having a shower, a sleep and a swim from the beach in water that was as warm as a tepid bath, they spent a heavenly evening. Later, in Manon's *bure* bedroom, Gregory felt as though thirty years had fallen from him. At his wish she remained passive or became temporarily a tigress. Her body was superb and he delighted in having her stand with him so that he could run his hands down the satin of her sides, waist and buttocks, then feel her crisp, dark pubic hair. Her laughter was infectious and by a dozen devices she incited him to further efforts. At last, in the small hours, he said that he must leave her to go down to the beach and flash a torch, as he had arranged for the speed boat to come in and take him off to the cruiser.

'Darling,' she gave a little giggle, 'for a man of your age and experience you are the greatest fool in the world. Joe-Joe, the other servants and the crew of the launch all realise that we are lovers. I'll bet you a hundred francs to a centime that if you went to the beach and flashed your torch the boat would not come off. The crew will be sound asleep. They and my servants would be utterly ashamed for me if they had reason to believe that you were not in my bed.'

He had wished to protect her reputation, but, willingly, he allowed himself to be persuaded that she was right. Their limbs entwined, they fell happily asleep. And, of course, a few hours later, wrinkle-faced, smiling Joe-Joe set a tray down beside them that held two breakfasts.

After a swim they went in the speed boat to Malolo, the main island of the group. Again they were expected. An elderly Chief greeted them with smiles and all the marks of respect. His village consisted of a clearing in which there were some twenty *bures*—all large, airy, thatched buildings set well apart. There was not a sign of squalor anywhere but, here and there, hibiscus bushes and rows of small white stones outlining the paths made it very neat. On the fringe of

130

the village there were tall coconut palms, breadfruit trees, mangoes, ugly, several-branched pandana palms, the leaves of which are used for thatching, and several very thin-stemmed palms with lovely feathery heads, a variety said to be inhabited by good spirits who kept away evil ones. From the forks of the trees orchids were growing, their blossoms hanging down in long strings.

In the middle of the village stood the Meeting House. Under a thatched roof it was open-sided except for a surround of low wall of woven bamboo about three feet high. They proceeded there for the welcome ceremony. At one end the Chief and the adult males of the village took their places, squatting with crossed legs on rush mats. Gregory and Manon sat down in similar fashion, facing the Chief. Before him was set a large, shallow wooden bowl on four squat legs, called a *tanoa*, tied to which there was a long string with shells attached.

To the accompaniment of chanting and rhythmic hand-clapping the dried and grated roots of the *Piper methysticum* bush was put in the bowl and mixed with water, to make the ceremonial drink known as *Kava* or *Yaggona*. A young warrior dipped a finely-polished, coconut half shell into the mixture. Holding the cup with his arms fully extended, he slowly sank down and offered it to the Chief. With hollowed palms, everyone gave three loud claps and the Chief drank from it. The same procedure was followed with Manon and Gregory, while the natives cried, '*Matha! matha!*' which means 'Empty it,' as the custom is to drink it straight down. They, too, clapped three times when they had swallowed the concoction, which Gregory found to be a milky liquid with a faint flavour resembling rhubarb. The remainder of those assembled then drank in turn to the continuation of hand-clapping.

The ceremony completed, the Chief led his guests to a bench shaded by a pink-flowered cassia tree, and sat down between them. In front of them a dozen or more men formed a double line. Their leader uttered a low note. The others took their key from it and began to sing. They were accompanied by a band which squatted a little to one side. One man

131

had a long, oval, double-ended drum upon which he beat incredibly fast with his finger-tips, others, with several different lengths of very thick bamboo, beat upon the ground. The harmony was magnificent. Some of the songs were primitive laments, others paeons of victory.

Later, a score of women performed *meke* for them, which is best expressed by 'dancing a poem'. Unaided, Gregory could interpret only a few of the movements, but the gently-smiling old Chief explained from time to time that his *corps de ballet* was expressing the surging of the sea, the sowing and the harvest, the growth of great trees and their destruction in a hurricane.

Under the midday sun the sweat streamed down the shoulders of the men and the rounded arms of the women, who were naked to the waist; but they did not appear to mind. Their singing and dancing seemed effortless and, obviously, they were enjoying every moment of it. Never, Gregory thought, had he seen such happy people. When the show was over he shook every one of them by the hand. Unabashed, the men who had a few words of English cried, 'Welcome! Welcome! Come again, yes. Big pleasure see you,' and gave him friendly pats on the shoulder.

At a loss how to express his appreciation to the Chief, Gregory asked him to accept his handkerchief. It was a large square of gaily-patterned rough silk, a speciality of Beale and Inman in Bond Street, and had cost two pounds. The old man was delighted and, not to be outdone, insisted on presenting him with a dozen beautiful, highly-polished shells.

He accompanied them down to their speed boat and had his men carry them out to it, then smilingly waved them away. Suddenly it had clouded over and on their way back began to rain. By the time they got home they were drenched, but the rain was so warm they laughed about it. They were wearing only the lightest garments, so within ten minutes they had dried themselves and changed, to sit down to a lunch of paw-paws, delicious, fresh-caught crabs, and mangoes from trees in the garden.

The following morning they swam with glass-masked snorkels out to the reef. Twenty feet down, the undersea garden provided a wonderful scene of colourful activity. Between the coral fans flitted shoals of tiny brilliant blue fish, and hundreds of big prawns. Occasionally there came into view bigger fellows, red, rainbow-striped, and dead black—octopuses with gently-waving tentacles, sea-slugs and hermit crabs. Later the speed boat swiftly circled the bay, trailing them in turn behind it on a surfboard. Gregory had mastered the art many years before in the South of France, and Manon was an expert.

For a week they enjoyed themselves immensely. To reach Tujoa, Gregory intended to charter a small, private aircraft; and if he was to be there by the time the salvaging machinery was expected he would have to leave Manon within the next two days. Until he raised the subject she had wisely held her fire. At the time they were sunbathing on the beach. Rolling over so that she could lie upon him, she looked down into his eyes and said:

'My love, be sensible. As you are so rich, why in the name of God should you risk your life just for the chance of bringing up treasure? If you continue to thwart Lacost and his gang you will be risking your life; make no mistake about it. I'm not suggesting that you should let James down. By all means provide him with the money to go ahead. But let him do it on his own.'

Gregory was greatly tempted to agree. Their long, happy days in the sunshine, swimming lazily in the warm sea, where an infinity of new sights could be seen among the rocks below: the starlit nights and love in the arms of a woman who was always willing but never pressed him beyond his own desires was as near Paradise as anything he had known since he had lost Erika. After all, he could easily send money to James; and why should he chance getting himself killed on Tujoa when he could continue this blissful existence with Manon? Smiling up at her, he said:

'I'll make no promises; still, I'll think about it.'

But next morning a small, chuffing steamer dropped anchor off the main island. Shortly afterwards a native in a canoe arrived with Manon's mail, a week-old copy of the

Fiji Times and a cable for Gregory. It was from James and read:

French Resident here insists permit required to salvage from wreck and ten per cent findings payable to Government stop proceeding Noumea but application cannot be made in company's name without producing articles stop suggest you meet me Noumea eleventh.

It was then the 8th and from Fiji too long a flight to be risked in a small, chartered aircraft. Even if Gregory left at once it might be several days before he could catch a connection. He had the Articles of Association with him but they had not yet been signed. Without them, James could get no further. Reluctantly he told Manon that he now had no option but to leave her. She begged him to take her with him. He pointed out that to get to New Caledonia he might first have to fly down to Australia, and said that it was pointless for her to make such a journey simply to be with him when he signed a few documents; but he promised to send for her as soon as he got to Tujoa. With that she had to be content.

That afternoon he left in the motor cruiser for Lautoka. There, as he had thought probable, to get to Noumea he would first have to fly down to Sydney, but, fortunately, the weekly QANTAS flight was due in next morning, and Hunt's got him a seat on it.

By Wednesday evening he was in Sydney. The heat there was even more sweltering than in Fiji, as the city lacked the cool breezes that made winter in the islands pleasant, provided one did not go out during the hottest hours of the day.

He had to wait two days there, but on the 12th an aircraft landed him at Toutouta airport on the south coast of New Caledonia. The airport was forty kilometres from the capital so, during the drive, he had ample time to form an impression of the eastern end of the island. The scenery could not have been more unlike that of Fiji. There was no lush vegetation, no riot of colourful flowering shrubs, no neat villages of thatched *bures*. Only an occasional palm was to be seen

134

and, had it not been for the heat, no-one would have taken it for an island in the tropics.

The road, which was excellent, curved away from the sea through sparsely-populated valleys between high, rolling hills that, in the distance, merged into mountains. It was no doubt this resemblance to the wilder parts of Scotland that had caused Captain Cook, when in the 1770s he had discovered the 250-mile-long, cigar-shaped island, to christen it New Caledonia.

The lower slopes were sparsely wooded by one variety of nearly leafless tree, which made the scene monotonous. Here and there, higher up, there were large patches of what looked like copper-coloured sand. These, Gregory's driver told him, were the nickel mines, the deposits of which were the richest in the world, and made New Caledonia a wealthy country.

On entering Noumea, the greater part of which stood on high land overlooking five large and one small bay, Gregory saw the huge factory that smelted the mineral. The chimneys belched clouds of reddish smoke, the deposit from which had coloured the roofs of the nearby buildings and the ships at the adjacent wharf in the first bay. The driver said the smoke was poisonous, but the *Societé de Nickel* contributed ninety per cent of the country's revenue and its position was so powerful that it could ignore all appeals to spend the large sum necessary to purify the surrounding atmosphere, and paid such high wages that it never lacked for labour. But, fortunately, the great plant was on the down-wind side of the town; so only the people living in its immediate vicinity were affected.

A mile further on they entered the town centre and Gregory bade his driver pull up in the big, tree-shaded main square, at the Tourist Office. There he telephoned several of the best hotels and located James at the Nouváta. Returning to his car, he was driven past the *Baie de la Moselle,* on the north side of which lies the port, then uphill across the base of a sizeable peninsula, along the shore of the even larger *Baie d'Orphelinat*. The southern side of the bay was indented by quite a small one that his driver told him was called Fisherman's Bay. In it there lay at anchor many privately-

135

owned vessels of various sizes and, beyond them, a battleship. The driver added that the Yacht Club was situated there and that the big building high up on the point was the Naval Headquarters.

Again the road left the sea front but, half a mile further on, returned to it, skirting the *Baie des Citrons*—a pleasant suburb where a number of typically French villas looked out across the road to long bathing beaches. Turning inland, they crossed the base of yet another peninsula, to come out on the last great bay, *Ansa Vata*. About half-way along it they passed a two-storey building set in an attractive garden, in which the flags of half a dozen nations fluttered from flag poles. The driver said it was the headquarters of the South Pacific Commission. Two minutes later, the car at last pulled up before the Hotel Nouváta.

Entering, Gregory found that most of the ground floor consisted of a restaurant and a large, circular bar. Beyond them lay a garden and swimming pool, round which fifty or more people, mostly in bikinis or bathing trunks, were enjoying drinks at tables under big, striped umbrellas. James was among them. On catching sight of Gregory, he jumped to his feet to greet him with delight.

Over dinner they discussed the situation. So far there had been no sign in Tujoa of Lacost and his friends; but, James having informed his Council of Elders that definite plans for the exploration of the wreck had been made, evidently Commandant Elbœuf, the elderly French Resident, had come to hear of it and had then proved obstructive. To start with, he had asserted that any treasure trove was the property of the French Government, but later, when James had insisted on seeing the text of this law, it had transpired that if a licence to search was obtained and the licensee paid all expenses, only ten per cent of the value of any treasure found would have to go to the Government. As Elbœuf was an old, and normally indolent, man, James was of the opinion that he had been gingered into this activity by Roboumo, the witch-doctor, who was most averse to any modernisation being introduced into the island.

After they had dined, Gregory and James signed the Articles of Association over the Fiji stamps already on the document, then had it witnessed by the manager of the hotel and his book-keeper.

The following morning, although it was a Sunday, Gregory rang up the Governor's secretary and requested an audience with His Excellency on a matter of urgency. By way of introduction he used the name of the French Ambassador in London, who happened to be an acquaintance of his. He was then told that the Governor had been flown to Paris ten days earlier to undergo a serious operation; but his Deputy, General Ribaud, would grant the requested interview at five o'clock that afternoon.

The Residency proved to be a large, modern building, in a small park on high ground at the extreme north-eastern corner of the town. On paying off his taxi, Gregory got a shock, as the meter read 1,300 francs. He already knew that New Caledonia had its own currency—the Pacific Franc—but, even so, to run in from the hotel had cost him just over one pound sterling.

After waiting for some ten minutes, when he was shown up to the Governor's office he received a very pleasant surprise. The bulky, blue-eyed, now grey-haired man seated behind a handsome desk had a familiar look. A minute later Gregory recognised him as one-time Lieutenant Ribaud of the Deuxième Bureau, with whom he had had friendly dealings during the early days of the war.

Recognition was mutual. Exclaiming 'It is—yes, I have the name, Monsieur Sallust!', the plump General stood up, beaming, came out from behind his desk, embraced Gregory and went on, 'What pleasure to see an old friend in this Godforsaken place. How do you come to be in Noumea?'

'First,' Gregory smiled, 'let me congratulate you, *mon Général,* upon having achieved this high rank.'

The General shrugged and threw out his hands. 'Our President is good to those who worked for him in the days of his adversity. It is as simple as that. As you know, after the fall of Paris I joined the Resistance. While a soldier I was not unsuccessful, so when the war ended I transferred from the Police to the Army. Things have gone well for me. But oh!

137

what would I not give to be out of this hothouse and back in Paris! Sit down, *mon ami*. A cigarette; cognac if you wish. Tell me now, what can I do for you?'

Accepting a *Gauloise*, Gregory lit it and gave particulars of his interest in the sunken *Reina Maria Amalia*.

The General screwed up his face in a grimace, 'It is true that the French Government is entitled to ten per cent of the value of any goods brought up. But alas, *mon vieux*, you come too late. Only a week ago I granted a licence to another man to salvage her contents.'

9

Outbreak of Passion

On hearing that a licence had been granted to someone else, Gregory was annoyed, but not surprised by the thought that Lacost had got in ahead of him. With a frown, he said, 'That is most unfortunate. In the hope of securing this treasure I have formed a company with Ratu James Omboloku, the hereditary ruler of the Nakapoa Group. . . .'

'I know him, of course,' General Ribaud put in. 'A handsome and very pleasant young man. But unfortunately, he is always asking us for funds to help him improve the lot of his people, and we have to refuse him because the money is not available.'

'It was for that very purpose that the Ratu intended to use his share of the treasure, if we could have got it up. That we should have been forestalled by a group of unscrupulous ex-Colons from Algeria, who will probably dissipate the money on drink and women, makes me see red.'

'Ex-Colons?' the General raised his eyebrows. 'I do not understand. Why should you suppose that such people are involved in this matter?'

'Was it not a man named Lacost who applied for the licence? But perhaps he made use of a nominee.'

Ribaud shook his round, closely-cropped grey head. 'I cannot think that the man to whom I issued the licence would act as a nominee for anyone. He is a Brazilian millionaire named Valentim Mauá de Carvalho.'

Gregory sat forward with a jerk. 'Well, I'll be damned! I met him in Brazil. Ratu James had gone there hoping to secure his financial backing. But de Carvalho was threatened by these Colons that they would make it hot for him if he put up the money. He told us that his reason for backing out was lack of evidence that there had ever been any quantity of gold in the ship. The records in Antigua show that there was, and later we learned that, and that de Carvalho had already seen them; so he lied to us. I naturally assumed that he had backed out from fear of the Colons. It's clear now that he's prepared to risk that, and double-crossed James to do him out of his share. Do you know where de Carvalho is now?'

'No. He has a fine, seagoing yacht and left in her the day after he obtained his licence; but not, I think, for Tujoa. He said something about making a trip to Tonga.'

'Do you think it likely that he will return?'

Hunching his broad shoulders, Ribaud spread out his hands. 'Who can say? The island is as flat as a pancake. It is covered almost entirely with plantations of coconut and banana palms; so there is nothing to see there except one mysterious old arch formed from three huge blocks of stone, and the blow holes on the coast, out of which the water spouts fifty feet into the air. But the new Date Line Hotel is one of the best in the South Pacific. It has an excellent restaurant, a beautiful garden and swimming pool, and it would be difficult to find more willing, happy servants anywhere. *Tout comfort,* in fact. De Carvalho likes that sort of thing and can well afford to pay for it. While they were here, instead of remaining on their yacht, he and his wife stayed out at the Château Royal. If you enquire of the manager there, he could tell you if, before leaving, they made another reservation.'

When Gregory had thanked him the General said, 'I trust, *mon ami,* that you are not engaged this evening. It would give me great pleasure if you would dine with me.'

Gregory accepted gladly, then returned to his hotel and broke the news about de Carvalho to James. The young Ratu was righteously indignant. After they had discussed the matter for some time he said, 'Of one thing I am certain. His wife could not have been aware of his treacherous intentions. She is as honest as she is beautiful and had she suspected this she would have found some way to warn me.'

'If you are sure of that, she might prove a big help to us,' remarked Gregory thoughtfully. 'That is, if they do return here or we can somehow get hold of them. No man likes to be shamed in front of his wife; and if he has told her some story about buying you out, there is a chance that we might persuade him to cut you in on the deal, as was originally intended. Anyhow, as I am dining with General Ribaud, you might go to the Château Royal this evening and see what you can find out.'

At seven-thirty one of the Governor's cars called for Gregory and took him to the Residence. Ribaud was a widower; so they dined alone, and over the meal swapped stories of the desperate times when Paris had been occupied by the Nazis. Later in the evening the conversation inevitably turned to de Gaulle.

'One cannot help admiring him,' Gregory remarked, 'although he is no friend to Britain.'

The General shrugged. 'What can you expect after the way your people treated him while he was in London? Churchill even refused to let him know the date fixed for the return to France. How would you have felt if, after all those years in exile as the leader of the Free British in Paris, the Prime Minister had invited you to breakfast and told you that at that very moment French troops were already on the Sussex beaches without a single British soldier to represent your Empire?'

'I'd have felt as mad as a hatter,' Gregory smiled. 'But there was a very good reason for that. You know as well as I do that, while the majority of your countrymen who came to England and joined the Free French were animated solely by patriotic motives, there were many bad eggs among them: crooks and adventurers who had nothing to gain and everything to lose if Britain succeeded in defeating Germany. Quite a number of them were completely unscrupulous and were selling to the enemy all the information they could get —and that goes for certain of the officers who held high positions on de Gaulle's staff.

'Our people knew that and could have pulled them in, but I don't have to tell you that in the counter-espionage game the devil you know is less dangerous than the devil you don't

141

know. Had we arrested them, it is possible that they would have been replaced by others equally treacherous; so the only alternative was to deny de Gaulle and his staff access to all the really important information about our plans.'

'Are you really sure that this was so?'

'Certain of it. When I was not on missions abroad I held a cover appointment as a Wing Commander on the Staff of the War Cabinet, and to do my job I had to be in on many secrets. The pity of it is that even after the war, when we were able to tell de Gaulle the facts, he refused to believe us and has remained anti-British ever since.'

'You must admit, though, that apart from withholding information from him your people treated him very badly. Time and again they refused him permission to go to North Africa and to France, and when he did get back they did their utmost to prevent him from relieving Paris.'

'There I agree, but for that you must blame General Eisenhower. And, strategically, he was right in his wish to bypass Paris; then, once he had the Boche on the run, use all the resources he could muster to throw them right back to the Siegfried Line. De Gaulle's premature dash to Paris wrecked the plan because, once the capital was liberated, its great population had to be fed by the Allies, and the offensive had to be broken off owing to the cost in petrol.'

Ribaud shrugged. 'Had de Gaulle not acted as he did, Paris would have been seized by the Communists and before long they would have had control of the whole of France. So the matter is arguable. But, if it is any consolation to you, the General's policy has been even more anti-American than anti-British.'

'I know, and more's the pity. Above all, his withdrawal from NATO. If ever there was a dangerous card to play it was that one. Mind you, for many years past it has been my view that China is the great danger and that we have little to fear from Russia. But one never knows.'

'I think you are right, and for that reason de Gaulle has shown great statemanship in his *rapprochement* with the Soviet Union.'

Gregory nodded. 'He also showed it in his conception of

combining Europe into a third Great Power block. Federated Europe would have a greater population and more resources than either America or Russia, and would have become independent of the dollar. But he muffed it by keeping Britain out of the Common Market. And, in view of the real menace that China is becoming, could Europe really afford to do without the United States? As I see it, unless a major war is fought to stop them, within another decade the Chinese will have overrun the whole of East Asia and India. Then we will definitely have to fight to defend Australia and New Zealand. For us to have any chance of winning against the Asiatic hordes, equipped with those ghastly modern weapons, there is only one thing for it—a Triple Alliance of the United States, Europe and Russia.'

With a rueful grin Ribaud said, 'Your reasoning is sound enough, but what a terrible picture you conjure up. So many of old Nostradamus' prophecies have come true, perhaps the one he made about Paris being destroyed in the year 2000 by a flock of giant, man-made birds coming from the East will too.'

It was one o'clock before Gregory got back to his hotel, so it was not until the following morning that he learned the result of James' visit to the Château Royal. The de Carvalhos were expected back there on Thursday the 16th, which was in three days' time.

Earnestly they debated their strategy. Loath as they now were to have de Carvalho as a partner, they could not possibly ignore that fact that he had secured the licence; and Ribaud had made it unmistakably clear that an attempt by anyone else to salvage the treasure would be a criminal act, equivalent to piracy, and so liable to heavy penalties. Therefore, the best they could hope for was to shame the Brazilian into the kind of arrangement that he had tentatively agreed with James in Rio before Gregory had come on the scene. Obviously the nature of the threat would render it futile if it was made in Olinda's presence, so somehow they must get him on his own, unknown to her.

James, being himself of a very upright nature, found it difficult to believe that any man of de Carvalho's standing

143

would allow himself to be denounced to his wife as a crook, so considered their chances good. The cynical Gregory was by no means so optimistic, but it was he who had first suggested that use might be made of Olinda's reactions to what had taken place, and he agreed that the idea would, at least, be worth trying.

The first move was obviously to find out what they could about the way in which the de Carvalhos spent their time while in Noumea, with a view to catching Valentim when Olinda was not with him. James said that the Château Royal was mainly staffed by New Caledonian natives. The latter were of the same Melanesian stock as his own people and, he felt sure, would talk freely to him. So it was decided that later in the day, while Gregory had a stroll round the town, James should pump some of the servants at the hotel.

The Château Royal was only a quarter of a mile further along the road out of town than the Nouváta. Soon after lunch, James set off in the broiling heat, to walk there, in order to catch one or two of the chambermaids and valets while they were off duty. Gregory, meanwhile, enjoyed a siesta, then a swim. When he went to the desk to ask for a taxi to be summoned, a young, brown-skinned New Caledonian was standing there. On hearing Gregory's request, he turned to him and said:

'Monsieur, I am from the Tourist Office, and I am about to return to the city. Allow me to offer you a lift.'

Gregory gladly accepted. As they went out to the young man's car, he introduced himself as Henry Maniquant and asked, 'Have you been up the height just behind here? If not, I will drive you up before we go downtown. It is well worth a visit.'

Maniquant proved right. Ten minutes' drive up a broad, steep, curving road brought them to the Naval Radio Station, several hundred feet above the sea. From there the panorama was magnificent. On one side lay the great sweep of *Ansa Vata* Bay, on the other the *Baie de St. Marie*. Between them, behind the town, in the low-lying neck of the peninsula, the Stadium, a large, open-air, drive-in cinema and Magenta Airport could be clearly seen. Islands, large and small, were

144

scattered round the coast in all directions, and inland to the north rose range after range of mountains. Gregory had to admit that although New Caledonia lacked the colour of Fiji, it certainly had some magnificent scenery.

On the way to the town young Maniquant proved a mine of information and extraordinarily enthusiastic about his job. Before they parted, he pressed on Gregory half a dozen pamphlets with useful information. Among them was one that Gregory thought must be unique in tourist-attraction literature. It listed over two hundred and fifty French and New Caledonian dishes, giving against each particulars in English of the ingredients.

Gregory had not previously realised that Noumea was by far the largest town in the South Pacific, with a population of thirty-five thousand. Even so, as he strolled in the still-strong, late afternoon sunshine, through streets named after famous French statesmen and Generals, he was surprised to find that the blocks contained many large stores, as well as scores of good shops, restaurants and travel agencies. As in Suva, the majority of the people were coloured; but here there were few Indians, a higher proportion of Chinese and many Indonesians.

By the cocktail hour he arrived back at the Nouváta, where James met him, grinning with satisfaction. He had located the quarters occupied by the de Carvalhos, and had talked to both the floor waiter and the chambermaid who had looked after them. The Brazilian couple had spent most of the days together. During the mornings Valentim sunbathed in the garden while Olinda swam in the sea, then in the late afternoons they went shopping or for a drive in a car. After dinner they always went up to their suite together, but, apparently, Olinda liked to have a last swim before going to bed; so, leaving him there, at about ten o'clock she went down again in a wrap and spent twenty minutes or so in the pool.

'That provides us with the opportunity, then,' Gregory smiled. 'The next thing is to devise a way of catching him in his suite without warning, or any of the hotel people questioning us as strangers when we go upstairs.'

Having thought for a few moments, he went on:

'I have it. Tomorrow I will move out to the Château Royal and take a room as near their suite as possible, anyhow in the same wing. Then on Thursday, when they are due to return, so that I don't run into them I'll pretend that I have a tummy upset and remain in my room all day. You will telephone in the evening to make certain they have arrived, then go out to the hotel about ten o'clock and post yourself in the garden under cover. As soon as you see Olinda come down for her swim, go into the hotel and ask for me. I'll say you are to be sent up, then the two of us will go along to the suite and catch Master de Carvalho napping.'

After dinner that evening Gregory walked along to the Château Royal and said that he did not like the Nouváta, so wished to move. Then, having rejected two rooms that he was shown, he settled on one which was only two doors from the suite the de Carvalhos had occupied and reserved for their return.

Next morning he made his move and, in daylight, was able to appreciate fully how preferable was the Château Royal to the Nouváta, for those who could afford it. The Château Royal was the only hotel on the sea side of the highway; so the guests had immediate access to the beach. In the main block the spacious lounge and restaurant were glass-walled, so that one could look out to seaward on a tree-surrounded swimming pool and, beyond it to the left, a separate beach bar where people could enjoy snack lunches while still in bathing things. To the right there was another two-storey block consisting only of bedrooms. It was there, on the upper floor, that Gregory had his room. The walls were panelled with *toile-de-jouy*, the furnishings were elegant, and it had a wide balcony where he could breakfast looking out on the sea.

Having unpacked, he changed into bathing things and went down to the beach. The best part of a hundred people were sun-bathing, drinking at tables under gay umbrellas, or in the sea. There were pedallos and canoes, a speed boat behind which a pretty girl was waterski-ing expertly, a big raft anchored a quarter of a mile out, and several small yachts in the distance.

146

On the debit side, the water was neither so clear nor so blue as in the Fijis, and by no means so warm. But Gregory enjoyed his swim and, having changed back into casual clothes, he went down to the restaurant for lunch. The meal he chose proved a revelation. Only in Paris could it have been equalled, and it hallmarked the Château Royal as the finest hotel in the South Seas. Dinner that night confirmed his opinion.

General Ribaud had told him that if he wished to make some motor trips he had only to ring up and a car would be placed at his disposal. So on the Wednesday he availed himself of the Governor's kind offer. After a swim, having had two picnic lunches prepared, he picked up James and they set off to see something of the interior.

The island was more than twice the length of Viti Levu, but not so large, as in no place along its two hundred and fifty miles was it much more than thirty miles wide. A long range of mountains, some rearing up to five thousand feet, divided it into two very different types of country. To the west lay great areas of flat, cultivated land; to the east deep valleys and rocky heights running right down to the coast. The roads crossing the Chaîne Centrale were most picturesque, as they passed through forests with, here and there, lovely vistas of waterfalls, reed-covered hills and rugged mountains.

Their French-speaking driver spoke proudly of the immense wealth in minerals that the mountains contained— nickel iron, cobalt, chromium and manganese—but sadly of the many rich crops that used to be grown in the lowlands owing to the exceptionally favourable semi-tropical climate, until the repatriation of the Vietnamese settlers who had farmed them.

Thursday Gregory spent in his room reading in bed, reluctantly supporting the fiction that he was unwell by denying himself the Chef's superb *Terrine Maison*. At six o'clock James telephoned him to say that 'their friends' had arrived, and he got through the evening with such patience as he could muster. Soon after ten, the office rang him. The Ratu James Omboloku was in the hall asking if he might come up. A few minutes later James reported that Olinda was taking

147

her nightly dip. Together they walked the few yards to de Carvalho's suite and, without knocking, went in.

Valentim, in a silk dressing gown, was seated at a table studying some papers. At the sound of the door opening, he turned his head. Amazement and consternation showed on his dark features. Coming to his feet, he exclaimed angrily:

'What the devil are you doing here? How dare you enter my room uninvited!'

'It is for your own peace of mind,' Gregory replied quietly. 'That is if you wish to retain your wife's respect. There is no need to go into details. But you have double-crossed James here, with the intention of getting the *Maria Amalia*'s treasure all to yourself. Can you deny it?'

De Carvalho shrugged. 'Why should I? Business is business. I am simply one move ahead of you, that is all.'

'What story did you tell your wife?'

'That is no concern of yours, but I led her to believe that the Ratu had decided to leave the whole matter in my hands.'

'We will not quarrel with that, or disillusion her—provided you are willing to sign an agreement, as originally proposed, that the Ratu should receive sixty per cent of the value of all treasure salvaged.'

'Why should I?' Valentim scowled. 'I hold the licence, so I alone have the right to salvage the treasure, and the authorities in Revika will protect that right for me until I am ready to exercise it. But I am in no hurry to do that. You may recall that while I was in Rio I was threatened, and I do not mean, by going to Tujoa just yet, to run my head into a hornet's nest. These people, whoever they are, will learn in a week or two that I have outsmarted them, then leave me a clear field. And that already goes for you.'

'You do not care, then, if we let your wife know that you are a crook?'

De Carvalho shrugged again. 'She is aware, from other operations that my friends and I have carried through, that in business there are times when one must act somewhat unethically, unless one wishes to lose money. It has been apparent to me that she has rather a soft spot for Ratu James; so I have no doubt that in this instance she will be annoyed

148

with me. But what more can she do than sulk for a few days?'

Matters had turned out as Gregory had half expected. De Carvalho's admission that he had been involved in other shady deals, and that Olinda knew about some of them, obviously robbed of any potency the threat to expose him. He preferred to have a scene with her rather than forgo a share of the treasure. Their little plot to force his hand had failed. There seemed no more to be said.

Suddenly the door opened and Olinda came into the room. She was wearing a white swim suit that set off her dark beauty to perfection. In a casual voice she got as far as saying, 'I left my cigarettes behind. . . .' Then she caught sight of James, smiled and exclaimed. 'This *is* a pleasant surprise! What are you and Mr. Sallust doing here?'

James bowed. 'Senhora, this is not a social visit. We have come . . . we have come. . . .'

While Gregory had done all the talking, James had contained his rage, but now he suddenly gave full vent to it.

'We have come to unmask your husband for the filthy crook he is. Like an innocent I placed myself in his hands, believing him to be a friend. And now, now, see what he has done! In Rio he lied to us, he said there was no evidence that the *Maria Amalia* carried treasure; yet he had already been up to Antigua and seen the records showing that she had a great sum in gold on board. He pretended that he was no longer interested. But what does he do? He comes to Noumea like a thief in the night and secures a licence to salvage from the wreck. That means the authorities will stop anyone else from attempting to do so. Behind my back he means to take all. He cannot deny it. He is a swindler! A cheat, a dirty cheat!'

As he flung out these accusations, James' long arm stretched out, indignantly pointing at de Carvalho. His dark eyes had gone black with rage and his great quiff of hair quivered as his head jerked backwards and forwards.

With distended eyes Olinda stared at him: then, as he ceased, she turned to her husband and cried in a shrill voice, 'Valentim, is this true?'

'More or less,' he admitted sullenly. 'But it is I who am

149

going to risk the money, isn't it? Not him. He produced the idea. All right. I'll give him the price of his journey to Rio and a bit over. But cut him in for sixty per cent? Why should I? I'll be damned if I will.'

'But, Valentim,' Olinda's voice had become hoarse and earnest, 'you cannot do this. It is robbery. It is as bad as going to his island and stealing valuables while you were a guest in his house. He trusted you. And you lied to me about it. You said he had left everything to you and that you were going to pay him his share when the salvaging was completed. I insist that you give James a fair deal. I insist! I insist!'

Glowering at her with half-closed eyes, her thick-set husband snarled, 'This is none of your business. Go and have your swim! Get out of here!'

'I won't!' she cried. 'I'll not stand by and see you cheat a simple honest man who is worth ten of you.'

De Carvalho ran his tongue over his thick lips then began to bellow at her in Portuguese.

Her beautiful face livid with rage, she screamed insults back at him in the same language.

Suddenly he lost his temper completely. Taking a swift step forward, he smacked her hard across the face with his open hand.

There fell a deathly silence in the room. Olinda stood with her mouth half open, a look of shocked surprise on her face. De Carvalho, his jaw thrust forward, was staring at her. Gregory, his eyes narrowed, waited tensely to see which of them would prevail. For a moment in time they all remained as rigid as statues. Then James erupted.

With the speed and savagery of his forbears, the brown-skinned giant launched himself at de Carvalho. In one movement he grasped him by the neck and under one knee, then swung him high over his head. Before Gregory had the least chance to stop him, he burst through the flimsy mosquito screens, bounded out on to the balcony and hurled the Brazilian over it.

There came one thin, wailing cry, the sound of a heavy thump from below, then again silence.

Wiping the back of one big brown hand across his eyes, James staggered back into the room.

'My God, man!' Gregory cried. 'Are you mad? You may have killed him.'

James gave a gasping sob. 'The swine! He hit her. I could not bear it. I love her! I love her!'

Olinda's face suddenly lit up and a spate of words poured from her. 'So it is true! I hardly dared hope; yet in my heart I knew it. Yes, from the very first moment. But you are so honourable. I feared you would despise me if I confessed my illicit passion for you. Oh, I love you! My wonderful one! I love you too.'

As she spoke, she held out her arms. James seized her in his and began to smother her face with kisses.

Gregory gave vent to an unprintable Italian oath and ran out on to the balcony. It was not yet half past ten. Many people were still dining in the restaurant on the ground floor of the main block; strains of music came up from it. Others were strolling in the garden that ran down to the beach. A little crowd of men and women had run over to de Carvalho. They were now grouped round him. One man was half-supporting his limp body.

As Gregory peered over, the voice of an American woman came excitedly from only a few yards away on his right. 'There he is! Help! Help! Murder!'

Almost immediately a man's voice followed, 'No, that's not him. It was a huge guy, a fuzzy-wuzzy.'

Glancing round, Gregory saw two figures beyond the partition that screened off the balcony from its neighbour. Evidently the American couple next door had been sitting there enjoying the cool of the evening, and had seen James throw de Carvalho over.

Ignoring them, he again leaned over the rail. He had to know whether the Brazilian was alive or dead. The crowd round him were exclaiming in several languages, 'Get a doctor!' 'Stand back!' 'Give him air!' 'We must carry him inside.' 'Lucky that he fell on his back and not on his head.' 'His right arm's broken.' 'His heart's all right.' 'Just unconscious, eh; don't wonder the fall knocked him out.'

151

Turning about, Gregory dashed back into the room. James and Olinda were still embraced and murmuring incoherently to each other between kisses. Seizing them each by an arm, Gregory dragged them apart and snarled at James:

'You lunatic! This is no time for lovemaking. Thank God he didn't break his neck. He's alive, but he may well die from internal injuries. Then you'll be had for murder. At best you'll be charged with attempted murder and get four or five years in prison. We've got to get out of here. And quick!'

His angry tirade acted like a douche of cold water on the lovers. 'He's right,' Olinda said in a frightened whisper. 'Oh, my darling, my heart bleeds that you should be in such danger on my account. But you must go. At once. Have you money?'

Gregory nodded. 'I've plenty in my wallet.'

'This way then.' She ran to the door. 'I'll go down with you and engage anyone we meet in conversation.'

They followed her out into the open corridor that served all the rooms on the upper floor of the block, and down the stairs. At the bottom they came face to face with a waiter. He was wheeling a trolley holding a cold supper for four—evidently a meal ordered by a party that intended to make merry in a private sitting room. At the sight of them running towards him, the man's mouth opened to give a shout. Before he could utter it, James darted past Olinda and struck him a single blow. He went down like a pole-axed ox.

As the other two ran on, Gregory pulled up short beside the trolley. Already he was thinking ahead. To escape arrest they would have to go into hiding and food might be difficult to obtain. Flinging a bowl of fruit salad and an orange jelly on the floor, he gathered up the four corners of the small tablecloth that covered the trolley, so that all the other food cascaded into the middle, heaved the bundle up and swung it over his shoulder.

At the circular drive outside the front entrance to the hotel, the others had halted to wait for him. Olinda had wrenched a ruby cross from a necklace she was wearing and thrust it into his hand as she said, still breathlessly, 'Go to the harbour. Go aboard our yacht, the *Boa Viagem*. Show this to

152

Captain Amedo. Tell him it is my order that he should take you where you wish.'

She did not hear Gregory's words of thanks, for she had turned away and was again in James' arms, crushing his mouth with violent kisses. Suddenly she pushed him from her and cried, 'Go now, go! Tomorrow I will burn a thousand candles. May the Holy Virgin protect you.'

In the drive stood several parked cars. Among them was a tradesman's Citroen van which had probably made a late delivery. No-one was about. Running to it, Gregory wrenched open the near door and jumped into the driver's seat. James ran round and scrambled in on the other side. The self-starter whirred, the clutch slid in and they were off.

There came a tense moment as they drove out through the arched entrance to the hotel grounds, but no-one attempted to stop them. James then relaxed, lay back in his seat and sighed ecstatically, 'She loves me. She loves me.'

Gregory could have hit him for the mess he had landed them in, and snarled, 'You bloody young fool! You should have bided your time and she would have fallen in your lap. As things are, after this little demonstration of your affection for her, you'll be darned lucky if you ever see her again.'

'That cannot be,' James declared with fatalistic optimism. 'The gods made us for one another. It is certain that they will smile upon our love. And owing to her we have little to fear. We shall sail away in the yacht.'

Tightening his grip on the wheel, Gregory took the bend opposite the Headquarters of the Pacific Commission at forty-five miles an hour. When they had made it he snapped angrily, 'You poor boob. With a couple like the de Carvalhos, who do you think the Captain takes his orders from? Him or her? Him, of course, unless she happens to be on the yacht without him. If we showed the Captain that trinket she gave me he'd immediately jump to it that we'd stolen it with all her other jewels, and had thought up a clever plan to make use of him for a quick get-away. It's all Lombard Street to a china orange that he'd have his crew grab us while he sent for the police.'

Subsiding, James asked dolefully, 'What then are we to do?'

'I don't fancy taking to the mountains,' Gregory replied after a moment. 'Our best bet would be to try to find another yacht—or, rather, a small cabin cruiser—with no-one aboard. If we could make off in her, and be well out of sight of Noumea before dawn, we'd stand a fair chance of getting away.'

Five minutes later they turned into Fisherman's Bay. The waterfront was almost deserted. As they drove past a long line of sheds Gregory noticed one with the doors standing open. Swerving, he drove the van into it. They got out, closed the doors, then walked quickly along to the wharf, to which a number of the smaller boats were tied up. A few of them showed lights, but none of their occupants was on deck. A patrolling gendarme came into view.

'If we try to hide, and he spots us, we'll be in trouble,' Gregory whispered. 'We'll just stroll casually past him, talking about anything, but stick to French.' In a louder voice, he added, 'Have you ever been to Europe?'

'No,' James replied. 'But I would like to, particularly to England; oh, and of course France. Paris must be wonderful.'

They were just under one of the arc lights when they drew level with the gendarme, so they saw that he was a native. He gave them a sharp look, murmured 'Bon soir' and walked on. Two minutes later he was hidden from view behind some sheds. Swiftly Gregory ran his eye over the twenty or more launches that were moored along the quay. Pointing to one about twenty-five feet in length, he said, 'That looks about our mark. You will make less noise than I should. Slip aboard her and make certain that there is no-one sleeping in the cabin, then check the tanks to see if she has plenty of petrol and water. I'll keep watch here and give a loud warning cough should the gendarme come back this way. If he does, lie doggo and don't worry about me.'

While Gregory hauled in the painter, James took off his shoes, then dropped almost silently into the stern of the launch. Two minutes later he called softly, 'O.K. Come aboard.' Gregory untied her and joined James on the deck.

154

Going forward he took the wheel, started the engine, and nosed the launch slowly out. A minute later a figure emerged from the cabin of one of the boats that had lights on further along the row, and a voice called:

'Where are you off to at this hour, Mathieu?'

It was a nasty moment, as Gregory had no idea how well the man who had hailed him knew 'Mathieu', and what type of man Mathieu was. But to have failed to reply would have been certain to arouse suspicion, so he took a chance. Praying that his voice would not give him away as a stranger, he called back facetiously:

'Maybe Marseilles; maybe New York.'

To his relief a laugh greeted his sally. Switching on the navigation lights, he headed at half-speed for the harbour entrance. When they had cleared it he asked James, 'How far do you reckon it is from here to Tujoa?'

'About four hundred and fifty miles. As I once told you, it is nearer Fiji than New Caledonia. By rights it should have been included in the Fijis, but it is our misfortune that in 1853 the Nakapoa Group, as well as New Caledonia, came under France.'

'Do you think you could navigate us to Tujoa? If not, we'll have to head down the coast here and try to hide up in some lonely inlet.'

James laughed. With his mercurial nature, now that they were temporarily out of danger, he seemed to have forgotten that barely an hour ago he had probably killed a man. 'Of course. I come of a race of great seafarers. I could take you anywhere in the South Pacific with my eyes shut. As a youth I spent many nights at sea. Even when the stars are hidden I would know my way by the feel of the wind, the look of the water and the smell of the air.'

As the night sky was clear, he had only to look up for a few moments to give Gregory a course. Then he said, 'The prevailing wind is against us, so it will take us three, perhaps four, days to make it. In these seas there is little traffic, so the danger of our coming into collision with another boat in the dark is negligible. But there are numerous islands and many reefs; so, although we can lash the wheel, one of us must always keep watch. Reefs can be seen at some distance because of the phosphorus in the waves that break over them. We call it "the breath of *Daucina*", the great Shark God who is the light-giver and protector of seafarers.'

When the lights of Noumea had become pinpoints behind them, Gregory murmured, 'So far, so good. Owing to your height, you and I make such a conspicuous couple that the gendarme we passed on the wharf is certain to remember us. I was afraid that soon after we left, a general police alert might reach him, then they would tumble to it that we had pinched this launch and got away by sea, and come after us in a speed boat. But, as they won't know which direction we have taken, we've got far enough now for the odds to be all against their catching us.'

James made up one of the two bunks in the small cabin and split the remainder of the night into two watches. The morning dawned cloudy and by eight o'clock it had begun to rain. On examining their food supply, they found that the things Gregory had whipped up from the trolley had become a glutinous mess, embedded in which were four thick slices of the delicious *Terrine Maison,* a score of prawns that had been in aspic, and four small birds. With care it would be enough to last them four to five days and if they did run short James said they could always pick up some coconuts and wild bananas from one of the many deserted islands they would pass or, failing that, they could catch fish. The supply of water was also satisfactory, but Gregory had serious misgivings that the petrol would not prove sufficient for so long a voyage.

By midday the sky had cleared and the sun blazed down. Soon the roof of the cabin became so hot that they could not bear to touch it. All through the long afternoon, sweltering and sweating, they alternately dozed and kept watch. Over their evening meal, Gregory asked, 'Have you decided what to do if and when we reach Tujoa?'

James looked at him a little unhappily. 'Stay there, I suppose. What else can I do? If I have killed that swine, they will come after me; but my people are loyal and would hide me up in the mountains.'

156

'Sooner or later someone would betray you, and the police would run you to earth. Even if you haven't killed de Carvalho they will institute a search for you and you'll get a long prison sentence if you are caught. I think the best plan would be for us to go on to Fiji. As that is British territory, they would have to get a warrant to extradite you. They will, of course, if de Carvalho dies; but if he is only injured they may not bother. Once we are in Fiji, too, we could probably get to Manon's island without being traced and lie up there.'

Putting a long arm round Gregory's shoulders, James said, 'Dear Gregory, what a good friend you have been to me. But for you I expect I would already be in prison. Yet you got me away and came with me, when you need not have done. You had no part in my act and Olinda would have sworn to your innocence.'

Gregory laughed. 'Perhaps, but they would have found out that we were partners; so they might have taken the line that I could have prevented you from throwing him over the balcony, and charged me as an accessory. Anyhow, forget it, dear boy. We are in this thing together.'

On the second day the good weather continued, but Gregory suffered severely from the sun. However careful he was, he had from time to time to expose himself to it: and his face, arms and insteps began to hot up until he knew that he was in for a bad bout of sunburn.

Soon after dawn on the third morning, a wind got up. The sea became choppy and flecked with white horses, then became really rough. They kept the launch head-on to the waves, but it bounded and bucked like a bronco, jarring them badly with each jolt. Spray broke over the boat in sheets and the bilge began to fill with water. Both of them set to baling frantically, but by midday the cabin was awash. In the afternoon the storm eased a little, but about four o'clock the engine sputtered and died. As Gregory had feared might happen, their petrol had given out.

Now the launch veered from her course and was at the mercy of the sea. All that they could do was to keep on baling and pray that the boat might be washed up on an island. James broke out into lamentations about the vulnerability

157

of modern vessels. The Pacific peoples had sailed in safety thousands of miles in their canoes—at one time even carrying out a great migration right through the East Indies and across the Indian Ocean to Madagascar. The Fijians, Tongans and his own people, he said, had long been famous as canoe-builders and their catamarans—big double canoes spanned by a deck with a palm-thatched house on it—were more comfortable to voyage in than anything short of a large, modern pleasure yacht. King Thakobau had once owned such a double canoe, one hundred and two feet long and eighteen feet wide, which he had presented to King George of Tonga.

But James' unhappy grumblings did nothing to lessen Gregory's anxiety. It seemed certain now that, unless the sea went down before nightfall, the launch would sink. Then, just as the sun was setting—a great orange ball on the horizon —they sighted and island. Ten minutes later it became certain that they were being carried towards it.

Darkness soon shrouded the scene, but fewer waves were now breaking over the boat and the stars came out. There followed an anxious two hours, then ahead of them they sighted a line of breaking surf. Some way behind it the island loomed up. The lights of the launch were still working, and Gregory switched them on. Had the engine not failed, they might have manoeuvred the boat until they found a gap in the reef, but she had no steerage way. As they were swept towards the reef, the waves pounding on it seemed to become higher until they towered overhead. Then came a grinding crash. The boat splintered to pieces on the rocks and they were both thrown into the sea.

As they came spluttering to the surface, they found that they were inside the reef and in calm water. Having called to each other, with infinite relief they swam for the shore. It was about a quarter of a mile away and they had only covered a third of the distance to it when, from the beach, a searchlight flashed out and began to sweep the lagoon until it focused on them. The lights of the launch had evidently been seen. Joyful at the thought that help was at hand, they redoubled their efforts and staggered ashore.

On the beach a soldier with a Sten gun was waiting to receive them. In a language of which Gregory understood a little, but James had never heard spoken, the man called out something and motioned to them to put up their hands. Surprised and breathless, they obeyed. Signing to them to go ahead of him, he marched them along the beach towards the searchlight. About a hundred yards before they reached it they were met by an officer at the head of a group of soldiers. In halting French the officer asked their nationality and where they had come from.

'We are British,' Gregory replied; and, in the hope that they would be sent on there, he added, 'We come from Fiji.'

'This island is forbidden to all persons,' said the officer harshly. 'You are under arrest.' Then he signed to a Sergeant and two men to escort them away along a path that led inland through the jungle.

As they moved off, James turned to Gregory and asked in a puzzled voice, 'What do they mean to do with us? Who are these people, anyway?'

'What they will do with us, God alone knows,' replied Gregory grimly, 'or how they come to be here. But these men are Russians.'

10

And the Bill to Pay

'Russians!' echoed James. 'But they are soldiers, and the Russians own no islands in the South Pacific. What are they doing here?'

'Ask me another,' Gregory shrugged, although he had already conceived a possible explanation. He was too wet and weary to wish to talk, and would anyhow not have speculated on the matter in the hearing of their escort, even though it was unlikely that any of the men understood English. But he did take that small chance by adding, 'If you have anything on you that will give away your identity I'll distract our escorts' attention for a moment while you throw it into the bushes.'

'No, I've nothing,' James murmured. 'I left everything behind at. . . .'

'In the launch,' Gregory cut in loudly. 'So did I.'

After trudging about a mile the ground sloped up and they came to a mound crowned by tall bushes. In the uncertain light it was not until they were quite near that Gregory realised that it was actually a low building, but so well camouflaged that even in daylight it could not have been detected from the background of jungle at more than a hundred yards. Apertures in the otherwise solid front showed it to be a small fort that commanded the bay. Hidden behind it were some storehouses and an open space in which stood two jeeps. A sentry who was on duty there shouted something and an officer emerged from the fort. The Sergeant reported to him. They held a brief colloquy; then the prisoners, prodded with machine pistols, were herded into one of the jeeps.

160

After half an hour of bumping along a dirt track they came down into a valley in which there were a number of lighted buildings, evidently forming a base camp. The jeep drew up in front of an office block. The Sergeant went inside, came out again and called to his men. The prisoners were taken up on to a veranda which ran the whole length of the building, marched some way along it, then put into a room furnished only with two tables, a few chairs and some filing cabinets. One of the soldiers went in with them, then the door was locked.

Wearily, Gregory sat down on one of the hard chairs. Looking up at James towering above him, he gave a just perceptible wink and said with apparent severity, 'Well, Johnny Olourna, what have you to say for yourself? Before we left Suva your father told me that you were to be relied upon. He assured me that you could take me in safety for a fortnight's cruise among the islands and were much too knowledgeable ever to leave port when there was a threat of bad weather.'

For a moment 'Johnny' looked surprised, then he got the message and replied, 'I am sorry, sir. But such storms do blow up quite unexpectedly.'

The soldier who had been left with them growled something, which Gregory knew to be an order not to talk; but he had no intention of giving away the fact that he knew even a little Russian, so he went on:

'And where are we now, I would like to know? What island is this?'

'It must be Yuloga. A solitary island that lies about half-way between the Loyalties and the Nakapoa Group.'

Angrily their guard stamped a heavily-booted foot, put one hand over his mouth and with the other waved his machine pistol; so they accepted his demonstration and fell silent.

After a wait of twenty minutes the door was unlocked, the Sergeant reappeared, and they were led along to a larger and much-better-furnished office. Behind a desk was seated a square-jawed Russian who, by his rank badges, Gregory knew to be a Colonel. Beside him stood a French officer wearing the uniform of a Captain of Artillery. Poker-faced,

161

the Russian threw the questions and the Frenchman interpreted.

Actually, owing to their hurried flight from Noumea, it
was there that the two prisoners had left their passports and
other papers, so there was little chance of their being identi-
fied; but Gregory took the precaution of choosing a false
name for himself, the initials of which would tally with the
monogram on his silk shirt. Showing great indignation at the
treatment they were receiving, he said that he was George
Simonds, a British subject who had come on a winter holiday
to Fiji. At home he owned a motor launch, and spent several
weeks each summer cruising across the Channel or North
Sea. Thinking that it would be pleasant to cruise among the
islands, he had hired a launch from a Mr. Olourna in Suva,
with his son Johnny to pilot her. They had been caught in a
storm, etc. He requested a passage back to Fiji as soon as
possible.

James substantiated Gregory's story. But the Russian did
not appear interested. He was concerned only with security.
At length the French Captain said, 'No-one is permitted to
land on this island unless he carries a special permit. That
you should have been wrecked on it is your misfortune. You
will have to remain here during the pleasure of the Commandant.'

At that Gregory blew up, declaiming on the Rights of
Nations and the Freedom of Individuals. But he was only
making a demonstration which he hoped would lead his captors to regard him as a person of some importance. He knew
only too well that, even could he have communicated with
Whitehall, the days were gone when the British Government
could protect her nationals the world over, and, should they
be unjustly imprisoned, send a warship to secure their release.
The birthright of Britons had been sold for a few sacksful of
dollars and a Socialist mess of pottage, based on liberal fan-
tasies that in the sacred name of Independence all peoples
were now entitled to kill their political enemies and imprison
foreigners whenever they wished.

As the prisoners, still protesting, were led away, Gregory
shouted to the Captain, 'We have not fed for over twelve

162

hours; so at least send us food and something passable to drink.'

They were taken a few hundred yards on foot to an enclosure of one-storey buildings. There the Sergeant handed them over to a Sergeant of Military Police, who led them across a compound, then locked them into two adjacent cells, each of which was furnished with a truckle-bed, a chair, a slop bucket, a rack that held a tin jug of water and a mug. But at least the prison had been built recently, so the cells were clean and hygienic. Above head level the walls on all four sides consisted of iron grilles covered with fine-gauge wire mesh, to provide through-currents of air and protect the prisoners from mosquitoes. There were no lights in the cells, but illumination from a great arc-lamp in the middle of the compound came through the grilles, giving enough light to see by, yet not sufficient to prevent sleep.

The island being forbidden to ordinary citizens, Gregory felt sure that the prison must be a military detention centre, so it was most unlikely that the cells were 'bugged'. Owing to the solid partition that separated them he could not see James, but they were able to talk to each other through the open-work iron grille above it. As Gregory did not feel like talking, he called out, 'We're in a fine mess, Johnny; but we had best sleep on it and discuss what can be done tomorrow.'

The thin clothes he was wearing had already dried out owing to the warm tropical night air, and were only a little stiff from salt. He was about to take off his trousers and get into bed when the door opened and an orderly thrust in a mess tin holding some pieces of meat, a yam, two bananas and what Gregory rightly took to be a mug of strong tea. The meat was tough and the yam unpalatable; but after his long fast he ate the greater part of them and the bananas with pleasure, then drank the dark brew of tea, comforted a little to think that their captors were not altogether inhuman. Partly undressing, he lay down on the bed, pulled the rough blanket over him and, utterly tired out, soon fell asleep.

When he woke the big arc-lamp had been switched off and instead the pale light of early morning filtered into the cell. Recalling the events of the past night, he endeavoured to con-

163

sole himself for having been made a prisoner by the fact that he was lucky to be alive at all. His waterproof watch was still going, and a glance at it showed the time to be a little before six.

Both he and James had been frisked for weapons, but not searched, and none of their few belongings had been taken from them. He put that down to their having been imprisoned not for any criminal act, but simply as detainees. His wallet had fallen out of his pocket when he had been thrown from the wrecked launch, but that did not particularly trouble him, as he still had plenty of money on him. During the long spells he had spent on secret missions abroad during the war he had always worn a money belt containing a hundred or more gold coins as well as wads of bank notes of the country in which he was operating. More recently, since he had been travelling further afield, he had resumed his practice of wearing the money-belt as a precaution against pick-pockets and hotel thieves. Now it had in it a considerable sum in dollar bills and Swiss franc bank notes.

Had he been searched, the money might have been taken from him; and he was still congratulating himself on having the wherewithal to bribe his way out of prison, should an opportunity arise, when his cell door was unlocked and a guard beckoned him out. James had already been released and, as they wished each other a rather gloomy 'Good morning', the guard led them along to a wash-house.

In it there were already two men who, from their light skins and only slightly crinkly hair, looked to Gregory like Polynesians. Soon afterwards they were joined by two white men and two fuzzy-haired Melanesians. The two white men were both fortyish, lanky, fair-haired and blue-eyed. Surprised and pleased at the sight of Gregory, they introduced themselves as Willy and Frank Robertson, Australians who had long been in the copra trade. Two months earlier their schooner had been driven on to a reef by a hurricane. They and the two Melanesians, who were members of their crew, had succeeded in getting ashore in a boat, only to be promptly arrested and imprisoned. The Polynesians, they said, had

164

been there for considerably longer, but for quite how long was uncertain, as neither of them spoke any English.

The guards, who stood by while the prisoners washed, did not prevent their talking, so 'George Simonds' and 'Johnny Olourna' duly told their story, then obtained as much information as time allowed from the Robertson brothers about conditions in the prison.

It emerged that it held two types of prisoner: themselves —castaways who were being held illegally on security grounds—and a number of Russian soldiers serving sentences for various derelictions of duty. The two groups were never allowed to mix and were exercised at different hours. There was no common dining hall, probably as a precaution against the detainees being together long enough to plan a mass attempt to break out. Food was brought to them three times daily in their cells. It was not too bad, but very monotonous. The heat was one of the worst afflictions, although they were allowed morning and evening to use the showers adjacent to the washroom. Another disadvantage was that no books or radio music were provided to help while away the intolerable monotony. And, last but not least, there was the terrible uncertainty about when, if ever, they would be restored to liberty.

Back in their cells they were given for breakfast bowls of maize porridge and tea. At eight o'clock they were let out for an hour's exercise, being made to walk and run alternately in single file round the compound. The midday meal consisted of a hot stew containing both meat and vegetables, a pancake for pudding and two bananas. At five o'clock they were again let out, this time for a game of volley-ball, then, after taking a shower, they were brought their evening meal —cold pork, yam, and a sort of fruit salad consisting largely of diced coconut.

In the intervals between exercising and meals Gregory had plenty of time to contemplate the possibility of escape. An attempt to suppress and overcome the guard who brought the meals was out of the question. Even if that could be done there were plenty of others about, all of them armed, and he had no doubt at all that they would not hesitate to use their weapons. An attempt at bribery appeared equally hopeless, as none of those to whom he had spoken understood English, French or German, and his Russian was so limited that he could not have put up a proposition to one of them. Even when he had tried to get them to fetch the French Captain, so that he could ask him for the loan of a few books, as a lead in possibly establishing regular communication with him, they had only shaken their heads, not in refusal but clearly because he had failed to make them understand his request.

Short, therefore, of some unforeseen development, there remained only the possibilty of finding some way to break out of his cell during the night. As the prison was a modern one, the lock on the cell door was prisoner-proof, a steel plate covering the whole inner side, so that no keyhole offered any opportunity to pick the lock from within. The floor was solid cement, making it impossible to dig a tunnel; so were the walls. The ceilings were corrugated asbestos, so could not be broken through without some heavy tool. But the grilles . . . ?

Gregory's keenly searching eye had lit on the sector in which the prison architect had slipped up, and he smiled to himself. The wire mesh-covered grilles on all four sides of the cell were each kept in place by from eight to twelve fair-sized screws. They had only to be removed and the grilles could be lifted out. Fortunately, too, the cell on his other side from James was unoccupied; so if he could get to work on the screws there was no-one there who might give away what he was doing and, as the guards never made a round of the cells after midnight, no fear of interruption.

But had the architect really slipped up, or had he simply settled for the cheapest way of securing the grilles? The prison would have been originally designed only for defaulting soldiers. Should a Russian private or N.C.O. show the initiative to break prison, which in itself was unlikely, what chance would he stand of escaping from a tropical island? That, and the harsh punishment he might expect if caught, were the real deterrents; and Gregory had no illusions about the difficulty of getting away from Yuloga. But, regarding himself as considerably more resourceful than the average Russian peasant in uniform, he comforted himself by recalling Napoleon's saying, 'It will be time to talk of the Vistula when we are over the Rhine.'

As James was in the next cell there was nothing to stop their talking and if they stood on their beds they could even see each other through the grille above the dividing wall. That night, adopting this means of coming face to face so that they could keep their voices low, Gregory told James of his plan and that the first thing needed was something with which to loosen the screws. Neither of them had anything in his possession that would serve, but they agreed to keep their eyes open.

On the third evening James was lucky. While they were playing volley-ball he saw on the ground a small half-moon of shining metal. It was the worn-down part-heel with which Russian soldiers' boots are reinforced, and this one had come off. Pretending to slip and fall, he palmed it; then, a few minutes later, bumped into Gregory and passed it to him.

The cells were longer than they were broad, so the grille in the outer wall had only eight screws in it; but, having only a small implement which was awkward to handle and, even standing on his bed, only being just able to reach the top three screws near the ceiling, it took him several hours' work during two nights before he had all the screws loosened.

The following day he passed the worn metal heel to James so that he could start work on his grille, but he had no intention of waiting until his friend could accompany him on a first reconnaissance. Gregory had always maintained that, in inverse ratio to the old saying 'one boy working in a garden is a boy and two boys only half a boy', two operatives working together doubled the danger to each of them, so, whenever possible, he had played the role of a lone wolf.

That night, having waited until well after midnight, he removed the grille. Standing on his bed, he peered cautiously out. Having made certain that no sentry was patrolling outside the prison, he had no difficulty in straddling the exposed top of the wall and dropping down on the other side.

After listening intently for a few minutes, he made his way

167

slowly round the perimeter of the military establishment, watching every step and, instead of walking toe and heel, putting his feet down flat. A few lights were on here and there, but no-one was about, so he edged his way between some buildings until he could get a view of the office block in which he and James had been interrogated. In front of it a sentry was patrolling. Satisfied now that provided they kept outside the area of buildings there was nothing to stop their getting away into the jungle, he returned to the prison, climbed back into his cell and, while replacing the grating, told James, who had been anxiously awaiting his return, what he had so far discovered.

Next night he went out again. On his first reconnaissance he had seen that, while several tracks led out from the settlement, all except one were dirt roads. The exception was metalled. It led uphill out of the valley and he followed it until he reached the crest of the ridge. From there he could see down into another valley. A rising moon now lit it quite clearly and, as he had expected, he was able to verify a supposition he had formed on finding that the island was garrisoned by Russians. The moonlight revealed blocks of hutments, tall gantries and a number of great launching pads from several of which there rose giant rockets. Clearly the French had allowed the Russians to take over Yuloga as a base for launching inter-continental missiles. It was no wonder that the Russians were taking such extreme precautions to ensure that no-one landed on the island without their knowledge and to protect the secret of their presence there by arbitrarily detaining anyone who came ashore.

Cautiously advancing further to get a closer look, Gregory disturbed a parrot roosting on the branch of a nearby tree. The bird flew off with a squawk. A moment later a challenge rang out from only twenty yards ahead. Instantly Gregory froze and held his breath, his heart hammering wildly. The challenge came again, then heavy footsteps advanced towards him. He felt a terrible urge to turn and run, but fought it down. The footsteps stopped. There fell an utter silence. For ten minutes that seemed an age he remained absolutely motionless. The sound of footsteps came again, but this time

168

they were moving away. For another ten minutes he stayed completely still, breathing gently but evenly. Then he turned and, placing each foot with the greatest care, slowly stole away, blessing the bird that had saved him from running slap into the sentry. Three-quarters of an hour later he was safely back in his cell.

By this time, James' greater height having enabled him to loosen more easily the top screws securing the grille in his cell, he had freed it. Now they could both leave the prison any night they liked; but, as they were quite reasonably treated there, to leave it for the jungle would have been pointless, and they were still faced with the much more difficult problem of how to get away from the island.

James produced the idea that the solution was to get in touch with the natives. It seemed certain that an island of that size must have long been inhabited and, although the dialect of the natives in each island differed, he felt confident that he would be able to enlist their help.

Gregory agreed, and it was decided that James should explore the surrounding country until he came upon a village of some size where the headman could put him in touch with the High Chief. But Gregory would not allow him to start on his quest for the time being, because the moon was waxing and during its bright period he feared that James would run too great a risk of being spotted by a Russian sentry.

From time to time it rained and on three nights in the next ten the sky was overcast, which enabled James to sally forth without undue danger; but total darkness proved a severe handicap and he did not succeed in finding a native village.

When the moon began to rise later, James went out every night. On one expedition he found a village up in the hills, but it was deserted. Then, three nights afterwards, having followed the valley for three miles to the sea, he came upon half a hundred or more *bures* sited on the estuary of a small river. But they, too, had been abandoned. The size of the place seemed to indicate that it was the principal township of the island, so, when he discussed his findings with Gregory, they came to the conclusion that, to make certain of guarding

169

their secrets, the French had evacuated the whole native population of the island.

This was a sad setback, as they had hoped the natives would provide them with a canoe in which to get away. It then occurred to Gregory that they might not have taken all their canoes with them. So James went again to the township and returned to report with no signs of satisfaction that, some way up a creek, he had come upon a boathouse in which a large canoe was chocked up.

When Gregory asked why he showed no pleasure in his find he replied, 'Because she is a thirty-foot war canoe, and much too heavy for the two of us to launch. What is more, her great sail is half rotten and without a sail we could not possibly get more than a few hundred yards in her.'

This gave Gregory furiously to think. The Robertson brothers had proved likeable fellows and very pleasant to exchange snatches of talk with while in the wash-house or during exercise periods; but, adhering to his sound conviction that the more people there were privy to a plot, the greater the danger of its discovery, he had strictly forbidden James to say anything to the Australians about their nightly excursions. However, now that their help was necessary to carry out his plans he was by no means sorry that circumstances forced him to give them this chance of joining in an attempt to escape.

Next day they were guardedly let into the secret, and Willy was slipped the metal half-heel so that the brothers could unscrew the grilles in their cells. It took them four nights and on the fifth they accompanied James down to the boathouse. When they got back James passed on to Gregory the views of these seasoned Pacific copra traders. They were confident that, with rollers, the four of them could launch the big canoe, but the sail remained a problem. It was useless as it was, but could be repaired if *tapa* cloth was available; and they had found that there was plenty of that in good condition to be had from some of the larger *bures,* where it had been used for decoration. However, only men skilled in such work were capable of making good the great sail. The brothers were not, but they said that their two Melanesian

170

crew men, Woggy and Punch, could do the job if Gregory was willing to include them in the party.

Reluctant as Gregory was to do so, he saw no alternative; so, on the Robertsons' vouching for the loyalty of their two Melanesians, they were in turn lent the precious steel half-heel that was the key to liberty.

By the time they had both got their gratings unscrewed, the bright period of the moon had come again and for the ten days that followed Gregory would not allow any of them to risk leaving the prison. At length this tiresome wait was over, but even then Gregory was averse to more of the escape party being absent from the prison on any one night, in order to minimise the risk of their all being detected should the guards at any time become suspicious and make a night inspection. So Willy alone took the two Melanesians down to the township.

That night they first inspected the canoe, then spent two hours collecting *tapa* cloth from the *bures*. Woggy and Punch had pointed out that needles and fibre twine would be needed to mend the sail. The former they could soon cut from bamboos, but if they had to collect the right form of tough liana, then shred it to make the twine, that would take a considerable time. However, on their second night down there with Willy they were lucky, as they came upon a long coil of twine in the back of the boathouse. Nevertheless, as between going and returning they could not safely work for more than two hours each night, it was six nights before they finished patching the great sail to their satisfaction.

Gregory's next concern was how to plan their get-away. According to James, Yuloga was not a large island. It therefore seemed probable that the Russians had posts and searchlight stations covering every sector of the coast; so there was a very considerable risk that, as the big canoe emerged from the mouth of the river, it would be spotted and their attempt to escape brought to nought. In order to estimate their chances Gregory decided that, on the last night that the Melanesians were working on the sail, he and James should carry out a reconnaissance.

A quarter of an hour after Woggy and Punch had set out,

Gregory and James left the prison together and walked in company down to the deserted town. There, while Gregory remained on the right bank of the river, James swam across to the left. They then set out to explore their respective sides of the coast.

Working his way through the fringe of jungle, Gregory had gone no more than a quarter of a mile before he came upon a searchlight party. Fortunately, the sound of men talking warned him in time to halt, then go down on his hands and knees and cautiously worm his way forward until he could get a view of the Russians. Near a searchlight on a tripod, four of them were seated round a small fire, quietly smoking and making an occasional remark. Gloomily he noted that the searchlight was in a position to sweep the estuary of the river and that it was well within range of a machine gun which had been set up nearby.

Withdrawing with equal caution, he walked back to the creek up which the canoe house lay. Willy and Frank Robertson had been taking it in turns to accompany the Melanesians, in order to take charge should these simple men run into a Russian on their way to or from their work, or be surprised at it, and Frank was with them that night. From the amount of patching that had been required, Gregory saw that they must have worked hard; but, as with any of the party who went out at night, there were many hours each day when, locked in their separate cells, they could make up for lost sleep.

He was just about to praise them for their work when he caught the sound of distant shots, then the rattle of a sub-machine gun. That could only mean that James had run into trouble. Gregory's heart missed a beat. He had become very fond of the cheerful young Ratu, and the thought that he might now be lying dead in the jungle or on the beach distressed him terribly.

At the same moment Frank exclaimed, 'That shooting must have been at Johnny Olourna! Hope to God they didn't get him.'

Gregory moved quickly towards the entrance of the canoe

172

house. 'I must go and find out. He may have got away but be lying wounded in the bushes and need help.'

'No!' Frank caught him by the arm. 'Don't go yet, George. Maybe he's got away unhurt. If so, in half an hour he'll be back here. If you go after him you can't shout his name or they'll be on to you too, and you may easily miss him. Besides, you're our leader. We're relying on you to get us away from this damned island. 'Twouldn't be fair to the rest of us to risk yourself while there's a chance that Johnny will get back all right.'

Seeing the sense of the argument, Gregory reluctantly agreed. With Frank, he walked along to the big cluster of *bures* on the river bank and, standing in the shadow of one of them, they waited anxiously. For the first time Gregory regretted having backed James in his project of salvaging the gold from the *Reina Maria Amalia*. He had done so in the first place simply as a new interest to relieve his boredom. Then it had developed into an exciting intrigue in which he had found himself up against Lacost and later de Carvalho. But in Noumea, owing to James' passion for Olinda, things had suddenly taken a shockingly bad turn, and already landed them for seven weeks in prison. De Carvalho was probably dead, so James, if caught, was liable to be charged with murder. The Brazilian had said that he did not mean to hurry about exercising his licence to salvage the gold, because he was confident that the French Resident would prevent the Colons from raising it illegally and that, fed up, they would abandon the idea, leaving him a free field. During the interval Lacost might have decided to ignore the Resident and by now have made off with it. Or, if de Carvalho had died and Lacost had learned of it, by this time he might somehow have acquired the licence. So, after all these weeks, the chances of James' securing the treasure seemed extremely slender. Instead, as had so often happened in other cases, it might well be that the pursuit of gold would cost the charming young Ratu his life.

After twenty minutes Frank's keen eyes detected a movement on the far bank of the river. Next moment there was a splash and a glitter of phosphorus in the churned-up water

173

made them feel sure that it was James swimming across. Running forward they helped him up the steep bank. Grinning and unwounded, he panted:

'That was a nasty one. They nearly got me. There is a searchlight party a mile or more away, round the end of the point, covering the next bay. They were dozing and I nearly walked right into them, but I pulled up in time and dashed back into thicker cover.'

'Thank God you're safe!' Gregory exclaimed. 'But they'll know now that either a prisoner has escaped or that someone has landed on the island without their being aware of it; so the hunt will be up.'

James shook the glistening drops of water from his big pouffe of hair. 'No, I don't think so. None of them could have actually seen me, and there are wild pigs on all these islands. As I crashed away through the jungle, I made the loud grunting of a startled old boar.'

'Good for you, Johnny!' cried Frank, slapping James on the back. 'Then we've not been rumbled and can still make our bid for freedom with a good chance of success.'

On their way back to the prison they decided that the three of them, with the addition of Willy, would meet the following night, to agree a detailed plan for their escape.

At one o'clock in the morning the four met at the rendezvous they had selected—a group of tall breadfruit trees a quarter of a mile from the prison. As Willy and Frank occupied adjacent cells, they had, during the day, spent a considerable time discussing the venture. Now Willy spoke for them both:

'Seeing where those searchlights were located last night, getting clear out to sea without being spotted is going to be near impossible. Of course, on leaving the river, we'll head east—that is round the coast to the left of the estuary—so we won't actually have to pass the searchlight party near the village; but the moment we hoist our big sail, it's for sure they'll see us.'

'Then we must not hoist the sail,' Gregory replied. 'About direction you are right. Fortunately, the searchlight party that Johnny ran into is well over a mile away and round the

174

point; so we should be able to work our way along the coast for half a mile or more without attracting their attention. By then darkness will have hidden us from the hoodlums near the village, and. . . .'

'But, George,' Frank interrupted, 'you haven't got Willy's point. That war canoe is a twenty-seater and as heavy as a ton of bricks. It's going to be hellish hard to get her out of the creek to start with. Then it's quite a stretch before we're clear of the river mouth. The six of us could never paddle her as far as you suggest. Without the sail, come dawn the odds are we'd still be inside the reef and a sitting pigeon for those Russian bastards.'

'Well, what do you suggest?'

'Neither Willy nor I think much of the idea, but we might get by if we took in the two Polynesians. Two extra paddles in the canoe could just make the difference.'

Gregory did not like the idea either. The Polynesians had shown by their grins and gestures that they were friendly enough, and James had succeeded in establishing a sketchy form of communication with them, but sufficient only to learn that they were father and son and had come down from Samoa. The reason for their adventurous voyage remained unknown. After a moment Gregory said:

'I'm afraid that's not on. I don't doubt that they would be willing enough to join us, but how could we possibly explain to them about unscrewing the grilles in their cells? And no-one can do it for them. Besides, even if during the next few days Johnny could manage to put them wise, we can't afford the delay. Two nights hence is the darkest phase of the moon. Then will be our best chance and we've got to take it.'

Willy nodded. 'You're right, George, but it's going to be one hell of a gamble.'

'Not too bad,' Gregory smiled. 'We have one thing in our favour. All of us have spent quite a number of hours down at the estuary and none of us has ever yet seen those search-lights turned on to sweep the bay. I am sure they never make use of them unless they see a vessel approaching, and then simply to ensure that no-one manages to get ashore from it unseen. We'll make an early start, though, so as to gain extra

175

time for paddling the canoe as far as we can before we set her sail.'

Previously they had never left their cells before midnight, which doubtless accounted for the fact that none of them had ever run into a Russian when going to and from the river mouth; but on the night of their great adventure they met by the group of breadfruit trees at ten o'clock. There were many more lights in the settlement than they were accustomed to see and music was coming from one of the buildings. As they were surrounded by jungle, that made it almost certain that such amusements as the Russians provided for their troops all took place inside the buildings; but at this hour there was the danger that a few of the troops might be returning from late strolls and that relieved or relieving squads might be moving from or to the beaches, so the six escapers made their way along the jungle path with extra caution.

When they had gone some distance they caught the sound of a faint drumming. The sound rapidly increased and was coming towards them. Hastily they left the track and plunged into the rank vegetation that grew in abundance on both sides of it. They were not a moment too soon. From round the bend ahead there appeared a horseman, and a Russian officer came cantering by. In such surroundings it seemed as though they must have seen an apparition, but Gregory swiftly demolished such a fantasy by saying:

'He has been visiting the outposts. And a jolly sensible way to do it. This track is not wide enough to take a jeep, so why walk or have yourself shaken to bits on a motor-cycle when God gave man the horse? Some of these Russians are not such fools as they look.'

At the canoe house the short lengths of tree-trunk for launching the canoe had been left in a stack on one side. Quickly they placed the first half-dozen in position, then took a grip on the side of the canoe and endeavoured to slide her forward. Hewn out of one great tree-trunk of hard, tropical wood, she seemed as heavy as lead. Their efforts failed to shift her. It was James who said:

'Four of us must get right underneath the bottom and attempt to lift her by taking the weight on our shoulders, while the other two pull on the prow and guide her down.'

They did as he told them. The strain was back-breaking, but their third heave was well timed and they got her moving. Once the fore-part was on the rollers, it needed only their full strength, applied in unison, to get her to the water. As she splashed into it, they stood away, sweating and gasping from their exertions.

Now they had to raise her mast. At its base it was nine inches thick, and tapered up to twenty feet in height. Normally the job would have been done by a dozen men; but, somehow, they managed it and hammered the chocks home to keep the heel firm. Puffing and blowing, they took a five-minute rest.

Having got their wind back, they set about hoisting the yard, an outsize bamboo even longer than the mast on to which the great single triangular sail had already been bent. That done, James stepped into the stern of the canoe and took the steering paddle. The others grouped themselves amidships. James gave the word, they dipped their paddles and the canoe moved forward slightly.

Launching the canoe and getting her ready for sea had taken over an hour; and another three-quarters of an hour slipped by before they got her to the mouth of the river. Long before then Gregory realised how right the Robertson brothers had been. Unless they unfurled the sail, it would be impossible to get the heavy craft far enough out to sea before dawn to escape the Russians' sighting her.

For another hour they laboured on, forcing her gradually up the east coast away from the village; but although the water in the lagoon was relatively calm, owing to the breakers that constantly rolled in, the strain of keeping her heading in the right direction was terrific.

By then it was getting on for half past two in the morning, and their efforts were clearly slackening. When they had set out, not only had it been at the apex of the dark period of the moon, but by good fortune the sky had been cloudy. Since, it had gradually cleared. A million bright stars now

177

faintly lit the scene and Gregory could easily pick out the Southern Cross.

As this increase of light gradually came about, he had become ever more reluctant to risk drawing attention to the canoe by setting her sail. But now he and his companions were clearly near exhaustion and the canoe was barely making steerage way. Grimly he decided that their only hope of getting out of the lagoon before dawn lay in making use of the sail.

When he consulted James and the Robertson brothers they all agreed that unless the risk was taken they would either be recaptured or killed by machine-gun fire; so Gregory told Woggy and Punch to ship their paddles and free the sail from its lashings.

A light breeze at once caught the great spread of *tapa* cloth. James set a course for an opening in the reef and, from having moved at a crawl, the long canoe suddenly leapt forward. As they relaxed, all on board listened with heartfelt delight to the rushing of the water alongside. James tacked once, twice, thrice, then there came a faint shout from the shore.

Within seconds a Sten gun began to stutter. Next minute the searchlight came on, swept to and fro, then fixed them in its beam. A heavy machine gun came into play. The occupants of the canoe ducked down behind her gunwale and crouched there, fearful that any moment would be their last. Bullets thudded into the hull of the canoe and ripped through the sail. But James, courageously plying his steering paddle, swung her round on a new tack. For a brief interval they were out of the line of fire, then the bullets came again, several smacking into the mast. The canoe had heeled right over, spray ran in sheets from the prow and she was now racing at twenty knots for the gap in the reef.

Two minutes later they were through it and shortly afterwards the machine gun ceased its murderous chatter. Sitting up, Gregory cried triumphantly, 'We've done it, chaps! No need to worry any more. They have no boats, so can't pursue us.'

Steered by James, the big canoe rode the seas splendidly.

Having studied the stars for a few moment, he set a course for the Fijis. The Australians would have preferred to make in the other direction—for the Loyalties—but Gregory having enabled them to escape from an indefinite captivity, they good-humouredly accepted his decision. When dawn came Yuloga was only a smudge on the horizon.

For some thirty hours, against a contrary breeze, they beat to eastward. Then a storm blew up. It was far from threatening a hurricane, but the gusts were powerful. Just before ten o'clock, without a moment's warning, disaster overtook them. There came a sudden squall, accompanied by driving rain, and the mast snapped off a few feet above the gunwale. The upper part of the mast, the yard and the great sail heeled over and came down with a splash in the sea. The canoe lurched sideways and came to a stop, tilted over at a dangerous angle.

Frantically, with two axes that had been left in the canoe by the natives, they hacked through the liana cords that held the mast and sail trailing alongside. Ten minutes later they had cut the canoe clear, and she righted herself. But they looked at one another in consternation. They had nothing they could rig as a jury mast and no spare *tapa* to make even a jib mounted on paddles, so were now at the mercy of the ocean.

They were, for the time at least, in no danger from thirst or starvation, as, while the Melanesians were repairing the sail, Willy and Frank had stored several dozen fresh coconuts and hands of bananas in the fore and aft parts of the canoe. But, the wind and tide being against them, they now began to drift rapidly back in a westerly direction.

On examining the stump of the mast, the reason for their calamity became clear. It had been hit by four bullets from the Russians' machine gun, so was weakened to such an extent that, when carrying a big sail, any strong gust of wind would have been enough to snap it off.

For twenty-four hours they were swept back, more or less in the direction of Yuloga, but had fair reason to suppose that they would be carried past it. Then, shortly before midday on the third day after their escape, they sighted a small

179

vessel steaming towards them. As she came nearer, they saw that she was a frigate, flying in her stern the Tricolor.

Gregory and James were both extremely loath to go aboard a French warship, but beggars could not be choosers. Hailed with relief by the others in the canoe, the frigate hove to alongside and took them all aboard.

While the frigate was approaching, Gregory fabricated an account of themselves which they must all adhere to, so as to conceal the danger of the French possibly returning them to Yuloga. It was that he and James had been passengers on the Robertsons' schooner when she had been wrecked, then they had all got ashore on a desert island and found the canoe abandoned there. When they told this story to the Captain of the frigate Gregory and James had good reason to be thankful that while in prison they had retained their aliases—George Simonds and Johnny Olourna—and all the more so when they learned that, having been on a cruise, the frigate was returning to Noumea.

Two days later she put into port. The rescued crew of the canoe were paraded before the Immigration Authorities and duly interrogated. The Robertsons were known there, so they and their crew boys, Woggy and Punch, were passed through, with condolences on the loss of their schooner. Gregory and James were more closely questioned, but their story that they were British subjects from Fiji was accepted.

Greatly relieved, they were about to leave the office when into it walked the brown-faced gendarme belonging to the harbour duty squad, who had bade them *bon soir* shortly before they had stolen the launch. As they were standing side by side he recognised them immediately, and cried:

'I arrest these two men. They are the ones sought in connection with the affair at the Hotel Château Royal.'

11

Out of the Frying Pan into the Fire

It was a shattering blow. They had escaped from Noumea on the night of February 17th and it was now Monday, April 18th. For eight weeks and four days they had been subjected to constant anxiety about their future, and either imprisonment, with its accompanying hardships, or the danger of losing their lives. And all for nothing. Here they were back again where they had started; they might just as well have given themselves up two months earlier. Into Gregory's mind flashed the awful question—Was de Carvalho dead or alive? For if he was dead James would go to the guillotine.

The Robertsons were still standing nearby. Their surprise overcome, loyalty to comrades with whom they had shared great perils came uppermost in their minds. In atrocious French Willy cried belligerently:

'Hi, what's all this? Must be some mistake. Mr. Simonds and Johnny Olourna are as straight as any men I've ever met. They can't be criminals.'

'That's right,' Frank backed him up. 'You're on to the wrong men for sure.'

A white Sergeant had joined the coffee-coloured gendarme. Now he said abruptly, 'I cannot think there is a mistake. My man here saw the fugitives on the dockside under a strong light just before they made their getaway in a launch they stole. Anyhow, I'm taking his word for it. And their names are not Simonds and Olourna but Sallust and Omboloku. This is none of your business, so you had better keep out of it.'

Gregory raised a smile for the brothers. 'He's right about

181

our names. No use denying it. But we haven't done anything to be ashamed of. I'm only sorry that we should have to part like this when we'd been looking forward to celebrating with you.'

'I'm sorry, too.' Willy shook his head. 'Still, if there is anything we can do to help, let us know. We'll be staying at a little pub called the *Maritime* until we can collect the insurance on our schooner and buy another.'

When he had thanked them and the brothers turned away, Gregory, acutely anxious to learn if de Carvalho was alive or dead, asked the Sergeant with what they were to be charged.

The Sergeant, a surly man with a walrus moustache, replied, 'You'll learn that when we get to Headquarters.' Then, tapping his pistol holster significantly, as an indication that he would use his weapon should the prisoners attempt to escape, he told the gendarme to lead them away, and followed a few paces in the rear.

As they walked along the wharf, Gregory was thinking bitterly of the plan that he and James had made soon after the Captain of the frigate had told them they were to be landed at Noumea. They had counted on the hue and cry for them having, after more than two months, long since died down. James was to have taken a room under his assumed name at some small inn and pretended illness so that he could remain there while Gregory used some of his dollars to arrange for them to be smuggled out on a ship leaving for Australia or New Zealand, from either of which they could fly back to Fiji. Even if it took him several days to find a ship he had thought that, provided they did not go into the better part of Noumea, the chances against their being recognised were a hundred to one; yet they had hardly stepped ashore when they had had the extraordinary ill-fortune to come face to face with the one gendarme who could identify them.

At Police Headquarters, despite Gregory's protestations, they were locked into separate cells, still with no charge being made against them; and the suspense of being left in ignorance was well-nigh intolerable. Until he knew the worst they

182

had to face, he was at a loss to formulate a line of policy. He could only take a little comfort from the thought that here in Noumea French law would ensure James a fair trial, and that he himself had the means to employ the best Counsel available to defend his friend.

About himself he was not particularly worried. Although he might be censured for not having prevented James from throwing de Carvalho from the balcony and, as James' partner, be thought to have tacitly condoned the act, it could certainly not be proved that he had inspired the deed or played any active part in it.

He would, of course, be charged with stealing the launch, but, as with so many hazards in life, money counted. Very rich men do not steal launches, although they may, in certain circumstances, borrow them without permission. His defence would be that he had done so, intending to return the launch from Fiji with handsome compensation to her owner for having been temporarily deprived of her. As she had been wrecked, he would, naturally, offer to pay her full value in addition; so he thought it as good as certain that he would be let off with a fine.

James' chances depended, he felt, on the line the prosecution took. If it *was* known that they were partners and had conspired to catch de Carvalho on his own to call him to account for cheating them, matters might go very badly. It would be argued that, having failed to get satisfaction from the Brazilian, with or without Gregory's approval, James had avenged himself by attacking de Carvalho with intent to murder him.

On the other hand, should the truth be accepted—that James was in love with de Carvalho's wife and, on seeing her husband strike her, had temporarily gone berserk—then it could be hoped that the well-known leniency of French courts in cases of *le crime passionel* would be exercised. But to prove that would require Olinda's presence as a witness. And where was she? Whether de Carvalho was dead or alive, having no reason to believe that James would return to Noumea, it seemed very unlikely that she would have remained there for over two months. Even if she could be produced as a witness at the trial, James would be found guilty of murderous assault, so the least he could expect was a sentence of several years.

At length, after nearly three hours of agonising suspense, the prisoners' cells were unlocked and they were conducted to the office of a Police Inspector. They then realised the reason for the delay in charging them. In the office, as well as the Sergeant and the gendarme, was the waiter from the Château Royal whom James had knocked down and whose trolley of food Gregory had looted. Evidently the police had been searching for him to support the gendarme's identification. Delighted at now having the chance to get his own back, the grinning waiter eagerly said his piece.

The prisoners were then charged—James with having assaulted de Carvalho with intent to murder, and with assaulting the waiter; Gregory with having been an accessary before the fact and having stolen food from the Hotel Château Royal; and both of them jointly with having stolen the launch of one Mathieu Serieu.

With *intent* to murder was, for both James and Gregory, the salient point in the indictment. Evidently de Carvalho was not dead. With a gasp of relief James exclaimed, 'Monsieur de Carvalho! He is alive! How seriously was he injured? Where is he now?'

'He was in hospital for some time, then he rejoined his wife at the Château Royal and spent a month or more there, convalescing,' replied the Inspector. 'Where he is now I have no idea. He and his wife left Noumea in their yacht about ten days ago.'

That Olinda could not be called to give evidence was a pity, but that was far outweighed by the fact that de Carvalho had survived. With a smile Gregory asked the Inspector if they might have legal aid for their defence.

'Certainly, Monsieur,' the Inspector nodded. 'Do you know of a good *avocat* here in Noumea, or would you like me to recommend one?'

'I would prefer it,' said Gregory quietly, 'if you would be good enough to provide me with pen and paper, so that I can write a line to General Ribaud and ask his advice. It so happens that he is a very old friend of mine.'

Gregory had long since learned that, while name-dropping without cause is regarded as a social gaffe, there are times when it can achieve most valuable results. Such was the present. Perceptibly, a new note of respect crept into the Inspector's voice. Of course he would oblige with writing materials, and if there were any other requests Monsieur Sallust cared to make they would receive due consideration. He even smiled and added that, the beds in the cells not being so comfortable as those in the Château Royal, extra pillows might be acceptable, and that if the prisoners cared to pay, no objection would be made to their sending out for wine to drink with their evening meal.

Back in his cell, Gregory felt very much happier about the situation. De Carvalho, praise be to the gods, was still alive and now clearly in no danger of dying as a result of his injuries. But James was still facing a charge of attempted murder. The mention of Ribaud had nullified any possibility of police hostility; but meant no more than that, while in prison, he and James would enjoy certain small comforts that they might otherwise have been denied. The real nub of the matter was, could Ribaud in some way be manœuvred into secretly influencing the court in James' favour?

That a Governor General was in a position to do so the cynical Gregory had no doubt at all. There were, of course, limits to which any high official of a non-totalitarian State could go; and in a democracy no upright judge would have acceded to a request to set free a man proved guilty of murder. But if he could be convinced that political expediency required that he should turn a blind eye to some lesser crime he might feel that it was his patriotic duty to do so.

Gregory had no illusions that out of friendship for him Ribaud would agree to procure a verdict in James' favour. In some way pressure had to be brought to bear upon him. The question arose: how could that be done?

For the moment he contented himself with writing a letter to Ribaud, simply saying that the General had perhaps been informed that he and the Ratu James Omboloku had re-

185

turned to Noumea, been arrested and were now in prison; but during their absence they had obtained some information which might prove of considerable value. He then requested a private interview with the General so that he might discuss the matter with him.

The following day, late in the afternoon, Gregory was taken to the Residence. Ribaud received him in his office, told his escort to wait outside, invited Gregory to sit down, then offered him a cigarette and said:

'*Mon ami*, I was much distressed to learn of the situation in which you find yourself.'

Gregory smiled. '*Mon Général*, I thank you for your concern for me. But I am not particularly worried about myself. I had intended to return Monsieur Serieu's launch to him with a handsome sum as compensation for having borrowed her. As she was wrecked that is now impossible, but I am in a position to offer him so large a sum for her loss that I feel confident he will agree not to prosecute.'

Making a little grimace, Ribaud remarked, 'I would that I were rich enough to think nothing of parting with a year's pay, for that is about what such a transaction would cost me.'

Into Gregory's mind there flashed the thought that this might be an indication that his friend was open to the offer of a heavy bribe. Knowing that the French Government was by no means lavish in the payment of their officials, the idea had already occurred to him; but, believing Ribaud to be a man of integrity, he had dismissed it, on the grounds that if such an offer was taken as an insult, the results could prove disastrous. Meanwhile the General was continuing:

'One can hardly suppose that Serieu will be such a fool as not to accept. But stealing a launch is only a minor matter and, no doubt, with a few hundred francs you can also pay off the waiter whom the Ratu assaulted. There still remains the more serious charge of being an accessary before the fact to attempted murder.'

'True. But that I can refute by proving that I am not guilty.'

'When de Carvalho was sufficiently recovered he made a statement to the effect that he had got the better of you and

186

the Ratu in a business deal, and that the two of you surprised him in his room, with the deliberate intention of revenging yourselves upon him.'

'That is only partially true. We went there to remonstrate with him, but with no thought at all of doing him an injury. By the by, I have not yet heard what injuries he did sustain.'

'You were very lucky, for his neck might well have been broken. As it was his fall was slightly checked by his crashing through the branches of an oleander bush before he hit the ground. He broke an arm and two ribs, and hit his head on a stone, which rendered him unconscious. After a fortnight in hospital he was over the worst, then he stayed on here convalescing until about ten days ago.'

'I see. And did his wife, the Senhora Olinda, make any statement?'

'No. Had you and the Ratu been caught, she would naturally have been called as a witness at your trial. But as you had both escaped, there seemed no point in bringing her into the matter.

'Well, she is the key to the whole business. Having reproached de Carvalho for double-crossing us, we disclosed to her that her husband was a crook. She took our part and abused him, then he lost his temper and smacked her face. It so happens that young James is desperately in love with her. As you can well imagine, he saw red. Before I had a chance to stop him he had picked up de Carvalho and chucked him over the balcony.'

'Do you swear to the truth of this?'

'Yes, and the Ratu will, of course, take full blame for his act.'

'In view of the grudge you both held against de Carvalho, the court may not believe you. They may also take the view that the Ratu, knowing that he will be found guilty in any case, stands to lose nothing by protecting you and taking the whole blame upon himself.'

'Mon cher Général,' Gregory spread out his hands, 'I pray you, consider the matter in the light of your knowledge of me. Had I decided to beat up someone against whom I had a grudge, let alone murder him, am I the sort of man who would go about it in such a fashion? Having, by the exercise of extreme caution, come through innumerable dangerous situations during six years of war, is it likely that I should revenge myself on an enemy in such a way that I could not possibly escape having the crime laid at the feet of myself and my friend?'

'No; you have something there. Of course such an idea is absurd.'

'Besides, if need be I shall demand to be let out on bail until the Senhora Olinda can be found and brought back here, or a sworn statement taken from her. As a key witness for the defence, the court could not refuse to secure her testimony, and I have no doubt at all that she will exonerate me.'

Ribaud nodded. 'You are right. But it may not be necessary. If I go into court myself and give evidence that, in view of my personal knowledge of your past, it is inconceivable to me that you would have committed such a clumsy crime, I don't doubt that it will be accepted.'

Gregory gave a little bow. 'That is most kind and I should be deeply grateful to you.'

'Not at all. I think, then, we may regard you as good as cleared. But there remains the Ratu. After what you have told me I am sorry for the young man, but even your ingenuity will, I fear, prove insufficient to save him from a heavy prison sentence.'

For a moment Gregory was silent, then he said, '*Mon Général,* you will recall that in the note I sent you I mentioned that, during our absence from Noumea, James and I had chanced upon certain information of value that I wished to discuss with you.'

Ribaud's arched eyebrows lifted, wrinkling his forehead. 'I took that only as a pretext to secure this private conversation with me.'

'By no means. I have not yet disclosed to anyone the name of the island on which the launch was wrecked—it was Yuloga.'

In the silence that followed one could have heard a pin drop. The General remained poker-faced, but a hard note

188

had crept into his voice when, at length, he said, 'I see. Well, what of it?'

'Only that previously I had been under the impression that it belonged to France.'

'It does. it is a dependency of New Caledonia, and comes under my jurisdiction.'

'How strange, then, that it should now be garrisoned by Russian troops.'

The General frowned. 'In that you are mistaken. There are, of course, a number of Russians there—technicians who, under an agreement made by General de Gaulle in Moscow, are assisting us with the development of our nuclear weapons.'

Gregory shook his head. *'Mon cher Général*, it is clear to me that you have been misinformed. Ratu James and myself spent two months illegally detained as prisoners on the island. The story of how we, with two Australians and two Melanesian natives, succeeded in escaping is quite an entertaining one. I must tell it to you some time, over a good dinner. But preparing our escape took many nights. During that time we explored a good part of the island. We discovered that the native population had been evacuated—no doubt for security reasons—that there were at the least a thousand Russian troops stationed there and—er—I did see one French Captain. Most interesting of all, one night I looked down into a valley where several I.C.B.M.s had already been set up, ready for launching—and they were guarded by Russian sentries.'

Ribaud's frown had become a threatening scowl as he demanded, 'What are you trying to tell me?'

'Only that I have formed the impression that, in exchange for valuable information about the construction of nuclear weapons, General de Gaulle has, in effect, made over the island of Yuloga to the Russians, so the Soviet Union now has a base of incalculable value in the South Pacific.'

'That is not so,' the General declared stoutly. 'You can have seen only a part of the island. I have ample troops there and it is still under French control. General de Gaulle would never surrender French territory to a foreign Power, and the warheads to those rockets are in French hands.'

189

Matters were not going quite as Gregory had hoped. His private belief was that Ribaud was lying, but he replied suavely, 'Naturally, *mon ami*, I accept your word for that, but you must forgive me if I incline to doubt whether others would do so.'

'You intend to inform others, then, of what you saw while on Yuloga?'

'I admit to having considered doing so.'

'Such a disclosure, if wrongly interpreted, could prove highly embarrassing to France. I may feel it my duty to take certain steps.'

'I appreciate that. But however high you rate the security of this tie-up with the Russians, I hardly think you would go to the length of having me shot.'

'No; no! God forbid! But as you have obtained knowledge of a military secret of the first importance, I could treat you as a spy and have you clapped into a fortress.'

'You could,' Gregory smiled, 'but for how long could you keep me there? You know well that I make no idle boast when I say that I have escaped from captivity a dozen times. If you did put me to such inconvenience you may be certain that I would blow the gaff immediately I got out. Whereas. . . .'

'Whereas what?'

'Well, I have given much thought to the situation. Were I in the employ of the British Government it would obviously be my duty to report what I know. But, as a private citizen, it is a matter between myself and my conscience. Having weighed the pros and cons, I have come to the conclusion that the Russians possessing a base in the South Pacific—or perhaps I should say being established in one—with intercontinental ballistic missiles, is no danger to Britain. If they wished they could menace Britain from much nearer home. Of course, it brings them within easy range of Australia and New Zealand; but Australia has her own rocket range, so could give as good or probably better than she got. However, the salient point is that there is little likelihood of the Soviet Union and the British Commonwealth going to war in the foreseeable future.'

190

'I concur in that,' said the General, looking slightly less antagonistic. 'And, that being the case, the information you have obtained would not cause great resentment in London.'

'No, probably not. But it would in Washington. The Americans still regard Russia as very much a potential enemy. At the idea of France's having given the Russians a rocket base—I am sorry, I meant receiving visiting troops—in the South Pacific, the roof would blow straight off the White House. And the United States being Britain's ally, I have to consider whether I can really justify keeping this information to myself.'

Ribaud glared, then grunted. 'What's your price?'

'*Cher ami*!' Gregory raised his eyebrows in pretended surprise. 'I fail to understand you. We are simply discussing the dictates of my conscience. As I was about to say, when I had the pleasure of dining with you some nine weeks ago I expressed the opinion that the Power really to be dreaded by the Western world was China, and that our only hope of definitely containing this huge and dangerous Asiatic people lay in an alliance between the United States, Europe and the Soviet Union.

'Should this come about and a war with China be forced on the Western Allies, what could be more fortunate than that the Soviet Union should not only have rocket bases in Manchuria, to the north of China, but also to the south—in the Southern Pacific. In the past the State Department in Washington has not distinguished itself by its foresight. Clinging to the doctrines of the French Revolution, which were so acceptable in the United States when they were born, they are still obsessed by the idea that every people is entitled to self-rule. So blind are they that men like Foster Dulles did their utmost to undermine the power of their most reliable ally, the British Empire. During the years following the war Britain, financially, stood naked in the breeze. Without the support of the almighty dollar we could not have carried on. Dulles, and others of his kind, used that to force us to give independence to many of our subject peoples who were totally incapable of governing themselves. Only now, when it is too late, are they regretting their stupidity. Since the

Americans were incapable of foreseeing that their policy would lead to the loss of a million lives in India alone, and to anarchy, or the setting up of police States, in Africa, I cannot believe that they will appreciate the possible long-term value of the Russians being given facilities in the South Pacific. But you and I, *mon ami*, come of older nations more experienced in statescraft. It is on these grounds that I have decided that it would be a great mistake to let the Americans know anything about what goes on in Yuloga.'

Ribaud mopped his forehead with a handkerchief. 'I follow your reasoning, and it is sound, but I'm damned if I know what you are driving at.'

'Surely it is obvious that, having squared matters with my conscience, my wish is to assist you in maintaining security concerning this operation?'

'I appreciate that. And by agreeing not to disseminate this information you take a great load off my shoulders. I am most grateful to you.'

'Ah.' Gregory gave a sigh. 'But, alas, the matter does not end there. I was only one of six people who were imprisoned on Yuloga and escaped from there.'

Again anxiety showed in Ribaud's eyes. 'You mean those two Australian may give everything away?'

'Not everything. They will no doubt tell their friends that there are Russian troops on Yuloga and that they were held prisoner by them, but they did not see the I.C.B.M.s and they have no idea that the Russians have set up rockets there which could be blasted off at any moment. That is the really important thing. And, of course, the same applies to the two Melanesians. However, there remains James. After all, he is my friend and was my trusted companion throughout this unhappy experience. You can hardly blame me for having told him everything that I discovered during my midnight explorations.'

'Can you persuade him to keep his mouth shut?'

Gregory shrugged. 'It is not a question of whether I can or can't. When he is brought to trial, our having stolen the launch and what happened to us afterwards is bound to emerge. He will be under oath to tell the truth. You cannot

192

expect me to ask him to perjure himself. I hope that I have made plain the situation.'

'*Mon Dieu*, you have!' Ribaud snarled. 'You damn' clever devil! Now we know where we are. You have come here to blackmail me. If the Ratu is sent for trial, security is to be blown wide open. We'll have those damn' Yanks creating hell, and it may lead to an international incident.'

'Now, now, *mon vieux*,' Gregory laughed, 'do not be so irate about it. I am only doing my best to protect my friend, and you would do the same in similar circumstances. The Brazilian deserved all he got and was lucky to get off so lightly. To imprison the Ratu for several years can do France no earthly good. To bring him to trial could result in God knows what trouble; as a small incident in which you would probably lose your job for having failed to see the wisdom of blanketing the whole business.'

'What, then, do you suggest?'

'That you should send for your Chief of Police, tell him that this is a matter of high policy, have him arrange that James and I should escape, then have us flown to his island of Tujoa.'

Suddenly Ribaud's attitude changed and he smiled. 'You old villain. You have got the better of me. But your reasoning is sound. On the greater issue it is the best course to pursue. Very well, it shall be done.'

Gregory smiled back. 'Thanks. And I am sure you will admit one thing. I have made no attempt to bribe you.'

'No. And I am glad you did not, for I would have greatly resented it.'

'I thought as much. But now that we have settled matters I should like to ask you a favour.'

'What is it?'

'When we dined together you told me that you were due to retire next year. And I gather that you are not very well off. I, on the other hand, am very rich. I would like to have the address of your bank in Paris, so that I may pay into it a sum equal to that which I shall have to pay Serieu for his launch. It would at least buy you a magnificent automobile.

193

This, you understand, is just a friendly gesture from one *ancien de la guerre* to another.'

Ribaud beamed. '*Mon vieux, mon vieux,* this is true generosity. If you wish it, you and the Ratu shall have an aircraft apiece in which to be flown out.'

'Thanks,' Gregory waved a hand in cheerful protest, 'but one will be enough. What I do need, though, is a good lawyer to negotiate a settlement with Monsieur Serieu for the loss of his launch, and to arrange compensation for the waiter. I have ample funds in the United States, but I shall need my cheque book on that account.'

'The police will have taken charge of all the items that you and the young Ratu left in your hotels, so at the proper time the cheque book can be given to you. For the other things you will have to wait, since we must proceed with great caution in this matter. Even Governors General cannot obstruct the course of justice with impunity and your escape will be by no means easy to arrange.'

'That I appreciate, and if it will make things easier for you the Ratu and I must put up with spending a week or two in prison.'

'No, a day or two should suffice. Tomorrow you will be brought before a magistrate. You will, of course, reserve your defence. I will instruct my lawyer, Maître Dufour, to appear for you. Afterwards you will ask him to visit you in your cell and brief him about Serieu and the waiter. Then somehow we must get you out as soon as possible; otherwise there would be a risk of your being brought to trial, and that must be avoided at all costs.'

'Do you think that our escape will cause a great stir?'

'It would if de Carvalho were still here. He would be certain to raise a stink, but fortunately he will not learn for weeks, if ever, that you returned here and were arrested. Luckily, I can trust our *Chef de Police* and my *Commandant de l'Air* to co-operate with me when I have explained that this must be done to avoid an international incident. But subordinates will be needed, and I can only pray that they will choose their men wisely. Should one of them betray us, we shall all be in the soup.'

194

'I appreciate the risk you are running for us,' Gregory said gravely, 'but there is one way in which I can show my gratitude. Should we be betrayed and the escape fail, there will then be no avoiding the Ratu's being brought to trial. On his behalf I give you my word that if there is a trial neither of us will mention that we know there to be I.C.B.M.s under Russian control on Yuloga.'

Ribaud nodded. 'That is generous of you. And now, much as I should like to offer you a glass of wine, I must refrain. It would not do for your escort waiting in the corridor to get the idea that we have been fraternising.'

'I agree. Now that we have settled everything, it remains only for you to give me the address of your bank in Paris, then I am ready to be taken back to prison.'

The General gave it then, as Gregory repeated it three times, stood up. The two old friends shook hands. Ribaud sat down again and struck a bell on his desk. When the escort entered the room he gruffly dismissed the prisoner and half an hour later Gregory was back in his cell.

On the Wednesday morning he and James were brought before a magistrate. They had not seen one another since they had been charged, and the young Ratu looked greatly depressed; but Gregory found a chance to whisper to him:

'These proceedings will be only a formality. Plead not guilty and say nothing else whatever. You must refuse to talk, too, should a *Juge d'Instruction* visit you later in your cell to prepare a case for the Prosecution. Leave everything to me and don't worry too much. I think I have found a way to get you off.'

James gave him a grateful glance and followed his instructions. At the court they were met by Maître Dufour. The *avocat* was a tall, grey-haired man wearing old-fashioned pince-nez. In a private room Gregory gave him particulars of the situation; then offered him a handsome fee to take their case, and he smilingly agreed. The proceedings in court took only a few minutes; after which the prisoners were taken back to Police Headquarters. That afternoon Gregory was led from his cell to a sparsely-furnished room in which

Maître Dufour was waiting to interview him. With him, the lawyer brought Gregory's cheque book.

Having dealt with the claims of Serieu and the waiter, Gregory said that James would ask for the case to be treated as a *crime passionel*. Dufour then said he would like to have James' own account of the affair, but Gregory fobbed him off by saying that it would be preferable to leave that for a few days until the Ratu was in better shape, as, at the moment, the thought of his impending fate had caused his mind to become temporarily disturbed.

Later that afternoon a *Juge d'Instruction* questioned both of them. Gregory again gave the true story, but James, as instructed, refused to talk. Back in his cell, Gregory could now only wait and hope that Ribaud would succeed in arranging their escape without compromising himself, and that they would get away safely.

At ten o'clock that night an Inspector whom Gregory had not previously seen came to his cell and said abruptly, 'Now that you have been committed to trial, in accordance with usual practice, we are transferring you from this headquarters to the prison. Come along now.'

In an outer office Gregory found James, already handcuffed to one gendarme. He was handcuffed to another, then the Inspector led the way out to a large car. The gendarmes and their prisoners got into the back, the Inspector took his seat beside the driver, and the car moved off.

They had covered about a mile and were passing through a slum quarter when a lorry emerged without warning from a side turning. Their driver sounded his klaxon, then gave a shout. Next moment the police car hit the lorry amidships and, with a grinding crash, came to a halt. This, Gregory instantly realised, was it.

Even before the gendarme to whom he was handcuffed had said in a swift whisper, 'Out you get and pull me after you,' he had his free hand on the handle of the door. Turning his head, he shouted to James, 'Get out. Pick up your man and carry him if necessary. Then follow me.'

Pandemonium followed. The lorry driver, the Inspector and his men were all shouting. Gregory was no sooner in the road with his gendarme staggering after him than the man said, 'Quick; down that alley opposite.'

Gregory dived into it, dragging the gendarme, who put up only a token resistance, after him. James was hard on their heels, the gendarme to whom he was handcuffed slung over his shoulder. The Inspector had jumped from the car and drawn his pistol. Had the escape been unplanned, he might well have hesitated before firing at the fugitives, for fear of hitting one of his men. To the few onlookers who were about, he appeared to chance that, but actually sent three bullets swishing over their heads.

The end of the alley was crossed by another. 'Turn right, then left,' gasped the man Gregory was dragging along. It was dark there and as they pulled up, the gendarme said with a laugh, 'You boys in the Deuxième Bureau certainly lead exciting lives.'

'So that's who old Ribaud has said we are,' Gregory thought gleefully. 'Damned clever of him.' By then his companion had got from his pocket the key of the handcuffs. As he unlocked himself from Gregory, he said, 'You and your big friend are supposed to have knocked us out. Run on for a hundred yards and you'll find a car—a blue Citroën. It will take you where you are to go.'

Having said that, he knocked his forehead against a nearby wall, so that the skin was torn and began to bleed a little, then lowered himself to the ground. James, meanwhile, had set down his gendarme and had his handcuffs unlocked. After a hasty word of thanks to the men who had helped them escape, they ran side by side down the alley. At its end they found the Citroën. A man in plain clothes was sitting at the wheel. As they came pounding up, he threw open the rear door. They scrambled in and Gregory slammed the door behind him. Without a word the driver let in the clutch. Still maintaining silence, he twisted his way through several short, mean streets, then, by way of a long, straggling suburb, to the low land behind the town.

By then the moon had risen and by its light there could be seen a row of low hangars and a building surmounted by a squat tower. It was the Magenta airport. The driver did not

197

take them to the office but pulled up a hundred yards short of it. Putting his finger to his lips to enjoin continued silence, he got out and led them across the grass to the end of the line of hangars, signed to them to go round to the front, whispered *'Bonne chance'*, then turned and hurried back to his car.

Walking cautiously round the corner, they saw that a small aircraft was standing in front of one of the hangars. Beside it there were two men quietly talking. On seeing Gregory and James they stopped and waved a greeting. One was dressed in pilot's kit, the other was an Army officer.

'Messieurs,' said the officer, whom Gregory now saw to be a Major, 'you will appreciate that the fewer people who see you leave, the better. Be pleased to go aboard before I summon the ground staff.'

The plane was a four-seater reconnaissance aircraft. As James and Gregory settled themselves in the rear seats, the latter asked, 'What about our baggage. Is it here?'

The Major shook his head. 'No. Were you expecting it to be? If so, I am sorry; but I was told nothing of this. And we cannot delay. You must leave without it.'

Gregory was annoyed, as to land in Tujoa without his passport, his clothes and other belongings, was going to cause him considerable inconvenience. But he felt that in all other respects, Ribaud had planned their get-away so efficiently that he could not be greatly blamed for this one oversight.

The Major blew a whistle, then got in beside the pilot. Vaguely-seen figures of ground crew moved round the aircraft, the propellers began to turn, she glided down the runway, halted while the engines revved up, then took off.

The tension in case some hitch occurred to prevent their escape had been so considerable that neither of the passengers felt like sleep, and for Gregory the flight proved a fascinating one. Since the war, nearly all his air travel had been in jets, flying at a height of many thousand feet, whereas the small prop plane was travelling at an altitude of only about two thousand.

As the nearly full moon gradually mounted higher in the sky, he could see the scene below quite clearly. Rarely for

198

long were they out of sight of one of the innumerable islands
that in the South Pacific seem almost as numerous as the stars
overhead. The majority were no more than atolls set in a
blue-black sea that, here and there, broke in white foam on
these coral strands. But when they passed over some of the
larger islands in the Loyalty Group, mountains, rivers and
little clusters of white buildings could be made out.

After an hour or so he began to tire of sitting at an angle
peering down, and his thoughts turned to speculation on the
situation they would find in Tujoa. Lacost and his friends
had had two clear months in which to work. It seemed as
good as certain that their salvaging apparatus would have
reached the island many weeks ago. But they had no licence,
so it seemed probable that the French Resident on Tujoa
would have prevented them from starting operations. Would
Lacost have ignored the ban and endeavoured to salvage the
treasure clandestinely on moonlit nights or, as de Carvalho
apparently thought he would, got fed up and thrown in his
hand?

And de Carvalho? Having sailed from Noumea ten days
previously, he could have been in Fiji for the past week. Was
he idling his time away in Suva or had he decided that the
time had come to go to Tujoa and find out how the land lay
there?

Thinking of Fiji brought Gregory's thoughts to Manon.
What would she be doing now? The story of James' attack
on de Carvalho would for certain have been reported in the
New Caledonian papers, and their escape afterwards. As
James was a Ratu and the hereditary High Chief of the
Nakapoa Group, it was a news item that would have been
printed in the *Fij Times*, so Manon must have learned of it.
But, as they had taken to sea in a small launch and she had
heard nothing from him for over two months, the odds were
that she would assume James and himself to have been
drowned.

Cynically, Gregory decided that by this time she would be
consoling herself with another lover. The thought did not distress him, because he had never loved her. Love for him
meant Erika, and only Erika. Other *affaires* were just fun, to

199

be enjoyed as long as his virility remained. And Manon had been fun: a superb bedfellow, instinctively capable of providing as many amorous delights as if she had been a star pupil in a brothel and, to boot, a highly intelligent companion. In his mind's eye he could see her now: no true beauty, owing to her receding chin, overlarge mouth and sallow skin; but the skin of her body was satin to the touch, her figure that of a dryad, her commonsense refreshing and her laughter infectious. He decided that, as soon as the situation on Tujoa was cleared up, he would return to Fiji and seek her out. He felt fairly confident that if she had taken another lover he would find a way to induce her to give him up and again become his mistress. To spend further nights with her would be well worth taking quite a lot of trouble.

The aircraft droned on. James was dozing and so was the Major. Gregory decided that he now would also take a nap. As he settled back, he became conscious that the plane had started to come down. Sitting up again, he looked out of the window. They were near quite a big island. The moonlight threw up its mountains and cast deep shadows in its valleys. But there was one broad, open space almost immediately below them. As Gregory stared out, he could hardly believe his eyes. There were buildings down there clustered round a dozen huge rockets.

The truth flashed upon him. Ribaud had proved cleverer than himself. To make certain of keeping France's dangerous secret he had double-crossed them and sent them back to Yuloga.

Land Safely or Die

From having been half asleep, Gregory's brain instantly began to turn over as fast as a dynamo. He could not altogether blame Ribaud for having done this to him. The General's first duty lay not to an old friend, whatever trouble he might be in, but to France. Had Gregory been responsible for keeping a British secret of equal importance he felt he would have done the same. Short of having him and James shot, this was the only way in which Ribaud could make absolutely certain of ensuring their silence. That Gregory might have escaped from a fortress in New Caledonia he had accepted, but to escape from the Russians on Yuloga was a very different matter. As he had done so once, they would make certain that he was given no chance to do so a second time. And the first time had been difficult enough.

There flashed through Gregory's mind the many nights which they had spent laboriously working with the steel half-shoe-heel on the screws that held in place the gratings of their cells, the scores of hours spent cautiously exploring the island, the nerve-racking delay while the Melanesians repaired the sail of the big canoe, then the desperate risk they had taken of being shot to pieces before they cleared the reef and reached the open sea.

By now those gratings would have been made permanent fixtures and there would be surprise visits by the guards to the prisoners' cells, some time each night. Gone for good was any chance of carrying out midnight reconnaissances and, even if one could, there would be little point in them, for it was quite certain that the Russians would have scoured the island for any other abandoned canoes and would have destroyed them. All this made the possibilty of another escape about as remote as had been the chances of getting away from Devil's Island in the Victorian era.

The future, then, held the awful prospect of imprisonment for an indefinite period—certainly for many months, perhaps for several years—with no hope of a reduction of sentence or reprieve. Perhaps even worse. On finding that no fewer than six of their prisoners had escaped and got clean away from the island, the Russians must have been furious. Now that two of those escapers were being returned to them they might well take strong measures.

Gregory suddenly had an awful vision of himself and James tied to stakes in the courtyard of the prison while a firing squad lined up to shoot them—just as an example to the other prisoners of what might happen to them should they give any trouble. The Russians were a law unto themselves. No-one could call them to account for such an execution or, the odds were, would even hear about it. If Ribaud chanced to do so he would probably consider Gregory fortunate not to have met such a fate much earlier in life, drink an extra glass of cognac after dinner to the memory of an ace secret agent, then forget the incident.

All these thoughts rushed through Gregory's mind in a matter of seconds. Looking down again, he saw that they had passed over the rocket-launching site and that the aircraft was slowly circling to come down in another valley in which rows of lights showed there to be an airstrip. The fact that they were on was a clear indication that Ribaud had sent a signal to the Russian Commandant, telling him to expect the aircraft.

Gregory knew that there was only one thing for it. James, beside him, and the Major, in front of him, were still dozing. With his right elbow he gave James a fierce dig in the ribs. Throwing himself forward he flung his left arm round the Major's neck and jerked his head violently backwards. At the same moment his right hand descended on the pistol holster at the officer's side, wrenched it open and grasped the weapon.

Within seconds of Gregory's first move, entirely unaware of what he was about to do, the pilot cried, 'We'll be landing in a few minutes. Fasten your safety belts.'

At the unexpected sound of threshing limbs beside him, he turned. By then Gregory had pulled the pistol from the holster, struck the Major a sharp blow on the side of the head with the butt and had the weapon pointing at the pilot.

'Up!' he snapped. 'Up, or I'll put a bullet through your head! We are not landing, and if you won't fly this plane I will.'

The aircraft was down to a thousand feet. The pilot, his eyes staring, did as he was bade and pulled back his joystick, but at so sharp an angle that the aircraft shot up as though about to loop the loop. The manœuvre came near to giving back the mastery of the situation to Ribaud's men. Gregory and James, who had half risen, were flung violently back into their seats, and the gun was jerked from Gregory's hand. But, as he had already knocked the Major unconscious, the odds remained two to one against the pilot.

Grimly endeavouring the carry out his mission, the pilot brought the aircraft down again in a steep dive.

'Half choke him!' Gregory cried urgently, and as he stooped to grope about the floor for the pistol, James's great hands closed round the pilot's neck from behind. As the pressure increased, he let go of the controls and began to claw frantically at James's fingers. Still the aircraft descended.

At that angle Gregory could see ahead out of the forward window. The plane was plunging straight to earth. The flares on the runway seemed to be leaping up to meet them. Forcing his head and shoulders between the unconscious Major and the pilot, he grabbed the joystick and pulled it back. The aircraft shot up again at such a steep angle that he feared it must stall. But it was now flying at an altitude of no more than five hundred feet. Then, to his horror, he saw that it was hurtling direct at a rocky peak that rose up from the centre of the island.

By then the pilot, half strangled, had had enough. His eyes starting from his head, he stopped clawing ineffectually at

203

James' hands and let his own fall, then rammed down his left foot on the rudder bar. The plane banked steeply.

At that moment the stunned Major came round. Unaware of the acute danger, he gave a groan, turned sideways in his seat and grabbed Gregory by the shoulders, wrenching him away from the controls. James let go of the pilot's neck to come to Gregory's assistance. The back of his fist smashed into the side of the Major's face. With another groan, he fell back in his seat. The pilot gasped in breath, then, panting wildly, seized the joystick. The plane zoomed up. It was touch and go. They missed the side of the rocky peak by no more than twenty feet.

Seeing that for the moment disaster had been averted and that the pilot had come to heel, Gregory again groped on the floor until his hand closed on the pistol. Picking it up, he jabbed the barrel into the pilot's ribs and snarled, 'Now, damn you! Do as I tell you or I'll put a bullet through your guts. Take her up to two thousand and head due east.'

The man had no more fight left in him. Rapidly the aircraft gained height, banked again and came round on the given course. A few minutes later the island of Yuloga was fading away into the night behind them.

Blood was trickling from the side of the Major's mouth where James had struck him. His *kepi* had fallen off and he was sitting hunched up with his head lolling forward, but his eyes were open, showing that he was still conscious. To make certain that he would give no further trouble, Gregory handed the pistol to James, then, with his left hand, grabbed the man by the hair, pulling his head back, and with his right undid his tie. Thrusting him forward again he pulled his arms behind his back and used the tie to secure his wrists firmly together.

Turning to the pilot, Gregory said, 'You will now fly us to Tujoa.'

'Fly her yourself,' the man replied truculently. 'I'm not going to risk facing a court martial for having helped two dangerous criminals to escape from justice.'

Gregory had many times parachuted from an aircraft and knew a considerable amount about them, but; in spite of

204

what he had implied when first threatening the pilot, he was not a trained airman; so he snapped back, 'I could fly her, but I'd probably crash her on landing. Like it or not, unless you want to risk being burned to a cinder, you'll do the job for us. You've got your orders and you'll bring us down at Tujoa.'

The pilot gave a harsh laugh. 'Like hell I will! I haven't enough petrol to get her half that distance.'

'You're lying. Tujoa is quite a bit closer to Yuloga than Yuloga is to Noumea, and you would have had to make the return hop.'

'That's so, but I would have taken on fuel at Yuloga.'

Gregory swore under his breath. The petrol gauge told him nothing, because he did not know if the pilot was already using the reserve tank or if it was still full. He might be bluffing. On the other hand, if he was telling the truth this was a really nasty one.

After a moment's thought Gregory said, 'The ocean in these parts is peppered with small islands. You are to keep going for Tujoa as long as you can. If you do find the petrol getting low you are to bring us down on the nearest island. But I'd like you to be clear about one thing. Should you do that and when we have landed I find that there is more than one gallon of petrol in the tank I'll blow your brains out.'

'If you'd ever tried to land an aircarft on a coral atoll you'd not be such a fool as to ask me to,' the pilot replied in a surly voice. 'She'd rip her bottom to pieces and we'd end up like strawberry jam.'

'Then bring her down in a lagoon, or near enough for us to swim ashore.'

'You're crazy. Force me to do that and we'll either drown or the sharks will get us. I know you'll be clapped into jail if we land at Yuloga, but surely that's better than killing yourself and us as well? For God's sake let me turn back to Yuloga.'

It was a terrible decision to have to take; but knowing the Russians were not given to showing mercy to escaped prisoners who were recaptured, Gregory thought it more likely that if he and James did land at Yuloga they would be shot out of hand. Again he remained silent for a few moments, then he said:

'No I prefer to risk the sharks and a chance of freedom to the certainty of prison and the possibility of having to face a firing squad. Just let me know when the petrol looks like running out and I'll tell you what to do. Given a little luck we may be near a fair-sized island with a beach that we could land on.'

His decision was followed by a period of agonising suspense. Now and then they flew within sight of islands, but they were further apart than Gregory had expected, and nearly all were composed of cruel coral reefs, against which the surf was breaking in great swathes of white foam. Only two were large enough to have risked a landing, but even on them groups of palm trees would have made an attempt to land highly dangerous. Leaning forward across the semi-conscious Major, Gregory kept his eyes fixed on the petrol gauge with steadily mounting anxiety.

After twenty minutes it showed the tank to be nearly empty. As another patch of white waves crashing on land came into sight ahead, he grimly made up his mind that they must now risk their necks by coming down in it. Gruffly he said to the pilot:

'Down you go. I'm sorry that I've let you in for this. But if you can manage to save our necks and we can get back to civilisation you'll not regret it. As I happen to be a rich man, I'll give you a year's pay. Now, circle that island, then do your best for us all.'

The pilot gave a harsh laugh. 'Thanks for the offer, but you'd never live to pay up or I to receive the money. We're not going down. You win, damn you!'

As he spoke, he leaned forward and pressed a switch. The needle of the petrol gauge began to lift. The reserve tank had been full and he had switched it on.

James gave a great sigh and laid a hand on Gregory's back. 'That was the worst twenty minutes I've ever lived through. But thank God you called his bluff. After the way we made fools of those Russians I'd have bet any money they would have shot us.'

While the aircraft droned on through the night they were now able to relax and savour to the full a wonderful relief at not having had to crash-land among the great waves pounding on what, as they passed over it, they saw to be no more than a crescent of barren rocks.

When they sighted Tujoa the sky was lightening in the east. Except for a once-weekly service and an occasional private plane no aircraft came down on the island, so it had no more than an airstrip, and that was manned only when information had been received that a plane was to be expected. But James was able to direct the pilot and by that time, with the suddenness usual in the tropics, full dawn had come. Having circled over the airstrip twice, the pilot made a good landing.

Pleased as Gregory was to have reached Tujoa, he needed no telling that he and James were as yet far from out of the wood; for the Tujoa group was French territory and they were wanted by the French authorities. Having double-crossed them, Ribaud must realise that Gregory would no longer feel bound to keep his promise to remain silent about the Russian rockets on Yuloga; so, as soon as he learned that they had escaped, he would do his utmost to have them re-arrested. There was also the question of what was to be done with the Major and the pilot. In no circumstances should they be given a chance to communicate with the French Resident or his gendarmerie, otherwise the fat would be in the fire right away.

Keeping the two Frenchmen covered with the pistol, Gregory looked quickly about him. At the far end of the airstrip there were a small one-storey building and two medium-sized hangars. Turning to James he asked:

'Are those hangars likely to be occupied?'

James shook his fuzzy head. 'I doubt it. No-one on the island owns an aircraft. They are used only by visitors who come here in private planes, and that doesn't happen often. I take it you are thinking of hiding the aircraft?'

'That's it. You go and open one of them up; or, rather, both of them, if both are empty.'

Squeezing past the Major, James jumped down and ran

along to the hangar. As soon as he had it open, Gregory made the pilot taxi the aircraft into it. Ordering the two Frenchmen out, he got out himself, then made them walk in front of him into the other hangar, where he told James to free the Major's wrists.

'Now,' he said, 'I fear that for a day or two you will have to suffer some discomfort. I'll treat you no worse than I have to; but until I have made certain arrangements you must remain prisoners. What are your names?'

The Major, who had remained sullenly silent ever since James had knocked him half senseless, now burst into a furious spate of words. Cursing Gregory and James for a pair of villainous crooks, he went on to say that if they thought they had got away they had better think again. The fact that the aircraft had not landed the prisoners on Yuloga would have been reported to General Ribaud. By now the General would have sent a signal to the Resident on Tujoa and as soon as they showed their faces they would be arrested. Then he flatly refused to give his name or co-operate in any way.

'You may be right, but not necessarily,' Gregory replied. 'The General cannot know that we overpowered you. Even if he suspects it, we might have doubled back to the Loyalties, or made for any one of a dozen uninhabited islands. But he will probably believe that the plane got out of control, came down in the sea and that we were all drowned. As to your name, I expect you have papers on you which will give it to me. About that we will soon know, for you are now going to strip. Get your clothes off.'

Indignantly the officer refused; whereupon Gregory turned to James, who was standing in the doorway of the hangar, and said, 'Would you oblige me by persuading this fellow to do as he is told.'

With a grin, the huge James advanced on the Major. Sudden fear showed in his eyes. Putting up one hand as though to fend James off, he began to unbutton his tunic. Two minutes later, with a hangdog expression he was standing there naked.

'Now you,' Gregory said to the pilot. Realising that it was futile to refuse, he, too, stripped to the buff. Meanwhile

James had been going through the Major's pockets. In one there were a couple of letters and he read out from an envelope, '*Comandante Andorache Fournier*.' He then picked up the pilot's jacket, fished a pocketbook from it and announced, '*Lieutenant Jules Joubert*.'

Gregory smiled and said, 'Messieurs Fournier and Joubert, I am happy to think that, in this delightful climate, being deprived of your clothes for a while will cause you no inconvenience, apart, perhaps, from a few mosquito bites. We will now leave you to contemplate the eternal verities; or, if you prefer, how extremely displeased with you General Ribaud will be when you try to explain to him how it came about that you failed to carry out his orders.'

James collected the clothes, carried them into the other hangar and dumped them in the aircraft, then locked the doors of both hangars. As they turned away, Gregory said, 'Naked and without shoes, I don't think there is much chance of their breaking out; but we daren't leave them there for long, in case someone comes out here and finds them. Do you know of a place where we could hide them safely for a few days?'

After a moment's thought, James replied, 'There are some caves a few miles away up in the hills. No-one would come upon them there, and some of my men could be relied on to guard them.'

'Good. I'm afraid, though, that Fournier was right. The erratic flight of the aircraft over Yuloga will have suggested to the Russians that a fight was taking place on board. Ribaud will be informed of that, and he is no fool. He is almost certain to assume that if we did get control of the plane we would make for your own island. Probably the best chance of keeping our freedom would be for us to retire to those caves ourselves, anyway for the time being.'

'Oh, we certainly need not do that.' James' voice had taken on a new note of authority. 'Commandant Elbœuf, the Resident, is a spineless old creature and there are no troops stationed on the island, only a Sergeant and six gendarmes. My people would never allow them to arrest us and the police would not dare force the issue. My *bure* is only about a mile away, on this side of the town. We will go there first and I'll send a reliable man down to find out if anything unusual is happening at the gendarmes' barracks. But I'm still in the dark about much that has been going on. What exactly did take place between you and General Ribaud?'

'Of course you are.' Gregory smiled. 'I had no chance to tell you while we were in prison, and I couldn't talk about it while we were in the plane with those two Frenchmen.' As they walked quickly along an upward-sloping dirt road through the jungle, Gregory then related to James how he had blackmailed Ribaud and what had come of it. When he had done he added:

'I ought to have foreseen that, although we were old friends, he might consider it his duty to trick me, and he darned near did. Unfortunately, too, we are far from having finished with him yet. Once he knows for certain that we are here he can fly troops in to get us. Even if we refuelled the aircraft, and forced Joubert to fly us on to Fiji, we'd still not be in the clear. There is a charge of attempted murder pending against you and he could apply for a warrant of extradition. You could go into hiding for a while, but not indefinitely; because to do so would mean your having to abandon everything. To do that would ruin your whole life; so, somehow or other, we've got to do a deal with him.'

'I don't see how we can,' James said gloomily.

'Neither do I at the moment. And the devil of it is we have precious little time to think in. The signal from Yuloga will be to the effect, "Aircraft failed to land, appeared to be out of control," so apparently only a mechanical fault, and Ribaud's people wouldn't wake him up in the middle of the night to give him a message of that kind. But it will be on his desk this morning; so at any time from nine o'clock on we can expect the sparks to fly.'

By this time they had mounted the rise and emerged from the jungle. Ahead of them, in a broad, open space, stood an exceptionally large and lofty *bure* with round about it a number of smaller ones. As they approached, a man appeared in the open doorway of the big *bure*. On seeing James, he gave a cry of delight, fell on his knees and bowed his head. His

master greeted him kindly but, instead of moving for them
to enter, he remained kneeling there. James turned aside,
smiled at Gregory and said:

'No High Chief ever enters his own or any other house by
the back door; and no inferior may ever pass behind a High
Chief when he is seated, even to serve him at table. In the
islands there are many such customs as these. The people
think them right and proper, so continue to observe them
willingly.'

To one side of the *bure* there was an oval swimming pool,
at the far end were shaded swing hammocks, basket chairs,
tables and a small bar; while round about were hibiscus
bushes, cannas and pepper plants in blossom, and frangipani
trees, the creamy flowers of which filled the air with a heady
scent.

As they came round to the front of the *bure,* Gregory
found himself looking on one of the most beautiful panoramas he had ever seen, A spacious garden sloped away down
the hillside. In the forefront there were carefully-tended beds
of many-coloured flowers. Along the side slopes and lower
down, so as not to obstruct the view, were splendid specimen
trees: mangoes, breadfruit, magnolias and giant figs that
bore only miniature fruit.

Below, shaped like a sickle moon, spread the long sweep
of the bay. In the centre, looking so clear in the early-morning light that one might have thrown a stone on to a roof-top,
nestled Revika, the island's capital. The town consisted of no
more than a few brick buildings and some half-hundred
wooden ones; but on either side of it along the coast, half-
hidden in groves of palm trees, there peeped out the thatched
roofs of scores of *bures*. The beach on the extremity of the
left horn of the bay was hidden by massed trees of vivid
green, the right horn was a mile-long stretch of gleaming
white sand.

In the little harbour of Revika there were several schooners
and a number of small motor boats, the phut-phut-phutting
of one of which could be heard clearly as it made its way towards the harbour mouth. Further out, half a dozen canoes,
with outriggers and great red triangular sails, were already

211

on their way to the fishing grounds, each leaving a rippling wake on the calm surface of the water inside the lagoon. Two miles out the waves broke in a thin, creaming line on the coral reef that protected it. Beyond the reef were two small islands that seemed to float between the deep blue of the sea and the paler blue of the cloudless sky. Both of them were thick with palms that, in the distance, looked like clusters of yellow-green feathers. Not far from the shore a patch of the mirror-like water suddenly danced and sparkled in the sunlight—it was a shoal of flying fish breaking surface.

'What a wonderful situation you have here,' Gregory remarked. 'It must be one of the most beautiful views in the South Seas.'

'It is,' agreed James. 'But down by the coast the scenery is not quite up to that in several other islands. The loveliest of all, I think, is Western Samoa. There is a stretch of forty miles there, where the road winds along within sight of the sea and for long distances only a hundred yards or so from it. You could not describe it as a built-up area, but for its whole length, instead of scattered villages, there are, at short intervals, houses with pretty gardens. They are mostly native *bures,* of course, and unlike those in Fiji or here, their thatched roofs are supported by poles between which are reed curtains that can be let down in times of bad weather. Normally the colourfully-clad people who live in them can be seen going about their daily tasks, and the interiors are always neat and clean. Against a back-drop of palms and jungle, which slope up to the heights behind them, they are enchanting.'

'How about Eastern Samoa?'

'That, too, is lovely; but in a different way. The coast road is a *corniche,* in most places a hundred or so feet above the sea and dropping steeply to a succession of charming little bays. The villages along it are few and far between, and consist mostly of tin-roofed, open-sided, brick bungalows, built by the generous Americans after a great number of the *bures* of the unfortunate natives were destroyed some years ago by a terrible hurricane.

'The principal attraction there is Pago-Pago. Hundreds of

years ago its site was occupied by an enormous volcano. One day it erupted with such terrific violence that it broke down a short strip of the coast, so that the ocean rushed in and turned the crater into a vast, almost land-locked lagoon. The little town of Pago-Pago stands along an inner arm of it. Not many years ago, on the extremity of the arm, overlooking the bay, the Americans put up their great Intercontinental Hotel, and the architect they employed did a splendid job for them. Instead of the usual big, oblong box, all the buildings, including about a score of separate *bures,* are copied from the local native design, and have roofs the shape of broad, upside-down boats. The hotel, too, has everything, and is one of the finest in the Pacific.

'The Americans also erected a cable railway which passes over the town and across the water up to their Radio Station at the top of Rainmaker Mountain, which dominates the country for miles round. I went up it, and was scared out of my wits. We were warned that the car stops and changes gear about a hundred feet from the top; but not that it would wobble violently, then suddenly run backward for about a dozen yards. I felt certain it was about to crash and, as the Rainmaker is over seventeen hundred feet high, I would have been smashed to atoms at the bottom. But my scare proved worth it, as the view from the top is fabulous.'

Gregory sighed. 'Why are we Europeans such fools as to spend our lives swarming like ants in hideous cities, when we might live in this South Sea paradise?'

With a smile James replied, 'If only a tenth of you settled in the South Pacific in no time things here would be just as bad. Even without that, our golden age of happy isolation is already over. Increases in population, science and modernisation are putting an end to true leisure and simple pleasures. We, too, are doomed to become the victims of the rat race.'

'Yet you plan to foster that unhappy state of things. That is, if we get the Spanish gold. To mechanise your native industries, build a canning factory and so on, is bound to do so.'

'The gold! Yes. My mind has been so occupied with the results of my folly in Noumea that I had almost forgotten

213

about it. I fear, though, that by now either Lacost will have made off with it illegally or de Carvalho will have divers at work salvaging it. In any case, the latter holds the licence, so it will not be easy to contest his rights. I shall, though. The *Maria Amalia* went down long before the French became the masters here. In the name of my ancestors who ruled here then, I mean to claim it.

'But you are right, of course, that the true welfare of my people and my plans for them conflict. Yet how can I stand by and watch them being exploited by the rising tide of Indians? Modernisation will come here anyhow. At least it will be better for them if I can succeed in controlling it on their behalf.'

As they turned to enter the *bure*, an old, half-blind man who appeared to be dozing on the doorstep suddenly saw them, stood up and went down on his knees. James spoke to him and said to Gregory, 'This is Sukuna. He has been our doorkeeper for longer than any of us can remember. In his youth people were still eating human flesh. I will send him for Kalabo, my head servant. We will have a bath while he has breakfast prepared for us.'

'By that I suppose you mean a shower?'

'You hate them, don't you?' James chuckled. 'But your luck is in. You seem to have forgotten that I was educated in the British manner. I, too, love to relax and lie soaking; so, when I succeeded my father I had three baths installed here.'

The interior of the *bure* was very similar to that of Manon's, except that it was much larger, the patterned designs of woven bamboo on the walls more intricate, and that on the great *tapa*-covered beams were imposed whole rows of precious whale teeth and the white cowrie shells that, by tradition, only Royalty is permitted to use for decoration.

Kalabo came in and made smiling obeisance. He was a huge man, as tall as and much broader than his Ratu, with a pouffe of black hair that must have measured close on eighteen inches from side to side. James spoke rapidly to him in the sing-song native tongue, then told Gregory:

'I have ordered him to send four of my men to guard the

214

Frenchmen and give them food. It will be quite unnecessary to remove them from the hangar, at least until our next weekly aircraft is due in, and that will not be for the next three days. Kalabo will also send his aunt down to the telegraph office. She is the mother of the operator there and, should a message come in from General Ribaud, we shall know its contents long before it reaches the Resident.'

Gregory did not even think of questioning the decision to leave the two Frenchmen in the hangar. Since they had arrived at the *bure,* James seemed to have become a different person. Although he was still in the travel-stained Western suit that he had worn for over two months, he had acquired an air of immense dignity. Even his movements and the tone of his voice had altered. About him there was an aura of complete self-assurance and unchallengeable authority.

In a bedroom *bure* to which another servant shortly afterwards conducted Gregory he found laid out for him a set of native clothes, and, in the adjacent bathroom, a safety razor, clean hairbrushes and everything else he might need. He lay for a long time in a tepid bath, then dressed. The colourful shirt, evidently one of James', was much too large for him; but the *sulu,* a form of kilt, was easily adjustable.

Having had to make do for many weeks on monotonous prison fare, they tremendously enjoyed an enormous breakfast. While they ate, James told Gregory that, at least concerning the gold, their luck was in. Contrary to expectations, despite their having been out of action for two months, no attempt to salvage it had so far been made. Through his servants James had obtained the following information.

The professional diver Hamie Baker, who had been engaged by Gregory in Fiji, had arrived with his salvaging apparatus in the second week of February. He had put up at the *Bonne Cuisine*, a guest house down on the harbour, and had remained there ever since, evidently awaiting instructions. Another professional diver, named Philip Macauta, bringing salvaging equipment from Tahiti, had arrived shortly after Baker and had also taken a room at the *Bonne Cuisine*.

But his employer, Lacost, and the other Colons had not put in an appearance until nine days previously. They had

215

turned up in a battered seagoing launch named the *Pigalle* and, according to the island grapevine, one of them had let it out, during a drunken evening ashore, that Lacost and one of the others had only recently completed a two-month prison sentence after having been caught smuggling drugs from Mexico into Tahiti. Soon after their arrival they had taken their launch and equipment out to the sunken *Maria Amalia;* but, having no licence, they had been warned off by the Resident and his Sergeant of gendarmes.

Lacost had defied them and refused to leave the site. The following day, de Carvalho had arrived in the *Boa Viagem*. He had brought no salvaging equipment with him, but had gone out to view the wreck. Both parties had then returned to harbour and two days ago both had sailed, it was thought, for Fiji.

In the light of the scanty information available, to find an explanation for these movements was not possible. It might be that Lacost, having sent his diver Macauta down to the wreck, had found there was no quantity of gold in her, after all. But if so why had he defied the Resident's order to leave the site, yet left after de Carvalho had gone out to it? Again, why, although the Colons had sailed from Revika in the *Pigalle* two days before, had they left Macauta and their salvaging equipment behind? And, biggest question of all, why should Lacost and de Carvalho have lingered in Revika for several days, then sailed on the same day for Fiji?

Only one thing was clear. If there was treasure in the wreck, it was still there; so, if James chose to ignore the fact that he had no licence, his rivals had left him a free field to send divers down right away to get it, provided Ribaud took no steps against him in the next few days. And James had made it clear that, regarding himself as the rightful owner of the gold, that was what he meant to do.

When they had finished their meal Gregory said, 'First things first. For the time being we must forget the gold and try to stave off Ribaud. While I was in my bath I did some pretty hard thinking, and if you'll give me a pencil and paper I'll draft a telegram I want to get off to him.'

From a fine old walnut Dutch bureau James produced

Gregory's requirements. After writing for a few minutes Gregory picked up the paper and read out:

'Your two compatriots deprived of clothes by natives here. Suggest you send replacements by air. Am arranging agreed transfer of money to Credit Lyonnaise 44 Boulevard St. Germain. Do you wish Charles Lorraine be informed of transaction? Expect reply by 1800 hours. Dantés.'

James gave him a puzzled look. 'I can't make head nor tail of it.'

'I'll interpret,' Gregory grinned. 'The two compatriots are, of course, Fournier and Joubert. You, anyhow, are a native of this island and that's good enough. Ribaud is an old Secret Service hand and so am I. When such types get hold of an enemy, and have no means of handing him over to someone else who will keep him for a while from becoming dangerous, it is common practice to take away his clothes and shoes. Then, even if he does break out from wherever he had been locked up, it is difficult for him get get very far or persuade anyone he happens to meet that he is not a lunatic. Ribaud knows that one as well as I do, so he'll jump to it that you and I debagged his two boys and left them to cool their heels in the nude.

'Having done that, it's obvious that at any time it suited us we could give them back their clothes. So "replacements" does not mean other sets of uniforms for them, but that Ribaud should send us our belongings. He'll get that one, too.

'Then there is the transfer of money. As I told you, I did not actually blackmail Ribaud; but when he had agreed to arrange our escape I offered to send quite a substantial sum of money to his bank in Paris. He accepted and gave me the address of his bank. It would have been round about four thousand pounds, but I felt that he would have earned it if he rigged matters with his police and had flown us to Tujoa.

'As things turned out, we've got to hand it to him as a conscientious servant of the French Republic. To make certain that we did not blow the gaff about the Russians and their rockets on Yuloga he attempted to send us back there, and

217

leave it to them to see to it that we had no chance to talk. And he knew that little gesture would cost him the four thousand he might have pocketed if he had really connived at our escape.

'But now I *am* blackmailing him—good, hard and proper. Only Fournier and Joubert believe us to be criminals and knew that he meant to give us back to the Russians. The other boys, all the police, obviously believed that they had been given the job of ensuring that we should escape because we were members of the Deuxième Bureau who had got ourselves into a fix.

'If there is an investigation and they are questioned, having no axe to grind they will tell what they believe to be the truth —and say that they were simply obeying the General's orders.

'If I send four thousand pounds to Ribaud's bank in Paris nobody will be able to contest the fact that he has received a large sum of money from me. And in certain circumstances somebody might require him to explain why I did so. In this telegram I have asked my old pal if he wishes Charles Lorraine to be informed of this transaction. Charles, of course, is General de Gaulle. You will remember that he took the double cross of Lorraine as his symbol for the Free French. Ribaud will pick that one up as swiftly as I would drop a red-hot coal.

'So, you see, he will be faced with a choice. Either he lets sleeping dogs lie and refrains for good from any attempt to have you and me arrested, or he will be called on to explain why he instructed his police to arrange our escape, and accepted a big bribe for doing so. I've given him until six o'clock this evening to make up his mind. Now, whether he gives in or, more maddened than ever by my threat, decides to go all out to get us, lies in the lap of the gods.'

13

Enter the White Witch

'He must give in; he must!' James cried, as Gregory sat back. 'He'll be ruined if he doesn't. But why are you signing the telegram "Dantés"?'

'Oh, that's because I can't use my own name. You and I have become notorious in Noumea; so, if I did, everyone there through whose hands the message passed would know that we are in Tujoa. Then, like it or not, Ribaud would be forced to do his utmost to recapture us. Dantés was the hero of Dumas Père's famous novel *The Count of Monte Cristo*. He was imprisoned on an island, in the Château d'If, and his getting away from it is the best-known escape story in all French literature. The name is by no means an uncommon one, so it won't ring a bell with anyone on Ribaud's staff, but it will with him.'

The young Ratu's eyes showed schoolboy hero-worship. 'What a man you are!' he exclaimed after a moment. 'No wonder you succeeded in fooling Himmler and the Gestapo all through the war. This is absolutely brilliant. The telegram gives nothing away to anyone who may read it. But to Ribaud its meaning will be as clear as crystal. He's got to let me go or be dismissed with ignominy as a corrupt official.'

'I hope you are right,' Gregory replied soberly. 'But we can't count our chickens yet. Ribaud is both a tough egg and an honest man. He may decide to face the music. You see, he just might get himself in the clear if he told the truth and brought Fournier and Joubert to witness that all the time his real intentions had been to return us to the Russians.'

'Even then it would be difficult to laugh off that big bribe.'

219

'Yes. It's that on which I am counting. So I want to send another telegram, when we send this, to my bank in New York. It will be an instruction, verified by a code word that only they and I know, to pay that four thousand into Ribaud's bank with the least possible delay, and to inform him by highest priority cable that it has been paid in.'

'Then you really mean to send the money?'

'Certainly. When he learns that it has actually been paid in that may prove the deciding factor.'

'It is a lot of money. And you are in no great danger, so you are really paying it out to save me. I must try to pay you back later on.'

'You'll do nothing of the sort,' Gregory replied sharply. 'It is my good fortune that my splendid old patron looked on me as a son and left me the greater part of his millions. The greatest pleasure money can bring is to be able to give help and pleasure to those one loves. And, dear James, I've become quite fond of you. In fact, I'd have liked to have you for a son. But for God's sake don't count on this. Ribaud is as clever as I am. Perhaps cleverer. He may pull a fast one on us yet. To know where we stand we'll have to wait until maybe nearly six o'clock.'

Pausing for a moment, Gregory yawned, then he went on, 'We must get those two telegrams off at once, and hope that the one to Ribaud will reach him before he has committed himself in any way—such as sending a signal to your Resident here to have us arrested. Now I'm for bed. The past twelve hours would have proved a pretty severe strain on any chap of my age. And I'm no exception.'

James shook his head. 'I'm sorry; terribly sorry. But I must ask you to stick it out for another few hours. Now that I have returned to Tujoa, I cannot possibly avoid the official ceremony of welcome. It is timed for eleven o'clock. My Council of Elders will assemble in our Meeting House to renew their homage. The fact that you have arrived here with me as my guest cannot possibly be disguised. They will wish to welcome you, too, and to refuse their formal welcome would be looked on as terribly discourteous. Please Father, if I may call you so, do not refuse me in this.'

220

Gregory smiled wryly. 'To have to stay up when they want to go to bed is the sort of price Princes must pay for being Princes. Of course I understand, my son. And I am entirely at your disposal. I'll go to my room now, and anyhow snatch an hour or two of sleep. Have me called a quarter of an hour before we have to start, and I shall be honoured to attend you.'

At a quarter to eleven Gregory rejoined James in the main *bure*. The young Ratu was now wearing his ceremonial robes. Except for a collar of thin ivory tusks, he was naked to the waist, round which was bound an elaborately-patterned sash of *tapa* cloth. Over his *sulu* there were concertina-like strips of brightly-coloured material, from his upper arms there hung a long cloak, and round his ankles there were fringes of coconut fibre; his feet were bare.

Gregory was congratulating him on his striking appearance when another man joined them. He was about thirty, as tall as James, with a splendid figure and noble features. When he had made his obeisance James introduced them. 'This is Aleamotu'a, my friend and herald; and this is Mr. Sallust, with whom my heart is one, for he has brought me safely through many perils.'

From that of a subservient courtier, Aleamotu'a's manner changed at once to that of an equal. Smiling, he shook Gregory firmly by the hand and said in excellent English, 'I am happy to meet you, Mr. Sallust. That you have served my Prince so well places every Nakapoan in your debt. And should the occasion arise I claim the right to be the first to honour that obligation.'

Gregory returned his smile. 'The Ratu makes too much of what I have done, and he omits to tell you that he has twice saved my life; so it is I who am the debtor.'

Leaving the *bure*, they walked down through the garden until they reached another plateau situated just above the town. In the centre stood the Meeting House, a large, open-sided, palm-thatched building. On both sides of the approach to it several hundred Tujoans were seated: the men in front, the women behind, all completely silent. Holding himself very erect and with a firm step, James strode forward, his

221

hands clasped behind his back. Gregory and Aleamotu'a dropped to the rear. As though at a given signal the whole crowd suddenly gave voice, beginning with a low murmur and rising to a fierce, tremendous shout. It was the *tama* greeting, given only as a sign of allegiance to Paramount Chiefs.

Inside the Meeting House the Council of Elders were seated cross-legged round the walls. At the far end two chairs had been placed for James and Gregory. When they entered the house the Elders broke into a low chant of welcome; then, as the newcomers took their seats, silence fell and the men who were to play the principal parts in the ceremony came forward to make obeisance.

The ceremony began with the presentation of three whale teeth, each by a different official, who made a short speech. On accepting the teeth, James handed them to Aleamotu'a, who was standing beside him. There followed the preparations for the age-old communion rite. This was the same as that which Gregory had witnessed while staying with Manon on her island, but more elaborate. The *tapa* mats that carpeted the floor were removed from a space in front of the Ratu and in the clearing the *tanoa* bowl—with its attached string of cowrie shells—in which the *yaggona* drink was to be mixed, set down. In the bowl was already heaped the powdered root and on it lay a bundle of hibiscus fibre for straining the liquid. Behind the man who was to mix the drink crouched a row of others, clad in grass skirts and with blackened faces, who were to act as cup-bearers. Two warriors then appeared, carrying over their shoulders long, thick tubes of bamboo. At a sign from the *yaggona*-maker they removed plugs from the top of the bamboos, tipped them up and poured into the bowl two streams of clear water. With intense concentration the mixer went to work, dipping and raising his hands rhythmically. There came a single wailing cry, then all the Elders joined in a melancholy chant punctuated by perfectly timed hand-clapping.

Impressed as Gregory was with the solemnity of the ritual, half his mind was given to wondering how Ribaud would react to the 'Dantés' telegram. Yet as he glanced about him he felt sure that no-one else present was giving a single thought to anything other than the mystic *yaggona* mixing.

Despite the danger in which James still stood, it appeared quite certain that he was not. With grave attention his gaze was fixed on the bowl and his handsome face had taken on a spiritual quality. Clearly he was completely at peace, his body unmoving but relaxed, his mind elevated above all mundane matters. The Elders too, intensely dignified, although many of them were wearing worn European jackets only partially hidden by the *leis* of sweet-scented leaves round their necks, sat utterly still, their eyes riveted on the preparation of the sacred brew.

At length the mixing was completed. The bundle of hibiscus fibre was thrown aside, the chanting stopped, a silence fell, unbroken even by the rustle of a grass skirt. The premier cup-bearer came forward and received with both hands the first coconut half-shell of *yaggona*. Approaching the Ratu, he held the cup with arms fully extended and lowered his body until his knees were doubled under him. The low chant began again. The man poured the drink into James' own beautifully ornamented cup, then squatted before him. Lifting the cup, James drained it in one gulp, then threw it back towards the *yaggona* bowl. '*Matha! Matha!*' shouted the assembly, clapping their cupped hands three times in rhythm.

The Ratu was offered, and accepted, a second cup. James received his portion next, then Aleamotu'a and afterwards, in order of rank, everyone else in the assembly. As each draught went down, everyone clapped three times, then the drinker clapped three times in response.

The atmosphere of tension continued until the last cupful had been drained, then a change took place. Everyone continued to behave with decorum, but became at ease as, with obvious appreciation of good things to come, they watched the food for the feast being carried in. There were roast sucking pigs, yams and breadfruit, two turtles and scores of chickens, baskets of mangoes, pawpaws, big tangerines and other fruit. A wizened Elder made a speech apologising for

223

the poorness of the fare, to which Aleamotu'a replied on the Ratu's behalf praising its quality and abundance.

It would have been against protocol for the Ratu to remain. A generous portion of the best food was set aside to be taken up to his *bure*. Walking slowly and with great dignity between the rows of kneeling Elders, he took his departure, followed by Gregory and Aleamotu'a.

The ceremony had lasted just over an hour; so when they came out from the shade of the Meeting House the midday sun blazed down upon them from almost directly overhead. Reluctantly Gregory faced the stiff walk uphill back to the *bure,* and before he had taken fifty paces he had broken out into a sweat. Glancing over his shoulder to speak to him James noticed it, halted and spoke to two big warriors who were kneeling respectfully beside the path until he had passed. They came grinning to their feet and advanced on Gregory as James said to him:

'My poor friend, you are not conditioned to exert yourself in this heat. These two men will carry you.'

'No; no!' Gregory protested. 'Although I may look on the thin side, I weigh a good twelve stone.'

'Don't worry,' came the airy reply. 'Some of our Naka-poan beauties weigh nearly as much as that, and they are always carried from the boats to the shore. These men will take it in turns and find it no hardship. Later they will beat their broad chests and tell their families with pride how they were given the honour of carrying their Ratu's friend up to the *bure.'*

Feeling rather a fool, Gregory submitted to being picked up like a baby, but he was relieved at not having to trudge up the steep hill. When he had been safely deposited at the top, both men, without a trace of shyness, extended hands for him to shake, then gave him friendly pats on the shoulder.

Back in his room he stripped, then decided that in such surroundings there was, after all, something to be said for a shower. Stepping into the bath, he turned on the spray above it and allowed the needles of cold water to reinvigorate his tired limbs. Nevertheless, within ten minutes of his having dried himself and lain down on his bed, he was fast asleep.

At five o'clock he was still sound asleep when James came in. The dignified calm that the young Ratu had shown earlier in the day had now deserted him. With unconcealed anxiety he said:

'I have just been informed that the Resident intends to call on me here at six o'clock. Do you think that means that he has received an order to have me arrested?'

Gregory yawned and knuckled the sleep from his eyes. 'It is quite possible. But you told me this morning that your people would not let you be arrested. Has nothing come in from Ribaud?'

'No. I sent orders to the telegraph operator that should any communication come in for Dantés it should be sent up to me immediately by runner. But no message has so far arrived. It looks as though Ribaud has decided to ignore your threat and do his best to get us.'

'It's early yet to be sure of that. As you have been away for two months, the Resident may be coming to see you on some other matter. Anyhow, if he does cut up rough, you can tell him to go to hell. Before troops can be flown in and deployed we should still have plenty of time to get out to another island.'

Reluctantly Gregory got up and dressed. James took him out to the swimming pool and fortified him with a long drink of well-iced passion-fruit juice laced with rum. Then they awaited with considerable anxiety the arrival of the Resident.

A little after six o'clock they caught the sound of the labouring engine of an evidently elderly car coming up the steep drive. Five minutes later Kalabo led Commandant Elbœuf round from the front of the *bure*. He was a small man, bronzed from living for many years in the tropics. His hair was white, he had a drooping, grey moustache and in his right hand held a thick stick, upon which he leaned heavily as he advanced towards them.

Appropriate greetings followed. The Commandant was happy to accept a neat cognac—in a tumbler, he suggested, because one could better appreciate the bouquet. When he had been furnished with a triple ration they settled down to talk—not of any serious matters, but whether James had en-

225

joyed his visit to Noumea, of the price of copra, of the prospects of the yam crop, and of the weather.

At length, with apparent casualness, the elderly Frenchman asked, 'Tell me, Ratu. In accordance with ancient custom, you are permitted to retain a private body-guard of fifty warriors. In the event of serious trouble here you are under obligation to order them to support my small force of gendarmes. But say it was simply a matter of enforcing law and order, so that the administration of justice could be carried out in peaceful conditions, would you be prepared to use them in that way or, if the matter in question was against your interests, order them to ignore the obligation to assist my men?'

This, thought Gregory, is it; for he took the question really to mean—should an attempt be made to arrest James, would he submit and order his body-guard to quell a rising of the townsfolk to protect their Ratu, or use his men to defy the gendarmes? Although James' spy in the telegraph office had failed to inform them of it, a signal must have come in. Possibly it had been graded 'Top Secret and Personal to the Resident'. Anyway, it looked as though, whatever the risk to himself, Ribaud meant to get them if he could.

James evidently thought the same, for he replied with caution, '*Commandant*, it all depends on the circumstances in which you requested the assistance of my warriors. Perhaps you would enlighten me further by putting a hypothetical case.'

At that moment Kalabo arrived at James' elbow with a buff envelope on a salver. With a murmured 'Excuse me, please', the Ratu tore the envelope open, read the flimsy it contained, then passed it to Gregory. The telegram was addressed to Dantés and read:

Replacements on way. Request return compatriots earliest. For security reasons instruct communicate with no-one and report direct to me. Grateful for execution of promise. Regard transaction as completed. Unnecessary inform Lorraine. Ribaud.

Gregory smiled across at James. After all, the shrewd Ribaud had decided to accept the handsome bribe rather than risk an ignominious end to his career. They had won, and had no more to fear from James' brainstorm act of having thrown de Carvalho out of the window.

The Commandant remarked, 'Good news, I see,' then went on, 'This is no hypothetical case, but trouble that we have been faced with during your absence, Ratu, which may occur again. It concerns the gold that is said to lie in the wrecked *Reina Maria Amalia*. Ten or twelve days ago a party of ex-Colons from Algeria arrived here, in an old tub named the *Pigalle*. They were headed by a man named Pierre Lacost. Ahead of them they had sent a professional diver, who had been here for several weeks and brought with him salvaging apparatus, so it was clear to me that they intended to attempt to get the gold up from the wreck.'

Under his heavy eyelids the Commandant gave a swift glance at James:

'As I informed you, Ratu, when you were here towards the end of January, for a salvaging operation a licence is required. Long before Lacost arrived here I had been notified by my superiors in Noumea that such a licence had been granted to the Brazilian millionaire Mauá de Carvalho. I therefore went out in my launch to the wreck and ordered Lacost to take his apparatus back to harbour.

'He proved extremely truculent. He and his companions were armed and they defied me. Naturally, I was loath to expose my gendarmes to a gun battle. But the following day he did bring his gear back to harbour. Apparently his visit to the wreck had been only for his professional diver to carry out a reconnaissance. As I understand it, one man could not possibly remove the heavy beams in the wreck that obstruct the passage leading to the place where the treasure is believed to be. Lacost had counted on the assistance of a dozen local Tujoa divers for this, but they all refused their services. Why, I do not know; but without such help he was forced to suspend his operations. Even so, he and his friends continued to linger on here, hoping, I suppose, to persuade our divers to change their minds.

227

'Soon after Lacost's arrival de Carvalho turned up here in his yacht. He brought no salvaging equipment, but he also had with him a professional deep-sea diver. They went out twice to the site of the wreck, then, for some reason unknown, sailed away again. By then Lacost seems to have abandoned any hope of securing divers here and also sailed away, but he left his salvaging equipment.

'Now, Ratu, this is what I wish to know. I am told that when Lacost left he intended to go to Fiji. It seems probable to me that his object is to collect divers there and bring them here. Should he succeed and, with them, defy my authority as an administrator of the law to protect the rights assigned to de Carvalho by the French Government, would you be willing to order your body-guard to support my gendarmes in, if necessary, using weapons to drive off these Colons? I ask this because I am aware of your own interest in the treasure, and, forgive me, but it had occurred to me that, as you failed to secure a licence, you might be employing Lacost to get the treasure for you.'

Gregory and James had difficulty in keeping straight faces. It was a most amusing twist in events that with legal backing they should be asked to prevent their most dangerous rival from getting at the treasure by openly attacking him.

James bowed gravely to the Commandant. 'Monsieur, you may rely on my full co-operation should a situation such as you fear come about. I would be happy to lead my warriors in person to prevent this man Lacost from illegally getting away with the gold. And now, please, permit your glass to be refreshed a little.'

With barely-concealed eagerness Commandant Elbœuf held out his tumbler to the attendant Kalabo. It was returned to him nearly full. Sipping happily, he said to James, 'It is a treat to come here, Ratu. Our government is not over-generous to *anciens de la première guerre* like myself, and even in the islands good French cognac is expensive for those who have ill-lined pockets.'

They talked on for a while until the old man had finished his brandy. A little unsteadily, he was then escorted by Kalabo back to his ancient car. As he disappeared from view, Gregory said to James:

'Thank God it worked. We have nothing further to fear from Ribaud now. As for old Elbœuf, he did his job none too badly; but if when we start on salvaging the gold he tries to make trouble I don't think we'll have much difficulty in dealing with him.'

After a moment he went on, 'Now about Ribaud's telegram. An aircraft bringing our belongings can be expected to land here within a few hours, and we don't want its crew to ask Fournier and Joubert what they are doing in Tujoa; so it would be best to get them off on their way back to Noumea as soon as possible.'

James nodded. 'I will arrange all that. I'll send Aleamoṭu'a down to see to it. He is fluent in French as well as English. I'll give him Ribaud's telegram so that he can show it to our prisoners and impress on them that they must keep their mouths shut until they report to the General. He will also arrange for a meal to be ready for the crew of the aircraft that brings in our baggage, and see them off on their return journey. Now, as we had no lunch, we had better have a snack; then get to bed.'

Gregory considered for a moment, then asked to see the telegram again. Having re-read it, he nodded. 'Yes, I think that should be all right. To prevent them from talking to anyone before they see Ribaud they must be shown this message. They will realise, of course, that he has now agreed to connive at our escape. But that can't be helped. They would tumble to that, anyhow, when he takes no further steps to get us. And he is clever enough to deal with that. He will probably tell them more or less the truth—that we've promised to keep mum about the Russians, so as a matter of high policy he thought it better to do a deal.'

Three-quarters of an hour later they were both in bed and asleep.

In the morning Aleamoṭu'a reported. Fournier and Joubert had been in poor shape, as for some fourteen hours the whole of their bodies had been exposed to mosquitoes and they were half-crazy from scores of bites. Cursing, but anxious to get away as soon as possible, they had flown off in their refuelled aircraft about eight o'clock. The plane from Noumea had not come in until after midnight. The crew of two had taken an hour for rest and refreshment, then cheerfully set out on their return journey. With him Aleamotou'a brought the baggage which Gregory and James had been forced to leave behind in Noumea two months before. On checking it through, they were pleased to find nothing missing.

After they had breakfasted they drove in James' jeep down to the town. It consisted of only one main street, parallel to the waterfront, with a few side-streets running inland from it. There were only half a dozen brick buildings; the others were of wood, the larger ones having arcades in front to shade the sidewalk, the roofs of the arcades being used as balconies. In the side-streets the buildings were mainly one-storey, their occupants sweltering under corrugated-iron roofs. At one end of the town there was an open-air market, protected from the sun by a thick thatch of palm leaves.

The shops were all run by sleek-looking Indians, many of the older ones wearing turbans, but the majority displaying their straight, black hair neatly oiled and arranged in contrast to the frizzy gollywog heads of the natives. The market, on the other hand, was the province of the Nakapoans. In addition to meat, fish, a wonderful variety of fruit, yams, *dalo, kasava* and *yaggona* root, there were stalls that offered for sale basketwork, cheap jewellery, *tapa* cloth dyed in patterns of black and brown, woven hats, and treasure from the beaches such as tortoise-shell, mother of pearl, coral, conches, cowries and many other lovely shells.

While walking down the main street, Gregory had noticed that, in addition to a small Roman Catholic Church and little Hindu temple, there were no fewer than three Nonconformist chapels, and he remarked to James upon there being so many religious buildings in so small a town.

With a shrug of his broad shoulders, James replied, 'I doubt if anywhere in the world such a high percentage of the population, as in the South Seas, now strictly observes some faith or other. Here, owing to French influence, the majority

230

of the Christians are Catholics. In the British and American territories they are mostly Protestants; but the different sects are innumerable and fanatically opposed to one another. The high spot of such rivalry is Tonga. There not only are there Lutherans, Baptists, Seventh-Day Adventists and many Latter Day Saints, as the Mormons call themselves, but three different kinds of Wesleyans: the followers of the original missionaries, a group that broke away and, as the King who preceded Queen Salote did not approve of either, a third sect that he created which practises a special variety of ritual invented by himself. Football and religion are the absorbing interests in all the islands. Believe it or not, one Sunday when I was in Tonga the charming head waiter at the Date Line Hotel actually mildly reproached me because I said I was not going to church.'

Having made the round, they returned to the *Bonne Cuisine* guest house, outside which they had left the jeep. The proprietor, a portly Indian, was standing on the doorstep, fanning himself. He wished them good morning politely, but showed James none of the deference which he received from his own people. When James asked for the diver from Fiji who was staying there, the Indian casually flicked his fan towards two men who were seated nearby, drinking beer at one of a dozen iron-topped tables under an awning.

Both were half-castes. The taller of the two was Hamie Baker, the man that Mr. Trollope had sent from Fiji; the other proved to be Lacost's diver from Tahiti, Philip Macauta, who had been left behind to look after their gear. Both being of the same profession, they had formed a friendship and were whiling away their time together.

Baker said that he had almost given up expecting the Mr. Sallust for whom he had been sent there to work; but, as he and the salvaging equipment had been hired for three months, he had meant to wait another week before writing to Mr. Trollope to arrange for the gear to be shipped back to Suva.

Gregory told him that they now expected to start work quite soon. Upon which Macauta made a grimace and said, 'Lucky for you, baas, that you seem to be on the right side of the Ratu. My lot couldn't get a single one of the divers here to work for them. Though why, beats me. They were offered good money.'

'My people are very independent,' said James, 'and easily offended. It may be that Monsieur Lacost approached them in a way that upset them. I am told that some days ago he left for Fiji, hoping to engage divers there.'

'That's right,' Macauta nodded. 'He and the Brazilian gent had several talks, then their two boats sailed away in company.'

After a few moments' further desultory conversation Gregory asked Baker how he was off for money; then, learning that he was pretty low, and wishing to gain his goodwill, he gave him some French banknotes that had been returned from Noumea with his passport and other papers.

As the two friends climbed back into the jeep, James said, 'This new development is very interesting.'

'Very,' Gregory agreed. 'It's evident that de Carvalho and Lacost have gone into partnership. On the face of it, that's quite a sound arrangement, as one has the licence and the other the equipment already to hand.'

'I find it rather surprising, seeing that de Carvalho wouldn't do a deal with us.'

'That was different. We had nothing to offer him, and he was then under the impression that after a month or two Lacost would get fed up and leave him a free field. When he got there he found, to the contrary, that the Colons were not only still in the game but intended to go ahead, licence or no licence, as soon as they could get divers. So he was faced with the strong possibility that they would beat him to it. All Lacost apparently has to gain is legalising his operations. But I wouldn't mind betting that it was he who put up the proposition, and that he is only jollying de Carvalho along until he can get his hands on the goods. Then he'll push the Brazilian overboard.'

'I do hope you are right,' James said, with charming candour. 'That would leave Olinda free, and I feel almost sure she would marry me.'

Gregory laughed. 'You are not taking into account that

Lacost has no reason whatever to do de Carvalho in until after they have got up the gold. And the odds are now all against them. While they are still busy engaging divers in Fiji, unless something quite unforeseen happens we shall have salvaged the treasure ourselves.'

'Yes, of course.' James' face fell. 'And I suppose the sooner we get to work, the better. I thought we might go out to the wreck late this afternoon, so that I can show it to you. We must get back by sundown, though, as my people mean to entertain you with a *meke*. Then I'll engage divers tomorrow and arrange for Baker's equipment to be towed out.'

'That will be fine,' Gregory agreed. 'No doubt, old Elbœuf will appear on the scene and start creating a fuss. He'll naturally believe that you lied to him when you said that Lacost was not employed by you, and think that the Colons having failed, you're now taking over. But. . . .'

'In such a matter I should never lie,' the young Ratu broke in indignantly. 'I shall tell him, as I have meant to ever since we learned that de Carvalho had got ahead of us in securing a licence, that as the Hereditary Ruler of Tujoa I consider the treasure mine by right. That I mean to take it and, if necessary, will fight my title to it in the courts.'

Soon after four o'clock that afternoon they again left the *bure* in the jeep. This time they took a road that led inland, mounting gradually as it wound through well-cultivated land. After covering a mile they were high enough to see over the tops of the trees that screened the left sickle point of the bay. Beyond them lay a small, well-wooded island, separated from the shore by a channel only a few hundred yards wide. Pointing to it, James said:

'That's where old Roboumo lives.'

'And who may he be?' Gregory enquired.

'I told you about him when we were in Rio. He is the great witch-doctor of Tujoa and, for lack of a better expression, my enemy.'

'Yes, I remember now. He runs a sort of protection racket, doesn't he? Blackmails the natives with the aid of a gang of toughs, who tell the people that he'll put a curse on them if they don't pay up?'

233

'That's it. And he's naturally opposed to modernisation of any kind, because it would tend to lessen their superstitious fear of him, or, rather, of the White Witch who is his partner. They think she is a kind of goddess and even a mention of her scares the pants off them.'

'The White Witch,' Gregory repeated. 'That rings a bell somehow. I've heard of her before, but I can't think where. Is she really a white woman?'

'I don't know, but I doubt it. I should think it more likely that she is either a very fair-skinned Polynesian or just one of our natives who paints her face and the exposed parts of her body white. Anyway, there is no question about her potency. I've had ample proof that her curses do bring misfortune and even death to people.'

'Then why don't you clear out this nest of vipers? Old Elbœuf mentioned your body-guard, although I haven't seen it. If you have fifty stout warriors at your disposal you should be able to overrun Roboumo's island any night.'

James laughed. 'My body-guard is really not much more than a piece of tradition. Six of them are my house servants; the rest are employed working in my plantations. They could, of course, be mustered in an emergency; but they have no modern weapons and have not been called on to fight for many years. All they do is attend me on State occasions, such as a visit from the Governor of New Caledonia, or at the funeral of one of my family. I've no doubt they would obey me in most matters; but, with the exception of a few of the more enlightened ones, like Aleamotu'a, not if I called on them to attack old Roboumo's stronghold and invite the anger of the White Witch.'

By this time they could no longer see the sea. The jeep had entered a valley, on one side of which there rose a mountain. Parts of it were covered with thick jungle, others consisted of sheer cliffs of brown rock. Down one of the cliffs there gushed a hundred-foot-high waterfall. Clouds of fine spray steamed off the tall white pillar that it made before crashing with a roar and churning wildly below a stone bridge over which they passed.

A few minutes later they came out of the valley and saw

234

the sea again, blue and sparkling, in another bay. The descent there was precipitous, but, with the ease of long practice in driving on such roads, James brought the jeep down to the white, palm-fringed beach.

Some way off, a launch was waiting and Aleamotu'a waved to them from her. Gregory and James were wearing only towelling robes over bathing trunks. Leaving their robes in the jeep, they waded, then swam out to the launch. As soon as they were aboard, Aleamotu'a headed her across the lagoon towards the reef. A few hundred yards short of the breaking waves, a buoy marked the site of the wreck. Near it a small speed boat, manned by two natives, was waiting. As they approached, its engine started up and, with spray festooning from either side of her bows, she began to race round in a narrow circle.

'What are those fellows up to?' Gregory asked.

'They are our shark patrol,' James answered lightly. 'Churning up the water scares the brutes away. And those boys have eyes like hawks. If they spot one they'll give us warning.'

Far from happy at the thought that sharks might be about, Gregory allowed Aleamotu'a to adjust on his head and shoulders the mask and cylinders of an aqua-lung, then put rubber flippers on his feet. He had believed that they were only going to swim on the surface with snorkels which would enable them to peer down at the wreck, and he did not at all like the idea of actually descending to her. But, not wishing to lose face, he followed James over the side without protest.

Through the shimmering waves on the surface he had been able to see nothing below from the boat, but once he was totally submerged, the undersea world became crystal clear for several fathoms down. On the shore side of the gently rocking launch a great cliff of tumbled rock rose up to within six feet of her bottom. Brightly-coloured fish darted in and out of hollows among the rocks, fans of coral waved lazily from it as he passed; he saw hermit crabs and sea anemones, a star fish and various kinds of seaweed that formed an underwater garden. On the seaward side of the launch there lay a deep valley. At the bottom of it was the wreck. Her outline was indistinct, as for over a century and a half submarine growths of many kinds had fastened themselves on her timbers. Apparently in some great hurricane she had been thrown right up on the nearby reef, had her bottom torn out, then sunk on her side to become wedged in the long pit between the reef and the cliff of rock.

He found the silent world below the surface fascinating and would have liked to linger ten feet down opposite the cliff face. But James grasped him by the ankle and pulled him further under. Lightly, his flippered feet touched the slowly-waving fronds of yellow-green growth that edged the broken bulwark of the ship. He then saw that the upper deck had caved in. The stump of a mast protruded from a chaotic cluster of planks, beams, spars and a cannon, all of which were so overgrown with barnacles and seaweed that they seemed to have coalesced into one solid mass.

With an arm that waved in slow motion, James beckoned him down towards a hole in the hillock of broken, slimy timbers, then disappeared into it. Far from happy, Gregory followed. He had always been a little vulnerable to claustrophobia. Now, the thought of being trapped down there, perhaps by another section of the deck collapsing, made the blood pound in his head and his breath come fast. It was almost dark and very eerie. As he pulled himself forward along the uneven passageway, his hand came to rest on a squashy substance that moved under it. His heart gave a lurch, then he realised that he was grasping a large sea-slug. Next moment a foot-long red fish darted out from a crevice, stared at him goggle-eyed for a moment, then streaked over his shoulder, only a few inches from his helmet. Automatically, he had thrown himself backwards. His right elbow came into sharp contact with the end of a small, jutting beam. It gave under the impact and other nearby pieces of the wreck shifted slightly. Deciding that he had had more than enough, he kicked out with his feet, thrusting himself back up the slope and out on to the slanting deck. There he encountered a squid the size of a croquet ball, with long tentacles. More frightened of him than he was of it, the squid discharged its inky fluid and made off, leaving Gregory enveloped in a cloud of blackened water. Jerking himself upright, he kicked and clawed his way towards the surface.

Aleamotu'a pulled him in over the side of the launch. Ripping off his headpiece, he sat panting for a few moments in the stern. He knew that if he had to go down through that dark tunnel to achieve something of real importance he could have forced himself to do it. But not for this, which amounted to no more than a gambling game. Others could play it if they wished, but it was not his idea of fun. Swimming slowly about below the surface of the deliciously warm sea, delighting in the colour and beauty of Nature's innumerable marine miracles—yes. But crawling about in a submerged wreck where at any moment a dislodged beam might glide down and pin one there for good—definitely no.

James stayed down for a further fifteen minutes, then reappeared, the drops of water glistening like jewels on his splendid bronzed torso. He made no comment on Gregory's early withdrawal, except to say, 'You were down there long enough to get an idea how much there is to be done before we can reach the treasure. As no work can be carried out during periods of rough weather, even with two fully-equipped professional divers it would take many weeks to clear away that mass of broken timber. But with a dozen good native divers to assist by clearing all the smaller stuff, while the crane lifts the big beams, we might do it during a single spell of calm weather.'

By seven o'clock they were back at the *bure*. When Gregory went to turn on his bath a loud croaking noise came up from the waste. Calling Kalabo, he asked what it was. Grinning, the man explained that it was toads, many of which made their homes in drainpipes.

After dinner they went out into the garden, which was now lit by half a hundred flaming torches fixed to long stakes, to witness the *meke*. Many people had assembled there, the majority well down the slope; but a number of notables were seated cross-legged in a line in front of the house. In the centre of the line two armchairs had been placed for James and Gregory. There were grave obeisances from the Elders, and

237

Gregory noticed that if any of them had occasion to pass in front of their Ratu they did so bent nearly double.

In the left foreground squatted a group of men. Several had guitars, one a long wooden *lali* drum extended across his knees, another a hollowed-out tree trunk to serve as a gong, a third a pair of clappers, while standing in a row behind them were six men holding upright bamboos of varying thicknesses, to imitate the noise of stamping on the ground. In front of the musicians squatted the singers. One of them opened on a high, single note, giving the others the key, then the rest joined in.

Presently the dancers emerged in a long, snake-like line from a group of trees. The heads of the women, crowned by their great puff-balls of black hair, swayed to the rhythm of the music. So did the *leis* of flowers swinging from their shoulders, and full skirts patterned in black, white and brown. By then each Elder had beside him a tin of black tobacco and a piece of dried banana leaf for rolling cigarettes. Courteously, they passed bowls of *yaggona* from one to another.

Now and then there came a precisely-measured series of hand-claps from the singers, or the guitars temporarily ceased, to allow the *lali* drum and stumping bamboos to dictate more clearly the intricate steps of the dancers. Like European ballet, each *meke* demonstrated in dumb show a particular theme; but, being a stranger to their customs, Gregory could not have told what their actions were meant to portray had not James explained to him in a low-voiced running commentary.

Later, six young girls came and sat in a line in front of James, then performed a different type of dance. It consisted of swaying their bodies while gracefully gesturing with their arms and outspread fingers. It was a delightful performance and recalled to Gregory the dances he had seen when in Bangkok. But there the Thai dancers had the advantage of displaying their beautiful sinuous bodies in the nude, but for jewelled belts, sandals and breast ornaments, and wore high, pointed, pagoda-like gilded helmets.

Shortly before midnight, James stood up. Complete silence

fell while obeisances were made by everyone. There followed three ear-shattering claps as Gregory followed him into the *bure*.

All the house servants were still outside, joining in renewed singing that had now become universal. In the great, lofty chamber only one benzine lamp had been left burning; so, for a moment, in the dim light, they did not notice a figure seated cross-legged on the floor.

The figure rose. It was a man: tall, gaunt, his face painted black, and dressed in barbaric splendour. Round the blackened face there was a complete aureole of white hair. From well back on the forehead it descended unbroken in bushy side-whiskers to a rounded beard. The sight of it at once reminded Gregory of the pictures he had seen of King Thakobau.

The old man made the customary genuflection to his Ratu, but as he rose, the light was sufficient for Gregory to see that on his face there was a mocking smile.

Abruptly James addressed him. His reply was soft-voiced, but held a tone of insolence. Turning to Gregory, James said, 'This is Roboumo, of whom I have told you. He has come here to talk to us about the wreck.'

Roboumo made a slight bow to Gregory and broke into pidgin French. 'Monsieur Salut. Have heard about. Interested in wreck too, yes? My spies very good. Learn everything. Others also wish Spanish gold. But no!'

The deep-set eyes in the wrinkled, leathery face took on a malignant glare. 'Frenchmens from Tahiti. They come here. make much plan. My spies, they listen. Frenchmens say. "With gold we make Revika tourist trap. Build hotel. Surfboarding. Deep-sea fish. Motor ride to waterfall. Make place for golf play. Plenty Americans, they come. We make much rich." But when I told, I say No! No! No! Will not have. To get gold from sea divers must have. I send the word. Divers not work. Diver work and I destroy him. White Witch will curse.'

So that, thought Gregory, is the answer to the riddle that has been puzzling me all day.

The tall, skinny old witch-doctor went on, 'The Frenchmens send Portuguese man to me. He argue; offer much money. I will not take. He very angry. He say I go to hell, he get divers from Fiji. I tell him, "Do that and the White Witch place curse of death on you. Forget gold or you live only till full moon. Full moon come, death strike you down".'

A moment after he had ceased speaking Roboumo uttered a high-pitched chuckle. Then he said, 'I have power to overlook Portuguese. You know that, Ratu. He seeks divers, I learn it. Then next week he dead.' Turning to Gregory, he added, 'This warning also for you. Leave bad gold where it lie. Try to get and White Witch curse you same as Portuguese man from Brazil.'

14

Midnight at the Grave

Without another word, the lean, sinewy old man turned away and, his naked feet making hardly a sound on the mats, disappeared through the rear door of the *bure*.

'A nasty bit of work if ever there was one,' Gregory remarked. 'Anyhow, we know now why the divers refused to work for Lacost, de Carvalho and Co. How is this likely to affect us? Do you think the divers will refuse to work for you?'

James gave an unhappy nod. 'I'm afraid so. The poor fellows will find themselves between the devil and the deep sea. They will feel terribly bad about refusing me, but they won't dare defy Roboumo. And there is another thing. In view of his threat to have the White Witch curse us, I don't think I'd now be prepared to go on.'

'My dear James!' Gregory's voice was a trifle sharp. 'You really surprise me. It is understandable that ignorant natives should be intimidated by such threats, but not an educated man like you.' As he spoke, he moved towards the drink table and added, 'May I help myself to a brandy-and-soda?'

'By all means. I'm sorry that, owing to custom, you've had to drink *yaggona* all the evening. It has very little kick in it, but it suits my people. They have no head for spirits, so I publicly discourage the drinking of them. In fact, in some Melanesian islands they are still prohibited altogether, because the "dragon" whisky and "crocodile" gin the traders used to sell them led to so many outbreaks of violence. But to get back to Roboumo. I feel that we must take his threat seriously.'

241

'All right, but let's examine it critically. What evidence have you that these spells really work?'

'Plenty. And there is no doubt at all that the *vuniduvas,* as the sorcerers are called, can overlook people when separated from them by great distances. They often produce information about happenings in the outer islands here that they could not possibly have known by normal means. And sometimes it is to do good. For instance, last year one of them told a servant of mine that he must buy certain medicines and take them at once to the small island where his family lived because his young son had had a serious accident. Of course, I at once gave him leave to go, and when he returned a fortnight later he told me that the sorcerer had been quite right. The boy had fallen from a tree while collecting coconuts, injured his leg and the wound had become infected. If it had not been treated within a few days he would have died.'

Gregory shrugged. 'That's fair enough. Thought transference has been scientifically proved, and distant vision is a form of it. But being capable of putting a curse on a person so that he dies is a very different matter.'

'It happens, though. Here witchcraft is called *drau-ni-kau,* and it is still widely practised. Men who have money will pay a big sum to a *vuniduva* to put a death curse on a really hated enemy. The victim simply weakens and dies. Then the man who has caused the curse to be put on him goes to his grave in the middle of the night and drives several sharp stakes down into the body, to prevent the spirit from returning to haunt him. I have several times seen such stakes in the graves of newly-dead.'

'I'm not doubting your beliefs, James, and, in spite of the fact that for the purposes of the war I once had to take a Satanist into partnership, I don't really know that much about the occult. But it is generally held to be a fact that curses do not work on people who are convinced that they will have no effect. How, otherwise, could comparatively few white men have subjugated many thousands of Negroes in Africa? Or the people here in the South Seas, for that matter? The witch-doctors would have killed them off in no time. Anyway, I don't believe for one moment that Roboumo and

242

his White Witch have the power to kill me by occult means. And it was I the old badhat threatened, not you.'

'True, it was to you that he actually spoke his threat; but only, I imagine, because he knows I would not be able to tackle the job if you withdrew your financial backing. If he finds that you refuse to be intimidated I think it certain that his next step will be to threaten me, in the hope that I have enough say in matters to make you throw in your hand.'

'And would you?'

'I hardly know,' James murmured miserably.

'Now listen, my boy.' Gregory spoke firmly but kindly. 'You know very well that this gold means nothing to me. If I had another sixty years to live I couldn't spend all the money I already have. In any case, I had meant to make my share of it over to you. But what does matter is not allowing either de Carvalho or Lacost to get the better of us. The one double-crossed us and the other did his best to kill us. And I'll bet you any money you like that neither of those tough eggs is going to get the jitters because that old buffoon has said that he'll have a magic put on them. In a week or so they will be back here with Fijian divers and going to work. The very idea of allowing those blackguards to lift the stuff in front of my eyes makes me as mad as a hatter. But this is your party, and I do appreciate that, your ancestry being different from mine, we have inherited very different mental reactions to certain possibilities. So if you'd rather that we chucked in our hands I'll agree, and think none the worse of you. Now: which is it to be?'

James hesitated for only a moment, then he said, 'You have been so very good to me. I can't let you down. You may be right, that your disbelief in the White Witch's powers will turn her curse aside. Anyhow, I'm game to go through with it.'

'Good man.' Gregory reached up and patted him on the shoulder. 'Then we had best not let the grass grow under our feet. I suggest that first thing tomorrow you find out if the divers here are willing to defy Roboumo and work for us. If they are, we keep the clear lead we have over the enemy. If they refuse, the enemy already has a lead of several days over us; so the sooner we can get to Fiji ourselves and collect some divers the better our chance of catching up.'

'I'll have myself called early and go down to the town with Aleamotu'a. Between us we can see several of the men, and I should be able to let you know the form at breakfast. While I am down there I'll call in at the church and arrange for candles to be burned to my patron saint every day from now on for your protection.'

'Thanks, that's very good of you.' Gregory had no great faith himself in the efficacy of burning candles, but he was strongly of the opinion that anyone who had could, by so doing, draw down spiritual strength and powerful influences to aid any good purpose. After a moment he added:

'I did not know that you were a Roman Catholic.'

'Oh, yes,' James replied cheerfully. 'Most people in the Nakapoa group are now at least nominally Catholics, although probably three-quarters of them pay only lip service to that religion. You see, the Catholic Fathers and the Protestant missionaries arrived in the South Seas at about the same period. Both, inspired by their faiths, set extraordinary examples of courage and self-denial. Here, owing to the influence of France, the Fathers ultimately triumphed. But in the Fijis the Methodists proved more successful; perhaps because they brought their wives with them.'

'What difference did that make?' Gregory enquired with interest.

'For one thing, that they should have wives at all made them seem more natural and human to the natives. For another, their women, both British and American, showed remarkable bravery. With the sweat pouring off them, as it must have seeing the layers of clothes they persisted in wearing, and bitten by myriads of mosquitoes, they still went out to nurse the sick and browbeat the natives into abandoning barbaric customs.

'In the middle of the last century cannibalism was still rife in all these islands. Before his conversion to Christianity King Thakobau boasted of having eaten meat from over a thousand corpses. He employed a whole tribe of warriors from the island of Beqa to do nothing else but kidnap people to supply his cooking ovens. Against all odds the missionaries and their wives fought with the greatest tenacity to persuade him to stop eating human flesh, and prevent a Chief's widows from being strangled and buried with him when he died.'

'Do the Chiefs still practice polygamy?' Gregory asked.

James shook his head. 'Not since they accepted *Lotu*, as Christianity is called. Many of them in the outer islands still keep concubines; but not the High Chiefs such as the Ratus of Fiji.'

'And how about yourself? Attached to the household of such a fine specimen of manhood I should have expected there to be half a dozen pretty young women.'

'There were four,' James admitted with a smile. 'But on the morning of our arrival I sent them away. I should have, in any case, when I married, as I expected to do, a Princess of the royal families of either Fiji or Tonga. But since I met Olinda in Brazil my thoughts are all of her. I have no desire for any other woman, although it seems that the chances of making her my wife are very slender.'

'I fear that is so. As she is a Roman Catholic, that rules out a divorce. I suppose, though, as she has no children, she might manage to get an annulment?'

'Even if de Carvalho consented—which I am sure he would not—that would prove a long and costly business. As things are, I fear it is equally out of the question.'

By then it was past one o'clock. Gregory yawned and stood up. 'Since you will be getting up early in the morning I think we'd best get to bed.' From the garden there continued to come the sound of low, rather mournful, singing, and he added, 'They are still at it out there. What time will they pack up?'

James looked rather surprised. 'They won't. That is, not until dawn. Later, when the *yaggona* begins to make them a little tipsy, the singing will get a bit ragged. But the idea is that they should sing us into pleasant dreams, and they are thoroughly enjoying themselves.'

When they met for breakfast James said, 'It is as I feared. Between us, Aleamotu'a and I saw five of our best divers, and they all refused to play. None of them acknowledged that it was because they had been threatened by Roboumo. They made various excuses—not well enough themselves, a member of their family very ill, the loss of a job which, if they threw it up, they might not get back later on, and so on.'

Gregory nodded. 'Then it has come to a race between ourselves and the others. Immediately after breakfast we'll get off a telegram to Hunt's to send a private aircraft to fetch us and to engage rooms for us at the Grand Pacific.'

'No!' James shook his big mop of hair. 'It's no good our going to Suva. The natives on Viti Levu, with very few exceptions, don't go in any more for diving as a living. They can make more money working in the hotels, driving trucks and acting as casual labourers for the shopkeepers. We must go to the outer islands to get the type of man we want. Probably the best are to be found in the Lau Group. But that is two hundred miles to the east of the main island; and we'll have to go in a big launch to pick them up. It would be much quicker to go to the Yasawas, on this side of Viti Levu. They are no great distance from Lautoka, and you could ask Hunt's to engage a big launch for us there.'

A message to that effect was duly written out and sent down by a runner to the telegraph office. They then collected their towels and went out to have a dip in the pool. When Gregory had walked the few yards from his bedroom *bure* to the main one he had noticed that the sky was overcast and that there was a slight drizzle; but as they went out into the garden he was amazed at the complete change of scene from the previous day. The distant islands could no longer be seen, neither could the horns of the big bay. The sea was no longer a deep blue, nor the sky a vault of azure. For the limited distance that could now be seen beyond the harbour, the sea was grey; the yellow had gone out of the palm fronds and they now looked a darkish green. Water dripped dismally from the big, shiny leaves of the nearest trees and much of the colour seemed to have left the flowers. Altogether, it was a gloomy and depressing scene.

Remarking on the change from the two previous days, Gregory asked, 'Is it often like this?'

'Oh, yes.' James shrugged. 'Sometimes it dries up in a few

246

hours; at others the rain goes on for weeks. When the breeze drops, as it has now, and the humidity increases, it can become very unpleasant. But we are quite used to it and everyone continues to work or go for a swim just the same.'

Gregory spent the morning reading, while James went down to the town and saw to numerous business affairs. He returned with a reply from Hunt's: an aircraft would arrive to pick them up at 1500 hours approximately, rooms had been booked for them at the Cathay Hotel, Lautoka, and arrangements about a launch were being made for them there.

Having lunched off a 'fish plate'—which consisted of delicious fresh crab meat, *walu,* the best local fish, and big prawns, followed by fruit, they were driven in the jeep down to the little airport. The weather had not improved and on the lower levels the mist was so thick that they feared the pilot might not be able to find the landing strip. But James had flares lit, and the aircraft came down safely only a quarter of an hour after its E.T.A.

Soon after they had taken off they passed out of the clouds and caught a glimpse of Tujoa's peak rising above them. Their journey was then uneventful. Hunt's had a car ready to meet them at Nandi, and by half past six they were at the Cathay Hotel, Lautoka.

After dinner there that evening Gregory said:

'I've been thinking, James, about the next few days. As I don't speak Fijian, I should not be the least help to you in arranging with the petty Chiefs in the islands for the hire of divers; and the Mamanucas lie only a little to the south of the Yasawas. By now Manon has probably given up all hope of ever seeing me again, but I'm sure she would be pleased to; so I'd like you to drop me off on her island.'

James grinned at him and raised one eyebrow. Gregory grinned back and went on:

'You're quite right, my boy. While you labour in the heat of the day I'll toil not neither will I spin, but I may do a few other things. When you have collected your team you can come and pick me up; then we'll make all steam back to Tujoa.'

247

Next morning, Hunt's representative took them along the wharf and aboard the *Southern Cross*, a cabin cruiser that could accommodate a dozen passengers, and introduced them to her Captain, Bob Wyndhoik—a tubby, brown-skinned little man who, it transpired, had a mixed ancestry of Dutch, Indonesian and Maori and had been born in New Zealand.

He said they were lucky to get him, as he had been booked to take a party of Americans for a week's trip round the islands, but it had been cancelled the day before; and, at the moment, there was no other boat of the size they wanted available at Lautoka.

When told what his boat was required for, he said that he would be taking on stores during the morning, so could sail that afternoon. But he stipulated that any divers they collected must sleep on deck. James said that was customary and a price was agreed; then he and Gregory went ashore to get some Fijian money from the bank on the corner of the main street, and do some shopping.

On the top of a slope opposite the hotel stood the Lautoka Club, which had a fine view over the bay and a big swimming pool. By courtesy of the secretary, they had drinks and a swim there before lunch. After the meal they had their baggage taken down to the *Southern Cross* and went aboard.

The weather was clement and the blue sea only slightly choppy, so, when they were well clear of the inshore reefs, Captain Bob Wyndhoik came and sat himself down beside them, under the awning shading the after deck. He proved a cheerful, garrulous little man and, having spent over fifteen years in the Fijis, knew a lot about them.

An outrigger canoe beating towards Lautoka swept past them, tilted right over, her triangular sail lying at an angle of forty-five degrees from the surface of the sea. 'Ah!' exclaimed the rotund Bob. 'Look at her! What a sight for you! Them Fijians certainly are good sailors. Time was when they built the finest canoes in all the Pacific. Great double ones with decks fifteen or more feet wide above the two hulls, and a thatched house on the stern for the Chiefs to live in when they went on long voyages. They was long voyages, too.

Down to Tonga, up to Samoa, across to Tahiti, way south to New Zealand or east to New Caledonia and the Solomons. Even all way up to Hawaii they went, and that's close on three thousand mile.'

'Still more amazing,' Gregory put in, 'many centuries ago great numbers of them decided to emigrate, and sailed in their canoes through the East Indies, and right across the Indian Ocean to Madagascar.'

'True enough, sir. That was the Polynesians, though. Them is a fair-skinned lot, and much more knowledgeable, as you might say. But the Fijians built the best canoes. Why, old King Thakobau built one as a present for his pal, King George of Tonga, that was over a hundred foot long, and could carry a hundred warriors. Took seven years to build her, it did. That was way back in the early forties, when the practice still was to christen a new canoe with a human sacrifice. Not content with that, they clubbed a few poor goops to make a nice foundation before they laid down the keel. In this case, a couple of missionary gents called Lyth and Hunt persuaded them to cut out any further bloodletting when the great canoe was launched and not to do the usual on her maiden voyage, which was to collar some unsuspecting feller at each port of call and bust his head open on the prow.

'But when they got her to Bau, the island from which eastern Fiji was ruled, there was an accident. As the tall mast was lowered for the first time, its heel slipped and it killed a man. Old King Thak took that as a sign that the gods were angry 'cos the usual sacrifices had not been made before she were delivered to him. He promptly put things right by having twenty-one undesirables hunted out and clubbed to death.'

'Keeping alive in those days must have been a pretty chancy business for ordinary people,' Gregory remarked.

'It was, sir. You'd never believe how cruel them old Chiefs could be. They bought it themselves, though, when they got old and sick. The young blood who was to step into a Chief's shoes just couldn't wait till his old man died. It was common practice for them to bury their pas alive.

'Another thing. Every time they built a *bure* they had a

249

special drill for keeping the evil spirits away. Into each hole where they meant to put one of them great pared tree-trunks that hold the building upright, they put a living man. Then they lowered the trunk, made the poor bugger embrace it, and shovelled in the earth atop of him, till he couldn't breathe no more and gave up the ghost.'

Looking across at James, Gregory gave a wicked little smile. 'I take it that goes for Tujoa, too?'

With a slightly embarrassed look, James returned his smile. 'I fear so. If anyone decided to do away with my *bure* they would find in the foundations quite a number of human skeletons. In view of the beliefs of my forefathers, I suppose that's quite understandable. But it does seem pretty awful that they did not club the poor wretches before stuffing them down into the holes.'

Bob took him up. 'For this purpose that wouldn't have seemed right to them, Ratu. All the same, the Melanesians were great boys with their clubs. They had spears and, some of them, bows and arrows. But they used them most times for hunting. Clubs were the thing. They even used them on girls they wanted for their wives. Just a light tap on the head, no more, then the young lady was carried back for you know what in the chap's *bure*. But early in the last century the Ratu Kadava Levu introduced a new custom at his capital, Bau Island. He assembled all the shy bachelors and unmarried girls. Made them sit in two lines facing each other. Then each man in turn rolled an orange to a girl he liked the look of. If the lady liked the look of the young man she rolled the orange back. Then, hooray, wedding feast a few days later. If not, nothing doing.'

'That was a much more civilised way of doing things,' Gregory commented with a smile.

Bob nodded. 'Pretty good idea, providing the orange ran to the girl it was aimed at. Later the missionaries took over and the marriage ceremony became a sort of hell-fire warning with "dos" and "don'ts". Many couples, though, escaped that. Old black-crow missionaries could not be everywhere and young people got tired of waiting. So when a British

250

Resident came round he just waved a Union Jack over the couple and that was O.K. by all.'

Half an hour before the sun was due to set they were approaching Manon's island. As Bob Wyndhoik brought the cruiser in to the anchorage, Gregory was having pleasant thoughts about Manon. In his mind's eye he visualised again her unusual but attractive face. Somehow the receding chin and sallow complexion did not seem to matter. Her eyes were magnificent and her laughter infectious. Her body was something to dream about: the firm, rounded breasts, the narrow waist, the perfectly-formed legs below the powerful hips, and that alluring 'V' of crisp black curls on the lower part of her flat stomach. He recalled, too, her wild abandon—gasping crying out endearments and pleas to be ravished more forcefully—each time he had possessed her. The week that lay ahead promised him a renewal of all those pleasures.

The motor cruiser anchored; a small speed boat was lowered from her stern and Gregory and James were taken ashore. On the beach old Joe-Joe met them. He smiled a greeting, but seemed downcast. When Gregory asked for his mistress he replied:

'Madame not here, Madame not here since ten, eleven days. She in Suva. But she lend house to friends. Frenchmen from Tahiti. They come in dirty old tub of yacht. Two live here all time. Others sail off up to Yasawas wanting to get divers. Last night all come back here. Make much merry. Then, this mornng, bad thing happen. They walk across island to swim from best beach on far side. On the head of one a coconut fall. They bring him back and he is dead.'

Gregory's brows knit and he asked sharply, 'What did they do with the body?'

Joe-Joe looked surprised. 'Why, Master, they bury it. Just beyond garden. Here peoples must bury soon after death. If taken back to Suva, long before they arrive body would have made great stink.'

'I appreciate that,' Gregory agreed. 'But I should like to see the grave. Please take us to it.'

Obediently Joe-Joe led them through the palms and an orange grove to a small clearing. In the centre there was the

251

mound of a newly-made grave. There were flowers on it and from one end rose a roughly-made wooden cross. Gregory leaned forward to look at the cross and saw that no name had been carved on it.

As they walked back towards the house, Joe-Joe offered hospitality. It would, he said, have been Madame's wish. Gregory thanked him, but declined, saying that they would dine on board and, later that night, return to the mainland.

When they sat down to dinner James looked across at Gregory uneasily. 'I can't understand this at all. It is most unlikely that two parties of Colons from Tahiti would have been out there seeking to engage divers at the same time.'

'I agree, and that Manon should have lent them her house as a headquarters is a very strange coincidence. Of course, as she had heard nothing from us for over ten weeks, she has very good reason to suppose that we are dead. I happen to know that she is extremely hard up. She is wildly extravagant by nature, and the house here cost her a small fortune. So she may have gone in with Lacost and Co. to earn a share in the gold. But there may be some other explanation.'

'Yes. She may have let the house to them through an agent, not knowing that they were Lacost's party. Anyhow, this fatal accident means that we have one enemy less.'

'But which? That's what I want to know. When they are all asleep in the house I'm going to find out.'

'What!' James exclaimed, with a horrified expression. 'You . . . you can't mean that you're going to desecrate the grave?'

'I am.' Gregory's voice was firm. 'Surely you don't imagine that the dead man's spook is going to jump out and bite me? You can come with me or not, as you wish.'

James shuddered. 'No, no! Forgive me, but I'll remain on board and stay up till you return.'

The following two hours seemed to creep by. As usual aboard such boats, the crew sat up on deck, strumming guitars and singing plaintively. James, after nervously flicking through the pages of a magazine for a while, gave up the attempt to read and sat listening to the nightly concert. Gregory, outwardly calm, but far from looking forward to the grim task he had set himself, downed four brandies-and-soda in succession while playing a game of six-pack bezique with Bob Wyndhoik. When the game ended he stood up and said to Bob:

'Have two of your boys man the boat, will you? I feel like going ashore for a stroll before I turn in.' With a glance at James, he added, 'Well, I'll be seeing you.' Then they went out on deck.

The boat had not been hove in, so was still alongside. The concert party broke up and Gregory followed the boys down into the boat. As she headed for the shore, phosphorus gleamed brightly in the little waves churned up by the bows. Five minutes later, having told the crew to wait for him, he waded through the shallows.

It was a wonderful night. The sky was free of cloud and a splendid moon dimmed the stars but made the scene almost as bright as in daylight. In places, contrasting with its brilliant illumination, there were patches of dense black shadow thrown by the groups of palm trees and the *bures*. The air was balmy and, but for the gentle lapping of the tide, it was utterly silent.

No light showed from the big *bure*. Cautiously, he moved from one patch of shadow to another, until he had made his way round it. The smaller *bures* behind it were also in darkness. Skirting them, he went to a tin-roofed shed. From his stay there early in February he knew that the gardener kept his implements there. Silently removing a spade from a stock of tools in one corner, he walked with almost noiseless footsteps through the orange grove to the small clearing in the jungle where the body had been buried.

Carefully removing the now wilted flowers and the wooden cross, he began to shovel the loose soil away from that end of it. As he had expected, the grave was quite shallow and the corpse covered with little more than a foot of earth.

The stillness of the night was eerie and the strong moonlight heightened the sense of tension that he felt. Sweat began to break out on his forehead but, setting his teeth, he laboured on until he had uncovered the dead man's head. Bright as the moonlight was, clots of earth still rendered the

253

corpse's features unrecognisable. Taking a torch from his pocket, he shone its beam down on to the now mottled face. Then grasping it by the hair, he pulled it up so that he could examine the skull. At the back was a deep depression of crushed broken bone clotted with blood, from which scores of frightened ants scurried. Letting it fall, he shovelled back the earth, replaced the flowers and the cross, threw the spade away into the nearest patch of undergrowth, then walked thoughtfully back to the beach.

On the deck of the cruiser, James was waiting anxiously for him. Bob had already gone to his cabin. As soon as the two boys who had taken Gregory ashore were out of ear-shot, wide-eyed, the young Ratu uttered the single word:

'Well?'

'It was as I expected,' Gregory replied grimly. 'De Carvalho.'

'Oh God!' James exclaimed. 'And it's the full of the moon! The White Witch's curse!'

'No. His death was not an accident brought about by occult means. He wasn't killed by a falling coconut. That would have hit him on the top of the head. The back had been bashed in. He was struck down with a club, by somebody walking behind him.'

'But why?' stammered James. 'Why? You . . . you said there was no point in their killing him until they had got up the gold.'

Gregory shrugged. 'I forgot one thing. To get clean away with taking the treasure, Lacost must have a licence. Otherwise the French authorities will hunt him down. If for no other reason, because they will want their ten per cent of the value. If he had murdered de Carvalho in Tujoa, after they had got the gold, it is certain that he would have been suspected. De Carvalho's having died here in Fiji, apparently from an accident, no-one is going to connect his death with what happens in Tujoa. And now the holder of the licence is dead, Lacost has a free field to apply for one himself. That is the answer. Anyway, this is a stroke of luck for you. With her husband out of the way, Olinda is now all yours.'

254

For a moment James was silent, then he burst out, 'Olinda! But don't you see? As de Carvalho's widow, she will inherit the licence. Before Lacost can apply for one for himself he will either have to come to terms with her—or kill her. And he must be on his way to her now!'

15

Night Race to Suva

Gregory raised an eyebrow. 'That could be, although I doubt it. I don't know much about Lacost, but I should think he's too clever to rush his fences. As it was while with his party that de Carvalho's death occurred, he will naturally go straight to Olinda and inform her of it. To fail to do so would be a hideous blunder. If he returned to Tujoa and left her to learn by some other means that she had become a widow she would immediately suspect that he had had a hand in it and set the police on to make enquiries. That is the one thing he dare not risk. An autopsy would disclose that de Carvalho was not killed by a falling coconut. Seeing that Lacost had motive and opportunity, he would find himself in a very nasty spot. But . . .'

Having listened impatiently, James broke in. 'What you say makes it more obvious than ever that he is on his way to Olinda. So we must go after him at once. Otherwise he may, as I said, kill her too, or at least trap her in some way. Perhaps he'll kidnap her.'

'No. As I was about to say, he is not to know that Olinda had come to hate her husband, so he will expect her to be grief-stricken by his news. It would be a most unnatural thing to force a business discussion on a woman in such a state, and a dangerous move, as it would draw attention to what Lacost hopes to gain by de Carvalho's death. As for killing or kidnapping her, he would be crazy to attempt to do either. Apart from the difficulty of getting away with it in a place like Suva, now he has collected his divers and it is known in Tujoa what he wants them for, the police would tumble to it in no time that he was sticking at nothing to get all the treasure for himself. And remember, he can have no idea that we know about de Carvalho's death and will soon be after him. Believe me, James, he'll take his time, do his best to comfort Olinda in her loss, then in a few days' time suggest to her that, as de Carvalho's surviving partner she should transfer the licence to him for a consideration— which, of course, he would have no intention of honouring.'

'She wouldn't do that. I'm certain she wouldn't. While Valentim was alive she had no chance to spike his guns. But she would have if she could, for my sake. Now that she is in control of the situation, I'm sure that she will refuse to have anything more to do with Lacost.'

'No doubt you are right. But only when she has turned Lacost down will he be forced to think up some scheme to get her into his power without being suspected of having murdered her husband. That is going to take some planning and should give us still longer to ensure that she is adequately protected. Meanwhile, we have a good chance to settle with Lacost and Co. once and for all. We'll go ashore again in the morning and carry out a very thorough investigation: take statements from Joe-Joe and all the other servants about the Colons and, as far as they know them, the exact circumstances of de Carvalho's death. I also intend to have his corpse disinterred, wrapped up in a lot of sacking and boxed, then take it back to Suva so that an autopsy can be carried out.'

'No!' James shook his bushy head violently. 'No! We must set off at once. Lacost is on his way to her. As I just said, I'm sure that when she learns that the licence is now legally hers her first thought will be of me. But she can have heard nothing of us for nearly ten weeks. She may believe me to be dead or that, not having found some way to communicate with her, I have ceased to love her. Fed up with this whole business, she might let Lacost have the licence for the asking, and return to Brazil. That's the least bad thing that can happen. We've got to work fast, I tell you.'

257

Gregory considered for a moment. 'There is something in what you say. But it would mean my abandoning the investigation I meant to carry out. If we leave that for a week or so the memories of the servants about what happened will have become faulty and de Carvalho's corpse will have become no more than a skeleton.'

'To hell with his corpse! Valentim was no friend of mine that I should be anxious to avenge his death. Besides, we can't prove that he was clubbed to death. Remember, a coconut falling from a tree is very different from one you see for sale on the stalls. It would not have had its husk chopped open and removed, so would have weighed anything up to twelve pounds. It is quite possible that, falling from such a height, it would have smashed his skull.'

'But it was the back of his head, not the top, that had been bashed in.'

'Yes; yes; I know. And I don't doubt that it was the Colons who killed him. But, if accused, they are sure to say that when the coconut fell he was bending over to tie up his shoelace, or pick a flower, or something. Naturally, I'd be delighted if we could pin Valentim's murder on Lacost, but the chances are we'd fail. Anyhow, I don't give a damn about that now. It's Olinda who matters. I've got to get to her. I'm going to rouse out Bob Wyndhoik and have him start the engines at once.'

As James turned away, Gregory shrugged resignedly. Although he did not believe that there was any immediate cause for anxiety about Olinda, he could not help sympathising with his young friend's urge to ensure that she had his protection at the earliest possible moment. Moreover, there was much to be said for the argument that it would be next to impossible to prove that when de Carvalho had, presumably, been hit by the coconut he was standing upright. There was also the factor that if the police were brought into the matter it was quite on the cards that he and James might have to kick their heels in Suva for perhaps several weeks until the trial came on, as they would be needed to give evidence about the reason why the Colons should have wanted de Carvalho out of the way.

258

All things considered, it seemed just as well to let sleeping dogs lie and, now that Olinda could so much improve their own position by legalising it, concentrate on securing the treasure before Lacost could get back to Tujoa, ignore old Elbœuf and make off with it.

The *Southern Cross* shuddered as her motors started and a moment later she was nosing her way out of the bay. Soon afterwards James joined Gregory in the cabin, where he was fixing himself a badly-needed drink. The young Ratu smiled and rubbed his hands together:

'Bob thinks we have quite a good chance of reaching Suva right on their heels. They can't have had more than a few hours' start, and from the account we had in Tujoa of Lacost's *Pigalle* she is a rotten old craft. For us, round the south coast of Viti Levu should be only about sixteen hours cruising, while she may take twenty or more.'

'Perhaps he's right,' Gregory conceded. 'But dirty old boats sometimes have good engines. If I were you I'd tell Bob to about ship and make for Lautoka.'

'Why? It's very unlikely Lacost will have gone there.'

'True. But it's only twenty miles away, and we could telephone a warning to Olinda from there.'

'You're right!' James exclaimed, and dashed away up the cabin steps.

When he returned the launch had heeled over and was making a sharp turn. Gregory finished his drink and remarked thoughtfully, 'There is one thing I don't understand. Why should de Carvalho have come to the Mamanucas in the Colon's old tub instead of in his own fine yacht?'

James shrugged. 'Goodness knows. But it does account for one thing, and I thank heaven for it on my knees. Normally, Olinda accompanies Valentim on all his cruises. From what Joe-Joe told us this afternoon it is clear that there was no woman with the visiting party, so Olinda remained in Suva. Obviously, her reason for doing so was because the accommodation in the *Pigalle* was too shoddy for an elegant woman to be willing to occupy it. Praises be things turned out like that, otherwise she would already be in the hands of

259

those devils. Or perhaps Lacost would have arranged a plausible double "accident", in which case she would be dead.'

'Yes. It's certainly a stroke of luck that she wasn't with them. There may be another explanation, though, why she was not. Perhaps there was a death in her family, or some other urgent reason why she should return to Brazil. If so, and de Carvalho sent her off in the yacht, that would account for his having come here with the Colons in the *Pigalle*.'

'I only hope you are right, although I would have thought that in such a case she would fly back. Anyhow, if she is no longer in Suva she will be out of all danger.'

After a moment James went on, 'One other thing puzzles me about this business. If Lacost had made up his mind to murder Valentim before getting the gold, why didn't they simply push him off the boat in the middle of the night, and let him drown? If they had done that, no-one would ever have been able to examine the body and learn the truth.'

Gregory slowly shook his head. 'The job they've done is much more subtle. If later any question arises of their having an interest in bringing about his death, they can say, "But if we had wanted to kill him we had a week or more at any time during which we could have thrown him to the sharks. His death was an accident of the sort that happens every now and then to a native in these islands. He died within a few hundred yards of the *bure*. It is only by chance that one of the servants there did not actually see what happened. We made no secret of his death, but gave him proper burial, and, instead of leaving for Tujoa, which was where we wanted to go, we at once returned to Suva to report the accident to his widow and the authorities".'

By that time it was two o'clock in the morning. Giving a yawn, Gregory added, 'We should dock at Lautoka in less than four hours, but that is time enough to get a good rest, and I need one. I'm going to my cabin. Tell Bob to give me a call ten minutes before we are due to land, will you?'

Soon after five o'clock, the *Southern Cross* reached Lautoka, and Gregory paid off the cheerful, garrulous Bob

Wyndhoik. As they walked the short distance to the Cathay Hotel, a wonderful dawn sky of gold and orange, streaked with narrow bars of black cloud, showed above the mountains to the east. At the hotel the servants were just starting work but the manager was away for the night, staying with friends, and was not expected back until after breakfast. However, his deputy, an Indian, proved most efficient and helpful. Having ordered coffee and fruit for them, he set about trying to put them in touch with Olinda.

Although it seemed certain that a yacht like the *Boa Viagem* would, if in harbour for any length of time, be connected to the shore by telephone, naturally there was no number for her in the book; so the Indian got on to the Port Authority. After a wait of ten minutes it was confirmed that the yacht was still at Suva and James was put through to her. He asked for her Captain and there was another, longer, wait until the Captain, very annoyed at being roused from his sleep, came on the line.

'Yes,' he replied, 'the Senhora Mauá de Carvalho is in the yacht, but I certainly will not rouse her at such an hour.' Angry and impatient, James began to shout. Realising that he was getting nowhere, Gregory pulled the instrument from him and said in a sharp voice:

'We are police officers. Do as you are told. Bring the Senhora to the telephone at once or you will find yourself in trouble.'

That had the desired effect. Six minutes later he was speaking to Olinda. The line was far from good, but he managed to make her understand who he was and that James was with him. Then, that at any time during the morning Lacost would probably arrive. She was to receive him in the presence of her Captain, who was to be armed. Lacost would tell her that her husband was dead. Whether she believed him or not, she was to show shock and pretend to faint, so that Lacost could be got rid of as soon as possible. In no circumstances was she to go ashore, and he and James expected to be with her within a few hours.

By leaving open the question whether de Carvalho was

261

really dead or still alive he had prepared her for the truth. The next matter was to get to her as soon as possible, so he asked for a car to take them to Nandi airport.

The Indian shook his head. 'I am sorry, sir, but that will not be easy so early in the morning. The garages will not be open yet. But wait; it is only ten or twelve miles to Nandi. Since your business is urgent, I will run you over in my little car. Our girl in the office here is very good. She will attend to any wishes our visitors may have during my absence.'

Gratefully, they accepted the offer of this most obliging man, and a few minutes later were on their way. It was a quarter to seven when they reached Nandi. An American jet liner had just come in from Honolulu, so the whole of the airport staff were fully occupied. James, still obsessed with the idea that Lacost would reach Olinda before they did and harm her in some way, could not conceal his impatience.

To take his mind off his worry while they waited, Gregory gently baited him by speaking of the kindness of the Indian who had motored them to Nandi, and mentioned that the Hindu and Pakistani immigrants had brought great benefits to the islands.

James rose to the bait and argued fiercely that they were usurers who swindled the natives out of their property, and were a menace to their simple but adequate standard of living.

Gregory took up the challenge and said that there were grasping men in every race. Here and there Indians might cheat the islanders, but the great majority were honest, industrious people. Rightly, he argued that the natives owed them a great deal. The better-off among them could now buy radios, fridges and electric gadgets that made housework easier, and even the poorest could buy good cooking utensils and gay cotton clothes from the Indian shops. The Indians, too, provided culture for the new generation of islanders who were ready to receive it. He instanced the Art and Botanical Societies in which they played such active part, and Mr. Desai's splendidly-stocked bookshop in Suva. Some of these things, he insisted, might be due originally to the white man's initiative, but they were supported and the increase in their activities made possible only by the capital contributed by the hard-working Indians.

The discussion served its purpose until an official was free to deal with Gregory's enquiry. He had hoped to secure a small charter plane which, as soon as it had been serviced, would fly them to Suva. But no such aircraft was available, and the public morning service did not leave until ten o'clock.

Gregory could not feel that after his talk with Olinda they had any real cause for anxiety, so he was in favour of waiting for the flight. But James, having in mind the way in which Lacost had attempted to kill them both on Lake Atitlan, remained convinced that such an unscrupulous enemy might quite well take a time-bomb with him when he went on the yacht to tell Olinda of her husband's death, and leave it behind to blow her to pieces.

As a result of his agitated pressing, a hire car was produced which, it was thought, could take them to Suva sooner than if they went by the 'plane and then had to drive from the airport into the city.

It was a little after eight o'clock when they set off, and Gregory had agreed to the plan because it seemed reasonable to suppose that on an almost clear road the drive could be accomplished in about three hours, which meant that they should reach Suva harbour a little before the E.T.A. of Lacost's *Pigalle*.

But neither he nor James had been aware of the condition of the road. They had assumed it to be similar to the good, smooth surface of that on which they had travelled from Lautoka to the airport. But it was nothing of the kind. For almost the whole way the surface was rutted, broken and, here and there, long stretches were pockmarked with dangerous potholes. Frequently the car bounced from side to side and, with only rare intervals, broken stones hit the bottom of it like an irregular fusilade of pistol shots.

In vain James alternately pleaded with their driver and offered him rewards to go faster. The man, quite reasonably, objected to having his tyres cut up more severely than could be avoided or having to force the pace to an extent where his car would be shaken to pieces.

Meantime, Gregory, jolted from side to side though he was, had an admirable opportunity to enjoy the tropical scenery as they followed the road, which for the greater part of the way was in sight of the sea, round the south of Viti Levu.

For some distance along the coastal plain there were thousands of acres of sugar cane and fields in which cattle and goats were grazing, but no sheep; while inland jungle-clad mountains, with many patches of bare rock showing, stood out against the sky. The villages became few and far between as they progressed into a country of rolling hills, not unlike Tuscany, then there came dense jungle again, with many mango, breadfruit and casuarina trees.

Along the second half of the way there was again wild, mountainous jungle, with tree-ferns, ginger plants and palms growing alongside the road. Then there came a long stretch of flat land—once rubber plantations that had since been abandoned. It was followed by the great area in which Fiji's dairy-farming industry flourishes. Their driver told them that eight thousand cattle were milked there every day. They left it for more jungle-covered mountain slopes, through which the road curved sharply and went up and down at steep gradients until they entered the huge semicircle of Suva Bay.

It was another quarter of an hour before their car brought them round the greater part of the long curve to the outskirts of the town, and by the time they found the berth at which the *Boa Viagem* was tied up it was well after midday.

Jumping out, James left Gregory to settle for the car and ran to the gangway leading up to the deck of the yacht. There he was halted by a sailor, which enabled Gregory to catch up with him. The man refused to let them pass until he had called an officer, so it was evident that Olinda was taking sound precautions. When they gave their names to the officer he said that the Senhora Mauá de Carvalho was expecting them, and led them to the saloon.

Olinda was there, looking at a fashion magazine. As she

264

saw them enter, she dropped the magazine and stood up, an expression of anxiety mingling with delight on her lovely face.

Again Gregory registered the fact that, although not his type, she was a splendid specimen of young womanhood. She was a big girl, at least five foot eleven in height, with a generous bust and full hips, separated by a waist that could not be said to be narrow, but was small enough to accentuate the curves of her upper and lower body. Her black hair was parted in the centre, Madonna-fashion, but fell to each side of her face and on to her broad shoulders in a glory of long curls. She had painted her Cupid's-bow mouth a bright red. Her big black eyes, under tapering arched brows, lit up as their glance became riveted on James.

Running forward, he clasped both her hands, raised them in turn rapidly to his lips and cried, 'Did you think me dead? I had no way of getting in touch with you. Mr. Sallust and I have survived all sorts of dangers. But we're still alive. And ... and ... thank God you are. Oh, how wonderful it is to see you again.'

'Yes,' she stammered. 'Yes. For me too. But Valentim? Is ... is it true that he is dead?'

Smiling, James nodded. 'Yes. He's dead. Lacost or one of the Colons killed him. We have not the least doubt about that. But it means that you are now in danger. I've been worried out of my wits about you. Oh, thank God, I've found you safe and well.'

'How ... how did Valentim die?' she asked, a little breathlessly. James told her; and of how Gregory had made certain by partly disinterring the corpse, that the man on whom the coconut was said to have fallen was Valentim.

She stared at Gregory with distended eyes. 'You did that? You opened up a grave? And in the middle of the night! How did you dare?'

He spread out his hands in the foreign gesture he sometimes used. 'Senhora, that sort of thing does not require anywhere near the courage that it does to grapple with an armed man. The dead cannot harm one. And while I have every

265

reason to believe in the existence of evil occult forces, I do not believe that they can harm anyone who has faith in his ability to defy them.'

Olinda shook her head. 'All the same, I think you are very brave, and it makes me happy that James should have you for his friend. After what you tell me there can be no doubt that Valentim is no more. I married him when quite young, hypnotised a little, perhaps, by his vivid personality and the power he exercised through his great fortune. Later he resented it that I did not give him children, although, according to the doctors, that was no fault of mine. Then his constant infidelities sickened me, and I began to hate him. I cannot honestly say that I am sorry that he is dead, but I will have many Masses said for his soul.'

As she crossed herself, Gregory asked, 'Has Lacost been here to see you? If he hasn't, he may arrive at any moment, and we must be prepared.'

'He was here over an hour ago. Very tactfully and, apparently, with much sorrow, he told me about Valentim's death —or, rather, about a falling coconut having killed him. To get rid of him quickly I pretended to faint, as you had told me to. Before he went off he left a message with Captain Amedo. It was to the effect that he had secured divers in the Yasawas and intended to leave shortly with them for Tujoa. He added that as soon as I had sufficiently recovered and the *Boa Viagem* was fit to put to sea he trusted that I would follow; as, now that my husband was dead, he naturally regarded me as his partner.'

James let go a sigh of relief. 'Then, if he's off back to Tujoa, you should be quite safe here.'

'If he does go,' Gregory added. 'But I wouldn't trust him.' Then, looking across at Olinda, he said, 'There seems to be a question about the *Boa Viagem*'s being fit to put to sea. What did he mean by that?'

'Oh, of course you wouldn't know,' Olinda replied quickly. 'Soon after we arrived here from Tujoa something went wrong with the engines. I know little about such things, but it was thought that some discontented member of the crew had damaged them deliberately. That is why Valentim went to the Yasawas in Lacost's boat, and I stayed behind.'

Gregory smiled. 'I suspected something of the kind. Evidently Lacost managed to put one of his pals on board to do a job of sabotage, or bribed one of your crew to do it. All the same, I'm a little surprised that he managed to persuade your husband to go with him in the *Pigalle*. After all, the Colons could have collected the divers quite well without Senhor de Carvalho.'

'That wasn't difficult. Valentim always enjoyed visiting the smaller groups of islands and he had never been to the Yasawas. There was also some talk of hula-hula girls, and having left me here in Suva, he wouldn't even have had to invent excuses for going ashore without me.'

'I see. I take it the engine has since been repaired, though?'

'Not yet. We are still waiting for one small part that has to be flown down from San Francisco. It should be here in a day or two.' Moving over to a cocktail cabinet, Olinda added, 'But both of you must be tired and thirsty. Let me mix you a drink.'

While she was busy at the cabinet, James said, 'You realise, of course, why Lacost murdered Valentim?'

'I assume it was something to do with the licence to get up the gold,' she replied. 'Holding it was Valentim's contribution to the partnership they entered into in Tujoa; the Colons were to do the actual work. After you escaped from Noumea I had no idea where you had got to, or whether you were alive or dead; so I could not let you know that they were making a deal, or do anything to stop them.'

'We guessed that was what had taken place. Anyhow, now Valentim is dead, you have become the licence-holder. Unless Lacost is prepared to risk being arrested he must either come to some arrangement with you or bring about your death; so that the way is clear for him to secure a licence himself. That's why we were so anxious about you.'

Her face lit by a lovely smile, she turned and handed him a frosted glass. 'Dear James. You must know that nothing would induce me to help him rob you of the treasure. It's

267

yours by right, and since you say that the licence is now mine, I will happily make it over to you.'

While James kissed her hands again and expressed his gratitude, Gregory took a long drink, then said:

'That's very generous of you, but it may not be possible. If your husband entered into a legal partnership with Lacost while they were in Tujoa, although you have become the licence-holder, you will still be bound by the contract. And there is another thing. If de Carvalho took the licence with him to the outer isles Lacost will have got hold of it.'

Olinda shook her head. 'They would have needed a lawyer to draw up a proper deed of partnership, and no lawyer came on board either while we were at Tujoa or here; neither did Valentim go ashore to see one. As for the licence, since it was registered at Noumea in the name of de Carvalho, what good could the possession of it do Lacost?'

'He might go to Noumea, show it to the authorities and say that he had bought it from your husband, then get them to cancel it and issue one to him.'

'I think it very unlikely that Valentim did take the licence with him. After all, why should he? If he didn't, it will be in the safe. As my jewellery is kept in it, I know the combination, so we can soon find out.'

The safe was cunningly concealed behind one of the mahogany panels that formed a front for the banquettes which ran along both sides of the saloon. Kneeling, Olinda removed the panel, twirled the knobs and opened the safe. In it, besides the cases holding her jewels, there were several folders. One of them was labelled *Reina Maria Amalia Treasure*. Pulling it out, she threw it up on to the table.

Gregory swiftly shuffled through the papers it contained. 'Here we are,' he said after a moment. 'This is the licence all right.' Then he handed the folder back to Olinda, who locked it up again in the safe.

'Well,' she asked, 'where do we go from here?'

Gregory remained thoughtful for a moment, then he said, 'We have to put ourselves in Lacost's shoes to make any likely guess at what he will do. It really depends on how much value he sets on obtaining a licence. James and I were prepared to go ahead without one, because the *Maria Amalia* having been sunk before Tujoa became a French possession, he could claim that he had inherited the right to the treasure trove as part of his ancestor's estate, and an international court might well have given a decision in his favour. But Lacost can claim no such right; so to make off with it would amount to an act equivalent to piracy, and for the rest of their lives he and his pals would be wanted criminals.

'He left a message to the effect that he now regarded Olinda as his partner, and expected her to follow him as soon as she could to Tujoa. No doubt when he left the message he was hoping that she would do so; then, covered by her legal authority, he could have salvaged the gold and later devised some way of swindling her out of her share of it.

'But he did not then know that James and I had reappeared on the scene. I don't suppose he does yet, but he will within a few hours because, to have sabotaged the engines of this yacht, he must have some contact with one of her crew; and the fact that we have turned up will alter his whole thinking.

'He must know about James having attacked de Carvalho in Noumea and possibly knows, or anyhow may suspect, the real reason for that—namely, that you two are in love. In any case, he will learn that the three of us are together in this yacht and on the most friendly terms. That will lead him to assume that, when Olinda arrives in Tujoa, James and I will be with her and that we will prevent him from getting the gold up under the legal cover of being her representative or, if having the lead on us he has already got some of it up, swindling her out of any part of it.'

'You have raised a point there,' James put in. 'He has got the start on us, and a good one. For one thing, he knows that this yacht is still out of action and may remain so for some days. For another, we have not yet secured any divers and can't procure them on Tujoa. If he sails at once and the weather proves favourable, he might scoop the pool and make off with it before we could get there.'

'That would entail defying Elbœuf and becoming a fugitive from the French Government.'

'If the haul is as large as we have reason to anticipate, he might think it worth it. To hunt for a handful of men among the innumerable islands of the South Pacific would be like looking for a needle in a haystack. If they lie up on one of the uninhabited ones that has water, and make do for a couple of years on wild pig, fruit and fish, it is very unlikely that they would be discovered; then they could separate and each unload his share of the spoil in a different country.'

'That is possible, but I don't see men of their kind having the patience to wait two years for the sort of life they hope to lead on their ill-gotten gains. It is a certainty they would quarrel. After a month or two some of them would plot to murder those who were in favour of sticking it out, get a double share of the loot and gamble on being able to evade the police when they got back to civilisation. Lacost is clever enough to realise the danger of rushing his fences. He would be all for continuing to lie doggo, so it would be him and anyone who stood by him that the others would murder. He must realise the risk he would run of having a mutiny on his hands or being knifed on a dark night. That is why I think he may be prepared to go to any lengths to make his operation legal. And the only way he can do that is to put Olinda out of the way. With her death the licence would lapse. Neither James nor I can return to Noumea; so he'd have a free field, go there, get a licence, pay the tax on the treasure and sail off with it, having nothing to fear.'

James' face took on a worried frown. 'Then you think Olinda is still in danger?'

'It's quite possible that she is. Lacost may send the *Pigalle* off on a cruise, but remain on here himself hoping to find some way of having a crack at her. But if she stays aboard her yacht I don't think he will stand much chance of doing her any harm.'

Olinda smiled. 'If you will both remain as my guests I'm sure I wouldn't lose a wink of sleep.'

'Thanks! Thanks!' James accepted eagerly. 'I was going to ask if I might stay. Just ... just in case ...'

Gregory, not relishing the idea of having to play gooseberry and conscious that his presence would put a damper

270

on much of their enjoyment at being together again, replied:

'Thank you, Senhora, but I feel sure that James is capable of taking care of you, and there are certain things I want to do in Suva; so it would be more convenient for me to live ashore. I think I will go back to the Grand Pacific.'

James and Olinda both refrained from pressing Gregory to alter his decision. Then James asked, not very enthusiastically, 'How about the future? What ought our next move to be?'

Gregory took his time about replying, then he said, 'Lacost may stay on here for a few days, in the hope of eliminating Olinda; but he may equally well do as he said he would—sail for Tujoa right away—even when he knows that he now has no chance of getting hold of the treasure legally. So, in spite of the fact that we now have the law on our side, we mustn't give him too great a lead—say five or six days.'

'We came here to get divers,' James remarked. 'We wouldn't be able to get them together in so short a time. We can't get them on Tujoa, and we can do nothing without them. All we can do is to confront Lacost when we reach Tujoa and stall him off. And we dare not leave him there with a free hand long enough for us to return here and get divers, so it would result in a stalemate.'

'We don't have to get divers,' Gregory smiled. 'That is why I suggested that we should give Lacost the best part of a week's start. We will let his divers do the job for us. Then we'll turn up unexpectedly and pounce.'

'That sounds all right,' James agreed, a shade dubiously, 'but when we get to the point of pouncing what do we pounce with?'

'Now we have the licence we can row in with old Elbœuf, whose job it is to see that no-one gets hold of the gold illegally and to collect the Government's ten per cent. With his gendarmes and the support of your body-guard—which you will remember you promised him in such a situation—we should have no great difficulty in overcoming half a dozen Colons and taking the treasure from them.'

'Say they have not got it up when we arrive there?'

Gregory shrugged. 'Providing we don't give them long

enough both to get it up and get away with it, we don't have to worry. With the help of Elbœuf's gendarmes we'll put Lacost and Co. out of business, then take over his divers. Our man Baker will do the job of directing them.'

There seemed no more to be said. James and Gregory had another long drink while Olinda changed into the only dark coat and skirt she had on board and draped a black scarf over her head. They then went ashore—Olinda, escorted by James, to buy a ready-made mourning outfit and arrange for Masses to be said for her husband's soul; Gregory to the Grand Pacific.

By then it was a quarter to two. Gregory felt very tired, but not particularly hungry. In the restaurant he made a quick meal off a few giant prawns, then had a bath, went to bed and immediately fell asleep.

Four hours later he woke, feeling both easy in his mind at the turn events had taken, and much refreshed. Putting on his bathing shorts and robe he went down to the garden for an evening dip. Now that May was only a week away it was considerably cooler than when he had been in Suva towards the end of January; but the sun still shone from a bright blue sky and it was as warm as one of those rare, really good days in an English summer. No one was in the pool but several people were scattered about the garden, sunbathing.

After he had had his swim he looked about for a place to lie and sun himself. In the garden there were half a dozen basket-work lounge chairs of a type he had seen nowhere else. They were shaped like a big, hollowed-out fish mould and on his previous visit he had found them particularly comfortable. Only one, some distance away, was vacant and it was next to another occupied by a woman lying on her face. As he walked over to it, he gave a sudden smile. That dark head of hair and beautifully-proportioned bronze body could belong to no-one other than Manon.

While still a dozen yards from her, he halted, took his cigarettes from the pocket of his robe, lit one and stood contemplating her. When on the previous day he had been on her island, Joe-Joe had given him to believe that she was staying with friends; so he had not expected to find her at the Grand

272

Pacific, and on his arrival that morning he had been too tired to enquire at the office if her whereabouts were known. That she should be there after all, and unaccompanied by a man, he took to be a piece of rare good fortune. But, as he again delighted in the sight of her seductive body, he wondered cynically what explanation she would give to account for having lent her house to Lacost and his murderous gang of Colons.

16

The Fire-Walkers of Beqa

Throwing away his cigarette, Gregory tiptoed over to Manon, stooped, and kissed her on the back of the neck.

Starting up, she turned over as swiftly as an eel. For a second her big dark eyes glared with offended dignity. Then they grew wide with astonishment and joy.

'Gregory!' she cried. Her arms reached out, closed round his neck and, drawing him down, she gave him a long, luscious kiss on the mouth.

As she released him, he smiled at her and said, 'Quite a surprise for you, eh? Anyhow, it's good to know that I still have a place in your affections.'

'Oh, darling!' She was a little breathless. 'Of course I still love you. But where have you been all this time? Why didn't you write me? I've been desolate, positively aching for you for months.'

'It's a long story,' he replied, sitting down on the other fish-shaped basket lounge. 'For most of the time I was in prison and it was impossible to write.'

'In prison?' she repeated. 'Whatever for?'

He then gave her a version of the tribulations which had befallen James and him, following James' assault on de Carvalho; but suppressing the facts that on Yuloga they had been prisoners of the Russians, the part that General Ribaud had played, his own knowledge that Lacost and de Carvalho had gone into partnership and that the latter was now dead.

When he had done he added casually, 'By the by, hoping to find you there, I went to your island yesterday.'

She could not suppress a start, and her eyes widened. For

274

a moment she was silent, then she said, 'I've been away from home for some time. As you know, it is a delightful spot, but if I am there alone for long I do get bored. So I spent a week with friends at the lovely new Fijian Hotel halfway down the south coast, then came on here for a few days to do some shopping before going back.'

Gregory's expression remained quite friendly, but his eyes bored into hers as he said, 'Meanwhile you had either let or lent your island to Lacost.'

Ready for him now, she raised her tapering eyebrows and repeated, 'Lacost?' as though she had never heard the name.

'Yes. The man who tried to kill me when we were in Guatemala.'

'Oh! Yes, of course. For the moment his name didn't ring a bell with me. But how can you possibly suppose that I'd let my island to a man who tried to murder you? I haven't even set eyes on him since we saw him at Mexico City airport.'

'The fact remains that up till two days ago, for a week or more, he and his Colons made your island their headquarters while they went round the Yasawas engaging divers. And Joe-Joe told me they were there with your permission.'

'Oh, Colons!' Manon exclaimed, her face suddenly brightening. 'Now I understand. One evening while I was at the Fijian I ran into an old acquaintance of mine. His name is André Gougon and I knew him both in Algeria and Tahiti. He told me he had come ashore from a boat in which he and a few other men were about to make a trip round the Yasawas. They were all nearly broke and fed up with Tahiti, where living has become appallingly expensive; so they were going to look for an island where they could settle and perhaps go into the copra trade. I said that if they liked to make my house their headquarters for a week or two while they looked round they were welcome; and I wrote him a note to take to Joe-Joe.'

Gregory shook his head. 'As it turns out that your Monsieur Gougon is now one of Lacost's gang, I fear having fallen on evil times must have driven him to crime—although he probably didn't need much driving. While I was in Tujoa I learned that Lacost had only recently been let out of prison.

275

Apparently, on his return to Tahiti, the police got him for smuggling. Maybe your friend Gougon was in that racket with him. Anyway, it set their plans back for a couple of months, which was a bit of luck for us.'

With a light laugh, he added, 'Still, you weren't to know that Gougon was one of Lacost's pals, so that explains everything. What a joy it is to see you again. You look positively ravishing.'

'Do I?' She preened herself and fluttered her long eyelashes at him.

'Indeed you do. How I wish that we were on a deserted beach instead of in this garden. I'd have that bikini off you quicker than you could take one sip at a dry martini. As it is, I'll have to make do with a good nibble of your lovely neck.'

As he spoke he took her by the shoulders and brought his face down close to hers.

'*Non, je t'en prie!*' she cried, squirming away. 'Not here! Not here!' Then, as he released her, she gave a happy laugh. '*Mon Dieu*, what a man you are! Such ardour. And at your age. You should be ashamed of yourself.'

He grinned at her. 'I'm not, my dear, because I can't help myself. It's the old candle flame and moth trouble. Lying about like this with next to no clothes on, you are a public danger.'

'Then let us go in, get dressed, then meet in the lounge for a drink,' she suggested. 'Anyhow, it is getting a little chilly.'

'Fine,' he agreed. 'And what about dinner afterwards? Or have you an attendant beau who has to drag himself from your side to do some errand for you?'

She shook her head. 'No. I am staying here alone, and can think of nothing nicer than to dine with you.'

'I can,' he responded with the suggestion of a quick grin, 'but maybe later.'

'About that we'll see,' she said, with mock primness, as they walked towards the hotel entrance. 'I have not yet forgiven you for deserting me for so long. Although I suppose I'll have to, as you spent most of the time in prison.' They then agreed to meet in an hour.

Up in her room Manon collapsed upon her bed and lay for a while staring at the ceiling. Her heart beat a little faster as she thought of the narrow escape she had had. It was quite a long time now since she had reluctantly come to the conclusion that, having had his fun with her, Gregory had found some other woman who appealed to him, so she had lost him for good. Her hopes of getting him to marry her having come to an end, no reason remained why she should endeavour to put a check on Pierre Lacost's activities. More than ever in need of money, she had become desperately anxious that he should secure the *Maria Amalia*'s gold, and to help him she had even connived at murder.

He had told her about the partnership that he had entered into with de Carvalho, then that he meant to get rid of him and how. She had agreed to lend her island for the deed, and only over lunch that day Pierre had told her that it had been satisfactorily carried out. Earlier he had wanted her to play hostess to de Carvalho, but, just in case some question about the way in which he had met his end should later be raised, she had refused, and had left her island before the Colons arrived so that, whatever happened, she could never be associated with de Carvalho's death. Now, she had good reason to thank the gods for that cautious streak in her nature; for, had she remained while the Colons were there, Joe-Joe would have told Gregory of it. Then she could not possibly have concealed from him her association with Pierre.

That Gregory had swallowed her story about lending her home to André Gougon without the least idea that he had become a crook she had no doubt. And here was this immensely wealthy potential husband back again, within her grasp. He had not met and gone off with some other woman, after all, but had spent the greater part of the time they had been separated immured in prison. He had made it obvious, too, that he was as mad about her as ever. What stupendous luck.

But she was very far from out of the wood yet. Along with his other activities, Pierre had continued as her lover and now, having returned to Suva that morning, he had taken a room at the Grand Pacific. Only her patron saint could have intervened to prevent Gregory from finding them lunching together, and over lunch Pierre had declared with gusto his intention of sleeping with her that night. Gregory obviously meant to also. Somehow a clash must be avoided, but it was going to tax all her ingenuity.

Jumping off the bed, she hastily began to dress, then made up her face. As soon as she had finished, she phoned down to the office and got the number of Pierre's room. Hurrying along to it, she knocked on the door. To her consternation, there was no reply. Half-running, she returned to her own room and swiftly wrote a note: *Sallust is here. You know my intentions towards him. Remember all you owe me. For God's sake keep out of the way and leave this hotel as soon as possible. In no circumstances come to my room tonight.*

Putting the note in an envelope she again hastened to Pierre's room and slipped it under the door. Then, endeavouring to still her agitation, she went downstairs to meet Gregory.

He, in the meantime, while washing and shaving, had been considering what he should do about Manon. Highly conscious that to sleep with she was a woman in a thousand, he was greatly looking forward to the night to come. But what then? He was expecting to leave Fiji for Tujoa in four or five days. That seemed all too short a time in which to enjoy to the full a resumption of their liaison. Should he take her with him? That was the question. After all, why not? Through her connection with the Colons she could be dangerous. But he credited himself with the ability to keep an eye on that.

If he did take her he would have, to some extent, to let her in on what was going on. But how much? Obviously that Olinda now held the licence, so that should Lacost and his pals attempt to salvage the gold they could be legally branded as pirates. Yet they must know that already. So, if he kept her in the dark about his day-to-day plans, what harm could she do?

When they met in the lounge for drinks it was overtly as old friends—lover and mistress who were happy with one another and had not a care in the world. Unaware that Manon already knew that de Carvalho was dead, Gregory related quite casually how, during his visit to her island, he had learned that the Brazilian had accompanied Lacost to it and had been hit on the head by a falling coconut.

Later, over dinner, he referred airily to de Carvalho's death being a stroke of good luck for James, as the handsome young Ratu had for some time been in love with the dead man's widow. He went on to say how well everything was panning out, as Olinda now held the licence and, as she reciprocated James' love, they would in future work together.

Having given Manon this handout of information, he felt that he had put her in the picture as far as was necessary. Then he laid himself out to charm her. While doing so, in fact during the whole of dinner, he had sensed that she was having difficulty in concealing nervous tension. That, he suspected, might well be accounted for by the possibility that, in spite of her having said that she had not got a beau, she was in fact having an *affaire* with someone in the hotel, or anyway in Suva, and feared that at any moment her new lover might put in an appearance.

It was not until they were having coffee and liqueurs in the lounge that she gave a reason for the nervy state in which she had been all the evening. Hesitantly, she said:

'*Chéri,* you must not come to my room tonight. I could not be sorrier. It is appalling luck when, after all this time, we have just met again. But there is no controlling nature. Fortunately, I am over the worst, so tomorrow I'll be all right. We'll just have to be patient and make up for lost time as soon as I'm well enough to have you love me.'

Naturally, Gregory was disappointed and, while her excuse might have been valid, it tended to deepen his suspicion that she was expecting another lover. To test the situation further, he said:

'Of course I understand. But never mind. It's so long since we have seen each other that we still have lots to talk about, so I'll come to your room anyhow. I'll bring along a bottle of champagne and we'll have a cosy chat. At least I'll be able to enjoy some of your luscious kisses.'

'No!' she protested hastily. 'No, please! When I am like this I can't bear to be touched. And I'm feeling rotten. I meant to go to bed early and take a sleeping pill. I promise you that tomorrow I'll make it up to you a hundred-fold.'

'That settles it,' he thought, and for a moment his sense of mischief led him to contemplate walking in on her a little after midnight. But he quickly dismissed the idea. Not only could it lead to a most unpleasant scene, as a result of which he might lose her altogether, but it would be a dirty trick to play. She had every right to take another lover. In fact, believing that he had deserted her, it would have been surprising if she hadn't. After all, what really mattered was that she had shown real delight at his return; and if she had another lover she obviously meant to get rid of him as soon as possible.

When they had finished their liqueurs she went up to her room and shortly afterwards he also went up to read in bed; so he did not see Lacost when the Colon passed through the lounge soon after ten o'clock on his way upstairs.

On reading the note Manon had left for him, Lacost gave vent to a string of unprintable oaths. He had believed that, having made away with de Carvalho, the treasure was now as good as his. On reaching Tujoa, he had meant to tell Elbœuf that he was acting on behalf of the dead man's widow, hoping that if Elbœuf called on her for verification, she would reply in the affirmative. Then, by the time she arrived in Tujoa, he would have got up the gold and have devised some means of swindling her out of her share of it. Now the accursed Sallust and the young Ratu, of whom he had heard nothing for months, had suddenly appeared on the scene again and threatened to ruin all his plans.

He was made even more furious by the fact that he had taken a room at the Grand Pacific for the night only in order to sleep with Manon; otherwise he would have remained with his friends in the *Pigalle*. And now that pleasant prospect had also been scotched. It seemed certain that Sallust would want to sleep with her, and now she had been given a second chance to get her claws on his money it was most unlikely that she would refuse him.

Nevertheless he must ignore her forbidding him to go to her room. It was imperative that he should see her, in order to learn whatever she might know about Sallust's plans. As it was still early and unlikely that Sallust would join her much before midnight, he was tempted to go along to her at once. But, on second thoughts, he decided that he dare not risk it. If Sallust did come upon them together their secret association would be blown once and for all, and she was far too valuable as a spy in the enemy camp to be thrown away.

Seething with rage, he marched up and down his room. Then his glance fell on the bedside telephone. Snatching it up, he had the office put him through to her. When she answered he asked gruffly:

'Are you alone?'

'Yes,' she replied. 'I dined with him and had the very devil of an evening. I feared every moment that you might turn up and queer my pitch with him by, one way or another, putting your foot in it.'

'I suppose he will be coming along to you later.'

'No. That is, I've stalled him off by telling him I am unwell. But we can't be certain that he won't think up some excuse to come to my room. I'm sure he suspects that I put him off only because I was expecting someone else, so he may try to catch me out.'

'I can't help that. I've got to talk to you.'

'Listen!' Her voice was sharp with anger and apprehension. 'If you come to my room I'll scream the place down. Can't you realise what his turning up again means to me? It's the chance of a lifetime. If you ruin it I'll kill you! I swear I will!'

'If you made a scene you'd ruin yourself,' he retorted sullenly, 'because I'll spill the beans to him about you.'

'Then I'll spill the beans about what happened on my island,' she snapped back.

'*Grâce dè Dieu*!' he gasped. 'Keep a guard on your tongue, girl. Now, look. If you won't let me come to you, you must come to me.'

'What, and risk his finding my room empty? That would be as bad as if he found someone with me. He'd be certain to think I was keeping an assignation.'

'There will be no risk if you leave it late enough. Or, bet-

281

ter still, make it early tomorrow morning. Ask the office to give you a ring at six o'clock. Then if you meet anyone on your way here they'll think you are going for an early swim. The number of my room is 103.'

For a moment she hesitated, then she said, 'All right. I'll do that.'

Soon after six, having given a swift glance to either side up and down the passage, Manon opened the door of Pierre's room and slipped inside. He was lying on his back, snoring loudly. Putting a hand on his shoulder, she gave him a quick shake. The snoring stopped abruptly. With a grunt he sat up, blinked at her, then rubbed the sleep from his eyes.

Going to the window, she pulled aside the curtain to let in more of the early-morning light. Returning to the bed, she perched herself on the end of it and said, 'Well, here I am. What do you want to talk to me about?'

'Sallust, of course,' he replied, heaving his great bulk higher up against the pillows. 'Where has he been all this time, and what are his latest plans?'

'He and the Ratu were imprisoned by the French for two months. Apparently they went to Noumea and had a row with de Carvalho. The Ratu half-killed him and they were lucky not to have got a longer sentence.'

'I see. De Carvalho never said anything about that to me, but it explains why he was still pretty groggy when I first met him in Tujoa.'

'When they were freed they flew to Tujoa,' Manon went on, 'and they meant to start work on the wreck. But the witch-doctor there made trouble for them. He threatened to put a curse on the local divers, so they came on here to collect Fijians. The idea was that the Ratu should make a round of the Yasawas to get the divers, while Sallust put in a week or so with me.'

Lacost brushed up his long, yellow moustache and grinned. 'He's still got hot pants for you, then?'

'He certainly has, thank God. And I'll hook him yet if you keep your nose out of my affairs and don't mess things up for me.'

'I wouldn't dream of it—provided you behave yourself. What then?'

'It was lucky for you they didn't land on my island a day or two earlier or you might not have got away with . . . with what you did there. Lucky for me, too, that I had the sense to refuse to play hostess to you and the others. If I had I could never have put over my story that I had no idea you were one of the party to whom I had lent my island. Anyhow, Sallust got there only a few hours after you had left. Joe-Joe told him about de Carvalho's death and instead of going after divers he and the Ratu made straight to Suva.'

'To get hold of the luscious Madame Olinda, I suppose.'

'Naturally; knowing that, unless de Carvalho had taken the licence with him, she must have it. Even if he had, unless you had entered into an agreement with him for a half-share in it, as his widow she has inherited it and, by right of the registration in Noumea, can dispose of her title to it as she wishes.'

Lacost slapped a hand angrily on his big knee. 'What a fool I was not to have had a deed of partnership drawn up between myself and de Carvalho. If I'd done that she would be tied to me. But I deliberately refrained, because his heirs would have used the document to claim a half-share. And I had counted on being able to twist her round my little finger when I got back here.'

Manon's full lips opened in a malicious grin. 'That's what comes of trying to be too clever.'

Ignoring the gibe, he asked, 'What do you think the chances are of my persuading her to let me do the job as her nominee?'

'None whatever.'

'Why are you so certain? When we were together in Tujoa, and later here in Suva before I took her husband off to your island, she was quite pleasant to me.'

'Maybe. But she was not in love with you, and she is with the handsome young Ratu.'

'*Sacré bleu*!' Lacost exploded. 'D'you really mean that?'

'That is what Sallust told me.'

'*Nom d'un nom*! What cursed luck! And I had it all nicely

283

fixed to do the job legally, pay the French their ten per cent, then bilk her out of her share afterwards. Now she'll go in with the nigger and the English swine. Well, there's only one thing for it.'

'What is that?'

'Get the stuff up before they have a chance to. Jules smuggled himself aboard the *Boa Viagem* one night and sabotaged her engines. That was so that I could get de Carvalho to come along for the trip with us and away from his own crew. Now that will pay me another dividend. It will be days yet, maybe a week, before the *Boa Viagem* can put to sea. Another thing. I've got my divers. They haven't any yet and they can't get any in Tujoa because the witch man won't let the divers there play. With luck we'll have the gold and be off before they even get there.'

'What about the French authorities?'

Lacost shrugged his massive shoulders. 'To hell with them! The old Resident will kick up a stink, but we have arms and there aren't enough police in Revika to stop us. Afterwards we'll have to disappear. Still, the Pacific is a big place. If there is anything like the amount of treasure in the *Maria Amalia* that the records in Antigua led me to suppose, it will be well worth lying doggo for a year on one of the islands, to enjoy it afterwards. As for you, *mon petit chou*, I'll put your share aside for you. Meanwhile, do your utmost to delay Sallust and Co. setting out for Tujoa. And all the luck in getting him to the altar, then giving him half a dozen pairs of cuckold's horns.'

Manon nodded. 'I'll do what I can; but once he is set on a thing, it is next to impossible to dissuade him from doing it.'

As she stood up, he lurched forward and grabbed her by the wrist. 'Not so fast, little one. We've lost a night together, but there is still time to get up an appetite for our *petit déjeuner.*'

'No!' She tried to pull away. 'No, Pierre. I'm not feeling like that sort of thing.'

His good humour restored by his belief that he would be able to get away with the treasure before his enemies reached

Tujoa, he gave a great guffaw and cried, 'You will, *ma belle*, in another two minutes, I promise you!'

Still grasping her wrist, he jumped out of bed, swung her round and pushed her backwards on to it. Her struggle was brief and vain. Next moment his heavy body was pinning her down. Relaxing, she closed her eyes and, submitting to the animal ferocity which was his principal attraction for her, gave herself to him willingly.

At nine o'clock Gregory telephoned her, and they agreed to meet downstairs at eleven. When she appeared she was, as ever, dressed with exquisite taste and her make-up had been so skilfully applied that the sallowness of her skin was not perceptible. Her eyes seemed so large that they detracted attention from her receding chin. Her step was buoyant with the vitality of youth and as, smiling, she extended her hand for Gregory to kiss, he thought again that, dubious as her morals might be, he was lucky as a man no longer young to have acquired such an enchanting companion.

The weather being warm, but not too hot, they decided to walk the half-mile to the town and, perhaps, do some shopping. In a shop run by Chinese they saw some richly-embroidered jackets and wraps, so he bought several of them for her. Then, as they came out of the shop, they ran into Mr. Hunt.

When Gregory had thanked him for the excellent arrangements made by his travel service he said, 'If you would like to do something rather special tomorrow I could fix it up for you. The natives on Beqa are doing a fire-walk. That does not happen often, and it is unique. The Indian fakirs walk on hot ashes, but these chaps walk over white-hot stones—a far more hazardous test of faith and will-power. I've a boat going over to the island with a party of Americans, and if you like I could arrange for you to go with them.'

Gregory and Manon at once agreed that they would like to see this extraordinary performance. They then strolled on past the market, down to the harbour and went on board the *Boa Viagem*.

James and Manon greeted each other pleasantly, as old acquaintances, but it was the first time the two women had met. As they exchanged courtesies, Gregory was amused to see them sizing each other up. Olinda's eyes, he noted, swept over Manon's clothes, that singled her out, even in the tropics, as a *Parisienne*. Manon's first glance was at a solitaire diamond which Gregory estimated to be worth several thousand pounds that Olinda was now wearing on her engagement finger.

After a few minutes the four of them were at ease together and soon enjoying well-iced drinks. James was positively glowing with happiness, and Olinda kept glancing at him with obvious delight and pride. Gregory mentioned the expedition to Beqa, and asked if they would like to come, too. James said he had seen it before, when in his teens, but Olinda was enthralled by the idea; so Gregory rang up Mr. Hunt, who obligingly said that he would somehow manage to squeeze two more people into the party.

Olinda insisted that her visitors should stay to lunch, and it proved a merry meal, Manon contributing, by her wit and charm, an outstanding share to their gaiety.

Afterwards Gregory took Olinda aside and asked her if she would do him the kindness to invite Manon to accompany them when they left for Tujoa, and Olinda readily agreed.

Half an hour later Gregory and Manon drove back to the Grand Pacific in a taxi, went to their rooms for their siestas, then met again to swim in the late afternoon. Drinks and dinner followed. Having nothing more to fear from Lacost, she talked and laughed as though spring instead of blood coursed through her veins, so that Gregory was enchanted by her. Later that night, with her lovely body in his arms, he felt as though twenty years had dropped from him, and that from her soft, rich mouth he was drawing the Elixir of Life.

Back in his own room in the early hours, he thought again what a delightful travelling companion she would make. She had charm, wit, vivacity, was well educated and invariably *soignée*. No one could ever replace Erika for him, but Manon had everything—bar one thing.

Wondering about the future, he dropped asleep, but slept

only for three hours, as they had to make an early start for Beqa, and both of them had put in a call for six o'clock.

He had ordered a car for seven o'clock, as it was a drive of some twenty miles to the place where they were to take a boat out to the island. After picking up Olinda and James, they drove west out of Suva, passing the picturesque cemetery, and right round the bay into the flat, cattle country. From a lonely landing stage a small boat took them off to a tubby motor yacht some way out. The party of Americans was already on board and after exchanging polite greetings with some of them, they settled down for the ten-mile sea trip.

The sea was choppy and the ship far from comfortable. They were told that it had formerly been Queen Salote's yacht, but found that difficult to believe, as the one lavatory could be entered from the cabin only by climbing a steep ladder and through a narrow door; so how so large a lady could have reached it with dignity it was hard to imagine. Manon made Gregory laugh by whispering bawdy comments on the possibilities.

The yacht anchored a good mile off the island, and the water was so shallow that a motor boat could not have taken them more than halfway to the shore. Two native rowing boats came off; but they had to make several trips before the twenty-odd people in the party had all been landed by big, laughing fuzzy-headed men carrying them through the shallows. Even then, as the tide was out, there was a quarter of a mile or more of muddy sand to be crossed between the water and the tangles of exposed mangrove roots that fringed the coast.

On dry land at last, they entered the village. Like all the others they had seen, there was no trace of squalor. Each *bure* stood well apart from the others, with neat rows of small, white stones marking the path to the door and here and there a palm to give a patch of shade.

There they were greeted by the *Vunivalu* and his Council of Elders. The Chief, a very old man, explained to them in good English that, as he had recently been ill, he would not be presiding at the ceremony. Then, showing special deference to James, he said that he would explain the proceedings

287

to his party and led the way with them up a steep, grassy slope just beyond the village.

Halfway up the slope there stood what amounted to a small grandstand, with two rows of chairs shaded from the sun by a palm-thatch awning. The Chief bowed Olinda and Manon to chairs on either side of him, and when the rest of the party had taken their places he clapped his hands for the 'welcome' ceremony to begin.

The usual *yaggona* drinking followed, the coconut-shell *bilo* being first presented to James. Then, to the accompanying hollow hand-claps, everyone else drank in turn.

About fifty feet below them, where the slope flattened out on to level ground, there lay a circular pit some twenty feet in circumference. The surface consisted of smouldering logs from which smoke was rising. Using careful English, in a low voice the old Chief told Olinda and Manon about this ancient custom of his country.

The big pit was three-quarters full of large stones. By a log fire lit at seven o'clock that morning they had been made red-hot. Shortly now all the unburnt wood would be removed to expose the stones. The fire-walkers would then step down into the pit and walk once round it. Today there were eight of them. For twenty-four hours they had been fasting and in seclusion. Several of them had made the fire-walk before. Every healthy man born on Beqa did it at least once, when he reached maturity, otherwise he left the island. Some of the men, including the Chief himself, had done it many times, because doing it brought the favour of the gods and strengthened the spirit.

At a signal from the Chief's deputy, a dozen natives approached the pit in pairs, each holding one end of a long, very tough, rope-like liana. Throwing these across the pit, they ran from it parallel to each other, so that the middle of the liana formed a bight and, as it narrowed to a loop, caught round one of the smouldering logs; then, hauling on it, they dragged the log out of the pit.

This procedure took about a quarter of an hour. When the big stones had been cleared of the layer of wood the natives again approached the pit, this time carrying long poles.

288

Standing round the edge, they used the poles to prod at the stones, pushing them a little over so that above the roughly level surface no jagged points should be left, upon which a fire-walker might trip.

As they were doing this, one of the poles snapped and the end, about two feet long, fell on the stones. It had not been there for more than thirty seconds when it burst into flame. A murmur went up from the audience, some of whom had been convinced that they were about to witness only some clever trickery, for the flaming pole-end was incontestable evidence that the stones really were intensely hot.

From a nearby *bure* the eight fire-walkers now emerged in single file. They were naked to the waist, but wore short *sulus* of what looked like leather; their legs and feet were bare. Carrying themselves very upright, they walked with slow, dignified steps to the pit, down on to the stones, once round it, then out again. Not one of them faltered, made a murmur or showed any change of expression on his face.

There came a burst of applause from the onlookers. As usual on such expeditions, most of the Americans had been taking photographs every few minutes. Now several of them went down the slope to get close-ups of the men. Two of the fire-walkers lay down on their backs and raised their legs in the air, to show that there was not even a blister on the soles of their feet.

The old Chief then personally escorted James and his party back to the beach. Most of the villagers—men, women and children—came too. There was much hand-shaking and laughter, then the visitors were rowed back to the tubby, ill-found yacht. The Americans had spent the previous night at Korolevu, but now they were going on to Suva; so instead of returning to the landing stage, the cruiser set a course for the capital. The distance was more than twice as far, and it proved anything but a pleasant voyage. Halfway there a squall blew up, it rained in torrents, and the yacht bucked about abominably.

Several of the passengers were seasick, and Olinda and Manon prevented themselves from succumbing only with difficulty. Fortunately, the weather eased when they were within a few miles of the harbour; but on landing they all felt the need of a good, strong drink, so they walked the few hundred yards to the *Boa Viagem*.

On board, good news awaited them. The one piece of machinery which had been holding up the complete repair of the ship's engines had been delivered that morning. Captain Amedo reported to Olinda that the engineers had been working on the job all day, and that if a trial run in the forenoon next day proved satisfactory he could sail in the afternoon.

Lacost's *Pigalle*, they now learned, had left harbour the previous morning and he had been seen on the bridge when she sailed. This made it clear that, realising he had no chance of doing a deal with Olinda or of eliminating her, he had decided to make all speed for Tujoa, and attempt to get away with the treasure illegally before they could follow and stop him. But now that the *Boa Viagem* should be able to sail within twenty-four hours, he would then have only two and a half days' start.

Manon, unaware that this was less than half the lead that Gregory secretly intended to give him and anxious to carry out her promise to Lacost to delay them if possible, began to press them to spend a day or two at her island on their way to Tujoa. As she did so, it suddenly struck her that Olinda would not at all like the idea of visiting the place where her husband had been killed. But Gregory said he thought it an excellent idea, and to her surprise Olinda said she would like to do so in order to make arrangements for Valentim's grave to be remade and properly tended.

That evening the four of them dined at the Grand Pacific, but the party was somewhat marred by James' being unusually silent and appearing to be far from happy. When rallied on it, he excused himself by saying that he did not feel very well, which they put down to an after-effect of the tossing they had had that afternoon, and thought no more of it.

Next morning they did their final shopping. At lunchtime Olinda telephoned Gregory to let him know that the yacht's trial run had been successful and at four o'clock that afternoon he and Manon went aboard with their baggage.

Olinda showed them to their cabins, then they returned

with Manon to the saloon. James was sitting there, slumped on a settee, looking thoroughly miserable. Suddenly he came to his feet, stared at Gregory and cried:

'I'm not going! And neither are you. I won't let you. This cursed gold has brought us nothing but trouble. Let it stay where it is. Or let Lacost have it. I don't give a damn. Roboumo had the White Witch curse Valentim and the curse worked. He died at the full of the moon. Roboumo will have her curse us. Both of us. And we'll die there in Tujoa. I'm through with this business. Through with it. The whole thing is off.'

17

None but the Brave Deserve the Fair

Gregory and Olinda stared at James aghast. Manon regarded him only with curiosity while fighting down an
inclination to give a laugh of delight. James' unexpected
declaration that he meant to throw in his hand solved all
her problems. Not only would it leave Lacost a free field to
secure the gold, but Gregory would not now go to Tujoa
and risk his life disputing possession of it with the Colons.
Instead, she could get him back to her island, with nothing to
distract his mind from herself, and with a far better chance
of persuading him to marry her. Even should she fail in that
she would, as Pierre's financial backer, come in for a large
enough share of the treasure to be freed from her worries
about money. Still better, now that he would become a
wealthy man he provided, in addition to being an insatiable
lover, an admirable second string as a potential husband.

For almost a minute there ensued an intense silence, then
Gregory burst out, 'James! You cannot mean this! You
can't be serious?'

'I am,' James retorted sharply. 'I have been worrying myself sick about this for days—ever since I learned of Valentim's death. I'll have no more to do with it.'

'But damn it, man, we can't let those murdering devils get
away with it! I don't give a fig for the money I've put into
the venture, but I care a lot about being licked at the post
solely because my partner lacks the will-power to resist occult blackmail; and that is what it amounts to.'

'And I care too,' Olinda followed up, her dark eyes flashing.'Like Gregory, the money side of it means nothing to me.

But I am now the holder of the licence. Valentim paid for it with his life. As I did not love him I feel no desperate urge to be avenged on his murderers. All the same, I'm not prepared to sit still and see them profit from their crime.'

'I . . . I feel that I'm letting both of you down,' James stammered. 'But I just can't help myself. I don't want to die.'

'Die!' Gregory snapped angrily. 'Just because an old witch-doctor has performed some mumbo-jumbo? What nonsense!'

'It's not nonsense. Valentim is far from being the only man that I've known to die as the result of a curse.'

'Were any of the others white men?'

'No.'

'Did any of them die suddenly, as the result of a heart attack or, apparently, an accident?'

'Well, no. They just sickened and died.'

'There you are, then. This was no case of a man gradually losing vitality, then dying because he knew that a curse had been put upon him. De Carvalho was murdered—killed in cold blood while perfectly fit and with all his faculties—an entirely different matter.'

Gregory had not previously disclosed to Manon that he knew de Carvalho to have been murdered; so she gave a gasp of simulated surprise, as James retorted swiftly.

'That is neither here nor there. The fact remains that he met his end on the day of the full moon—just as the White Witch had decreed.'

'I don't believe for one moment that she had anything to do with it. You know perfectly well that we had already agreed that, sooner or later, Lacost would do de Carvalho in. That he killed him on the day he did is pure coincidence.'

'You may think so, but I don't. And I know much more about what goes on in these islands than you do. In Europe and the United States people may no longer believe in the Black Art, but *Draunikau* still works here in the South Seas.'

'I am not contesting that, but of one thing I am certain: it can affect only people who are afraid of it.'

'All right, then,' James gave a sullen shrug. 'There you

293

have the truth of the matter. I am backing out because I am afraid.'

'Oh, James!' Olinda exclaimed reproachfully. 'You mustn't say that. I'm sure you are not a coward.'

He turned sad eyes to her. 'I don't think I am in a physical sense, but I am about this.'

'I won't believe it,' she protested. 'It is quite understandable that the natives in these islands should still be affected by magic and curses; but you are an educated man, so should be capable of resisting that sort of thing.'

'I would have expected more sympathy from you, Olinda,' he murmured with evident distress. 'After all, magical practices are an everyday occurrence in Brazil. They call it *Macumba* there, don't they, and nearly everyone goes in fear of the *Macumba* priests.'

'The ignorant masses do, and plenty of other weak-minded superstitious people. But not those of the class to which I belong. That is, provided they lead normal lives and have sane, well-balanced brains. Only fools would deny the existence of occult powers, but that does not mean that one should allow oneself to become dominated by them.'

'I'm not. In the ordinary way I never give a thought to such things.'

'Then, for God's sake, stop doing so now,' Gregory put in. 'All you have to do is to exercise a little will-power. Keep your mind on normal things and ignore this other business.'

'That's right.' Olinda backed him up. 'I entirely agree with everything Gregory has said. If you allow your primitive instincts to get the upper hand, and start imagining things, evil people with occult powers can do what they like with you. But if you treat them as if they don't exist they can't possibly do you any harm.'

'You really believe that?' James asked hesitantly.

'Indeed I do.'

For a moment they were silent, then Gregory said, 'Now listen, James. Surely you are sufficiently sophisticated to appreciate that the human brain is like a wireless set, and can be tuned in to many wave-lengths. If you are stupid enough, and stubborn enough, to keep thinking of the awful things that, with the aid of the White Witch, Roboumo might possibly do to you, that will be giving them a chance to pull off something pretty nasty. But if you have the guts to switch to another wave-length their curses will prove as futile as stones thrown against a brick wall.'

James looked miserably from Gregory to Olinda and back again. 'That's all very well; and you may be right. But nothing will convince me that Valentim's death was not due to the White Witch's curse. And if we go on with this business she'll curse us and we'll die too, so how can I stop thinking of that?'

'If you can't ignore it, James, fight it.' Olinda spoke with great earnestness. 'It is either that, or to go on thinking about it, but with defiance—not in fear. If you don't you will fall under her evil influence for ever, and she will ruin your whole life.'

'But I have no occult power, so how can I defy the White Witch?'

'Everyone has occult power. What you mean is that you have never attempted to use yours.' Olinda paused for a moment, then went on. 'I am not suggesting that without prolonged instruction and training you could perform any great magics. But the exertion of will-power to influence others is in itself an occult phenomenon. You also seem to have forgotten that these people are your subjects, and that they are in rebellion against you. As a Ratu and a ruling Prince, it is no less than your duty to pit your will against theirs and subdue them.'

'If only I could,' James moaned. 'But I can't! I can't! They would get the better of it and inflict on me some horrible death. I just haven't the courage to challenge them. It's too much to ask.'

'Then you *are* a coward, and not fit to rule.' Olinda sadly shook her head. Her voice became almost a wail as she added, 'I'd never have believed it. How terribly I have let myself be misled.' Suddenly she burst into tears and ran from the saloon.

James started after her, then, utterly stricken, collapsed on

295

the settee and buried his face in his hands. His great shoulders began to heave and tears trickled between his fingers.

Manon had remained a silent observer throughout this unhappy scene. Gregory now signed to her to leave the cabin. Much relieved that James had not been persuaded to alter his mind, she was inwardly smiling, but before going up on deck she gave Gregory one of those expressive French grimaces in which raised eyebrows and down-turned mouth portray both puzzlement and sympathy.

As soon as she had gone, Gregory laid a hand on James' shoulder and said, 'Don't take Olinda's outburst too badly. When she has had a little time to think things over I'm sure she'll come round and understand your point of view.'

'No!' sobbed James. 'No, I'm sure she won't. She meant what she said about being disappointed in me. I love her so dearly, and now I've lost her love. Oh, this is terrible . . . terrible.'

In spite of what Gregory had said, he thought the odds were that James was right. At a loss for words to console him, he sat down on the settee and began vaguely to philosophise, in the hope of distracting his young friend's attention from his grief.

'If a man lived to be as old as Methuselah he could still not count on predicting every time what a woman's reaction to an act of his would be. That is because each one is an individual, with a different upbringing, past experience, background, morals, instincts and so on. But there are certain general principles that apply to most. Flattery in moderation never fails to go down well and, of course, generosity. Honesty, earnestness and endeavour they may respect, but they would far rather have a man who makes them laugh. Their attitude towards courage is illogical. They admire a man for his past deeds of valour, but if he wants to go out and fight again they do their utmost to restrain him. On the other hand, should he be faced with a challenge and refuse it, they send him straight to the bottom of the class.'

James suddenly looked up and said bitterly, 'That's where Olinda has sent me, and I've got to get back to the top. I've got to. But how am I going to do it?'

'My dear boy, with the best will in the world I can't give you any answer to that one, except to change your mind about facing up to this curse—unless . . .'

'Unless, what?' James asked eagerly.

'Well, there is another way; and I suppose if I felt as scared of the White Witch as you do, I should take it. You could return to Tujoa and put bullets through her and her pal Roboumo; then you could cheerfully go ahead with getting up the gold without anything to fear.'

'I wish I could.' James shook his head. 'But it's not possible. I'd never be able to get past Roboumo's body-guard. And, even if I did succeed in that, everyone would be after me for murder.'

They fell silent for a few minutes, then Gregory remarked, 'I don't know much about these matters, but I've always understood that there were ways in which curses could be turned aside and deflected back on to their originator.'

'You're right. And that is a by no means uncommon practice. If a man knows himself to have been cursed he seeks out a more powerful witch-doctor and, whatever it costs him, pays the man to channel the curse on to his enemy.'

'Then why shouldn't you do that?'

'Because I know of no witch-doctor more powerful than Roboumo. In fact, with the aid of the White Witch he has made himself the most powerful *Draunikau* wizard in all the South Seas.'

'What about trying your own hand at outmagicking him?' Gregory suggested.

'How could I? Such an idea is crazy. I wouldn't even know how to start.'

'Perhaps I could help you. Of course, this sort of thing is right outside my field. But I do know a bit about the sort of games that witches and warlocks used to get up to in Europe in the Middle Ages. We'll get hold of some wax and model two little figures of a man and a woman. On them we will scratch the names Roboumo and White Witch. Then we'll stick needles in the places where their livers would be and let them melt slowly in front of a fire.'

'Do you really think that would have any effect?'

Gregory shrugged. 'God alone knows. Naturally, I couldn't guarantee anything. With a bit of luck the two of them might be suffering all sorts of pain and grief come morning. But it's a long-odds bet, because I expect the sorcerer who does the job would have to mutter all sorts of gibberish over the images while they were melting, to make the curse effective. What we really want is for you to turn up in Tujoa with some sort of trick up your sleeve that will make everyone believe that you have become a more powerful magician than Roboumo. For instance, when a white man first killed here at a distance by banging off his musket, or showed that he could talk to his pals many miles away through the magic box that we call a wireless set.'

For a few minutes James considered this, then suddenly he jumped to his feet and cried, 'I have it! I've got it! I'll do a fire-walk.'

Gregory stared up at him. 'Good God, man! How could you? It's you who are being crazy now. You'd be burned to a cinder.'

'Why should I be?' James demanded. 'If the men of Beqa can do it, why shouldn't I? No training is required. The Chief there told me so. Only twenty-four hours of abstinence and concentration to gain faith in one's ability to walk over the hot stones without being burned. Nowhere else in the Pacific, or in the world, for that matter, do men perform this feat. If I could come safely through a trial on Beqa I could do another fire-walk in Tujoa, with my Council of Elders as witnesses. After that I would be publicly acclaimed as a more powerful magician than Roboumo, and could defy him with impunity.'

Silently, Gregory marvelled that a well-educated man who could not bring himself to face the nebulous possibility of being harmed by an evil occultist should be willing to face the very real danger of becoming crippled for life through attempting to walk on red-hot stones. After a moment he said:

'Well, James. you are a braver man than I am. Far braver. But if you can pull this off it will be a great spiritual victory

298

and once and for all you will have destroyed the evil influ-
once that Roboumo has over your people. Even should you
fail, I feel sure that your having undertaken this ordeal will
restore Olinda's faith in your courage.'

As Gregory had predicted, within half an hour James had
regained Olinda's good graces. Manon, on learning of James'
intentions, had to admit uneasily to herself that she had
counted her chickens before they were hatched, but she
could still hope that his brash audacity would result in his
being so badly burned that he would be put out of the game
for good. His decision to do the fire-walk necessitated a
change of plan as, instead of putting in two days at her
island, they would spend them lying off Beqa; but she consoled herself with the thought that the delay still gave Lacost
the lead that she had done her best to secure for him.

James, now keyed up with nervous tension, was anxious to
face his ordeal as soon as possible, so that evening the
yacht left harbour as planned, but set a course for Beqa instead of the Mamanucas.

When they arrived off the island darkness had fallen and,
as the waking hours of the inhabitants were governed by the
sun, it was decided that they should not go ashore that night.
Then, over dinner, James declared firmly that he did not
want the others to come ashore at all; the reason he gave
being that, should he fail the test it would be bad enough
for him to have to confess it later, but more than he could
bear that they should actually witness his failure.

To that they all readily agreed, and Gregory suggested
that to fill in the two days that James would be ashore the
rest of them should amuse themselves by big-game fishing in
nearby waters.

It was now the dark quarter of the moon, but the sky was
cloudless and the stars showed at their brightest. In countless
millions, from tiny pinpoints of light to steadily gleaming
beacons, they spangled the entire vault of the heavens, cast-
ing a soft radiance on the scene as the yacht rocked gently at
her moorings.

The night was made for lovers, and when James and Olinda went arm in arm to the after part of the deck, Gregory

and Manon tactfully settled themselves forward of the deckhouse, just under the bridge.

Next day Olinda confided to Gregory that she had spent three hours doing her utmost to dissuade James from risking mutilation by doing the fire-walk, but even when she had offered to tear up the licence and forget about the gold he had refused to be deflected from his purpose. For a moment Gregory was tempted to point out to her that it was she who had driven the young Ratu into this situation where he must either prove his courage or forfeit her love, but she was obviously so distressed and anxious that he refrained, then did his best to assure her that the friendly old Chief of Beqa would see to it that James came to no serious harm.

Meanwhile, at first light, James had gone off in the yacht's speed boat to within half a mile of the coast, then had been taken on to a native-paddled craft and carried ashore. As he had not returned by the time the others had finished a late breakfast, it could be taken as certain that the old *Vunivalu* of Beqa had agreed to allow him to attempt the fire-walk. The anchor was hauled up and the yacht headed for the deeper waters to the west.

The day's fishing did not prove very successful. Olinda showed no interest and Gregory's thoughts, also, were too occupied with James for him to concentrate fully on the sport. Manon did best by catching several medium-sized colourful fish and a large *walu,* fried slices of which they enjoyed at dinner. Gregory landed only an angel fish and a sea snake, then hooked some weighty, unidentified monster —probably a Tuna—which, after he had played it for only a few minutes, snapped his line.

That night they returned to the anchorage off Beqa and the following morning, as none of them felt like going fishing again, they decided to remain there, although it was uncertain whether James would rejoin them that day. If he had spent the past twenty-four hours fasting in seclusion and there had been nothing to prevent the fire-pit from being prepared that morning they should learn from him soon after midday of his success or failure. But it might be that, as he was not a native of Beqa, more prolonged preparation for the

300

ordeal was necessary, or that ancient custom dictated that fire-walks should be undertaken only at a certain phase of the moon.

This last possibility worried Gregory considerably, as if they had to remain off Beqa for any length of time that would give Lacost so long a lead that he might get up the gold and make off with it before they could reach Tujoa. But he endeavoured to console himself with the thought that securing the treasure was of secondary importance to James' being able, once and for all, to free himself from his fear of Roboumo.

By ten o'clock the sky had clouded over and it began to drizzle. Olinda, already in a state of feverish anxiety, walked the deck restlessly, cursing the weather; although Gregory assured her that, if the 'party' were on, light, warm rain would have no effect on the heat of the stones, so would not lead to a postponement. Manon alone had no reason to be worried, as James meant nothing to her, but she tactfully suppressed her normal high spirits and endeavoured to show the same concern as the others.

The morning seemed endless and, with poor appetites, they ate their lunch almost in silence. Up on deck again, they sat staring out into the mist that now nearly obscured the island, miserably aware that they might have to keep up their uneasy vigil for another twenty-four hours or more.

The dreary hours of the sunless afternoon dragged by. Wrapped in coats and rugs against the mist, they sat on, facing the vaguely-seen coast: Olinda telling the beads of her rosary and murmuring prayers, Gregory from time to time scanning through binoculars the partially obscured patches of jungle that stood between the village and the beach, and Manon doing her best to conceal her boredom.

A little before six they came to the conclusion that they would have to remain at anchor there for at least another day, and stood up to go below. It was then, as Gregory gave the murky vista a last sweep with his glasses, that he suddenly sighted a boat coming towards them. The now-fading light, added to the mist, had caused him to miss seeing it as it put off, and it was already some way from the shore. Quickly he pointed it out to the others; then Olinda shouted to Captain Amedo to send the speed boat in to meet it.

Now, lining the rail, they waited with almost unbearable impatience, striving to pierce the gloom and see if the native boat carried James, returning to them, or if it bore only a messenger to report that the fire-walk had had, for some reason, to be delayed.

The speed boat met the native craft about halfway from the shore and a figure transferred to it. But many of the natives of Beqa were as tall as James, so his friends could still not tell if it was him or a messenger.

Another agonising five minutes passed; then Olinda, to whom Gregory had passed the binoculars, cried: 'It's he! It's he! And he can't have been maimed, otherwise he wouldn't have been able to step so easily from one boat into the other. Oh, Holy Mary be praised!'

Gregory and Manon could also by then recognise the figure in the stern of the speed boat as James. He waved to them and they all waved back. But the all-important question still remained. Had he passed through the ordeal unscathed or had he, at the last moment, allowed fear to overcome him and refused the trial?

As the speed boat drew alongside the yacht, they had the answer. James' handsome face was lit with a radiant smile that told its own story. No man who had to confess failure through lack of courage could have worn such an expression. When he scrambled aboard, Olinda, sobbing with relief, threw her arms about him and, regardless of onlookers, kissed him again and again with fervid passion. No sooner had she released him than Manon went on tiptoe to kiss his cheek, Gregory and Captain Amedo shook him warmly by the hand, and the crew, although ignorant of his reason for having stayed ashore overnight, but realising that he must have achieved some triumph, cheered him lustily.

With flushed cheeks and sparkling eyes, Olinda told Captain Amedo that all the crew were to be given an extra month's pay and a good ration of wine with their meal that evening. Down in the saloon, the steward produced two magnums of the late Valentim's best champagne, and James' friends drank his health again and again as he told his story.

It had taken the whole of the previous morning to persuade the old Chief to let him attempt the fire-walk, so he had not started his twenty-four hours of segregation until well on in the afternoon. While in the darkened *bure,* he had followed the Chief's instructions and told himself countless times, hour after hour, until it had resulted in self-hypnosis, that he would feel no pain when he walked over the hot stones.

When he had emerged, everything had been made ready for the ordeal and the whole population of the village had assembled to watch. At the sight of the slight drizzle sizzling on the hot stones, thus turning into steam, his courage had ebbed, but the *Vunivalu* had taken him by the hand, told him that he must not look at the stones but straight ahead of him, then personally led him down into the pit. Concentrating his whole mind on Olinda, he had visualised her standing waiting for him on the opposite brink of the pit. His body had seemed to become lighter, the heat about him was so intense that it had vaguely crossed his mind that his clothes might catch fire, but he had felt no pain on the soles of his feet, only a swift tingling. Before he fully realised it, his ordeal was over, the *Vunivalu* was embracing him and giving him the nose-kiss, the villagers were shouting their applause and he was being escorted to the Meeting House for a *yaggona* ceremony.

He had only just finished his account when Olinda's chef appeared to say that, with the Senhora's permission, he proposed to put on a gala dinner. In the meantime quite a sea had got up, so Olinda told her Captain that they would lie under the shelter of Beqa for the night and not sail for Tujoa until the following morning. Manon, still anxious to delay their arrival for as long as possible, then renewed her invitation for them to visit her island.

Olinda looked across at Gregory, silently consulting him before making a reply. He did not want to give Lacost a free hand for too long at Tujoa, but the *Boa Viagem* would make the voyage more quickly than the *Pigalle,* and the Mamanucas lay almost on the direct course for the Nakapoas; so, knowing that Olinda would like to arrange about Valentim's grave, he said he thought it would be a good idea.

By midday on Sunday they anchored off Manon's island, and in the afternoon all went ashore to accompany Olinda, clad and veiled in deep black, on a formal visit to her late husband's grave. Meanwhile, old Joe-Joe had performed miracles with his staff to provide his mistress and her guests with an excellent dinner in the big *bure*.

That night they slept aboard. Next morning James gave Joe-Joe instructions about the reburial of de Carvalho in a stone-lined grave, and passed on to him a sum that Olinda had given him for the work and upkeep of the grave. After lunch they sailed again and dropped anchor off Revika shortly before midday on Wednesday, May 4th.

James had taken it for granted that the others would be his guests while on Tujoa but, when preparations were being made to go ashore, Olinda drew him aside and said:

'Darling, as we are to marry when my formal period of mourning is over, I do feel that, for both our sakes, I ought to protect my reputation in the eyes of your people. Manon is a gay and pleasant creature but . . . well, hardly the sort of woman who would be regarded in many quarters as a satisfactory chaperon. Of course, I shall love to come ashore and see your home and the island, but I think it would be best if I continued to sleep aboard the yacht.'

James agreed at once. 'Of course you are right, my love, and your decision is a wise one. If you were living up on the hill I'd be sorely tempted to pay you a midnight visit; and, although my servants must sleep at times, somehow they seem to become aware of everything that is going on.'

It was this brief conversation that led James a few minutes later to get hold of Gregory and say to him, 'Dear friend. You have made no secret of it that Manon is your mistress. How would you wish that situation to be treated while you are here? If I put the two of you in separate *bures* I take it you will want to join her in hers now and then. I have not the least objection, but the servants will be certain to learn of it, so, although they will be no less respectful, it will be goodbye to her reputation. How much you or she cares about

304

that, I have no notion; but if the thought disturbs you there is an easy way out. During your stay here we could refer to her as "Mrs. Sallust", then I could put the two of you in a double *bure*. How does that idea appeal to you?'

Gregory grinned at him. 'I don't think Manon is the sort of woman to care much what the servants say of her, but as far as I am concerned your idea is admirable. I have always hated having to leave the warm bed of a girl in the early hours of the morning and make my way back to a cold one. I'll tell her, and I'm sure she'll raise no objections.'

Far from objecting, Manon was delighted. To become, even temporarily, Gregory's official wife, seemed to her a splendid omen. Already, in eager anticipation, she could visualise her slim, short, pointed fingers manipulating the Sallust cheque book.

After lunching on board they all went ashore in the speed boat. When they landed at the harbour Gregory left the others, as he wanted to find out as quickly as possible from Hamie Baker how Lacost was getting on with salvaging the gold from the wreck.

Outside the *Bonne Cuisine* he found its fat Indian proprietor seated under an umbrella, just finishing his midday meal. Recalling their previous brief meeting, Gregory enquired for his diver. Continuing to munch a mouthful of bread and guava jelly, the landlord shook his head.

'He's not here. He's on the far side of the island, working on the wreck with the French Colons.'

That Hamie should have gone over to the enemy was a disconcerting piece of news, as for Lacost to have the assistance of two professional divers instead of one meant that he would be able to complete operations considerably quicker than Gregory had thought likely. Deciding that it would pay him to secure the good-will of mine host of the *Bonne Cuisine,* he invited him to join him in a cognac.

The landlord readily accepted and, as they sat over their drinks, Gregory learned that the *Pigalle* had arrived at Revika early on the morning of the preceding Friday, April 29th, remained there only for a couple of hours to take on supplies of fresh food and collect the two divers, then set off round

305

the coast to the site of the wreck. That meant this was the sixth day that Lacost's party had been at work there. Naturally, everyone in Revika was taking a great interest in the proceedings, and natives were frequently going off to the *Pigalle* to offer for sale fresh vegetables and fruit. The accounts they brought back were to the effect that excellent progress was being made. Lacost had been particularly lucky in having an unbroken spell of calm weather. The great beam that had blocked the entrance to the stern cabins had been lifted clear on the second day. Two more days had passed while the native divers cleared away the mass of rotted debris that had fallen in when the beam had been removed and it was reported that on the previous day they had begun to get up the treasure.

All this gave Gregory furiously to think. He now feared that he might have given Lacost too great a start. Leaving the *Bonne Cuisine,* he hurried up the hill to the Royal *bure*, told James of the situation and urged upon him the necessity for taking immediate action.

18

Triumph and Disaster

Having listened to Gregory's alarming report, James said that he had heard much the same from Aleamotu'a, and had sent a message to Commandant Elbœuf, asking him to come to the *bure* that evening, so that they could learn what steps he was taking to prevent illegal salvaging from the wreck.

By then, Manon, rejoicing in her wifely status, had unpacked for both Gregory and herself, and came jauntily into the main *bure*, provocatively clad only in a bikini. With her was Olinda, who, at James' suggestion, had brought ashore a vanity case and swimsuit and had changed at the same time. On their appearance, Gregory and James temporarily shelved the problem of how to deal with Lacost and ten minutes later joined the girls at the pool, where the four of them spent a most enjoyable hour.

Afterwards, when they were sitting with their drinks, Gregory said to James, 'These rumours we have heard give a rough picture of how things are going, but we must try to secure really accurate information. Above all, it is important for us to know when Lacost expects to be through with the job and make off with the loot. The only way I can think of to do that is to get hold of Hamie Baker. He is now living with the others in the *Pigalle*. For you or me to go out to her would almost certainly result in a showdown, and we daren't risk that in a place where the odds would be so heavily against us. But it is very unlikely that they would do Aleamotu'a any harm if we sent him out with a message; so would you agree to his acting for us?'

'By all means,' James replied. 'He wouldn't have to go

aboard the *Pigalle*, only hand a letter up for Hamie, and I'm sure he would be willing to do that.'

Accordingly, Gregory wrote a note for Hamie, in which he said that, on arriving back in Tujoa, he had found a letter from Hamie's boss, Mr. Trollope, which contained certain instructions that were to be passed on to him; so would he come ashore to receive them. Soon after five o'clock he set off in the jeep with the handsome Aleamotu'a, up through the mountain pass, past the great waterfall and down to the bay on the far side of the island in which the wreck of the *Reina Maria Amalia* lay.

They parked the jeep behind a screen of banana palms and, while Gregory waited there, Aleamotu'a walked on to the beach and had himself paddled out to the *Pigalle* in one of the boats used by the natives to peddle their wares to the Colons.

Three-quarters of an hour later he returned with Hamie Baker. Gregory greeted the diver with a frown and said abruptly, 'Well, Hamie. As the other party got in first, it seems that, instead of waiting for me, you decided to lend them a hand.'

The half-caste gave a sullen nod. 'That's so, baas. I got fed up sitting on my arse doing nothing all them weeks, and me an' Phil Macauta had become good buddies. Anyways, your contract wi' Mr. Trollope had run out and I'd heard nothing from either of you, so I didn't see why I shouldn't earn a bit o' extra money.'

'I gave you some extra money before I left here,' Gregory remarked, 'but we'll say no more about that. I've had you brought ashore to let you know that Mr. Trollope's orders are that you are to co-operate with me, otherwise you'll be out on your ear when you get back to Fiji. To that I should add that I am ready to make it very well worth your while if you do as I wish.'

At that Hamie brightened a little and said, 'I didn't mean no harm, an' I've no wish to quarrel wi' Mr. Trollope or yerself. What is it you want o' me?'

'For the moment only information. How have things been going out there?'

'We've done fine, baas. Got the big beam away much quicker than expected, an' yesterday started gettin' up the stuff. My! Yer eyes would pop at some o' the things we brought up. Crosses and cups wi' precious stones as big as 'aricot beans stuck in 'em, an' lumps of gold coins all bent and fused together as though they'd been half melted in a fire. But come evening we got a nasty jolt—a real nasty one.'

'In what way?' asked Gregory.

'Big part of the deck caved in, jus' as we was about to knock off for the night. Couple of native boys trapped down there, poor sods; an' half the hull full of debris. Mr. Lacost had hoped to be through by termorrer night, an' he fairly blew his top. There's lots more of the stuff still down there and buried deep. He's kep' us hard at it all day, clearing a way down.'

'How long do you reckon it will be before you reach it?'

'It's difficult to say. We—Phil an' I—working alone, it 'ud take us at least a week. But it's on this sort of job the native boys come in handy. Reckon we'll be down to the stuff again in another twenty-four hours.'

'Very well, then,' Gregory nodded. 'Now I'll make the position clear to you. These Frenchmen hold no licence to salvage the treasure. They are, therefore, committing what amounts to an act of piracy. I don't doubt that Lacost has offered you a pretty big sum for your help, but if you take it that will be regarded as accepting part of the swag, and you will be liable to be sent to prison. Unless you want to risk that, as soon as they do get down to the treasure again you will pretend to be stricken with sudden illness, or think up some other means of having yourself put ashore, and come at once to the Ratu's *bure* and let me know. Then you will be in the clear.'

Hamie shifted his feet uneasily, looked down at them and muttered, 'That's all very well, baas; but Mr. Lacost is treating me very decent. Thirty pound a day he's promised me, an' a whackin' good bonus when the job's finished.'

Gregory gave a laugh that had no humour in it. 'If you are counting on that, you don't know the man you are dealing with. He is a crook and a murderer. When he has no more

309

use for you the odds are that, rather than cash out, he'll cut your air-pipe on your last dive and leave you to feed the fishes. I need to have twelve hours' warning before the *Pigalle* is likely to sail. Bring it to me and you will not only be out of trouble but I'll pay you two hundred pounds.'

Obviously shaken by the picture Gregory had drawn of Lacost, Hamie cleared his throat, spat and said, 'O.K., baas. Anyways, I know yer on the level. I'll get ashore somehow an' give you the tip-off.'

Back at the Royal *bure,* Gregory found James and Olinda drinking rum-on-the-rocks. James had just finished showing her over her future home and, delighted with it, she was enthusing over its suitability to such a climate and its beautiful vistas. Gregory told them about his arrangement with Hamie Baker, then asked if Commandant Elbœuf had yet put in an appearance.

'He sent to say that he would come here after dinner,' James replied, then added with a laugh, 'I don't doubt the old boy picked his time so that he could get a good swig at my old brandy.'

As the dinner hour was approaching, Gregory knocked back the drink James had poured for him and went across to the twin-bedded *bure* that had been assigned to him and Manon. She was seated at the dressing table, putting the last touches to her hair, and, as he kissed her on the nape of the neck, he was struck by the warm domesticity of the scene. To go to bed with a woman was one thing, to live with her quite another, and, although the room was not her own, her possessions scattered about it gave it a delightful intimate atmosphere.

When he had shaved in the bathroom that had been built on to the *bure* they rejoined the others and afterwards sat down to dinner. As the Resident was expected, they did not linger over the meal, but moved to the other end of the long room for their coffee and liqueurs.

They had hardly settled themselves there when Elbœuf was announced. Limping forward with his stick, he gallantly kissed the hands of the ladies, condoled with Olinda on her husband's death, then accepted a large ration of old brandy.

310

Contrary to South Seas custom, James got down to business right away, and asked him what steps he had taken to prevent the Colons from attempting to salvage the treasure in the wreck.

Raising his grey eyebrows, the old man replied, 'None, my dear Ratu, and I have had no reason to suppose that any such steps should be taken. Monsieur Lacost arrived here on Friday last, and that evening he paid a courtesy call upon me. He told me of Senhor Mauá de Carvalho's most regrettable demise, that Madame here now held the licence to salvage from the wreck, that she would be arriving in Revika shortly and had asked him, in the meantime, to go ahead with the work on her behalf. When he and the de Carvalhos were in Revika some weeks ago, de Carvalho showed me the licence he had secured in Noumea and told me that he had entered into a partnership with Lacost. So I naturally accepted Lacost's account of matters, and have not attempted to interfere with his operations.'

'Then, Commandant, I must acquaint you with the true situation,' said James. 'There was no legal partnership entered into between de Carvalho and Lacost. The Senhora intends to make the licence over to me. Lacost is a crook and his salvaging operations are illegal. They must be stopped at once.'

'Dear me! Dear me!' Elbœuf exclaimed with a sudden show of agitation. 'While I am happy for you, Ratu, that you should have met with such good fortune, the situation now created may result in much unpleasantness. First thing tomorrow morning I will send Sergeant Marceau off with a couple of his gendarmes to the *Pigalle* to tell Lacost that he must desist from further salvaging and hand over any valuables that he may have already recovered. But what if he refuses?'

'He will,' Gregory put in. 'I am sure of that. So you will have to back up your order by a show of force.'

The elderly Frenchman sighed. 'I fear you are right, Monsieur. It seems that a situation has now arisen similar to one we envisaged some time ago. You will remember, Ratu, that I called upon you to enquire if I might count on your body-

311

guard to support my few gendarmes in the event of an illegal attempt being made to salvage any treasure in the *Maria Amalia.*'

'I do,' James smiled. 'And I don't mind admitting now that I was secretly amused, because your request implied my using force against myself. I have always maintained that this treasure is mine by right of inheritance, and I was quite prepared to defy your government on those grounds. But now, thanks to the Senhora, my position is fully legalised and I will give you all the support of which I am capable to prevent Lacost robbing me of my property.'

Elbœuf nodded. 'Then, Ratu, my duty and your interests are now one. But I understand that the Colons are armed, and I am most averse to provoking a conflict. So I think it best first to send off Sergeant Marceau, as I suggested, and only concert stronger measures should they refuse to obey the order he will convey to them.'

That having been settled, the old Resident began to talk of other matters, and would have stayed there until midnight, happily imbibing brandy, had not James, soon after ten o'clock, said that he must escort Olinda back to her yacht.

When they had gone, Manon did her best to persuade Gregory to come to bed; but, as he was anxious to talk to James about the morrow, he resisted her blandishments. In vain she pointed out that James might take hours in saying good night to Olinda on the yacht, but Gregory insisted that, however late James got back, he must see him again before morning; so, after a last drink, she went off in a huff to their *bure*.

Having settled down with a book, in anticipation of a lengthy vigil, Gregory was agreeably surprised when James returned after an absence of only three-quarters of an hour. Throwing the book aside, Gregory said:

'About tomorrow. Lacost will tell Sergeant Marceau to take a running jump at himself and we've no time to lose; so we've got to be prepared for the next act. D'you think old Elbœuf will agree to order his gendarmes to arrest Lacost and Co.?'

James nodded, 'I think he will, provided they have the backing of my body-guard.'

'Yes. But how much confidence have you in your chaps? Do you really think they will go in and fight? That is what has been worrying me.'

'It would have worried me, too, had the question arisen this time last week,' James replied with a smile. 'But not now. This afternoon I sent word to my Council of Elders that I intend to do a fire-walk. When they have seen me do that, my people will follow me anywhere. It was so that I could be up early in the morning, to supervise the making of the pit, that I denied myself the pleasure of a prolonged good night to Olinda, and left her as soon as I had seen her aboard the yacht.'

'Well done,' Gregory smiled back. 'I'm proud of you, James. We'll get the better of that gang of thugs yet.'

'Thank you. It is going to be a close call, though, because I'll have to spend twenty-four hours preparing myself to go down into the pit, and I can't start my vigil until I've seen the pit made. While the work is being carried out tomorrow morning, I intend to write two letters: one giving authority over my people to Aleamotu'a while I am out of action, and the other nominating you as my representative with the Resident. So that, if Lacost refuses to comply with the old boy's orders, as it's pretty certain that he will, you can exert pressure on Elbœuf to call on the authorities in Noumea to send him support.'

Gregory agreed these to be sound measures, and it warmed his heart to find again how, now that the young Ratu was back in his own island, he readily took decisions and assumed the leadership.

When they had wished each other an affectionate good night Gregory went to his *bure*, to find Manon sitting up in bed waiting for him, in anticipation of a night of connubial bliss. But in that she was to be disappointed. Firmly, Gregory told her that the next day might prove an unusually hectic one, so he meant to get all the sleep he could; but, kissing her fondly, he consoled her by saying that he had good hopes that the future held for them many happy nights together.

313

In the morning they walked down the lovely, flower-filled slope of garden to the Meeting House. Outside it, James was directing the preparations for his fire-walk. One gang of natives had already nearly completed the digging of a deep pit some twenty feet in diameter; another, under Aleamotu'a, was bringing up from the beach a number of carefully-selected large, smooth stones, and a third had been sent to collect the best type of logs for heating them.

James gave Gregory the letter for Elbœuf, and said he had given Aleamotu'a orders that the fire should be lit at seven o'clock the next morning. He added that he had told Olinda of his intentions before leaving her the previous night. Naturally, she was greatly concerned for him and had said she would prefer to spend the day on the yacht. He meant to ask Manon to go off and keep her company, to which he felt sure 'Mrs. Sallust' would readily agree.

As the news of the Ratu's intention had soon spread, it had created great excitement among his people. Most of the Elders and a considerable crowd had collected to watch the preparations in awed silence. The usual Ceremony of Welcome on his return to the island should have been held that day, but the Elders had accepted the reason for its postponement and were planning a great *meke* for the following night.

By eleven o'clock, the work on the pit was completed and, escorted by a large, silent crowd, James returned up the hill to start his twenty-four-hour vigil. Gregory then took Manon off to the yacht, where they found that Olinda had passed a sleepless night and was making herself ill with worry that, although James had done the fire-walk successfully on Beqa, here he might fail and become, instead of a paladin, the laughing stock of his people.

Gregory, too, was secretly harassed by that fear; but he strove to reassure her and could honestly report that James showed no trace of fear himself. On the contrary, he appeared perfectly calm and confident. Olinda being in such poor shape, Gregory would have liked to remain with her throughout the day, but it was essential that he should learn the result of the warning that had been given to Lacost; so,

314

at midday, he went ashore again, leaving Manon to do her best to distract Olinda's mind from James' coming ordeal.

From the harbour, Gregory drove out in James' jeep to the Residence, a large French-style Colonial villa built back in the nineties, and lying some way outside the town. On the broad veranda he found Elbœuf enjoying his morning *Amoer Picon*, and presented James' letter to him. The old Resident welcomed him courteously, sent a boy to make a Planter's Punch which, when offered a drink, Gregory said he would prefer, then said:

'It take it you have already heard from Sergeant Marceau that his mission proved unsuccessful?'

'No,' Gregory replied. 'If you sent him up to the *bure*, I missed him, as I left it over two hours ago. But I'm not surprised. What happened?'

'He went out to the *Pigalle* with two of his men about nine o'clock. Lacost would not even let them go aboard and flatly refused to abandon his operations.'

'Then we shall have to resort to force. As the law is on our side, I assume that, backed by the Ratu's body-guard, you are willing to order your gendarmes to board the *Pigalle*?'

The old man hesitated for a moment, then he said, 'I suppose we now have no alternative, but I am far from happy at having to give such an order. After all, the Colons have weapons and they are desperate men. There are six of them with, in addition, a native crew; and they will have the advantage of being able to fire on my people from the cover provided by their yacht; whereas Marceau has only six men, and they would have to attack in open boats.'

Gregory nodded. 'I appreciate the danger they will run, but they will have the support of about fifty warriors, so the Colons are bound to realise that they will be overcome by weight of numbers. The odds are that after a few shots have been exchanged they will surrender.'

'Theoretically, Monsieur, your argument is sound. But I have little faith in the courage of the Ratu's men. They are not warriors in the true sense. Unlike their forbears they have never taken part in tribal wars, and are untrained. Even a

315

few shots might scare them into turning tail and abandoning my men.'

'That might well have been the case yesterday,' Gregory replied, 'but I have good reason to believe that tomorrow they will show a different mettle.' He then told the Commandant about the fire-walk that James intended to undertake, and of his conviction that it would bring out in his men the fanatical devotion and courage that they had inherited from their ancestors.

After expressing astonishment at the Ratu's daring, Elbœuf said, 'Personally, I am an agnostic, so have no belief in occult powers. It is, of course, true that *Draunikau* is still widely practised in the islands and that if a native believes that the curse of death has been put upon him he will pine away and die. I have known many such cases; but that is attributable to self-hypnosis. The tales one hears of dead men being raised from their graves and imbued with new life as zombies, of fakirs lying on beds of nails without becoming scarred, walking through fire, yet remaining unburned, and so on, fall into a very different category. All of them are based on clever trickery, and I have no doubt that the islanders of Beqa long ago devised some means of deceiving onlookers. If they passed their secret on to the Ratu he may succeed in fooling his people. Otherwise, I fear he will be bitterly disillusioned and suffer a grave humiliation.'

Gregory, too, on considering the matter again that morning, had been subject to serious misgivings. He did not, for one moment, doubt that James had performed the fire-walk on Beqa, but he could not help wondering if he had been able to accomplish it only because the Chief had either hypnotised him into a deep trance in which he would not be conscious of pain or, unknown to him put some powerful drug into the last meal he had had before beginning his fast. Were that so, without such aid he must fail, which would have a most disastrous effect both on his own mentality and his prestige with his people. But to have raised such questions with James could only have undermined his confidence in himself so, the die having been cast, Gregory had decided that he must now let matters take their course, and he countered Elbœuf's scepticism by asserting that 'faith could move mountains'.

When he had finished his drink the Commandant pressed him to stay on to lunch. As he now had twenty-four hours to fill, he gladly accepted. Having spent most of his life in the South Seas, the old man was a mine of information about the natives and their customs, and his cook produced a Lobster Americaine, followed by a rum omelette that could not have been bettered outside France; so for a very pleasant couple of hours Gregory was able from time to time to put out of his mind his anxiety about James.

On returning to the Royal *bure*, he found that Aleamotu'a had mustered the body-guard and was endeavouring to instil a war-like spirit into it. They were a fine-looking collection of men, with muscular bodies, holding themselves very upright and, including their great puffs of crinkly, black hair, averaging not less than six foot three in height; but their weapons left much to be desired. Only eight of them were armed with comparatively modern repeating rifles; the rest had shotguns, and a few only ancient muzzle-loading muskets. Nevertheless, laughing and chattering, they were entering into the spirit of the game like happy children.

After two hours napping on his bed in the *bure* still faintly redolent of Manon's seductive scent, Gregory went down to the harbour; for it had occurred to him that, with James in seclusion, it was very probable that no arrangements had yet been made for the body-guard to carry out a sea-borne attack on the *Pigalle*.

At the small police station he introduced himself to Sergeant Marceau, whom he found to be a paunchy little man with a ruddy face, close-cropped hair and an indolent manner—the last, no doubt, having been acquired during years spent in a tropical backwater where there was little serious crime to occupy him.

Having given Gregory a personal account of his abortive mission that morning, the Sergeant went on to say that he hoped his master, the Resident, would not order an attack on the *Pigalle*, as he had only six men and no faith at all in the native auxiliaries who were to support them. However, it

317

transpired that his small arsenal was considerably larger than Gregory had expected. It contained one heavy machine gun, four Sten guns, a rifle and pistol for each man, and several dozen hand-grenades and tear-gas bombs.

Much comforted by this, Gregory suggested that the gendarmes should go armed with the machine weapons, and grenades, and loan the surplus rifles to members of the Ratu's body-guard. Marceau proved most reluctant to hand over any of his weapons to the natives, but finally agreed that to get the best value out of them it would be wise to do so.

For transport he could provide only one motor launch which was used for occasional anti-smuggling patrols. He added that the Ratu owned several large war canoes, but they were chocked up in boathouses and it was so long since they had been used that it was certain they would prove unseaworthy. Brushing aside the idea of canoes, Gregory declared that they must commandeer other motor craft, of which there were several in the harbour. To that Marceau agreed and they left the office together, the Sergeant to make the necessary arrangements and Gregory, feeling that there was no more he could do, to go off in James' speed boat to the *Boa Viagem*.

Down in the saloon, he found that Manon had inveigled Olinda into playing a game of six-pack bezique, but on Gregory's appearance she impatiently pushed the cards aside and enquired anxiously for news. He could tell her only that Lacost had defied the police and that, since a little before midday, James had gone into seclusion.

By then it was time for a drink, and Gregory decided that the kindest thing he could do for Olinda would be to get her good and high, so that she would, at all events, sleep a good part of the night.

Going to the bar, he compounded a killer cocktail, putting into each of three large goblets good measures of cordial Médoc, green Chartreuse and brandy, then filling them up with champagne. As the wine disguised the strength of the spirits with which it had been loaded, both the girls enjoyed the drink without suspecting its potency, and happily accepted a second ration. To Olinda he gave the mixture as before,

318

but did no more than flavour the champagne for Manon and himself. Manon, meanwhile, had switched on the record player and Olinda had become perceptibly more cheerful. Shortly before dinner was due, Captain Amedo came in to enquire if there was anything he could do for her and she invited him to make a fourth.

During the meal Gregory kept the champagne going, and to outward appearances it was a merry party; but the others were aware that Olinda was only putting a brave face on things and was all the while worrying herself into a fever about what might happen to James next day. She stuck it out until the pudding, a Zabaglione, was served. Then she suddenly burst into tears and hurriedly got up from the table.

Manon rose, too, but she was on the opposite side of the table and Gregory caught her arm while Captain Amedo took Olinda's and supported her out of the dining cabin. As they moved towards the door, Gregory snatched up a couple of dry biscuits from the cheese tray, thrust them into Manon's hand and said in a swift whisper:

'Now go after her. I don't want her to be sick, so you must prevent her from lying down. Sit her in a chair and make her nibble these while you get behind her and massage her temples with eau-de-Cologne. Talk to her soothingly and tell her we'll stay on board tonight, in case she needs us. When she has quietened down, undo her hair and keep brushing it until she becomes drowsy. The odds are she'll have some aspirins in her cabin. If so, give her a couple, then get her to bed.'

With a half-humorous grimace, Manon replied, 'You would make a good psychologist, but are a lousy husband. Drink and tears are just what the poor dear needed, though, and between us, with luck, we'll get her off for a good night's sleep.'

When Amedo rejoined Gregory they told the steward to clear the table and helped themselves to liqueur brandies. The Captain had heard enough of what was happening on shore to be aware of the reason for Olinda's collapse, but he knew nothing about the projected attack on the *Pigalle*; so Gregory told him what was being planned, then went on:

'Those Colons are real toughs, so it's certain that they will put up a fight and it is going to be a very nasty business. I would gladly have the help of yourself and your crew, but it would not be right to ask it. This is a private quarrel, and there would be no justification for risking you or any of them being killed or wounded. But there is one way in which you could help us.'

Amedo gave a courteous little bow, 'You are correct, Señhor, in that I have no right to expose my men to danger in such an affair, but, that apart, be pleased to express your wishes.'

'It is a matter of arms,' Gregory replied. 'Unfortunately, very few of the Ratu's body-guard have modern weapons, so they will be at a great disadvantage against the Colons. In a yacht such as this it is usual to carry a few firearms against emergencies and, if that is the case with you, I should be most grateful if I might have the loan of them.'

'We have two rifles, four sporting guns and, including my own, three pistols. Provided the Señhora gives her permission, I should be happy to place them at your disposal.'

'Thank you, Captain. I'm sure the Señhora will agree, and that will enable me to equip much more satisfactorily several of the Ratu's men who have only muzzle-loading muskets.' After a moment Gregory added with a smile, 'As they have never handled repeaters, we must hope there won't be any accidents, but that is my responsibility.'

For three-quarters of an hour they talked very amicably, then Captain Amedo excused himself and went off to his quarters. Shortly afterwards Manon came in, smiled at Gregory and said, 'Olinda wasn't sick and I managed to calm her down. I found her aspirin, too, and gave her a couple. Soon after, she dropped off and she is now sleeping soundly; so as a doctor you are to be congratulated.'

Giving a laugh, he stood up, crushed her to him in a tight embrace that almost drove the breath out of her body, and said, 'Well done, my sweet. And although a cabin won't be quite as cosy as our *bure*, I'll show you that I can also be a competent husband.'

Gasping, she laughed back. 'Having made me half-tight,

320

you'd better, or I'll go along and seduce the handsome Captain.' Then her full lips melted on his in a long kiss.

In the morning, soon after half past ten, Olinda joined them in the saloon, pale but calm and, to their surprise, dressed entirely in white, with her dark hair falling to her shoulders. Seeing their expressions, she gave a faint smile, and said:

'I didn't meant to go ashore, but I have changed my mind. I know James was against our seeing him do his fire-walk at Beqa, but this is different. Hundreds of people will be watching and I've decided that I ought to be present. If he succeeds, that will be wonderful. But if he fails, at least I shall be there to comfort him, and I'll make it known to all his people that I mean to marry him.'

Realising that for her to watch James undergoing his ordeal would mean almost as severe a one for her, Gregory and Manon both praised her courage; but she waved aside their compliments and led the way on deck. The launch was brought alongside and, after a word with her Captain, Amedo had the weapons and ammunition he had collected put into it. By eleven o'clock they were landed on the harbour. James' jeep was still there where Gregory had parked it. The arms were loaded into it, then he drove the two girls up through the town to the Meeting House.

As was to be expected, the whole town had turned out to witness the fire-walk. The sloping hillside was black with people, only an area round the pit being kept clear by Sergeant Marceau and his gendarmes. Near it were grouped the Council of the Elders. With them was Commandant Elbœuf, and, standing a little apart, the sinister figure of Roboumo. The Elders solemnly welcomed Gregory and his party and brought out chairs for them to sit on.

Aleamotu'a was in charge of the proceedings. From time to time he glanced at his wrist watch and, as they sat watching him, the time of waiting seemed interminable. At last, he gave a signal. A score of men then ran forward and, giving excited cries, began with long, wire hawsers to drag the smouldering logs out of the pit. It took nearly a quarter of an hour before they had cleared the crater down to its level of large rounded stones, and another ten minutes before they had finished prodding the stones with poles until Aleamotu'a was satisfied that no rough corners upon which his Ratu might trip were left protruding. He then took a cardboard carton from a nearby man, who had been holding it ready for him, and hurled it into the centre of the pit. Within seconds it burst into flame and in less than a minute was reduced to ashes. A gasp of awe ran through the watching multitude.

There followed several minutes of appalling strain, then faintly there came up to them the tinny chime of the clock in the tower of the little church down on the harbour, striking midday. Suddenly, all heads were turned towards the garden sloping up to the Royal *bure,* and a great sigh went up from the huge crowd. Walking slowly and very erect, James, alone and unattended, was advancing down the slope.

An utter silence fell as everyone, from the Resident to the humblest present, stared at him with fascinated expectancy. When he was within fifty feet of the pit, Olinda stood up, walked forward to the edge of the pit opposite him and held out her arms.

Instantly it flashed on Gregory why she had decided to come ashore. James had said that when he did his fire-walk on Beqa he had had a vision of her on the far side of the pit. Now she was bringing that vision to life. Clad all in white, like an angel come to earth, she stood there, her arms extended and her eyes fixed on his, willing him to come to her.

Without a second's hesitation he stepped down into the pit, walked with quick, firm steps across the twenty feet of stones, came up on the far side and took her in his arms.

The shout of applause that went up was ear-splitting. For minutes on end the crowd cheered itself hoarse. As though at a given signal, James' subjects threw themselves on their knees and bowed their heads to the ground. Coming to their feet again, they swarmed towards him, hoping to touch his sacred person. Only with the greatest difficulty did the gendarmes and Elders fend them off and get James and Olinda into the Meeting House.

They had to remain there for half an hour before order was restored. Meanwhile, James told the Elders that after his

322

ordeal he needed complete rest, so the *yaggona* ceremony they had planned and a great *meke* for that evening must be postponed until the following day.

It was two o'clock before James and his party, accompanied by the Commandant, Sergeant Marceau and Aleamotu'a, at last got back to the *bure*. There luncheon had been prepared and, having fasted for twenty-four hours, James ate heartily, but when he learned what had been taking place during his seclusion his exuberant happiness became overshadowed by the thought that if the treasure was to be saved they now had no alternative but to attack the *Pigalle*.

After his fire-walk there was no longer any doubt that his body-guard would wholeheartedly support the gendarmes and, that being so, Elbœuf showed no further qualms about ordering in his men. But it seemed certain that there would be casualties and James was loath to risk the lives of his people. However, when Gregory told him how, owing to Sergeant Marceau and Captain Amedo, the majority of them were now equipped with modern weapons and that motor boats had been commandeered to give them swiftness of manœuvre, he agreed that the attempt to capture the *Pigalle* must be made. The question that remained was—when?

Gregory at once said that if casualties were to be minimised, surprise was essential; so the best hour would be about three o'clock in the morning. But the Commandant would not hear of that. He maintained that, although the Colons were breaking the law, to launch an armed attack upon them without warning would make all who were concerned in it, above all himself, as the principal authority responsible, subject to prison sentences. Hostilities were permissible only if the Colons had been called on to surrender, refused and then offered armed resistance.

James and Aleamotu'a backed up Gregory; but Elbœuf and Sergeant Marceau insisted that unless the law was strictly observed they would all land themselves in very serious trouble. The argument had been raging for a quarter of an hour when the head houseboy, Kalabo, came in to say that there was a man outside asking urgently for Gregory.

On going outside, he found it to be Hamie Baker. The

323

diver reported that, with the help of the natives, they had cleared the fallen debris in the wreck sooner than had been expected and had again got down to the treasure. To keep his pact with Gregory, he had slipped overboard during the break for the midday meal, and had swum ashore.

Asked how long he thought it would take to get up the rest of the treasure, he replied, 'Can't say, baas. Depends how much of it there is. Might be another couple of days, but maybe they'll be through by tonight.'

This alarming news created a new situation. Having renewed his promise to pay Hamie two hundred pounds, Gregory handed him over to Kalabo, to be given food and drink, then hurried in to report the tidings he had just received.

On consideration, he thought it most unlikely that the *Pigalle* would sail before morning, so he was still in favour of a surprise attack in the middle of the night, but the chance that she would make off before then could not be ignored. The weight of opinion now went against him, so he had to agree that the showdown should take place that evening.

The Sergeant left to muster his gendarmes and Aleamotu'a to mobilise the body-guard. Elbœuf stayed for another brandy, then drove off in his ancient car. By then it was half past three, and they had agreed to rendezvous down at the harbour at five o'clock, so Gregory, true to form when about to face trouble, decided to take an hour's siesta. Manon tried for a while to think of a way in which she could warn Lacost of the pending attack, but gave it up as hopeless and went out to sit by the pool. James, still transported with delight at the success of his fire-walk and the way in which Olinda had aided him, took her to his *bure*, where she willingly submitted to his passionate embraces.

A little before five, the two girls, now fearful that their men might be killed or wounded, sadly kissed them good-bye and watched them set off for the harbour. Everything there was in readiness. Altogether, with the gendarmes and body-guard, the contingent now numbered some sixty men, and the flotilla to carry them consisted of eight motor boats. In case the one carrying the leaders should come to grief, it was decided that James should go in his own launch, Gregory in the *Boa Via-*

gem's speed boat and Sergeant Marceau and Aleamotu'a in others. The gendarmes were also separated, so that each could show an example to a boat carrying members of the body-guard. Old Elbœuf, excusing himself on account of his age and infirmity, contented himself with wishing them good luck and waving them away.

Adjusting their speeds to keep in convoy, the flotilla made its way round the point, through the channel which separated Roboumo's island from the mainland, and so to the bay in which the wreck of the *Maria Amalia* lay. As they approached the *Pigalle*, they saw that great activity was taking place about her. Fuzzy-headed natives were diving from her every few minutes, then bobbing up again clutching unidentifiable objects and two men in the stern were working hard at a hand pump, which was obviously feeding air down to Lacost's professional diver, Philip Macauta.

Then there came a sudden change in these activities. There were shouted orders, the native divers scrambled back on board. Macauta's big, round helmet glinted in the evening sunlight as he surfaced and climbed a ladder on to the deck. In a matter of minutes everyone in the *Pigalle* had taken cover, with the one exception of Pierre Lacost, who remained standing on the bridge.

As the official leader of the expedition, Sergeant Marceau's launch was some way ahead of the others. When it was within a hundred yards of the *Pigalle* he stood up in the stern, put a megaphone to his mouth and shouted:

'Ahoy there, Monsieur Lacost. You are committing an illegal act. In the name of the Republic I summon you to weigh anchor and accompany us back to harbour.'

For a second Gregory held his breath, as he waited to hear what the response would be. It came almost immediately. Lacost gave a shout and darted back into the bridge cabin. Then there was a spurt of flame from the stern of the *Pigalle,* followed by the crack of a rifle. Sergeant Marceau's *kepi* seemed to jump from his head, he staggered, then jack-knifed and crouched among the other men in his boat.

This opening episode was immediately followed by a ragged fusillade from all the boats of the flotilla, but the attackers were handicapped by being unable to see the men aboard the *Pigalle*. Splinters flew from woodwork here and there, the glass of the deckhouse windows was smashed and tinkled as it fell, but no cry or scream proclaimed a hit.

'We'll have to board,' Gregory shouted to the motorman in his boat. 'Get going, full speed ahead now.' But next moment a machine gun opened on them. The gendarme beside him was shot through the chest, and one of the bodyguard screeched as a bullet seared his arm.

Everyone in the flotilla was firing now and bullets by the score were thudding into the hull of the *Pigalle*. Within a minute a second machine gun had opened up from her. It raked one boat, killing or wounding the majority of the crew. Then it was turned on another, hit it in a dozen places below the water-line and it swiftly began to sink. The first machine gun blazed off again at Sergeant Marceau's boat. This time he was not so lucky. A bullet caught him in the shoulder, spun him round, and he fell overboard, while half his crew were massacred.

By then all the other boats had shut off their engines, none daring to approach nearer, but their occupants continued to pepper the *Pigalle* uselessly with bullets.

Gregory, seething with rage at this senseless débâcle, shouted to James, 'We must board her! Don't you understand? If we can once get into her, they'll stand no chance against our numbers.'

Even as he shouted, another boat received a fusillade, mowing down half the men in her. Two of the boats had now restarted their engines, turned about and were making off.

Cupping his hands, James yelled back, 'It's hopeless! I'd join you myself, but I won't see any more of my people slaughtered.' Then, raising his voice still higher, he shouted in his native tongue, 'Cease fire! Cease fire and return to harbour, all of you.'

The firing from the boats fell to a dribble, but the machine guns in the *Pigalle* continued their ugly chatter, inflicting more casualties as the remains of the flotilla turned tail and made off.

With fury in his heart, Gregory cursed Elbœuf. If only the old fool had not prevented them from carrying out a surprise attack in the middle of the night they could easily have overcome the Colons. Now he must resign himself to defeat. The game was lost and Lacost would get away with the treasure.

19

A Fateful Evening

As darkness fell, the remaining boats of the flotilla made
their way back to harbour. There they sadly counted their
losses. One gendarme and four of the body-guard had been
killed, and fifteen members of the force, including Sergeant
Marceau and another gendarme, had been wounded. Two of
the boats had been sunk and the casualties would have been
still higher had not all the Tujoans been excellent swimmers,
so that none of those in the sunken boats had been drowned.

James was in such distress about the dead and wounded of
his body-guard that Gregory thought him in no state to discuss the situation with Elbœuf, so he persuaded him to go
straight up to the *bure* while he himself went to the Residence. There he found the old Frenchman partaking of his
pre-dinner aperitif.

Nothing would have pleased Gregory better than to flay
Elbœuf verbally, but on the way back to harbour it had occurred to him that there was still a last chance of getting the
better of Lacost. He and his Colons had fired upon French
gendarmes who were in the course of carrying out their duty,
killing one and wounding two others; so, no reinforcements
being available locally, the Resident's proper course was to
call for troops to be sent in from Noumea. To get that done,
and swiftly, meant that Gregory must retain the good-will
of the Commandant. In consequence, he confined himself to
reporting the bare facts of the disaster, and asking that aid
to overcome the Colons should be asked for as a matter of
urgency.

On hearing what had happened, Elbœuf expressed great indignation, although he continued to maintain that he could not possibly have permitted the attack on the *Pigalle* to be made at night and without warning. But he readily agreed to radio Noumea for troops to be sent in by air, then set off for the town to send the signal and see his wounded Sergeant.

Returning to the *bure,* Gregory found James still in very low spirits in spite of the efforts of the two girls to console him; so dinner proved a gloomy meal and, soon after it, James escorted Olinda back to the *Boa Viagem*. On his return they went to bed: Manon greatly relieved that Gregory had come to no harm in the affray, but secretly glad that Pierre Lacost had had the better of it; James and Gregory both now with the depressing feeling that, unless help was sent promptly from Noumea, all the danger, distress and anxiety they had suffered during the past four months would have been for nothing.

A reply was not received until eleven o'clock on the following morning. Elbœuf brought a copy of it up to the *bure* and, to Gregory's fury, it was anything but satisfactory. Apparently, the old man had not fully explained the situation and its urgency, but had simply asked for troops to be sent owing to his gendarmes being insufficient in numbers to arrest a gang of desperadoes. It was, therefore, hardly surprising that Noumea requested further information before acting.

In view of the way in which Gregory had, not long before, got the better of his one-time colleague General Ribaud, he could still not be certain that a personal appeal from him would have the desired effect, so he wrote out a lengthy cable putting matters in a way that Ribaud, as the responsible authority, could not ignore, then made Elbœuf sign it, and sent it off himself.

Meanwhile, James had gone down to visit the wounded and condole with the relatives of the dead, promising the latter's dependants that he would arrange for their support. This occupied him for the greater part of the day, so Gregory and Manon lunched with Olinda on the yacht and spent an anxious afternoon with her. Soon after five o'clock James came out to them with a copy of a reply Ribaud had sent to Elbœuf's second signal. It read:

Now appreciate situation stop troop carriers on exercise so temporarily unavailable stop am despatching gunboat should be with you Monday.

Again their hopes were dashed. It was already Saturday evening and, from what Hamie had said, Lacost might have all the treasure on board and be ready to sail that night, or at latest the following day. The fact that the gunboat would give chase was small consolation. Even twenty-four hours' start would be sufficient for the *Pigalle* to elude capture for some days. During that time Lacost could anchor off one of the innumerable uninhabited islands between Fiji and New Caledonia, get the treasure and all his stores ashore, and scuttle the *Pigalle*, so that she would sink without trace. He could then lie low there for a year or more, until he and his companions felt it safe to signal some passing vessel and, under false names, have themselves taken off as the survivors of the shipwreck of a copra-collecting schooner; or at least until the more impatient Colons either mutinied or decided to murder him, and that was unlikely to happen for several months.

But with him James brought another document—a lengthy epistle in Nakapoan script. It was a letter from Roboumo, and its contents were roughly as follows:

Having witnessed his Ratu's fire-walk on the previous day, he was much concerned that the ability to perform such a feat would undermine the authority that he had enjoyed for so long; and this might lead to desertion by his followers. Therefore, he proposed a pact. The attack on the *Pigalle* had, he declared, been doomed to failure because it had been made in daylight. But a surprise attack by night, given over-whelming numbers, could not fail to prove successful. The Ratu's body-guard, he assumed, would on their own prove reluctant to face the Colons again, but he could offer rein-forcements of twenty-seven men, all armed with modern weapons. He was, he admitted, most reluctant to allow the treasure in the *Maria Amalia* to be salvaged, but this was for him a secondary consideration to losing his status as the great Magic Man of Tujoa.

If the Ratu would give a solemn undertaking to perform no more feats of *draunikau*, he would send his men to aid in the capture of the *Pigalle*. But the matter was urgent, because the White Witch had told him that the salvaging of the treasure was near completion, so, if the *Pigalle* was to be attacked again, it must be that night. If the Ratu was agreeable to treat, arrangements should be made that evening. Since the fire-walk, he was not prepared to risk his own followers deserting to the body-guard should the Ratu come to his island accompanied by armed men. But if he would come alone, as a guarantee of good faith in the future, they might agree an alliance which would confirm his status and enable the Ratu to secure the treasure.

From this, one thing stood out clearly. Roboumo's proposal did offer a real chance to stymie Lacost at the eighteenth hole. James then declared that, after his triumph, he felt such complete confidence in himself that he no longer had any far of Roboumo or his White Witch. He was quite prepared to go alone to a meeting. Smiling at him with pride, Olinda said that evidently it was now Roboumo who was afraid of him, so she was in favour of his accepting.

Having considered for a few moments, Gregory said to James, 'To get the better of that swine Lacost I'd be prepared to take very big risks. But I don't like the idea of your going to Roboumo's island on your own. The old devil is obviously more concerned about keeping his hooks on the people than he is about who gets the treasure. He might take a chance on having his boys murder you, so that he would be quite certain of continuing to rule the roost here. And, anyhow, would you be willing to enter a pact that would leave him free to do so?'

'I have no fear that he would harm me,' James replied at once. 'He would not dare. Although many of my people have been kept under his thumb, by far the greater part of them are devoted to me. They would rise up in their wrath, invade his island by the hundred and put an end to him and all his

331

followers. As for the situation should we make a pact, I look at it this way. I would stand by my bargain and let him continue his blackmail as long as he could. But my possession of the gold here would enable me to break his power gradually. If I could start industries here, that would not only ensure a decent standard of living for the majority of my people, but would also open their minds to Western ways of thought, so that they would no longer go in fear of being bewitched.'

'You are right,' Olinda agreed. 'All the same, darling, I spoke before without thinking, and I now agree with Gregory. To go alone to Roboumo's island would be an awful risk to take. Write to him or send a messenger, but I beg you not to go yourself.'

James shook his head. 'My love, that would be no use. I know my people and, bad man as he may be, I understand the way Roboumo's mind works. How could he trust me to keep my word in the future unless I show trust in him by placing myself unprotected in his hands?'

'I wouldn't trust him not to try to pull a fast one over me even if we were face to face and I was armed and he was not,' Manon remarked, using such little weight as she had on the side of preventing, if possible, an agreement which would lead to another attack on the *Pigalle*.

'Nor I,' Gregory agreed. 'The issue hinges entirely on how much store James sets on getting hold of the gold. As I have said on several previous occasions, I don't want any of it myself; so, although I'd hate to see Lacost get away with it, I'd rather that than have James run into serious danger.'

'It is not the gold,' James said earnestly. 'Not now. It is my people who were killed and maimed last night. Four of my body-guard killed and thirteen of them wounded; not to mention the three gendarmes. I would never again consider myself fit to be a Ratu if I neglected any possibility of being revenged upon those murdering Frenchmen.'

There fell a short silence. Obviously James had made up his mind and there seemed no more to be said; but, after a minute or so, Gregory did say, 'Very well, then. You will go in alone. But I mean to follow you. I'll keep well out of the way, but shall remain within listening distance of Roboumo's

332

kraal—or whatever they call it in these parts. And we'll have Aleamotu'a, and some of the other boys, just across the channel, on the mainland. Then, if any treacherous attempt is made on you, just start yelling at the top of your lungs and we'll do our damnedest to get you out.'

James laid his big, brown hand over Gregory's and smiled. 'You are a true friend: my father and protector. That's how it shall be, then. And if the attack is to be for tonight the sooner we put Roboumo's honesty to the test, the better.'

Again both girls were stricken with anxiety for their men. It was agreed that they would dine together on the yacht, then Manon should go ashore to the *bure* and there wait events. As soon as James and Gregory returned safely, she was to switch the light over the front entrance to the *bure* on and off three times, while Olinda sat on deck watching for this signal that all was well with them.

The two men then had themselves taken off to the wharf, walked up the hill and, without delay, put their preparations in train. While Aleamotu'a was getting the body-guard together, James and Gregory ate an early cold supper. By the time they had finished, darkness had fallen. When they came out of the *bure*, James addressed his men, explaining to them what it was hoped they would be able to accomplish during the coming night. All of them were eager to avenge their fallen comrades and, beating their chests, proclaimed their willingness again to follow their Ratu into danger.

As it was probable that Roboumo had spies in the town who would have set off post-haste to warn him if they saw an expedition being mounted from the harbour, it was decided to march inland by circuitous tracks, down to a fishing village only about a mile from the witch-doctor's island, and use the boats of the natives there.

The trek took the best part of an hour. It was by then a little before nine o'clock, and the moon, halfway through its first quarter, stood at about thirty degrees above the horizon. By the light it gave, any sentinel on the island could not have failed to see a flotilla of boats creeping along the coast. But the island at its nearest point to the mainland was only a quarter of a mile off-shore; so it was decided that Aleamotu'a

333

should march the body-guard along the beach to that point, then, if they were needed, they could within ten minutes wade across the shallow channel.

In consequence, when they reached the village, they took only two boats: a dinghy with an outboard engine, in which James set off steered by his coxswain, and a low-lying, one-man canoe for Gregory. For the first half-mile the dinghy towed the canoe, then dropped it off; so that, should there be a reception party expecting James to arrive, Gregory, paddling himself and arriving several minutes later, would stand the best chance of landing unobserved, while James was being escorted up to Roboumo's *bure*.

This plan worked admirably. The light was insufficient for Gregory actually to see James land at that distance, but the sound of voices coming clearly across the water in the quiet of the night told him that some of Roboumo's men had been waiting there to greet him. As the voices faded, Gregory altered course a little, then beached his canoe about two hundred yards from the place where the coxswain had landed James and was lying off until he returned.

The white coral beach extended inland for only some fifty feet. Darting across the open space at a crouching run, Gregory swiftly gained the shelter of a group of palms that cast dark shadows. Had his canoe been seen before he landed, it would have been taken for that of a native fisherman on his way further out to sea to spear fish attracted by the light of a torch, so his only real hazard had been that he might be spotted while crossing the beach. But no challenge had rung out. Considerably relieved, he now moved cautiously through the screen of palms and light undergrowth, working his way round until he came upon the path that led up to a group of *bures*.

The previous night the gendarme in Gregory's boat had been killed; so he had quietly 'naturalised' the man's Sten gun and two tear-gas grenades. Now, he switched the safety catch off the weapon, so that he could use it instantly, and proceeded with even greater caution up the path, keeping well into the shadowed side of it.

Two hundred yards brought him within sight of the nearest *bure*, which lay on the far side of a vegetable garden. Moving off the path, and stooping now, he crept stealthily from bush to bush until he could get a view of a good part of the village. It consisted, he guessed, of about thirty *bures,* with the tall roof of one, obviously Roboumo's, rising high above the others.

Normally, at this hour the inhabitants would have been asleep, but, although he could not see anyone, the low murmur of voices and an occasional laugh told him that there were people about. Selecting a position that gave him the best available field of fire into the village entrance, he settled down to await either James' emergence or sounds of trouble.

He had reasoned that, if Roboumo did intend treachery, it was most unlikely that James would be set upon when entering the village, as his coxswain might have heard sounds of a struggle and made off to give the alarm. It seemed certain that there would be a *yaggona* drinking ceremony and there was just the possibility that the witch-doctor might use that as a means of either poisoning or drugging James, taking it for granted that he would follow traditional custom and gulp down the whole contents of the cup. But James had a lifetime's familiarity with the drink, so he would almost certainly detect a different flavour the moment the first drop touched his tongue, and when he and Gregory had discussed this possibility he had promised to be on his guard. Endeavouring to think as Roboumo might, Gregory had decided that the most likely way he would attempt to rid himself of James was by some apparent accident after James had left his *bure* —perhaps by one of his men pretending to trip and at the same time shooting James in the back—so that afterwards any suggestion that he had been murdered could be disclaimed.

On the other hand, Gregory acknowledged to himself that his fears for James quite probably had no foundation. Clearly Roboumo's paramount interest was to retain the hold that he had over the many Tujoans who feared his evil powers; and, should James meet his death on the island, even apparently through an accident, that might lead to his people's

335

summoning up the courage to put an end to Roboumo and his following of bad men.

Making due allowance for the time the *yaggona* ceremony would take, and the usual prolonged palaver about irrelevant matters that normally preceded getting down to business when South Sea notabilities met, after half an hour Gregory became considerably more hopeful that James and Roboumo were really reaching agreement on a pact that, later that night, would bring about the death or capture of Lacost and his Colons.

Another ten minutes drifted by; then, suddenly, the silence of the night was broken by a loud shout.

Repressing the instinct to spring to his feet, Gregory remained crouching under cover, his Sten gun at the ready.

The shout was followed by a scream of rage and, immediately afterwards, by swift, violent banging on a drum. At these sounds, several men came running out from the small *bures*, some with arms and others without; so evidently the alarm had taken them by surprise.

A moment later, James appeared round the corner of a small *bure* that partially hid Roboumo's lofty one. In great bounds he dashed towards the path that led down to the shore. Two men ran forward to intercept him, a third, some feet to his left, raised a rifle to shoot him down.

Gregory's finger lightly squeezed the trigger of the Sten gun. Its bullets ploughed waist high into the man who held the rifle. With a single screech, he fell, riddled. His rifle flashed as it fell from his hands, but as he was hit he had jerked it up and the bullet passed high over James' head.

At the rat-tat-tat of Gregory's volley, it was as though the paralysing glance of an angry god had suddenly turned the villagers to stone. Their heads all turned in the direction of the shots, they remained for thirty seconds rigid and gaping.

James struck the nearer of the two men who had been about to intercept him a blow under the chin that sent him reeling, swerved past the other and ran on. Swiftly putting down his gun, Gregory pulled the pins out of his two tear-gas grenades, one after the other, then lobbed them into the centre of the little group of natives.

At that moment Roboumo appeared, brandishing a great war club and screaming with rage. By then James was well past Gregory and round the bend of the path. Even as the witch-doctor shouted to his men to give chase, the fumes from the bombs were catching them in the eyes and throat. Snatching up his gun, Gregory followed James, running all-out for the shore.

Two minutes later they were wading out to the dinghy. The coxswain already had the outboard motor going. As they scrambled aboard and the boat turned towards the mainland, the moon gave light enough for them to see that Aleamotu'a and the body-guard, having heard the shots, were already half-way across the narrow channel. But their help was not now needed. James shouted to them that he was unharmed and that they should return to the beach.

As the two friends landed, the Tujoans crowded round their Ratu with excited cries, congratulating him on his escape and begging to be told what had occurred. When he had calmed them down he told them that he would make an important announcement about Roboumo the following morning. Then he ordered Aleamotu'a to march them back to the Royal *bure*, where they were to be given a good meal and as much *kava* as they liked to drink. He and Gregory then reboarded the borrowed dinghy, as they could get home more quickly by water.

On their way round to the harbour, James gave Gregory an account of his meeting with Roboumo. It had opened with a solemn *yaggona* drinking, at which five of the witch-doctor's principal retainers had been present. After the ceremony and when many compliments had been exchanged, the discussions had begun well. The five chief warriors had said that they and their men would have no fears about boarding the *Pigalle*, provided that the attack was made during the hours of darkness during which they would enjoy the full protection of the White Witch. With muffled paddles they would approach the *Pigalle* from her seaward side, while the Ratu and his body-guard would come round the island, also in canoes—as the noise of motor engines might alert the crew of the ship—and attack from the landward side. In order that the two attacks should occur simultaneously, it was agreed that they would both go in half an hour after the moon had set. This would be at an early hour in the morning, and in order to ensure synchronisation to within a few minutes, one man in each party would, every few moments, imitate the cry of a seagull. When they came within sound of one another both parties would paddle in with the utmost speed and board the *Pigalle*.

Having listened to these proposed tactics and fully approved them, Gregory asked, 'Then what went wrong to cause Roboumo to quarrel with you afterwards? I am amazed, too, that you succeeded in breaking away from six of them and escaping as you did. You must have been born under a lucky star.'

James laughed. 'I think I was, but I didn't have to wage any desperate encounter or take on such heavy odds. After showing that he meant business, that his men were willing to fight and the details of the attack having been settled, Roboumo dismissed his five warriors, so that we could discuss in private the terms he asked for his assistance. I agreed to give no more demonstrations of my own powers as a *Draunikau*, and not to interfere with him, on one condition, namely that in future he should not threaten anyone with the death curse. After some argument he reluctantly agreed. Then I said to him:

' "It is known throughout the islands that your power is really vested in the far greater occult powers of the White Witch. Therefore I feel sure you will appreciate that I must also have her word that she will regard our agreement as binding upon her as well as upon yourself." '

'Ho! Ho!' Gregory murmured. 'That was jolly shrewd of you, James. Go on. I can hardly wait to hear what happened, though I'll make a guess. It turned out that he's been fooling everyone and that there is really is no such person.'

'You're wrong. There is, and I saw her. But I had the hell of a job to persuade him to let me. He said that, since she has been in Tujoa, no man except himself has ever set eyes on her, and no woman other than his three senior wives, who attend upon her. I took a firm line and told him that unless

338

she became a party to the deal it was off. Even as I made the threat, I regretted it, as I feared he'd call my bluff. But he didn't. After sitting in silence for a few moment he stood up and said, "Very well. Wait here, Ratu, until I return for you." Then he walked to the far end of his big *bure* which was completely screened off by heavy *tapa*-cloth curtains.

'He went behind them and remained there for about three minutes; then he opened the curtains a few inches and beckoned to me to come through. You can imagine how intrigued and excited I was, but I managed to keep up an appearance of calmness and walked across the room quite slowly. I had all my work cut out, though, not to show my amazement when I saw what lay behind those curtains.

'Apart from a few feet on the far side, the whole space was filled by a huge bamboo and wicker cage. It was about fourteen feet square by ten feet high, and furnished inside as a bed-sitting room. At one end there was a large, comfortable divan. The other held a round table, an armchair, a single elbow chair, a small desk, and one corner was screened off— no doubt concealing a washplace and privy.

'The Witch was seated in the elbow chair facing the front of the cage. I had always believed her to be a fair-skinned Polynesian, or a native of the islands who painted herself white. But she was neither. She was a white woman, all right. For her age—I put her down to be about sixty—she was still remarkably good-looking. Her face was very pale and slightly wrinkled; her hair was dead white, very long, parted in the centre and falling straight on either side of her face to her shoulders, hiding them and the upper part of a rich native dress that she was wearing. But her eyes, which were blue, were quite blank; and, although she was looking straight at me, she did not seem to be aware of me.

'Roboumo spoke to her—in his own dialect of course, but I understood enough of it to know that he was honestly giving her particulars of our agreement. When he had finished there was a moment's silence, then she replied to him, giving her consent, but in such a halting, toneless voice that I felt certain that when he had first left me to go behind the curtain he had hypnotised her.

'Turning to me, he asked, "Now are you satisfied?" Thinking that nothing further could be got out of her, I replied that I was. Roboumo then turned his back on the Witch and parted the curtains so that I could walk through to the main part of the *bure*. Just as I reached the curtains, I glanced over my shoulder to take a last look at her. Instantly I noticed a change in her expression. Her face was working. Clearly she was coming out of her trance and struggling to speak. Then, in a hoarse whisper, her voice came:

' *"Aidez-moi. Je suis prisonnière".'*

'God Almighty!' Gregory exclaimed. 'This is terrific. What happened then?'

'Naturally, I stepped back towards her, intending to question her in order to learn who she was, where she had come from and so on. But Roboumo, too, had caught her whisper. Swinging round he shouted at her, "Sleep! Sleep!" and made some swift passes at her with his outstretched hands. Her eyelids drooped until her eyes had closed and, her muscles relaxing, she sank back in the elbow chair. I turned on Roboumo and cried:

' "You are a swindler! A swindler! This woman has no power of her own. You have just used her as a means of terrifying the superstitious among my people."

'Pushing him aside, I advanced to the cage and tried to tear apart the bamboo bars, so that I could free her. They were thick and strong, so that I could do no more than bend them. While I was still straining every muscle to break into the cage, her head began to roll upon her shoulders. Again she partially emerged from the trance into which she had been thrown. Her eyes opened, then dilated. Suddenly her mouth gaped and she cried:

' *"Achtung!"*

'I don't know much German, but enough to understand that to be a cry of warning. Not an instant too soon I swung round and jerked my head aside. Had I not, Roboumo would have bashed in my skull with a big war club that he had snatched from the wall. I then knew that, as I had discovered the White Witch to be no better than a ventriloquist's doll that he was making use of, he meant to kill me rather than give me any chance to disclose his secret.

'It was then, knowing that you were not far away, that I gave my cry for help.

'I made a grab at him, but he eluded me. Before I had a chance to attempt to seize him again he had darted through the curtains. Another moment, and before I could stop him he had snatched up a long stick with a big, round head and was beating wildly with it on a drum.

'I needed no telling that he was summoning his warriors and that if I failed to escape within a matter of minutes I would pay for it with my life.

'As I raced past Roboumo I struck him a savage blow low in the back, somewhere in the region of the kidneys. He let out an ear-splitting screech, dropped the great drum stick and fell to the floor.

'Next moment I was out of his *bure* and running hell for leather through the village to save myself. I need not recount what happened after that. You, dear friend, saved me from being killed or captured and we reached this boat together.'

For a few moments Gregory was silent; then he said, 'What has happened tonight has created an entirely new situation. That, through entirely unforeseen circumstances, you failed to secure the help of Roboumo's warriors for an attack on the *Pigalle* is most unfortunate. But a new factor has emerged that just might turn the tide in our favour. If the White Witch is Roboumo's prisoner, and is being used by him under hypnotism as a helpless stooge, we now have a chance to prove him a fraud and discredit him with his followers. I can't yet see how this can be used against Lacost; but I am sure there is a way that it can, if only we can think of it.'

By then the dinghy was nearing the anchorage outside the harbour at which the *Boa Viagem* lay. James had the little boat go alongside, so that he could board the yacht, and let Olinda know that he had returned safely from his visit to Roboumo's island. As he went up the ladder to the deck of the yacht, Gregory called after him:

'Just tell her that you are all right, James; then come down to the boat again. Tonight is the night when we play the final hand against Lacost. Don't you dare linger with her. I'm not yet clear in my mind about what we ought to do; but we've got to take some sort of action, and without your authority I can do nothing.'

Impressed by Gregory's earnestness, James remained for only five minutes with Olinda, then returned to the boat. Ten minutes later it put them ashore, and a quarter of an hour's walk up the hill brought them to the Royal *bure*.

The aged doorman had long since gone to his bed, all the able-bodied servants were members of the body-guard and were still a quarter of an hour's march away. It did not surprise them to see that the paraffin lamps had been left burning in the main *bure*, but as they entered they were taken aback to see Hamie Baker sitting in an armchair with a glass of rum clasped in his horny hand.

'What the devil are you doing here?' Gregory asked.

Hamie gave a sheepish grin, got to his feet and replied, 'I bin left here, baas, as a sort o' go-between. Mr. Lacost, he got to know somehow that when I reported sick and slipped ashore I'd spilled the beans to you what were goin' on; so he thought I'd serve as a good sort o' mouth-piece.'

'That,' replied Gregory, 'was quite a sound decision. Well, what has he told you to tell us?'

'You got him worried,' Hamie said, solemnly nodding his head. 'He's got friends in the town he pays to let him know what goes on. 'S'evening he learned that a gunboat was being sent from Noumea to collar him an' his pals. The Frenchies wouldn't have had much on him 'bout gettin' up the treasure, provided he'd paid their tax. But you an' the Ratu attackin' the *Pigalle* lars' evenin' made things very different. Ter keep the stuff he's got he had ter shoot a lot of the islanders an' maybe one or two gendarmes. That 'ull have made the Frenchies mad as hatters. So for him there's only way way out. He's got to have that licence wot Mrs. de Carvalho holds transferred to him, and pre-dated. Then he could claim that he'd done no more than fight off pirates who were tryin' ter rob him of his legitimate gains. See?'

'Yes, I see,' Gregory agreed. 'He has let himself and his friends in for the death penalty if they are caught. And, believe me, he will be. You'll be for it, too, since you failed to take my advice, and rejoined him.'

'No.' Hamie gave a twisted grin. 'Not me, baas. I were still malingerin' at the hospital when the attack on the *Pigalle* took place. I rejoined her only this mornin' ter claim the money wot they owed me. And my! You should see wot they got up. Gold is worth sixteen pounds an ounce these days, an' they've salvaged half a ton of it, not ter mention crosses, crooks, mitres an' whatnot, stuck all over with jewels like plums in a Christmas puddin'. But no-one's got anything on me. That's why Mr. Lacost left me here to be his mouth-piece.'

'O.K., then; you are in the clear. But why should Lacost suppose that we would persuade the Senhora de Carvalho to make the licence over to him?'

Hamie's mouth twisted into a toothsome grin. 'Because, baas, he's kidnapped your missus. He an' his pals come here an' took Mrs. Sallust off to their yacht. I bin left ter tell yer that unless yer goes aboard the *Pigalle* by two o'clock this mornin' an' hands him that licence dated three days back, he's goin' ter pull her toenails out an' slice off them pretty ears she's got. You still has two hours ter work in, but you'd better get on wi' this job.'

'The swine,' James burst out. 'My God, if I could only get my hands on him! And as for you, I'll . . .' Breaking off, he strode towards Hamie, obviously intending to seize him by the throat.

Whipping a pistol from his hip pocket, Hamie snarled, 'Keep off, Ratu! Another step an' I'll drill yer full o' holes.'

As James halted, Gregory said to him, 'There is nothing to be gained by trying to take it out on Baker. He is simply a go-between. Lacost left him here to deliver his ultimatum only because if he had set it down on paper it would have incriminated him. Of course he is right that, had the licence really been transferred to him three days ago, he would have had fair reason to assume that our attack on the *Pigalle* was an attempted act of piracy; and that, somehow, we had managed to fool the gendarmes into putting up a front for us. After all, anyone who thought he was about to be robbed of

343

many thousands of pounds' worth of treasure and had only a handful of men to protect it against a force of three score armed natives could plead justification in firing to drive them off before giving them a chance to come alongside and swarm aboard.'

'Perhaps you are right,' James agreed reluctantly. 'But when the gunboat from Noumea arrives and we tell our story, with Elbœuf to support us, the warship will give chase.'

'If we do let Lacost have a pre-dated transfer of the licence how can we prove that we did not make a secret deal with him without Elbœuf's knowledge? Lacost, too, is quite shrewd enough to leave a letter for Elbœuf, giving a guarantee that he will pay up the ten per cent tax to the French Government as soon as he has had time to dispose of the treasure.'

'In any case, the gunboat will pursue the *Pigalle*. The Government in New Caledonia could not ignore the killing of a gendarme and a number of my people. They will regard it as essential to hold a full inquiry, and that could not be held without the interrogation of the men responsible.'

Gregory nodded. 'About that I entirely agree. But you have to catch your hare before you can cook it. If Lacost sails tonight he may disappear for good. Even if he and his pals are caught such an inquiry would take weeks. If he has said that he will pay the tax and he holds the licence I think the odds are against the Colons being convicted.'

'I suppose they are.' James gave a heavy sigh. 'The question is, what do we do now? We can't possibly leave Manon to be subjected to hideous tortures. As I think I told you, Olinda made the licence over to me two nights ago. So we can go off to the *Pigalle* right away and ransom Manon with it. On the other hand, to attack the ship during the hours of darkness would be very different from exposing ourselves again in daylight. So I feel sure my body-guard would jump at the chance to avenge their comrades. When they get back we could set off with them at once and, with luck, both rescue Manon and capture these filthy Colons. But there is the risk that if we attack they may kill Manon before we can get

344

her. So it is for you to say. My feeling is that we must throw in our hand and let Lacost have this accursed licence.'

'Maybe you're right,' Gregory muttered. 'We have to bear in mind that if we attack, although we'd have the cover of darkness, we won't catch the Colons napping. They will anticipate that we may, so be ready for us. In any case, even if they don't think we'll dare risk it they will be up and about, waiting for us to arrive with the licence. But since you told me about your dust-up with Roboumo I've been toying with an idea, and I've still got to think a little. Meantime I want to pump ship, so I'm going to my *bure*.'

Leaving James and Hamie staring at each other in silent hostility, Gregory walked out of the big room and across the few yards to the smaller *bure* which he had shared with Manon. As he entered the bathroom his glance immediately fell on a piece of paper lying on the lavatory seat. Picking it up, he saw a few pencilled lines hurriedly scrawled by Manon. They read:

On no account come off to the Pigalle. *If you do I feel certain Lacost intends to murder you. But, provided he gets the licence, I'm sure he won't vent his spite on me if you don't bring it yourself. Send Hamie Baker with it, then they will let me go.*

Evidently, before the Colons had carried off Manon, they had allowed her to use the bathroom, and she had seized the opportunity to leave this message. It confirmed certain ideas that Gregory had already formed and decided him to take the course he had been contemplating. With a grim smile he pushed the paper into his pocket, had a quick wash to rid his hands and face of the dirt he had picked up on Roboumo's island, then returned to the main *bure*.

James was still glowering at Hamie. As Gregory appeared, he turned to him and asked, 'Well, what have you decided? My body-guard is back. You can hear them singing outside, as they are getting down to the food and *kava* which I ordered to be left ready for them. Do we lead them in another

345

attack, or do you and I go off to the *Pigalle* and sign away the licence?'

'We do neither,' Gregory replied quietly. 'Manon left a message for me in the loo. She's convinced that Lacost will not take it out on her if I fail to turn up with the licence. But all the same I want you to go out and get your boys on parade again before they've drunk too much *kava*.'

'You *do* mean us to attack the *Pigalle*, then?'

'No. We are going to attack Roboumo's island.'

James' eyebrows went up. 'In God's name, why?'

'Because, with the Colons on the alert, your body-guard might not be sufficiently strong to get the best of things. We've got to have Roboumo's toughs with us to make certain of overwhelming Lacost and his pals.'

'But damn it, man, after what happened an hour ago he'd never allow them to become our allies.'

'I mean to put him in a spot that will render him powerless. The fact that you got away from him unharmed will both have shaken his own men's confidence in him and stiffened the morale of yours; so I don't think we need fear very serious opposition. And after you told me about what happened in his *bure* I hit on the key to the whole situation.'

'The key to the situation?' James repeated in a puzzled voice.

'Yes; it's the White Witch. She is a prisoner. We are going in to rescue her. And she will be on our side. Without her, Roboumo will be a busted flush and his men will take your orders. With their aid the *Pigalle* and the treasure will be in our hands before morning.'

20

Death in the Dark Hours

As the body-guard had arrived back from their hour's march only ten minutes earlier it was decided that they should be given a further quarter of an hour to rest and refresh themselves. James went out to warn them that he meant to lead them on another expedition and to tell Aleamotu'a of the new plan, leaving Gregory alone with Hamie.

The half-caste diver had been a silent listener to all that had passed, so now Gregory said to him, 'I am afraid you are in for an uncomfortable time these next few hours, Hamie. I can't risk your making off as soon as we have gone, getting back to the *Pigalle* and warning Lacost of our intentions. As there are no locks on the *bure* doors, I'll have to tie you up securely until we return.'

Hamie grinned. 'That's all right by me, baas. Warnin' Mr. Lacost wouldn't prevent you attacking the *Pigalle*, an' I wouldn't care ter be aboard her when that happens; not wiv half a hundred of them fuzzywuzzies swarmin' on to her bangin' off rifles an' yellin' murder. I ain't done so bad, wot wiv the two hundred quid you give me an' the nice little wad he were fair enough ter pay me for me divin', before he left me here. Though I guess that were really so I'd feel it were up ter me ter stick around an' give you his message, 'stead of makin' off while no-one were about. But ter my mind you're actin' stupid.'

'You think so?' Gregory smiled. 'May I ask why?'

'Well, wot abart yer missus? Two o'clock were the deadline Mr. Lacost set fer you to go aboard the *Pigalle* wiv that licence, an 'it's arter midnight now. Maybe you'll put paid to

347

the old witch guy by makin' off wiv his girl friend. But you can't do that an' get back ter attack the *Pigalle* in under a couple o' hours, can yer?'

'No. You're right about that. It would take at least three hours.'

'O.K., then. An' that Lacost is an impatient type. Maybe he'll give you half-an-hour's leeway, but come half past two, or thereabouts, he'll decide you ain't goin' ter play an' start pullin' yer wife's toenails out.'

'I don't think he will. He's got nothing to gain by doing that.'

For a moment the diver remained thoughtful, then he said, 'It's your gamble, baas, not mine. But I wouldn't take a chance on it if he'd got ahold o' my gal. Still, p'raps there's somethin' in wot yer say. Be a pity ter make a mess of a lady like her to no purpose. In fact if I were in his shoes I'd act quite different. I'd up anchor, then take her down to me cabin an' do you know what.'

'That is an unpleasant possibility that I have already considered,' Greory replied. 'But I have no means of preventing him from doing that at any time between now and when the moon goes down. And I must wait until then to attack; otherwise, if he can see us coming in, he might succeed in driving us off.'

'Blimey! Yer not goin' in till moonset? If yer wait that long, baas, you'll miss the boat. Time's runnin' out fer him. He's gotter get well clear o' Tujoa before the warship from Noumea turns up. If he don't he'll be good an' proper sunk. He jus' daren't hang around fer more than an hour or so arter two o'clock.'

'Yes he will,' Gregory declared with conviction. 'The gunboat can't possibly reach Revika in under thirty-six hours from now, and the licence means everything to Lacost. With it, the odds are that he would be able to argue a committee of inquiry into believing that yesterday he honestly believed the Ratu to have have tricked the police into aiding him in an attempt to rob the Colons of the treasure they had salvaged legitimately. Without it, he and his pals will be hunted men for the rest of their lives. Sooner or later the French

348

authorities will get them, then they will go to the guillotine.
When I fail to turn up he'll think of some way of trying to
make a deal with us—perhaps sharing the treasure or, as a
last resort, turning the whole lot over to us in exchange for
the licence. But you can take it from me, the *Pigalle* will still
be lying off Tujoa until at least midday tomorrow.'

'My! You're a cool customer.' Hamie shook his head.

Gregory smiled. 'I've had quite a lot of experience in dealing with bad men, and I'm very sensible of the fact that he
has Mrs. Sallust in his power. But there is nothing I can do
about that for the time being. When you are as old as I am,
Hamie, you will know that it is only asking for trouble to hit
out at your enemy until you are certain you can strike him
down.'

At that moment James re-entered the *bure*. He said that his
body-guard was ready and eager to be led against Roboumo
and, once and for all, destroy the power of that evil man who
had for so long terrorised and blackmailed so many of their
friends and relatives.

Hamie was told to move from the armchair in which he
was lounging to a stout upright one; then, unresisting, he allowed himself to be lashed securely to it with a score of strips
of stout *tapa* cloth which James produced from one of his
handsome wooden chests. That done, the two friends poured
themselves stiff drinks, drank to the success of their expedition, then went out to join the reassembling body-guard.

This time, instead of taking the circuitous track through
the jungle, they marched straight down to the harbour. There
they piled into the six speediest motor boats available and,
with James leading in his own cabin cruiser, set a course
round the coast for Roboumo's island.

In accordance with instructions that James had given before they set out, when the boats were within half a mile of
the island they separated, so that each crew would land at
some distance from their nearest neighbours. Then the engines were shut off and paddles used to bring them inshore.

As they neared the beach, no lights were to be seen through
the trees and no sentry challenged them; so evidently Roboumo and his men had no suspicion that they were about to re-

349

ceive unwelcome visitors. The boats dropped anchor in the shallows; jumping from them, the crews waded to the beach and the six groups, with weapons at the ready, cautiously made their way across the beach to the screen of vegetation. The moon was still well up, but the palms, magnolias, breadfruit and bau trees threw heavy shadows and in places where they were close together there were areas to which only a very faint light penetrated.

It was in the group Gregory was leading that the accident occurred. They had proceeded no more than a hundred yards among the trees when one of the body-guard tripped on a protruding root. He was within a yard of Gregory and clutched at him for support. Most unfortunately, in the darkness he grabbed the hand on a sub-machine gun Gregory was carrying at the ready. He had his thumb on the safety catch and his finger on the trigger. The sudden, unexpected pressure on both thumb and finger caused the gun to go off.

The eerie silence was shattered by the burst of fire that followed. Fortunately, the bullets whistled through the trees, harming none of his companions; but the swift series of explosions raised an appalling clatter.

Next moment a furious barking of dogs sounded in the village. But it was only three or four hundred yards away; so, although all hope of achieving complete surprise was now gone, Gregory still hoped that the attacking force might reach it before any serious defence could be organised. Yelling to his men to follow him, he dashed forward through the trees.

Before they had covered half the distance they heard the deep booming of Roboumo's drum sounding the alarm. Then, on reaching an open space, they saw the village, the roofs of its *bures* clearly outlined in the moonlight. But to Gregory's consternation he also saw that they were heading for a six-foot-high cactus hedge. Earlier in the night when he had covered James' visit to the witch-doctor they had both approached the village by the path up from the beach. It had never occurred to him that only by that way could one enter it. Now they were faced by this apparently impenetrable barrier.

He had to take a swift decision. Should he turn left and run on along the hedge until he struck the path, or should he attempt to force a way through the spiky barrier of cactus? It was a foregone conclusion that, apart from the group led by James, which he had elected to lead in by the path, all the other four groups would come up against the hedge and, most probably, make their way round to the unprotected entrance. It was there the fight would rage for possession of the village and every one of Roboumo's men would be engaged in it. If, therefore, Gregory could force a way through the hedge the odds were that he would be able to reach the witch-doctor's *bure* and rescue the witch without opposition.

On looking over his group before they had left harbour he had seen that, in addition to firearms, four out of six of them had machetes slung at their waists. Only two of them could speak a few words of English; so, instead of trying to explain his intention, he snatched the machete from the man nearest him, ran forward and began to slash frantically at the wall of cactus. The others similarly armed, shouting their war-cry and waving their sharp blades, immediately came to his assistance.

By then pandemonium had broken out in the village. Yells of defiance mingled with the barking of dogs and the screams of terrified women. Single shots rang out in swift succession, but no bursts of machine-gun fire, as James had been anxious to avoid a massacre and had given orders that the few men so armed should not use their weapons except in an emergency.

Five minutes, which seemed an age to Gregory, went by before he and his men had succeeded in hacking a gap in the cactus wide enough for them to get through without their limbs being torn or pierced by the hundreds of three-inch-long spikes as stiff as steel needles.

Leading the way again, he dashed between several smaller *bures* until he reached the rear of Roboumo's big, high-roofed house. A single sharp push on the back entrance door showed that it was not locked or bolted. Thrusting it open, he almost fell inside, to find himself at the back of the White

351

Witch's cage. She was lying on her big divan, her face turned away from him and half hidden by her long, white hair.

Three elderly native women were seated cross-legged on the floor on the far side of the cage. As Gregory burst in, they sprang to their feet. For a moment they stared at him in terror and amazement. He lifted his Sten gun as though about to fire at them through the cage. Screaming, they turned and, tumbling over one another, fled through the *tapa*-cloth curtains.

Gregory had supposed the White Witch to be asleep; but, to his surprise, the screams of the women did not rouse her. Raising his machete, he slashed at the bamboo bars of the big cage until he had cut a hole large enough to get through. On a low table beside her divan stood a mug. Picking it up, he sniffed. It had a strange, strong odour and still gave off faintly the type of fumes one associates with neat spirits. That confirmed his guess that before Roboumo had left the *bure*, fearing that the attackers might break in and question his prisoner, he had forced her to swallow some potent drug that would cause her to fall into a coma.

Turning towards her, he looked down into her face. His eyes widened. For a moment he held his breath, then let it go with a sharp, rasping sound; but for a full minute he remained there, staring at the lined but still beautiful features framed in long, dead-white hair. Suddenly pulling himself together, he stooped, swiftly wrapped her in the light rug under which she lay, picked her up and carried her out through the hole he had cut in the cage.

Their eyes wide with astonishment and awe, his men gaped at the limp body of the woman whom, with Roboumo as her mouth-piece, they believed to have terrorised the people of Tujoa for so long. To the two of them who understood a little English, Gregory said quickly:

'Go find Ratu. Tell him I have White Witch. She ill. I take her to yacht—the *Boa Viagem*.' Then he beckoned the other four to follow him out of the *bure*.

The Witch was very thin and, at a guess, Gregory thought she could not weigh much more than seven stone; even so, by the time he got her down to the beach he was panting heavily

352

There the largest of the men with him—a broad-shouldered giant—insisted on taking her from him and carrying her out to the motor boat. On reaching it, they laid her gently upon the cushions in the stern. As the engine was started up, Gregory sat down beside her, pillowed her head on his lap and tried to rouse her; but his efforts proved fruitless.

A quarter of an hour later they reached the harbour. It had been Gregory's intention to get her aboard the yacht, give her an emetic and enlist Olinda's help in looking after her. But, as they came round the high, curved mole that protected the harbour from the worst gales, a surprise awaited him. The *Boa Viagem* was no longer there.

Why she should have left her mooring Gregory could not imagine. Ever since she had arrived at Revika she had lain at anchor in deep water about two hundred yards from the wharf.

What possible reason could Olinda have had for giving orders for her yacht to put to sea? Greatly puzzled and not a little perturbed, he had the motor boat land them on the quay. The departure of the yacht meant that another quarter of an hour must elapse, while the Witch was carried up the hill to the Royal *bure*, before she could be given an emetic; but that could not be helped and was not a matter of great urgency.

On reaching the *bure*, Gregory took the Witch from the big native who had carried her up the hill, then made signs to the four men who had accompanied him that they should go round to the kitchens and refresh themselves. As they bowed and turned away, he eased the position of the White Witch in his arms and carried her into the *bure*. On entering, he was confronted with another surprise. Hamie Baker was no longer there; but the big, lofty room was not unoccupied. Manon was reclining with her feet up on one of the sofas, smoking a cigarette and with a drink by her side. Coming to her feet, she exclaimed:

'*Mon Dieu*! Where have you been? And who in the world is that?'

'I've come from Roboumo's island,' he replied, as he laid

353

his still-unconscious burden down on one of the other sofas, 'and this is the White Witch.'

'The White Witch?' Manon echoed. 'How different she is from what I had imagined. I've always thought of her as some great, fat, forceful-looking half-caste. And now she turns out to be an old, frail, white woman. But why have you brought her here?'

'We rescued her in order to get the better of Lacost. As you know, in the afternoon of—yes, yesterday, although it seems now weeks ago—James received an offer from Roboumo to enter into a pact. James went to the island and all was going well, but he insisted that the Witch should be a party to the pact so Roboumo let him see her. She was under hypnosis, but managed to struggle out of it sufficiently to let James know that she was a prisoner.'

Manon shook her head. 'What an extraordinary affair.'

'It certainly is. When James found out the truth, Roboumo tried to kill him; but he got away. Of course, all prospect of a pact had gone up in smoke. We were stuck again with the fact that, with only the body-guard, our chances of capturing the *Pigalle* were far from good. It was then it struck me that, although the Witch was not really a witch at all, Roboumo's men believed that he owed all his power to her; so, if we could rescue her, they would come over to us. We attacked the island an hour ago and I got her out. She had been doped to the eyebrows and we must bring her round as soon as possible; but that can wait for a few minutes while you tell me how you come to be here. Did you escape, or did Lacost let you go?'

'Tell me first why you failed to act on the message I left for you.' Manon's voice held an angry, resentful tone as she went on:

'I know you had it, because when I got back here I went to the loo and found it gone. And you already had Lacost's ultimatum from Hamie Baker about pulling out my toenails and cutting off my ears unless he received the licence.'

Gregory gave a slight shrug. 'My dear girl, I should have thought that would already be clear to you. In your note you said you felt certain Lacost would do you no harm if I failed

354

to go aboard the *Pigalle* and, even if we did not send him the licence by someone else, he would have had nothing to gain by taking you to pieces. To leave without it would have meant that, sooner or later, he and all his pals would go to the guillotine. Therefore I felt certain that the time limit of two o'clock which he had given me could safely be ignored. It was a sure bet that he would hang on here till the very last moment, hoping in some way that he'd get the licence from us; and, as the gunboat from Noumea can't arrive before Monday morning, he could safely stay on in Revika until midday. You must know that the body-guard is made up only of house servants and peasants: not real fighting men. That's why we had to delay until we could secure the support of Roboumo's toughs.'

Before Manon replied she lit another cigarette; then she said more mildly, 'I suppose the view you took is understandable. As a matter of fact I learned quite a bit from Hamie about what was going on.'

'I take it that it was you who released him?'

'Yes. You tied him up so tightly that the poor fellow was in agony. He meant you no harm and only acted as Lacost's messenger; so I set him free and let him go.'

Gregory's face darkened into a scowl, so that the scar that ran from the end of his eyebrows up into his forehead showed livid, and he exclaimed angrily, 'Damn it, you may have ruined everything! Hamie's only interest is money. It's quite on the cards that by now he is on his way to the *Pigalle* to get himself another wad of notes by warning Lacost of our intentions.'

'No, he won't be able to do that, even if he tries to. By the time he gets across the island to the site of the wreck, where the *Pigalle* was anchored, he will find her gone.'

'D'you mean . . . d'you mean that Lacost has thrown in his hand and sailed?'

Manon nodded. 'Yes, but not for good. He remained there until half past two. Then, as you failed to turn up, or someone sent by you, he got under way and set off to put into operation an alternative plan by which he hoped to get the better of you.'

355

'Good God! Do you know it?'

'I do. That's why he released me. The *Pigalle* sailed round to the harbour and later he had me put ashore; so that I could act as his messenger and bring you a second ultimatum.'

Instantly there flashed back into Gregory's mind the fact that the *Boa Viagem* had disappeared. With a gasp of dismay he exclaimed, 'Hell's bells! I've got it! He seized Olinda's yacht and swapped you for her as a hostage.'

Manon gave a sigh, looked down at her feet and said, 'I'm terribly sorry that it should be I who have been forced to bring you this bad news. But you are right. It was easy to capture the yacht. Everyone aboard her was sound asleep. The *Pigalle* came alongside, the Colons boarded her and took her over without a shot being fired.'

Putting a hand to his head, Gregory groaned. It was he who had persuaded Captain Amedo to lend him all the weapons from the yacht's armoury, and the body-guard still had them; so the crew of the *Boa Viagem* had been deprived of the chance of putting up any resistance.

Meanwhile, Manon was going on, 'One must admit that Lacost is no fool. Unfortunately for him he made one mistake. He naturally believed that Olinda still held the licence. His plan had been to take over the yacht, transfer the treasure to her, then scuttle the *Pigalle* and make off in the much faster *Boa Viagem*. But in that he was foiled. Olinda declared that the licence was no longer hers, that she had transferred it to James two days ago. When threatened with torture she convinced Lacost by opening her safe and showing him that it was not among her valuables and papers. It was then that he decided he must make another bid for it. Possession of the licence could clear him and the others of having fired on the flotilla of boats in which you attacked him yesterday. Seizing the *Boa Viagem* was, of course, an act of piracy; but by threats of torture he can force Olinda to write a letter to the effect that she was being held by James in Revika against her will, and asking Lacost to come to her rescue.'

'Yes, he's a clever devil,' Gregory admitted; then he added, 'How comes it that he told you so much about his plans?'

She raised her eyebrows and spread out her hands. 'Why not? It was natural that he should, since he meant to use me as his emissary. How could I give you a clear account of his intentions unless he told me of them? His spies have informed him that James is in love with Olinda, so he is counting on that to bring the two of you to heel and send a transfer of the licence out to him as her ransom. Of course, he knows nothing about how you and James have been away for a good part of the night attacking Roboumo's island. But he has given you a few hours to think it over. Either you send out the licence to him before dawn or he means to up anchor and make off into the blue with Olinda. I am most terribly sorry to have to tell you all this, darling. But there it is. I had no option.'

'What has he done with the *Pigalle*?' Gregory asked.

'When he had me put ashore he was about to tow her out to the far side of the mole, then, after he had transferred the treasure and his stores to the *Boa Viagem*, scuttle her. The Colons must have been working on shifting their cargoes from the *Pigalle* for the past hour.'

It was at that moment that James burst into the room. His handsome face expressed a queer mixture of triumph and concern.

'We've done it!' he exclaimed. 'It was all over in ten minutes. We had to shoot half a dozen of Roboumo's men then he arrived on the scene himself, and urged them to greater efforts. Aleamotu'a brought him down by a bullet through the thigh. It has always been a custom in the islands that immediately one leader or the other is rendered *hors de combat* his followers should cease fighting. That is what happened. His men surrendered.

'Then your two messengers reached me with the news that you had got away with the White Witch. When I announced it Roboumo's men went down on their knees and grovelled to me begging for mercy. I assured them of my forgiveness and protection, provided they obeyed me without question. My first order to them was that they should tie Roboumo to a tree and shoot him. It was a tense moment, but they did; so

357

summary justice was done on him and he will give us no more trouble.

'Next I told them that I required them to show further their loyalty to me by aiding in an attack on the *Pigalle*. There were more than a score of them unwounded and still fighting fit. Unhesitatingly they beat their chests and cried, "*Bole! Bole!*", their challenge to an enemy, and followed me down to our boats.

'From your two men I learned that you were on your way back to the harbour, so we went there to pick you up. I expected to find that you had taken the White Witch to the *Boa Viagem*. But the yacht was not there. She has gone. I was amazed and filled with fear. What has become of her?'

As quickly as he could, Gregory told James of the new and menacing situation.

When he realised what had occurred James let out a wail of grief and cried, 'Olinda! My love; my sweet one! She is in the hands of those devils. We must go at once. I will transfer the licence to this brute Lacost. It is the only way to save her.'

'No,' said Gregory firmly. 'I'm damned if I'll let you throw the sponge in now, when the odds are in our favour. With the body-guard and Roboumo's men to give them a lead, we'll have the upper hand. Lacost is there waiting for us; but by now the moon must have set. Under cover of darkness we will be able to approach the yacht unseen. The Colons number half a dozen at the most. We will have ten times their numbers. With twenty ruthless, well-armed fighting men, backed by forty others, they won't stand a chance against us.'

Manon, wide-eyed, cut in. 'You'll not pull it off. I beg you not to try. I don't think I told you, but Lacost said I was to let you know that if more than one motor boat with three or four men in her approached the yacht he would open fire with his machine guns. Such an attempt could not possibly succeed. It would lead only to a massacre.'

'You are right,' muttered James miserably. 'Oh, you are right! The only way I can save Olinda is to go out and transfer the licence to Lacost.'

'Pull your wits together, boy!' Gregory snapped. 'Haven't you the sense to see that transferring the licence will not now

358

be enough? Possession of it might just be sufficient to excuse Lacost having fired upon us and those French gendarmes yesterday. But not for this act of piracy in having boarded and seized the *Boa Viagem*. If he is caught, and he certainly will be, the only way in which he can clear himself of that is by coercing Olinda into writing a series of letters, purporting to show that you had been detaining her here against her will, and begging him, as her late husband's partner, to rescue her. Convincing letters of that kind cannot be thought out and written in the space of half an hour while we lie alongside the yacht in a motor boat. Lacost will take the licence from you, then tell you to go to hell and carry Olinda off with him. How could you possibly prevent him from doing that? If you mean to save Olinda the only chance you've got is to go in and get her.'

'You have reason on your side,' James muttered unhappily. 'I suppose that is the only hope of saving her. But if Lacost intends to fire on us should we approach the yacht with more than one boat, how can we possibly hope to get the better of him?'

'God knows! I don't,' Gregory said with a shrug. 'But with luck I'll think up some way to trick him.'

Turning towards the white-haired woman who still lay unconscious on the sofa, he looked at her, then added, 'At the moment the last thing I want to do is to leave here. I want to bring our pseudo Witch round and hear her story. But it is up to you, James. If you want to get your girl back I can't let you down, so I'll come with you. But dawn can't be far off, and we'll stand no chance at all unless we can attack under cover of darkness. So if we are going to make the attempt we must leave at once.'

James nodded. 'Thank you, dear friend. Yes; let us go.'

Gregory took another long look at the Witch, then he said to Manon, 'I don't think for a moment that Roboumo would have been such a fool as to give her a deadly poison, because he would have thought there was a good chance of his warriors successfully defending the village. But he must have made her swallow something pretty potent for her to have fallen into such deep unconsciousness, and the sooner it is out of her system, the better. Get some mustard from the kitchen, mix it with hot water, then force it down her throat. Even if she doesn't come to, it will make her sick. And remember, she has never been our enemy, but an unhappy prisoner; so if she does come round, treat her with the greatest kindness and get her to bed.'

'Of course I'll look after her,' Manon promised. Then Gregory turned and followed James out of the *bure*.

Directly they were outside James said, 'The whole of our force is down on the harbour. I brought Roboumo's men back with me in our boats, so that they would be with us to receive our instructions about attacking the *Pigalle*. I came up to the *bure* only because I was told that you had taken the White Witch up here; and I would not have dreamed of launching the attack without your counsel.'

'We've not lost much time,' Gregory replied. 'The moon cannot have set much more than a quarter of an hour ago; and instead of having to go right round to the site of the wreck, where the *Pigalle* was anchored, we now have to go only a mile or so on the far side of the mole.'

James, who was in great distress, then began to give vent to his fears for Olinda, but Gregory cut him short by saying, 'Dear boy, I know how you must feel, but please don't talk about it now. I've got to think—to think hard—of a way in which to trick Lacost, and I've got little enough time to do it in.' So, for the rest of the way down the long slope of the garden, across the open space in which the Meeting House stood and through the sleeping town, they walked in silence.

When they reached the harbour Gregory said, 'What we have to do is to prevent Lacost from taking alarm, ordering the yacht to forge full speed ahead and shooting us to pieces before there is time for our flotilla to come up. I've had one idea how we might achieve that. Whether it will come off or not, God alone knows. If it doesn't, you and I will be dead within the next half-hour. But I see no alternative to trying it. To play this trick I'll need two pieces of strong fishing net, each about twenty feet square, and a dozen pieces of wire all about three metres long and a third of a centimetre thick.'

Beckoning to one of his men who normally was a wharf

hand, James told him what was required; and he went off to knock up a nearby ship chandler, who would have the type of wire required, and who could quickly cut it into lengths. Aleamotu'a then joined James, and Gregory briefed them on the tactics that he had thought out.

The Ratu's cabin cruiser was to be used by the two of them, James' coxswain and Kalabo. The boat was to approach the *Boa Viagem* unaccompanied, and tie up under her stern. James was to parley with Lacost and refuse, for the time being, to go on board. He was to show the licence, upon which Lacost would say that it was useless to him without a transfer. James would then go into the small cabin and spend several minutes writing one out. Lacost would require that it be witnessed. James would have this done by Kalabo and his coxswain. Next, James would refuse to hand over the papers until Olinda was lowered into the boat. It was certain that Lacost, suspecting that he meant to make off with her, would refuse. An argument, which James was to keep going as long as possible, would then ensue. When they reached stalemate James was to flash a torch on to the papers and hold it there for some moments, pretending to do so in order that Lacost, by peering over the stern rail, might see that they were in order, then offer to hand them up simultaneously with Olinda being put over the side. As Lacost leaned over, James was to drop the papers, throw the torch high into the air, leap up, seize Lacost by the wrists and endeavour to drag him over into the boat. If he succeeded he was to hold Lacost in front of him as a shield against being fired upon.

Meanwhile, the other nine most speedy motor boats in the harbour would have been manned. The crew of each was to take with it two or three anchors from small rowing boats and canoes. These, with lengths of thick rope attached to them, were, when the boats came alongside the yacht, to be thrown up as grapples, so that they would catch on the rail of the yacht and boarding parties could swarm up the ropes dangling from them.

The flotilla was to muster on the inner side of the mole. Two watchmen were to be stationed on it. When they saw the light of James' torch, as he threw it up into the air, that would be the signal. Led by Aleamotu'a, the boats were to round the end of the mole and make at all possible speed for the yacht. Each crew was to act independently of the others, board the yacht and show no mercy to the Colons, capturing them if they surrendered or killing them without hesitation should they put up the least resistance.

Aleamotu'a translated into Nakapoan such parts of Gregory's instructions as applied to the main force, shouting them so that all could hear. They responded eagerly, crying 'Bole! Bole!', beating their chests and each boastfully declaring that he would kill two—three—four Colons at the least.

As they dispersed to make their preparations, Gregory's party went on board James' cruiser, taking with them the pieces of fishing net and wire for which Gregory had asked. Five minutes later the cruiser rounded the end of the mole and headed towards the *Boa Viagem*, the position of which could be seen by her riding lights as she lay at anchor about a mile away.

Gregory went into the low cabin, took off his clothes and emerged a few minutes later, stark naked. As he appeared, James exclaimed anxiously, 'What on earth ...! Oh, my dear friend! What are you about to do?'

'Have a dip,' Gregory smiled. 'The wash from our propeller will scare off any sharks that may be about. I shall be dropping over the side when we get to within about two hundred yards of the yacht. You must slow down so that I can continue to hang on. Then I want you to drape the bundles of fishing net over each side of the boat's bows so that they look like bumpers.'

'How do you mean to use them?'

'You'll see, if my idea comes off. I wish to God that we had half a dozen of the gendarmes' grenades, but we couldn't possibly spare the time to dig old Elbœuf out of bed and get his authority for the police to let us have them. Still, I'm hoping the nets will serve our purpose.'

By then they were within a quarter of a mile of the *Boa Viagem*. They could make out her outline quite clearly, but there was no sign of the *Pigalle*, so evidently the Colons had by this time transferred the treasure to the other yacht and had scuttled their old tub.

A few minutes later the cruiser slowed down and Gregory slipped overboard into the warm sea, with the lengths of thin wire looped round his neck.

As they approached the yacht, a hail came from her and a small beam light was switched on; but when it focused on the boat Gregory could not be seen as his head was below her gunwale and he was being drawn along with her only by the clutching fingers of one hand on it.

James answered the hail and was told to come alongside. Instead his coxswain brought the boat close in under the stern of the yacht. As the beam of light showed clearly that there were only three men in the boat and none of them was carrying arms, no protest was made at this manœuvre. A moment later, Lacost, holding a pistol in one hand, was peering down into her and speaking in French to James.

The conversation between them proceeded on the lines that Gregory had planned. Meanwhile, he had drawn the whole of one of the bundles of fishing net into the water and, as swiftly as he could, was wrapping it round the starboard propeller of the yacht. It was no easy task as the propeller, being well under water, could not be seen in the darkness caused by the overhang of the stern of the yacht, and every minute or two he had to come up for air.

When he had managed, as well as he could, to entangle the propeller in many folds of net, he twisted six of the lengths of wire round the bundle to keep it in place.

Coming up for a longer breather, he listened anxiously to the conversation going on above. It had reached the stage where Lacost, now angry and impatient, was telling James that the transfer of the licence he had just written out would not be legal unless it was witnessed.

Swiftly Gregory dived under the prow, came up on the far side and drew the other bundle of net down into the water. Alternately going right under, fumbling wildly in the dark, then coming up to gasp in air, he fouled the port propeller in the same way as he had the starboard one.

But after having firmly twisted together the ends of four

363

lengths of wire he felt he dare stay no longer, and surfaced with the two remaining lengths of wire still round his neck. Immediately he saw that a stronger light glowed in the vicinity of the boat, so knew that the critical stage had been reached when James would be holding up the documents for Lacost to see, and shining his powerful torch upon them.

A moment later the light dimmed, for James had thrown his torch high into the air. There came a cry, the crack of a pistol and a tremendous thump. That told Gregory that Lacost had fallen into the trap that had been set for him. James had jumped, grabbed Lacost's wrists and pulled him over the rail so that they had crashed on to the deck together. But that shot. Had James been killed or wounded?

In awful suspense Gregory waited, holding on to the prow of the boat with one hand. He heard the sounds of curses and a struggle only a few feet above his head. Excited, angry shouts came from the stern of the yacht. Then James' voice came clear and loud:

'I have your Captain! Now I've got him, I'll kill him unless you do as I say. Bring the Señhora. Bring her and lower her into the boat and I'll give you the papers and him in exchange.'

James' inspiration for making the best use of his captive was an improvement on Gregory's hastily-made plan, and he gave him full marks for it. The offer must result in creating just the delay needed for the flotilla to make the greater part of its way from the harbour. And, in making the offer, James must know perfectly well that if he had to carry out his promise to give up Lacost and the documents, he would get both back after his men had captured the *Boa Viagem*.

A heated argument broke out up on the stern deck of the yacht. Evidently all the other Colons were assembled there. One cried, 'Don't shoot! Don't shoot! You will kill Pierre.'

Another was for abandoning Lacost and making off.

Lacost's voice came from close overhead in a furious bellow, 'Felix, you are an imbecile! Without me as your leader you would be captured in a week.'

The others, too, shouted down the man who wanted to cut and run.

364

'No! No! Pierre has the brains. And we must have the licence.'

'Yes, we dare not sail without the licence.'

'The licence! Yes, it would be as much as our necks are worth to leave without it.'

'Pierre is the only one among us capable of marketing our haul.'

'What does the woman matter? Once we get the money we'll have scores of the bitches.'

Again Lacost's voice broke in—urgent, commanding. 'Alphonse, go and fetch the Senhora.'

The excited shouts fell to swift murmurings. Now that the babel had subsided, Gregory, his face only just above water, listened intently. At once he caught the purr of motor engines. Down there at sea level was the best place to catch distant sounds, but he knew that in a few minutes the men above him must also hear them.

Another two minutes passed. Again the voices up on the stern deck grew louder. Then came James, his voice vibrant with relief and delight. 'Olinda! Olinda! Thank God you are all right. I have been worried out of my wits.'

She called back to him, 'James! My James! How wonderful! I . . . I can hardly believe I am not dreaming.'

Racked with anxiety Gregory continued to listen. He could now hear the approaching flotilla more distinctly.

Suddenly one of the Colons cried, 'Listen! Motor boats are coming in our direction.'

Another laughed. 'You fool. It is only the fishermen going out to spear fish.'

'Not at this hour,' the first man snapped. 'Listen, I say! Listen! There are many boats heading towards us. I swear it!'

A sudden silence fell. The roar made by the engines of the flotilla could now be heard by everyone. One of the Colons shouted, 'Look! I can see them! Four! No, six—eight—a dozen.'

The man who had wanted to abandon Lacost yelled, 'We are betrayed. We are betrayed. I sensed it. We should have left at once.'

365

Another, more resolute and commanding, voice took over. 'Keep calm. Provided we can prevent them from boarding us, we'll get away.'

Lacost's voice came—urgent, pleading. 'For God's sake, save me. Throw the woman down into the boat and I'll climb aboard somehow.'

James cut into his plea by shouting to Olinda in English, 'Pretend you have fainted. Slide down on the deck and lie there, then none of these brutes will harm you.'

Ignoring Lacost's appeal, the man who had taken charge bellowed, 'Jean! To the bridge! Run! Give her full speed ahead and we'll outdistance them. Raoul! To the forward capstan! Get the anchor up. We drag it till it's in.'

In spite of the almost total darkness beyond the area lit by the light of the yacht, the phosphorescent bow waves, churned up by the leading boats of the flotilla, could now be seen as they rushed swiftly towards the prow and midships of the *Boa Viagem*.

Suddenly her engines began to throb. But she made no movement. Gregory's strategem had worked. Both her propellers turned, but, clogged by a mass of netting and wire, were unable to force her forward.

As the boats came alongside, the men in them were shouting war-cries that had not been used for a generation. Throwing their grapples on to the rails of the yacht, they swarmed up the ropes on to the deck. A machine gun opened fire, Sten guns clattered, the staccato crack of dozens of rifles pierced the din.

Gregory grasped the bow of the motor boat and hauled himself, dripping, into it. James had been holding Lacost in front of him, one hand round his waist, the other clutching his throat. Letting him go for a moment he pulled a pistol from his pocket and, as Lacost lurched forward, hit him a hard blow with it on the back of the head. The Frenchman gave a gasp, staggered for an instant, then fell forward, unconscious, on the deck.

At Gregory's appearance, James cried, 'Well done! Well done! It must be your work that prevents the yacht moving and getting away from us.'

366

Gregory nodded. 'Yes, I fouled her propellers. Now our chaps are aboard, the Colons don't stand an earthly chance.'

'Praise be! A thousand times I bless you!' James responded in great excitement. 'But Olinda is up there on deck. I must get her. And my men are fighting. I must show myself to them.'

With a gesture that embraced the coxswain, Kalabo and Gregory, he added, 'Come, all of you. Up on to the deck and show these swinish Frenchmen that we are not afraid of them.'

Jumping at the stern rail of the *Boa Viagem*, he seized it low down and scrambled up. Kalabo and his coxswain followed him. But Gregory did not. He was no longer young and his efforts to foul the propellers of the yacht had exhausted him. Staggering to the stern of the boat, he collapsed on to a seat and remained there, his head in his hands and lolling forward so that it was only a few inches above his knees.

As he strove to regain his breath and still the violent beating of his heart, he thought, 'We've got Lacost, the yacht can't move and it's certain there won't be any serious resistance. This is James' show. He no longer needs my help. I'll leave him to handle it now, then he'll get all the credit for rescuing Olinda.'

From Olinda his thoughts drifted to the White Witch. Instantly he jerked erect and, sitting rigid, stared wide-eyed into the darkness. A sudden flash of memory had recalled to him the occasion when he had first heard the White Witch mentioned.

It had been in Brazil at the beginning of the Great Rain—on the night that he had first met Manon. They had gone to the *Macumba* ceremony, then taken refuge in the *Macumba* priest's bungalow. He had cast the bones for Manon—told her that she would have a new lover and was already involved with one with whom she was concerned in a financial transaction. He had gone on to ask her if she had ever killed anybody, and she had admitted that she had. Then he had told her that a White Witch would cross her path and that she

367

must kill again. Unless she killed the White Witch when she had the chance, her life and all her hopes would be ruined.

His brain reeling, Gregory forced himself to his feet. He had left the White Witch unconscious and in Manon's power. He must return at once. But would he be in time to save her?

21

A Fateful Dawn

His tiredness forgotten, Gregory made for the bow of the
boat. To get to it he had to step over Lacost's unconscious
body which lay sprawled face downward on the deck. On
reaching the bow, he fumbled frantically to undo the painter
that kept the nose of the boat close up under the *Boa Viagem*'s stern. As he was no seaman, he found the knots intricate and the pull from the rocking boat had tightened them.
Moreover, splashes of water had made the rope wet. Cursing,
Gregory tore at the knot. A good three minutes passed before, at the cost of two broken fingernails, he had managed
to undo it.

Jumping back over Lacost's prostrate body, he reached the
stern, switched on the boat's engine and flung the gear into
reverse. His thoughts were now miles from the *Boa Viagem,*
away up in the Royal *bure,* with Manon and the Witch; so he
was aware only subconsciously that the firing above had
ceased.

As the boat backed away, James appeared at the stern rail
of the yacht, with Olinda beside him. 'What the devil are you
doing?' he called to Gregory. 'Why have you cast off?'

Gregory made no reply, switched the gear into neutral and
gave the wheel a sharp twist that brought the boat round
broadside on.

James, thinking that he was about to nose in again, cried
in excited triumph, 'It's all over! One dead and the others
prisoners. Bring her under the stern and I'll lower Olinda to
you.'

To his astonishment, instead of complying, Gregory pushed the gear lever into full speed ahead and again gave a twist to the wheel. The boat leapt forward, churning up great sheets of spray on either side of the bow and curving round in a wide half-circle until she was heading for the port.

In vain James shouted after him. Gregory had forgotten the very existence of the yacht. His mind was in a turmoil. The White Witch had been heavily drugged. He had been convinced that Roboumo would not have given her a dose that was likely to kill her—or deliberately have poisoned her. He would never have done that as long as he had the faintest hope of keeping her as his prisoner, so that, through the natives' fear of her, he could continue to exercise his evil power. But people had often been known to die of an overdose of a normally harmless drug. If Manon also recalled the *Macumba* priest's prediction, and decided to poison the Witch, she could get away with it. Everyone would believe that the Witch had died as a result of Roboumo's drug.

And Manon had the means to poison at hand. The sweat broke out on Gregory's forehead as he remembered the ring she always wore—the so-called Borgia ring—the secret of which she had revealed to him in Rio. In his mind's eye he could see her again now, sitting on the side of his bed and showing how, if pressed, a hidden spring caused the big amethyst to slide back, revealing a hollow in which there lay a cyanide of potassium pellet.

The first grey light preceding dawn had begun to lighten the scene while the fracas on the yacht was in progress. By the time Gregory was halfway to the harbour the light had increased perceptibly. Suddenly he noticed a movement in the fore part of the boat. Peering forward, he saw Lacost struggle up into a sitting position. Evidently his thick yellow hair had prevented his being put out for more than ten or twelve minutes after the blow on the head James had given him with his pistol. He was now coming round.

Gregory gave vent to the unprintable Italian oath which he used only on very rare occasions. This was hell's own luck. At the speed the boat was going he dared not leave the wheel, even for a minute, in order to knock Lacost out again. He could only pray to all his gods that the big Frenchman would not be sufficiently recovered to attack him before they reached harbour.

While the boat roared on, bumping abruptly as it lifted over small waves, Gregory kept a wary eye on his dangerous passenger. Another five minutes passed, and he had good reason to believe that his worst fears were to be realised. Lacost lurched to his feet and, swaying slightly, stood staring at him across the cabin roof.

His anxiety on account of the Witch was now replaced by a more immediate one. What was he to do if Lacost did rush him? The automatic he had brought, anticipating that he would take part in the capture of the yacht, was in the cabin with his clothes. A swift glance round had shown him that no weapon, such as an iron bar or a marlin-spike, with which he could defend himself, was in sight. Worst handicap of all for any man in a fight, he was still stark naked.

Lacost took a shuffling step towards him. Gregory knew now that he stood no chance of rounding the mole and bringing the boat alongside the wharf, where he could have shouted for help, before the murderous Colon would be upon him. Again his thoughts flashed for a second to what might be taking place up at the Royal *bure*, and the urgency of getting there. But he knew that his best chance of overcoming Lacost lay in tackling him before he had recovered the full use of his wits. With agonised reluctance he pulled the boat's gear lever over, bringing her down to half-speed.

At that moment Lacost stopped to pick up something from the deck. Gregory's heart missed a beat, for he felt certain that his enemy had found a weapon; but as Lacost came upright again he was holding two sheets of paper. He had stumbled on the licence to salvage the treasure and its transfer to himself which James had signed while Gregory was fouling the propellers of the yacht.

Gregory swore beneath his breath. Should Lacost succeed in overcoming him that would now mean a double defeat. Not only would the Frenchman be able to get away in the motor cruiser to some other island, but, if he was ever caught, the possession of those documents could enable him to plead justification for having fired on the gendarmes.

Lacost pushed the papers into his jacket pocket and moved a step nearer. 'It is now or never,' Gregory decided. 'He is just near enough for me to jump him.' Stretching out a hand, he switched off the engine.

Guessing his intention, Lacost stepped quickly back, at the same time thrusting a hand into his trouser pocket. Next moment he had withdrawn it, holding a jack-knife. With a swift movement he flicked it open. By now there was light enough for Gregory to see his face clearly. Under his long moustache his slightly protruding teeth showed in a sardonic smile.

Although Gregory had been tensed to spring, his enemy's quick retreat had given him pause. The flash of the knife had deterred him altogether. Naked as he was, he knew that it would now be suicidal to attack Lacost unarmed.

For the first time the Frenchman spoke. 'Fate has favoured me, after all, Monsieur Sallust. It is you who have been the ruin of my enterprise. Temporarily at least I have lost the treasure; although later, now that I have the necessary documents, I may yet appoint nominees to put in for me a legal claim to it. But at least I'll have the satisfaction of settling with you. When we met in Guatemala I recall you said that, should occasion arise, you would take pleasure in throwing me to the sharks. Now it is I who will throw you to the sharks. The smell of the blood that will flow after I've stuck my knife in your stomach will bring them racing to you.'

As he ceased speaking he made a sudden rush at Gregory. Abandoning the wheel of the now slowly-rocking boat, Gregory dodged to the port side of the cabin roof. Lacost followed, hurling blasphemies at him. Three times they sped round the roof. The tall Frenchman had the longer stride, but Gregory the greater agility and, being barefooted, a firmer purchase on the deck. The chase ended with them on either side of the low roof, panting for breath and glaring at each other.

Suddenly Lacost sprung on to the roof. A wave caused the boat to tilt a little. He staggered, but regained his balance.

372

For a moment he stood there, huge and menacing, a towering bulky figure outlined against the pale light of the pre-dawn sky. Then, his boots thudding on the cabin roof, in three strides he was across it.

The movement was so sudden that Gregory had no chance to jump aside and, had he turned, Lacost would have knifed him in the back. Lowering his head, he threw himself forward and butted the Frenchman in the stomach. Lacost gave a choking gasp and somersaulted over Gregory's shoulders, but the impact of his heavy body brought them both crashing to the deck.

Winded and retching, Lacost doubled up; but he still grasped the jack-knife. Gregory struck the wrist above it a savage blow with the hard edge of his right hand. The knife tinkled against a grating and slithered away. Clutching wildly at one another, they rolled across the deck.

They brought up against the stern seat, Lacost on top. Pressed down by the Frenchman's weight, Gregory could not wriggle from underneath him. Making a great effort, he kneed him in the groin. Lacost gave a groan, but there was not sufficient force behind the stroke to disable him. A moment later he had his hands round Gregory's throat. In vain Gregory tried to break the hold. His chest felt as though an iron band were being screwed tight about it. There came a singing in his ears. Making the first and second fingers of his right hand rigid, he jabbed desperately with them at the Frenchman's eyes. One finger went home. Lacost gave a scream of pain. Letting go of Gregory's throat, he rolled off him.

Gregory staggered to his feet. Lacost lurched to his and, although half-blinded, came at him again. Seizing Gregory round the waist in a bear-like hug, he lifted him from his feet and strove to throw him overboard. Being much the weaker, Gregory knew that he was now at his enemy's mercy. It could be only a matter of minutes before his breath would be squeezed out of his body.

Suddenly there came to him a way in which he might possibly save himself. When the fight had started, the last two long strands of wire which were left because he had not had the time to make the net fouling the port propeller more secure had still been looped round his neck with the ends hanging down his back. During his wrestle with Lacost on the deck one of them had fallen off; but as he clung to his enemy, clutching his shoulders and with their faces pressed together, he could feel the bite of the remaining wire now under his chin.

Releasing his hold on his antagonist with one hand at a time while continuing to cling to him with the other, he felt down over his shoulder until his fingers had found the wire. In turn, he pulled the ends of the wire up and jerked them forward so that they were hanging down behind Lacost's back instead of his own. Letting go of his enemy for a moment, but still clasped round the waist by him, he got his hands behind his neck, crossed the long ends of wire and pulled them together.

Suddenly Lacost realised what was happening and made frantic efforts to thrust Gregory from him. But, with his legs now round the Frenchman's waist and his hands behind his head, Gregory succeeded in clinging to him. As the garotte tightened, Lacost gasped. His eyes started to bulge. Ceasing his attempts to throw Gregory overboard, he staggered round, lurched forward and attempted to crush him against the cabin roof. But he could no longer draw breath. The strength was seeping from his great limbs. Gregory gave a savage jerk on the two ends of the wire, so that their loop cut into Lacost's throat, then twisted them over one another. He began to make a horrible gurgling noise. Only seconds later his grasp of Gregory relaxed. His arms fell to his sides, he heeled over and slumped on to the deck, bringing Gregory down with him.

Gregory was underneath, his muscles aching intolerably and sobbing for breath. It was minutes before he had regained sufficient strength to push Lacost off and stagger to his feet. In the dawn light the Frenchman's face was going purple. Gregory did not want him to die there, but to stand trial for his crimes and go to the guillotine. As he could always tighten the garotte again before Lacost was in any condition to renew the fight, he eased it a little; just enough for the Frenchman to draw painful breaths.

The struggle had ended near the stern of the boat. As Gregory moved to switch on the engine, his glance fell on the other length of wire. Picking it up, he used it to secure Lacost's hands behind his back. Then he eased the garotte a little more and firmly tied the ends of the wire that formed it to a cleat. Without the use of his hands Lacost could not free himself from the garotte, and should he attempt to get to his feet it would strangle him.

Within another two minutes the fact that he had so recently been fighting for his life had passed from Gregory's mind. As the boat again surged through the water, now not far from the extremity of the mole, his mind had once more become obsessed by the question of what Manon had done, or might do, to the Witch, up in the Royal *bure*.

Rounding the mole he brought the boat alongside the wharf and hastily tied her up. Lacost, blood seeping from his neck where the wire had cut into it, lay unmoving. The only people about were a few early-rising longshoremen and none of them was near; but if he could manage to shout for help, that might bring one of them to the boat. Anyone finding him would be sure to fall for a story that he had been set upon by robbers, and would release him. To prevent such a happening, greatly as Gregory grudged the time, he spent a few minutes taking precautions against it.

While retrieving the papers from Lacost's pocket, he found a handkerchief in it and used that to gag him. Then, lest the gag in addition to the wire should cause him, after all, to die from suffocation, he again eased the wire until it was quite loose, but would still tighten if Lacost tried to sit up. Lastly, to conceal him from any passer-by, Gregory flung over him a tarpaulin that was normally used to cover the stern end of the boat when she was not in use.

Satisfied that the unscrupulous brute who had brought death and pain to many people would, in due course, meet his just deserts, Gregory dived into the cabin, remained there only to put on his trousers and shoes, scrambled ashore and set off at a run through the town.

Even had he been forty years younger he could not have run the whole way from the harbour up the long slope to the *bure* but, at a quick walk for most of the way, with bursts of running now and then, he flogged himself into the utmost speed he could manage.

When he reached the *bure* his breath was coming in sobs and the sweat was streaming down his naked torso. As he burst into the big room Manon, who was standing at one end of it, gave a cry of fright. In his haggard state, for a moment she had failed to recognise him. When she did, she exclaimed:

'Gregory! Whatever has happened? You look absolutely ghastly. And why are you only half-dressed?'

For a full minute he stood there panting as he stared at her. Then, still fighting to get back his wind, he wheezed out. 'The Witch? Is . . . is she all right? Where . . . is she?'

'She's better,' Manon replied. 'I gave her the mustard and hot water, as you said, and she was sick. After a while she came round. That is, not enough to talk; but she began to moan and move her limbs feebly. So I put her to bed in our room.'

'Thank God!' Gregory murmured. 'Oh, thank God!'

Manon gave him a puzzled look and said, 'You seem to have worked yourself up into a frightful state. Why are you so concerned about her.'

'Because . . .' Gregory replied slowly. 'Because she is rather a special person.'

'D'you mean you still need her help to induce the natives to fight? I thought you'd found her out to be a fraud—only a sort of puppet, used by Roboumo to scare people with threats that she would curse them. But I suppose the natives are not yet aware of that; so now she is on our side, when she is well enough, she would be willing to frighten them into fighting the Colons for you.'

'No; it's not that.' Gregory shook his head. 'The fighting is over and the Colons are finished. James and his men captured the *Boa Viagem* three-quarters of an hour ago. Olinda is safe and I've got Lacost down at the harbour. He did his

376

damnedest to kill me, but I half killed him and left him trussed up like a chicken.'

Manon was silent for a moment. Then she smiled. 'So at last this terrible business is over. What a wonderful relief. I've been so worried that you would get yourself killed, darling; then all my dreams would have been shattered and I'd be miserable ever after.'

'What dreams?' he asked, looking at her curiously.

'Why, that you would make an honest woman of me. We are already living here as man and wife, and you know how I adore you. If you have ever doubted that, I proved it last night. I took a great risk in leaving that note for you saying I felt sure that Lacost would not harm me. He very well might have, but I preferred to chance it rather than let you risk your life by going on board the *Pigalle*.'

Gregory had noticed that on a small table beside Manon there was a bottle of champagne and two glasses, one of which was full of wine. Walking forward he gave a twisted smile and said:

'I suppose you thought that if I got the better of Lacost my triumphant return would be just the moment to ask me to become engaged to you; and you raided James's cellar for this bottle, with a view to celebrating.' As he spoke, he stretched out a hand to take the full glass of wine.

'No! . . . No!' Her eyes widened and she quickly pushed his hand aside. 'I hadn't counted my chickens that far. I got up and opened this bottle only for medicinal purposes. But don't take that glass. Fill the other, and I'll get another for myself.'

'What's wrong with the full one? he asked, eyeing her intently.

Manon shrugged. 'As I've told you, I fetched it from James' cellar only to serve as a medicine; although I'll admit I meant to have a glass myself. I was just about to take the full one to the Witch and leave it by her bedside, so that when she rouses and becomes fully conscious she'll drink it. I've put a couple of sleeping pills in it and sleep is what the poor woman needs.'

Taking a step forward, Gregory seized Manon's wrist. The

thumb and first finger of his other hand closed upon the big Borgia ring. He pressed the secret spring. The jewel slid back. The cavity that it normally concealed was empty.

Giving a scream of rage and fear, she wrenched her arm away from him.

He was smiling. But it was so grim a smile that it filled her with terror. His voice was hard, cold, scathing, as he lashed her with his tongue.

'Murderess! Liar! Whore! Did you think you could fool a man like me indefinitely? I've been on to you for a long time. But you are a gay companion and marvellous to go to bed with. So, cynic that I am, I decided to let you continue to play your treacherous game. I got quite a lot of fun out of watching you at it and speculating how you would manage to wriggle out of tight corners.'

With a harsh laugh, he went on, 'I learned that Pierre Lacost was your lover months ago—back in Antigua. You will recall that, on our first night there, he paid me a midnight visit. The following night I decided to pay him one, in order to find out a bit more about him. When I reached the door of his room I could hear that he had a woman with him. I felt that it might prove useful to find out who she was, so I concealed myself nearby and waited very patiently. I was well rewarded, for it was you who came out of his room.'

The blood had drained from Manon's cheeks. In a hoarse voice she whispered, 'I admit that I knew him. But . . . but . . .'

Ignoring her, Gregory went on, 'After I had given the matter a little thought the pieces began to fall into place. The old *Macumba* priest had said that you were about to take on a new lover. Myself, of course. He also said that you had one already, with whom you were involved in a financial venture. Him I discovered while in Antigua to be Lacost. Far from making a secret of it, he informed me of his intention to salvage the gold from the *Reina Maria Amalia* and threatened me with dire consequences should I attempt to contend with him in that venture.

'Nothing could have rung a louder bell for me, as far as you were concerned. The same threat aimed at freezing out competition over the same major project had been made to de Carvalho—and by a woman. His description of the woman who had threatened him was somewhat vague, but not too vague to fit you. And, seeing that you had no friends in Rio, nor the money to travel so far from Fiji only for a holiday, what reason could there have been for your going there other than as a partner of Lacost's, to protect the interests you had in common?'

'It's not true! It's not true!' Manon protested.

'Had I needed further confirmation of my theory, you gave it to me yourself,' Gregory retorted. 'You did your damnedest to convince me that the treasure was not worth going after and, time and again, endeavoured to persuade me to accompany you instead to your island and remain there with you, lotus-eating.

'You knew that I was very rich, and I soon tumbled to it that you hoped to induce me to marry you. That being so, I can well imagine in what a difficult position you must have found yourself with Lacost, who wanted to kill me. But it was in your interests that I should continue to live. That is why you did your best to prevent me from going up to Lake Atitlan. That, too, is the reason why you left that note last night ,warning me not to go aboard the *Pigalle*.'

'No! No! No!' Manon cried, violently shaking her head. 'It was because I loved you.'

'Love!' sneered Gregory. 'You don't know the meaning of the word. It is greed that inspires your every action. And what a shock it must have been for you when I turned up again so unexpectedly in Suva. Having just learned about the brutal murder of de Carvalho by your friends, I was in half a mind to have a showdown with you then. That you had lent your island to Lacost and his pals was beyond doubt. But I had no proof that you were aware of what they intended to do there, so I gave you the benefit of the doubt about that. Although I knew you were lying, I even had a sneaking admiration for the way you put up a very plausible story, to the effect that you had no idea that the Colons to whom you had lent your island had any connection with Lacost.

379

'You have played it both ways—hoping to get your share of the treasure by helping Lacost, and also hoping to hook me so that you could get your claws on my money. Lacost is now down, out and finished; and so are you.'

'Please!' she began to plead desperately. 'Please! Seeing all we've been to each other, you can't turn me adrift. Now that Lacost is finished and has lost the treasure, I'm ruined. I mortgaged my house to finance him. I'll be left penniless and starve.'

He shrugged, and his eyes were as hard as agates. 'In recognition of the pleasure that you have given me, I might still have forgiven you, and given you enough money to keep you going for a year or two. But for one thing. You have revealed yourself tonight as not just an adventuress but true spawn of the Devil, utterly evil and unscrupulous.

'You admitted to the *Macumba* priest that you had killed a man. I never asked you why, but assumed that you had been in a spot during those troubled times in Algeria, and had been justified in doing so. But the old priest told you that, in due course, you would come into contact with a White Witch and that if you failed to kill her when you had the chance you would lose everything.

'Well! The White Witch is here. She has done you no injury, but you intended to give her poison in that wine. Presumably because you believed that if you did not kill her she would, in some way, prevent me from marrying you. But you were acting on false premises. You make an admirable mistress, but that is one thing and taking a wife is quite another. Even before I knew you to be a liar and a cheat I wouldn't have considered it for one moment.'

The tears were now running down Manon's cheeks. After pausing for a moment, he went on harshly, 'And now I will answer your question why I was so concerned about the White Witch. It was not only because what the *Macumba* priest had said to you came back to my mind an hour or so ago and I suspected your truly evil nature. It was because when I broke into her cage tonight, as soon as I saw her face I recognised her. She is the love of my life. My beloved Erika, whom I had believed to have been long since drowned.'

As Gregory ceased speaking, Manon gave a wailing cry. 'Then . . . then I've lost my share of the gold and I've lost you, too. I've nothing . . . nothing left to live for.'

Before Gregory could stop her, she had snatched up the glass of wine and tipped half its contents down her throat. The action of the cyanide was almost instantaneous. Her eyes bulged, her limbs went rigid and she fell dead at his feet.

Epilogue

Dear Readers,

So many of you wrote to me after having read *The Island Where Time Stands Still*, saying that I could not possibly let Erika die, and begging me to write another book in which Gregory found his great love. In this story I have acceded to those requests.

Needless to say, Pierre Lacost and his surviving companions went to the guillotine. James and Olinda married, were beloved by their people and had several beautiful, golden-skinned children. Erika had suffered in no way, apart from her long imprisonment, and after a few weeks became again her old charming self. So our hero and heroine, once more united, lived happily ever after.